MUNCH

LESLEY BAILEY

MUNCH
LESLEY BAILEY

This book is a work of fiction and any resemblance to
actual persons, or places is entirely coincidental.

Produced by: Eden Valley Publications
Cover Design by: Blueice Graphic Design
Images: @ shutterstock
Typeset in Adobe Garamond Regular

Printed in the UK by: Clays.

ISBN: 978 1 7384377 0 2

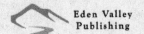
Eden Valley
Publishing

ABOUT THE AUTHOR

Lesley Bailey has enjoyed writing creatively for many years. She and husband, Richard divide their time between rural Northamptonshire and the Eden Valley in Cumbria.

Now a retired company director she has more time to devote to writing. As a result, Munch is her debut novel. When not writing, Lesley enjoys reading, walking, and gardening. Family is extremely important, and she is proud of her two grown children and four grandchildren.

PRAISE FOR MUNCH

"What can I say? Munch is absolutely brilliant. Pitch perfect. An absolute joy to read. Funny. Thoughtful. Excellent pace. Wrapped up in nature and a sense of place. Characterisations very quickly established and lots of lovely, lovely touches everywhere. When I got to Part Two, I wanted romance....and I wasn't disappointed! Lesley's debut novel reveals an incredible new talent."

Claire Bowles, Literary Publicist.

DEDICATED TO BEAR

PART ONE

ONE

Evelyn watched from the window of the drawing room with some misgivings. Another money-raising scheme was unfolding before her eyes. Devised by her son Toby, it threatened to undermine the unassuming quality of her home, Melchett Hall.

The three-hundred-year-old estate had been established and was still owned by the Bursill-Brookes family, Evelyn Bursill-Brookes being the current incumbent and matriarch of the extended family and the staff who lived and worked within the estate. Evelyn resided in the west wing of the house and whilst still involved in the workings of the estate, she'd passed most of the responsibility of running the business to Toby. At seventy-three years of age her interest in the estate hadn't waned but her growing frailty and tendency to bronchitis had caused her reluctantly to pass the reins on.

She turned from the window and cast a stern glance towards her son, "I don't want this…" She whirled her hand in the air, whilst searching for the right word, "This concert to ruin our reputation, Toby."

Toby momentarily closed his eyes, keeping a lid on his frustration. "No, Mother. And it's a music festival, not a concert."

Evelyn took a deep breath. "Toby, we are stewards of this estate, mindful of those who went before us and those who will come after us. I know I introduced the market garden and tearooms, tasteful and appropriate additions to the estate income in my opinion. But really, the farm park, weddings in the orangery, and now music festivals... Darling, they are so horribly vulgar. I know what you are going to say – the roof needs replacing, and our farm profits are down."

"We've got to move with the times, Mother, provide visitors with reasons to return time and again."

"Quite so, Toby, but look at the Christmas fair – it was a complete disaster, darling!"

Toby wasn't surprised his mother had mentioned the fair. She waved it like a flag of vindication every time she wanted to make a point. He said nothing, but turned to leave the room, desperate to get on with his busy schedule.

Evelyn watched him reach for the door handle before saying sharply, "Oh, and darling?"

"Yes, Mama?" He used the endearment to try and soften what was inevitably coming.

"I can *still* see that monstrous wedding marquee from the drawing room. It's going to have to be moved."

As Toby left the room, she smiled and then chuckled. Poor Toby! She often wondered what Peter would have thought. Dear, dear Peter. She still missed his wonderful company every day. Five years had passed unbelievably quickly since Peter had died, and Evelyn, being the woman of sturdy character she was, would never show how deeply she felt his loss. No. Chin up and carry on, old girl. She was still surrounded by many wonderful people, and though her manner towards them was always very formal and bordered on brusque, she loved them dearly.

She had Jim Gamble and his wife Marion. Jim had been her estate manager for over thirty years, and as Evelyn liked to say to anyone who cared to listen, "One simply couldn't find a more dependable man upon whom to rely – bloody good chap!" Jim and Marion lived in one of the small but comfortable cottages that formed a terrace towards the north side of the estate. Marion worked in the house, assisting the housekeeper with meeting the household's domestic requirements.

Evelyn's tearoom was managed by Lisa Brown, a quietly spoken but capable girl who lived in nearby Market Braithwaite, and she in turn was assisted by a variety of part-time ladies whose plump, pink faces beamed at customers as they entered the shop.

That was the thing about working at Melchett Hall – once the atmosphere of the place infused into the staff, they became melded to the community, part of her Melchett family.

Over the years, none had embodied this better than Pedro and Maria Santoro. They had migrated to England from Italy in the early 1990s and, as luck would have it, had arrived just as Evelyn had been looking to employ good, solid, reliable people to work in her new tearoom and market garden. Pedro became one of her estate gardeners and eventually her head gardener before he retired. Maria had made a wonderful tearoom manager – she baked the most fabulous food, exchanges with customers only enhanced by her heavily accented English, her charming nature won over the customers again and again.

Their son Giovanni had been eight when they arrived on English shores. He was a strange little boy, and his sullen nature had been at odds with his parents' sunny dispositions. He used to disappear for hours within the grounds of the estate and got into tremendous trouble for continually being absent from school.

Poor chap had been like a fish out of water. His Mediterranean looks had set him apart from the other boys. He was a big lad with black, crisp hair which lay in tight curls around his face and neck and caused him no end of bother from his classmates' cruel teasing. No doubt his domestic situation being so different from that of the other lads only served to exacerbate his isolation from them. He had spent his spare time helping his father in his dour way or exploring the grounds of the estate.

Evelyn knew that his parents had been called to the school on many occasions to discuss their son's difficulties; the language barrier, the apparent inability to form friendships, the misbehaviours. When he was fifteen, he hit a boy who had called him that name he hated being called – only hit him the once, but the boy went down like a felled tree and woke up in hospital with a broken jaw. Gi, poor chap, was summarily expelled.

Evelyn had suggested to Jim that Gi could work within the

protection of the estate as a junior gardener. And that is what happened. Pedro and Maria had worked for Evelyn until they retired. They had remained living at the little gatehouse paying a peppercorn rent until they had both passed away some six years previously, and within weeks of each other.

Gi, now in his mid-thirties, still lived in the gatehouse, quite alone, but he had chosen to lead a solitary life, and Evelyn was in no doubt it was an arrangement that suited him. The house was situated away from the main entrance to the hall and, as such, left him in perfect isolation. He rarely left the confines of the estate, only occasionally making the trip into Market Braithwaite to stock up on provisions. Sometimes she saw him walking down to the local pub, the Melchett Arms where, she had been told, he drank alone standing at the bar. His life was his work on the estate, the collection of Italian art books his father had bequeathed him and his extraordinary ability to sketch and draw with precise accuracy the flora and fauna he came across in and around the grounds of the estate.

As he had matured, he had developed into a beast of a man. At least six three or four; his black crispy hair cascaded over his shoulders and his dark eyes were sullen and hooded. The physical demands of his work kept him in excellent shape, and Jim had told Evelyn that he often compared Gi to a carthorse. Willing and able to work incredibly hard, he would always do Jim's bidding, though Evelyn noted the healthy respect shown by Jim – wise man, for Gi could have wiped him off the floor with one swing of his arm. Evelyn knew that Jim didn't completely trust the man, but he showed empathy towards him and had certainly taken responsibility to care for him since his parents had died. Jim had told her that he couldn't put his finger on quite what it was about Gi that caused him concern, but there was something off, something that just wasn't quite right about him.

*

Toby Bursill-Brookes was excited and filled with nervous

anticipation. Toby, Jim and all the staff had been working around the clock to prepare for the music festival which was taking place on the last weekend in August.

The weather had been settled since the first of June when there had been a ferocious snowstorm which had taken everyone by surprise. Since then, nearly every day had been amazing, hot sunshine beating down until the landscape was faded and dusty and the local newspaper the *Braithwaite Mail* was warning of a drought and impending hosepipe ban.

The festival was situated away from the hall towards the western edge of the estate. A river separated the various tents, caravans, and motor homes from the formal gardens of the hall. The river was often mistaken for a lake because Toby's great-grandfather had excavated the land around the banks of the river and flooded a large area of ground. This gave the impression of a lake which formed an attractive margin between the lawns, flower beds and the landscaped meadows beyond.

The festival itself would remain self-contained and separate from the grounds of the hall, allowing access to the usual amenities and attractions which the hall offered to the public, six days of the week. However, just the knowledge that the festival event was being held on the estate would be enough to attract a far larger contingent of local people to the hall that weekend, some of whom Toby was sure would have passed the hall many times previously but had never visited.

Toby had allowed for this eventuality; indeed, he had been banking on it. He had organised additional car parking space in the field by the house and extra catering in the form of a large barbecue. The gardens looked wonderful with hollyhocks, dahlias, sweet peas, and roses in bloom, and the grass trimmed to Jim's exacting standards.

As the gates were opened to allow a steady stream of vehicles through, Toby and Jim stood on the front steps of the entrance to the hall observing the attendants as they directed cars into the field to park.

"I think it's going to be a great success, Jim." Toby looked across at his estate manager with satisfaction.

"I hope so, Toby. There's a lot of hard work gone into it, that's for sure, and the… Mrs Bursill-Brookes will be on your case if it flops." Jim had been about to say "the old bird" which was the private name he gave to Evelyn. He only ever used it openly when speaking with his wife Marion, but he'd nearly slipped up there! He smiled gently, thinking that Toby probably had his own private name for his mother that was possibly much worse.

"Yes, well, let's not go there, Jim, thank you. God, do you remember last year when the Christmas event flopped? I don't think she'll ever let it go. She can be a harridan, you know."

"Well, I wouldn't like to say, but you wouldn't have it any other way now, would you?"

Toby's laughter barked out across the lawn as the two men walked around the side of the building and towards the tearoom.

"Come on, let's get a quick coffee before it all kicks off."

*

Gary and Louise Bosworth had already fallen out twice that morning and neither was particularly in the mood for a family outing. However, they had made a commitment to Louise's mother that they would bring her and the girls to Melchett Hall for a picnic that weekend, and if they fancied it, they could wander down to the folk festival too.

In fact, the very idea of taking Wendy, Louise's mother, out at all was the cause of the first argument. Gary was sulking, because whilst he had agreed to it when Louise had mentioned the idea some weeks ago, as the day had approached, he had felt less and less inclined to spend his weekend with his mother-in-law or, as he called her, the 'monster-in-law'. So that had led to sharp words at the breakfast table.

Then as they sat in the car whilst queuing to enter the grounds of the hall his girls had had a disagreement… well, more of an all-out fight really, and Gary had ended up shouting at them which had caused tears and Wendy's admonishing looks. So, by the time they had parked the car, Gary couldn't wait to get some fresh air and distance from all the women in his life.

*

Around the same time, another local family, Tom, Maggie, and Jennifer Pritchard were also waiting in their car to enter the estate. The atmosphere in this vehicle was somewhat more amiable, with Tom and Maggie chatting about the history of the hall and recalling the memories of a family wedding which had taken place there some years earlier.

Jennifer - Jenny or Jen to her friends, was engrossed in the workings of a new camera she had just received for her birthday. This would be the first occasion she would have the chance to use it properly and she had brought it, together with her sketch pad and pencils, to capture some of the wonderful flowers she knew would be on display.

At fourteen years of age, Jennifer Pritchard was an unusual girl. She loved to draw and did it very well indeed, to the point where she had announced that she was going to become a professional artist when she left school. Her parents had smiled indulgently as she informed them of her somewhat unusual career choice.

Tom, her father, who was an accountant, was a sensible and pragmatic man who really didn't give much thought to the opportunities that a creative flair could bring his daughter. Whilst Maggie, who was a part-time seamstress in the local dry cleaners, secretly hoped her daughter could find some route to escape the humdrum and somewhat boring life that she had managed to carve out for herself. Not that she begrudged it, of course. She was happy with Tom and had been delighted when they managed to have a baby following years of trying. But if her Jen could do something exciting with her life, well, good on her was what she thought.

But Maggie was anxious at times for her only child. Jen was a bit of a loner who was quite happy in her own company, and she had never sought out friendships with girls of her own age, preferring instead to draw and take herself off on long walks with

Bounce her springer spaniel.

It had been the source of some friction in the house when Jenny refused to invite girls home and rarely went to anyone else's house. There were strict rules as to where she was allowed to go out walking on her own and rules about what time she had to be home. Her parents insisted that she took her mobile phone with her when she was out so they could keep in touch by text to reassure themselves that she was safe, and she was happy.

Maggie worried that her daughter didn't appear to want to, or worse still, couldn't form lasting friendships with people of her own age. In fact, she wondered at times if her daughter was being bullied at school, but Jenny maintained she was not and that she was perfectly content with life. Maggie had spoken at length to Tom about the issue, but he had wisely said, "You shouldn't try and change her personality, Mags. Let her grow up in her own way. If she's serious about going to art college, that's bound to bring her out of her skin a bit."

Maggie reluctantly agreed with Tom at the time, but it didn't prevent her from being concerned.

*

As the Pritchard family climbed out of the car, the grounds of the hall were already crowded with families wandering around the gardens, setting up picnics in the meadow leading down to the river and browsing around the nursery plant sale.

Tom Pritchard unloaded the boot of the car, handing the picnic rug and a folding chair to Jen whilst he hoisted the hamper and another folding chair under each arm. Maggie reached up to close the boot and locked the car before she stuffed the keys into Tom's trouser pocket.

"Steady on, Mags! You nearly got me in the…"

"Dad! Please, that's sick." Jen groaned. Her parents never seemed to worry about embarrassing her with their playful innuendo. Her mother compounded the moment by pinching her father's bottom playfully and then giving it a squeeze.

"Come on, gorgeous, let's get you on that rug." And then she started singing in her pseudo-American accent, *"On the blanket on the ground..."*

"Right, that's it!" Jenny admonished them both. "I'm going to the walled garden to do some sketching." And she handed the chair and the rug to her mother.

"Okay, love, we'll set up the picnic down by the lake, so don't be too long or we'll have eaten all the food."

"It's not a lake, Dad – it's a river, okay."

Tom rolled his eyes and, putting on a sulky teenage voice, said, "Whatever."

Jenny left them to it. *What a pair*, she thought. What other teenager had to put up with lovesick parents? For heaven's sake! She smiled. She was lucky and she knew it. Most of the people in her class seemed to live part-time with each parent who all appeared to be going through vicious separations or divorces. One poor kid had just found out before the summer holidays that his dad was leaving his mother for another bloke, which had been a shock. Jenny thought she must make the effort to speak with Josh when they went back to school in September.

She instantly felt that familiar squeezing sensation in the pit of her stomach and her throat felt dry as she contemplated going back to school. For a horrible moment she thought she was going to cry but her mouth gave that little twist it always did when she felt her anxiety getting the better of her. God, but how she hated school. Even the smell – that disgusting mixture of school dinners, floor polish, and whatever else went into making the unmistakable aroma of the building... yes, even the smell could make her feel anxious.

Another four years of bloody purgatory and then she would be free! It wasn't the academia that got to her – it was all that humanity, rushing and pushing, the jostling in the corridors, the boys and their infantile manners and behaviour, and the girls and their silly cliques and obsession with fashion and celebrity. And matters had taken a horrible turn last term when a new girl, Cheryl Bosworth, and her sister had started at the school, picking on Jen, through no fault of her own. They were all morons so far as Jen was concerned. If she could spend all day in the art classroom, working alongside sexy Mr Ashburn, that would be her idea of heaven.

She shook her head to try and rid herself of the depression that had begun to settle inside her like a stone. She only had a few days left of freedom, so she had better make the best of it.

She arrived at the walled garden and pushed on the weathered door, which was warm and dry to her touch, stepped through the doorway and into the beautiful, secluded garden. The ancient red-brick wall surrounding the garden stood around twelve feet high, and it completely enclosed the acre of borders and pathways inside. There were several water features, and gazebos with seating for quiet contemplation. Most of the beds were filled with a sensational mixture of late summer perennials, hollyhocks, dahlias, asters, and roses. At the far end of the garden, there were beds of vegetables planted with great precision and symmetry. The walls were ablaze with climbing roses and the air was heady with the perfume of honeysuckle.

Jenny settled herself on a stone bench, tucking one leg up onto the bench for comfort. She gazed for a moment at the array of flowers on show. There was a large tea rose which was emerging from bud to display the most perfect deep apricot petals, and they seemed to glow with a shimmering light in the warm sunshine. She took several photographs of the flower using her new camera and then flicked open her sketch pad and was lost in concentration as she began to reproduce the flower on paper using her sketching pencils.

*

Giovanni was also in the walled garden. He had spent the morning clearing and preparing one of the flowering beds, before planting a mixture of narcissi and crocus bulbs for the spring. It was hot work and as he forked the last of the cuttings and roots into the barrow by his side, he wiped the sweat from his forehead using the back of his arm which glistened damply as a result. His stomach growled loudly so he wiped his hands on the back of his trousers and stepped over to the old rucksack which lay on the pathway. He picked it up, slung it over one shoulder and wandered over to a wooden bench that was set on the grass between the flower beds and vegetable patch.

His lunch comprised of a large and roughly made ham sandwich, a flask of cold water, an apple, and an orange. He managed to demolish them all in less than five minutes. He swilled the last of the water around his mouth and wiped the crumbs from his lips with the back of his grimy hand.

That task completed, he took a sketch pad out of his bag and contemplated the garden before noticing a young girl who was seated and completely absorbed in her task of drawing a rose. He was utterly transfixed by her.

Her hair swung down, partially covering one side of her face. She had tucked the hair on the other side behind her ear so that her ear emerged pixie-like from her head. He could almost see the curve of her lashes as her eyes were cast downwards in studied concentration and the tip of her tongue emerged every now and again through her lips as she raised her pencil to her mouth whilst considering her composition.

Gi felt slightly guilty at his fascination with her, felt as though he was somehow violating her with his eyes. But he couldn't help himself, nor could he help feeling a connection with her, a synergy. And so rather than sketch the butterfly, which was resting on a nearby buddleia, he turned his attention to the girl and began to sketch her instead.

*

At the same moment, the Bosworth family entered the walled garden, Gary and Louise led the way, with Louise's mother following behind making a bit of a fuss with the door as her cardigan caught on a protruding nail.

"I knew I should have worn my old cardie – Louise, look at this catch on my new cardie, what a shame! You would think they would make sure the grounds were safe."

"Mum, it's just a catch; it'll pull through." Louise rolled her eyes.

Gary could barely conceal his contempt. "Isn't that the cardie you got from Oxfam for three quid, here…" He shoved his hand in his pocket and pulled out a five-pound note. "Treat yourself to a new one, Wendy."

"Oooh, you are a card, our Gary," Wendy simpered, but took the note anyway before he could put it back in his pocket.

"Hey!" Gary stared in disbelief at his hand.

"Serves you right." Louise dug him in the ribs before turning back to check on the girls. "Come on you two, catch up!"

"Hey! Look at that." Gary shoved Louise with his shoulder.

"What now?"

"Have you seen who's over there? Bloody hell, I never thought I'd see him again."

"What? Who?" Louise peered around the garden in the general direction of her husband's stare.

"It's that Italian bloke from school. You remember. You know, the bloke that floored Terry Goss and broke his jaw. What did we used to call him?"

"It's Munch," Louise said quietly. "You all called him Munch."

"Yeah, that's right! Bloody hell, he's a biggin now, isn't he? Wouldn't want to get on the wrong side of him."

"Shut up, Gary."

"What's the matter with you now?"

She shrugged off his attention, turning instead to stare again at Giovanni.

Gary wasn't the most intuitive man in the world, but even he sensed the disquiet that had settled on his wife. She was clearly flustered by the presence of their old fellow pupil.

"Is it to do with him?" He jerked his head in the direction of Giovanni who seemed to be closely watching a young girl on the other side of the garden.

"No, don't be silly, I just… I just feel a bit funny and need to sit down." She passed her hand over her face, emphasising the point.

"Here!" Gary grabbed her somewhat roughly by the arm. "Sit down here," and he propelled her to a stone bench, pushing her none too gently back and down so that she had no option other than to sit down for a few moments to regain her composure. Her mother took this as a sign that she too could plonk her bottom of ample proportions onto the bench.

The girls scooted off down one of the paths. As they came to a junction in the path, the older girl, Cheryl, hissed to her sister, "OMG, look who it isn't!"

"What?"

"Look over there, stupid. It's Pritchard the Bitchard. Come on, let's go and have some fun."

They sidled over towards Jennifer who didn't notice their advance, so engrossed was she in her drawing, until they were standing directly in front of her.

"Hi, bitch. Still swotting in the holidays, I see." Cheryl put her hand on her hip and blew a tiny bubble with her chewing gum so that it popped and stuck momentarily to her lips. She sucked it back into her mouth, chewing on it again.

Jennifer froze but kept her head down, not wanting to make eye contact with the girl.

"What's the matter, then? Cat got your tongue, bitch?"

Still, Jennifer did not respond. In fact, she felt like jumping up and stabbing the girl in the eye with her pencil, but that would just be a waste of a good sketching pencil, so she quietly started packing her pencils and drawing away.

Gi was watching this small drama as it played out, and he frowned to himself, not liking the stance of the two girls and their obvious threatening behaviour.

He slung the remnants of his lunch into his backpack and closed the sketch pad carefully before sliding it lengthways into a pocket in the pack. Then he placed this, together with the gardening implements he had been using, in the wheelbarrow so that they lay on top of the foliage which was already wilting in the heat of the day. He hoisted the handles of the wheelbarrow and swivelled around until he was facing the direction of the small gathering of girls.

Jenny was fastening her own pack in readiness to leave the garden. The older two girls appeared to be blocking her path, and as Gi approached, they turned and looked at him sullenly, but then a little fearfully as his vast frame loomed above them. He jerked his head in the direction of the door through which they had passed to enter the garden.

"Garden is closing now." He said slowly, whilst eyeballing them both in turn.

They stared at him, rooted to the spot, so he jerked his head again and growled roughly, "Out now!"

"Alright, keep your hair on, man," Cheryl said impudently, thinking, *He's only a gardener, for God's sake*. But she felt something else – a creeping fear of the man that made her shiver and grab her sister's arm. "Come on, Laura, let's go. We'll see you on Tuesday at school, bitch!"

When they were far enough away from the man, Cheryl said in disgust, "What a creep!"

"Are you gonna tell, Dad?" Asked Laura.

"Yeah, I might just see if I can get that bloke into trouble, threatening little girls!" Her lip curled nastily, and Laura thought, not for the first time, that sometimes she really didn't like her sister at all.

"Dad, that bloke's a creep. He told us to get out of the garden."

"Why, what you been up to now? Anyway, what did he say to you?"

"He told us the garden was closing and then he shouted at us to get out."

Their father stood up quickly and said loudly, "I'm not having that, I'm not! Bloody cheek!" Then he turned in the direction of Giovanni and shouted, "Here, I know you, mate. You leave my girls alone d'you hear?"

Louise stood up and grasped his arm. "Gary, leave it."

Giovanni turned and placed the wheelbarrow down, at which point Gary hustled his family together and said, "Come on, you lot, I'm gonna find the manager and make a complaint about him."

Jenny had watched everything from the bench with a growing sense of horror. The very last thing she needed was to compound the already awful situation she had experienced last term when Cheryl, and to a lesser extent her younger sister Laura, had singled her out for some nasty treatment.

This encounter was almost certainly going to make matters worse. For a moment she stared at the man who had spoken to the girls and warned them off. As the family scooted through the old doorway, which led back to the main grounds of the hall, he turned to pick up the handles of his wheelbarrow again. As he was set to go, he looked across to where Jenny stood. She knew she should remember her manners and thank him for his assistance but there was something about his demeanour which dissuaded her from doing so. Instead, she raised her hand in a half-hearted acknowledgement to which he gave a small nod before trundling off up the path. He left the garden through the same door which the Bosworth family had so recently passed through.

*

Jenny found her parents some ten minutes later. They had set up the chairs and the picnic rug near to the riverbank and Maggie was feeding the ducks with the crusts she had saved for them from her sandwich.

"Hello, love, I thought you'd got lost. Fancy some picnic?"

Jenny shrugged. "What is there?"

"What's the matter, bumble?" Her father placed the newspaper he had been reading on his lap.

She shrugged again, "Nothing, just… bored, I s'pose."

"Come and sit next to me," Her mother patted the rug at her feet. "And I'll find you something yummy. How's about a sausage roll to start with?"

Jenny's mood brightened at the news that her mother had packed sausage rolls, "Are they from the bakery?"

"Of course, where else? And I heated them and wrapped them

in tinfoil before we left home, so they are still lovely and warm."

As Jenny settled down to enjoy her picnic, leaning back against her mother, she pushed the incident in the walled garden to the back of her mind. "Mum?"

"Yes, love?"

"What are you wearing to the christening tomorrow?"

"I'm pleased you asked me that, Jen, because I wanted to ask you whether I should wear my skirt and raspberry-coloured top or my white-and-blue dress… What do you think?"

Their conversation continued whilst Jenny ate her lunch, and when she had finished, she lay on her back and watched the clouds pass overhead as her parents' chatter turned to discussing where they should go for their next family holiday.

*

Gary Bosworth by this time had found the manager's office and he puffed his chest out before rapping loudly on the door. The family were seated nearby at a table usually allocated to the patrons of the café, but Gary felt entitled to have them sit there, under the circumstances. A solidly built, older man opened the door in response to Gary's knocking. He had a pipe in his hand and a tweed cap pulled low over his head. "Help you?" He enquired pleasantly.

"Are you the manager?"

"Yes, I'm the manager. Jim Gamble the estate manager. How can I help you, Mr…?"

"Bosworth. Mr Bosworth. I've come to make a complaint about one of your staff."

"Oh! Really, that does surprise me. What's the problem here?"

Gary turned and pointed towards his family. "My girls, my little girls have just been shouted at by a big bloke in the walled garden, told to get out and that the garden was closed. And I know he's trouble cos I went to school with him, till he got expelled, that is. What you going to do about it?"

Jim Gamble looked at the man and took an instant dislike to him, but he knew customer relations were important. "Look, Mr

Bosworth, I am sure there has been some misunderstanding here. I will of course have a word with my member of staff."

"Too bloody right, mate, or I'll be going to the local paper with my story, okay?" He shook his finger at Jim.

"That won't be necessary, Mr Bosworth, I can assure you. May I take a contact number and I will telephone you in the week, if I may, to bring you up to date about the outcome of any investigation into this matter."

"Hmmm, I suppose that'll have to do. I don't want you giving any of my details to that bloke though, understood? He's trouble, for sure."

"Your details will remain confidential I can assure you of that, Mr Bosworth. Now, if you could give me your number, I will make enquiries straightaway."

Jim Gamble took Gary Bosworth's mobile telephone number, bade him good afternoon, and said he hoped he and his family would enjoy the rest of their day and visit again soon. Then he turned and walked away from the office door so that the man couldn't continue with his onslaught.

"What a pain in the arse!" He muttered to himself when he had finally removed himself from earshot. But then he shook his head and said just as crossly, "What have you been up to now, Giovanni?"

TWO

It wasn't until the next morning that Jim managed to have his chat with Gi. Jim had risen very early and had already been around the estate in the old Land Rover. He reckoned they would be able to finish bringing in the oil seed rape crop from the huge field that was situated towards the northern edge of the farm. They were one farm hand down thanks to a twisted ankle, and the remaining men would need Gi's help if they were to get it in that morning.

The weather forecast was good but threatened showers in the afternoon, so Jim wanted it done before then. Even though they could and often did work on into the night using the lights from the farm machinery, he wanted this job completed before the rain came. That would be the last of the main harvest, leaving just a few acres of maize which they used for cattle feed.

He pulled the Land Rover up outside Gi's cottage and killed the engine, waiting a moment or two to consider how he would frame his conversation regarding the previous day's complaint. The engine started to cool and tick as he pondered the best approach to take. The back door to the cottage stood open and the early morning sunlight was spilling over the step and into the interior beyond, so Jim knew that Gi was up and about, even at this early hour.

As Jim slid down from the Land Rover, Gi's hefty frame filled the cottage doorway. He lifted his hand by way of greeting his boss and pointed to the mug in his other hand.

"Morning, Gi, it's a fine one. Yes, I'll have half a cup with you, thanks."

When Jim reached the cottage door Gi was lifting the kettle from the cooking plate to pour boiling water onto the teabag which he had dumped unceremoniously into a chipped mug, one of only two he had in his possession. Milk and sugar followed, and the tea was stirred using the spoon that lay on the side from earlier.

"Cheers!" Jim took the mug from Gi and lifted it towards his mouth appreciatively.

Jim looked around the tiny kitchen. It looked like he had interrupted Gi in the middle of some task, as papers and notices lay upon the old pine table. It appeared they had been taken down from the tatty cork board that was propped up on the top of the bookcase. The remaining shelves held Gi's treasured Italian art books.

"Having a tidy up?" Jim nodded towards the papers.

Gi shrugged and tilted his head by way of response, pulling his mouth down, as if to say, *Maybe I am and maybe I'm not.*

"Gi, can you come and help out on the top field this morning, going to get the last bit of that rape in whilst the weather holds."

"Sure, boss."

"I meant to mention, had a bit of a set-to with a visitor yesterday. Funny bloke."

"Oh?"

"Seems his girls were ticked off by a member of staff."

"Yes."

"Gi, you don't make things easy for me, do you? Did you have a go at them in the gardens?"

He shrugged in response.

"Come on, Gi! Did you, or didn't you? What happened to rile you?"

"They're not nice girls. I told them to go, that's it."

"Okay, I can see I'm not going to get anywhere with you on this one. Look, Gi, I know the public are a pain in the arse and they get in the way of our work, but no public, no income, no job – you savvy?"

"Yes, boss."

"Okay, consider the matter closed, but also take it as a warning, Gi. I can't have members of the public upset – bad news travels fast in this community."

They drank their tea in silence whilst the clock ticked like a metronome, emphasising the awkwardness of the moment. Jim noticed Gi's sketchbook lay on the corner of the table, there was a sheet of paper protruding from it. As Gi turned to the sink with the mugs, Jim pinched the corner of the paper and drew the sketch out from the encasing pad. He froze and almost gasped at the image which lay before him. It was a pencilled drawing of a young girl, stunningly pretty. The artist had captured the essence of her, half girl, half woman. The picture conveyed innocence and eroticism together – it was quite extraordinary.

"Christ Almighty!" Jim said, finally managing to speak.

Gi turned at the expletive, took one step from the sink to the table and took the picture away from Jim.

"Who is *that*, Gi?"

The man shrugged.

"You did it?"

A small nod.

"I recognise the background. This is the walled garden."

Again, a nod.

"Who is it, Gi?"

"She is the girl in the garden, that's all."

Jim passed his hand over his face. "Gi, was this recent? Yesterday, maybe?"

The nod again and a steady piercing stare which made Jim feel uncomfortable.

"This is one of the girls you told off?"

"No!"

"Then who? I'm confused."

"It's just a girl in the garden, that's all."

"Gi, take some advice from me, yes? This is not appropriate. Someone could misunderstand this, okay?" He pointed to the picture. "It's not right!"

Gi studied the image critically, a frown forming.

"I don't mean technically not right, man! I mean morally not right. You could be accused of…" He shook his head in exasperation. "Stick to flowers, Gi. I mean it – stick to flowers.

I'll see you at the top field in half an hour." With that Jim stalked from the room, and across the yard. He jumped up into the Land Rover, keyed the engine and with a grating of the clutch and gears he roared away up the lane, sweat breaking out on his forehead.

Gi waited until he heard the roar of the Land Rover pulling away and then crossed the small room and picked up the picture of the girl. He found four drawing pins on the table and pinned the picture to the centre of the empty cork board. Then he leant back against the ancient kitchen worktop, folded his arms across his barrel chest and stared at the image, a small smile forming on his lips.

*

Jenny had also woken early, so early that the light still held that quiet and secretive pre-dawn quality. She turned over to glance at the alarm clock that sat upon her bedside table. It was six o'clock. She pushed back the bedclothes, rolled off her bed and squinted out of the window. The sun was on the verge of breaking over the top of the hill to pour its warmth on the land and it looked like it was going to be another beautiful day.

With a sigh, Jenny considered her options. She could climb back into bed and have a cosy lie-in or get up and start preparing her stuff for the dreaded school due to recommence on Tuesday morning. Or she could creep from the house and take her bike up to the woods or to the reservoir for some bird-spotting and sketching. She could still be back in plenty of time for her cousin Sophie's christening. She decided upon the latter, and as she knew her mother would forbid her from going, she did her best to get dressed without making any noise.

Her parents' bedroom was on the opposite side of the large galleried landing, so it wasn't difficult to make her way downstairs without disturbing them. She closed the kitchen door softly behind her before switching on the light and proceeding to the fridge to find some food to take with her. She spotted some cooked chicken on a plate, under which was a bowl of salad from the previous evening's meal. Using these ingredients, she made two filled rolls.

She placed a generous squeeze of salad cream on each before wrapping them in cling film. Then she took a packet of biscuits from the cupboard and a selection of fruit from the bowl. Finally, she made up a big bottle of juice and carried this and her other provisions through the door at the back of the kitchen and into the utility room.

There, she was greeted by Bounce her dog whose tail played percussion against the side of his crate. Shushing him she let him out for a moment into the garden to relieve himself, and then feeling guilty, she coaxed him back inside and persuaded him back into the crate with a couple of pieces of dried dog food. Bounce gobbled up the food and immediately sat down fixing her with his most baleful of stares. She smiled at him and scratched his head through the top of the crate, "Sorry, Bounce, not today."

The dog seemed to realise he was out of luck, so he turned in several tight circles before settling back on his bed and emitting a snorting sigh of disgust.

Jenny carefully unhooked her rucksack from the peg and checked the contents. A rug lay folded in the bottom together with her field glasses, her sketching kit, and a new bird book which her aunt and uncle had given to her for her birthday. The side pocket, as always, contained whistle, torch, compass, her camping knife, and matches. She pushed the food and drink into the top of the bag and, as a secondary thought, grabbed her one-man tent. She fastened this onto the bag with the cords designed for just that purpose.

Jenny felt a little guilty so went back into the kitchen and scribbled a note to her parents.

> *Hi! Gone out to the woods for a bit,*
> *back in time for the christening,*
> *promise! Love Jen XX*

She spotted her mobile phone and grabbed it off the table as she went back through the utility room and into the garage where her bike was stored. Within minutes she was cycling up the lane feeling the wonderful sense of freedom she experienced every time she ventured out on her bike.

*

Maggie Pritchard turned over in bed and smiled as she looked out of the window. Sunlight was flooding across the field. It would be a lovely day for the christening, and with a family barbecue planned afterwards to celebrate, the fine weather would really add to the occasion. She prodded Tom who was still deeply asleep. "Hey, sleepy, would you like a coffee?"

Tom stuck his thumb in the air by way of a response, so Maggie rolled out of bed, and once she had found her slippers and dressing gown, she moved across their bedroom and the landing and headed down the stairs to the kitchen to put the kettle on.

She of course noticed the hand-scrawled note as soon as she entered the kitchen, and when she read it, she exclaimed in irritation. "Oh, Jenny, no! Not today, surely. It's no good, my girl, you're coming straight back home." She glanced at the kitchen clock which showed a quarter past seven and she wondered how long Jenny had been gone.

There were breadcrumbs and the remnants of the chicken and salad left on the side, and a big blob of salad cream had dripped down the front of the cupboard door. "Great! And a mess to clear up – sometimes I despair of that girl."

She looked around the kitchen for her handbag, but it wasn't there. She crossed the hallway and went into the living room where her bag, sure enough, was lying by the side of her chair. She bent down and rummaged around inside until she felt the sleek firmness of her mobile phone.

Sitting on the edge of the sofa she unlocked the screen and scrolled down until she found Jenny's number, then she stabbed the dial button and prepared herself for the disagreement that was bound to ensue with her daughter. Annoyingly, Jenny's phone rang and rang and then clicked to the voicemail message, and Jenny's cheerful voice: "Hi! Sorry I missed you. Leave a message and I'll call you back. Bye!"

"Jenny, it's Mum. I'm not surprised you're not picking up, young lady. Can you please make sure you are home by ten at the very latest, otherwise you will be for the high jump! Call me to let me know you got this okay."

Maggie killed the call and swore softly under her breath as she made her way back to the kitchen. She put her phone on the kitchen table next to Jenny's note, and feeling irritated with her daughter, she took her frustration out on the fridge door, letting it crash shut after taking out the milk. It was a moment of pure petulance, but it did make her feel better.

*

Jenny had reached the top of the lane when her mobile phone rang, chirping and vibrating in the pocket of her jacket. This part of the lane represented decision time for her: right, into the woodland with its criss-crossing of pathways; or left, onto the little used track which would take her to the reservoir.

She pulled the bike to a halt, and balancing the frame against her leg, took the phone from her pocket and screwed her face up in discomfort when she saw the word 'mum' flashing on the display. For a moment she considered answering it, but then what little courage she had, evaporated, and she let it ring off and divert to her voicemail. Looking at the display on her phone she noticed she had six new text messages, so she clicked on the envelope icon to open them. The first one was from one of her friends from school.

Hi hope yr ok, CB got yr number, sorry x

The second and subsequent ones were horrible.

Hey Pritchard Bitchard c u @ school

Whats matter bitch cat got yr tongue

Don't ignore me you whore

You're going to get it nxt week

We'll b waiting at gates on Tues morn

Just what had she done to deserve an enemy like Cheryl Bosworth? She hardly knew the girl or the gang that trolled around with her, but they had somehow latched on to Jenny and had made life at school a kind of hell. Jenny felt a cold dread settle on her, and her hand was shaking as she hit the exit button on the messages, hoping that not seeing them would banish them from her mind.

The inbox remained empty for seconds before another text message popped onto the screen, and in a moment of fear and desperation, she flung her phone away across the lane where it bounced, skittered, and disappeared into a ditch.

She lay her head on the handlebars of her bike and allowed her emotions to get the better of her. Realising she shouldn't have been so rash with her phone, she groaned, crashing her bike to the ground so she could look for it. A full five minutes passed and still she couldn't find it. She had searched the lane and tried to search the ditch by thrashing through the vegetation. The stinging nettles were vicious, and it was all too much to bear.

Jenny knew she would be in terrible trouble with her parents for losing her mobile phone – they had given her a long lecture about looking after it and how much it had cost. She wiped the sleeve of her jacket roughly across her face which was wet with tears running from her eyes and snot streaming from her nose. Then she sighed deeply, climbed back on her bike, and paused for a moment at the top of the lane. She turned resolutely left in the direction of the reservoir.

*

Maggie looked anxiously at the clock again. It was almost ten o'clock and there was no sign of Jenny. She had telephoned her daughter's mobile number several times and had given up leaving messages. She had gone through the whole gamut of emotions, from mild irritation to outright anger, but now a new feeling was wriggling in the pit of her stomach. Dark thoughts had begun to creep into her brain. Jenny could had fallen off her bike; she could have been knocked down by a hit-and-run driver and be lying in desperate need of help. Maybe she'd got lost in the woods, getting confused by the myriad of pathways that crisscrossed each other and wound for miles. Or maybe something worse, someone... She shook the thought from her mind.

She felt helpless and picked up the phone again to dial Jenny's number once more. Her heart leapt when she heard the rustling sound of the phone being answered. "Jenny, thank heavens – where on earth are you?" But then her heart leapt in a different way, and she felt the blood draining from her face when she heard a strange male voice say, "Hello, hello."

"Who's that? Is my daughter with you?"

"Oh, hello. I'm actually just walking my dog and heard a mobile ringing – it was in a ditch."

"A ditch? Oh my God, oh God. Tom! Tom! TOM!" Maggie screeched his name, the panic and fear gripping her until she felt her bowels turn to liquid. She turned back to the phone. "Who are you? Where are you? That is my daughter's phone." Her voice cracked at this last statement.

Tom came through the door with great long strides, hastened by his wife's distress. He took the phone from her. "Hello, yes, I'm Tom Pritchard and I think you have found my daughter's phone." He paused and grabbed the note Jenny had left, using it to scribble down directions, "That's very good of you, thank you... Yes, I'll be there in about ten minutes, so if you don't mind waiting... You're sure? Okay, I'll look out for you in the car park. Okay, yep... Yep, sure – see you in few minutes then. Thank you. Goodbye, bye."

For a moment they just looked at each other, then Tom said, "Maggie I think we had better call the police. This is out of character for Jenny and now her phone has been found, well..."

"Oh my God, my God. I've been sat here all morning when I could have been out looking for her. Tom what if something..." She gasped at the darkest of thoughts as they crowded into her mind.

"Mags don't think about anything but the here and the now, okay. Call the police and explain the situation. I'm going to fetch her phone."

"Don't you think you ought to wait for the police, Tom? I mean, won't they want to see where it was found? It could be a… well…" A sob escaped, and she couldn't finish the sentence.

Tom finished it for her. "A crime scene." His own voice shook as he uttered the words. "Look, I'll go up there and you call them anyway, and I'll stay there until they get there."

"So, do I dial the local number, or three nines? I don't know…" Maggie wiped a shaking hand across her mouth to bring her emotions under control.

"Christ! I don't know, love… three nines, I guess. And you'd better phone your sister – there's no way we'll get to the christening. Tell her I'm unwell or something; we don't want to set the whole family in a panic until… well… unless… Shit, this is difficult." He scrabbled furiously at his hair with both hands, snatched up his car keys, the recently updated note, and his mobile phone. He briefly pulled Maggie towards him in a clutching embrace and left the house.

*

The harvesting of the rapeseed went well, and the team of men were finished by twelve thirty, which they reckoned was a record. Jim Gamble had told them, "We work till it's finished – early, we get to go down the pub for a pint or two and see the footie; late, and we don't." That was sufficient to concentrate the efforts of the men who sweated, cursed, and shouted over the roar of the farm machinery.

At twelve forty the gate to the field was padlocked and the men hauled themselves up into the back of the trailer which rattled down the road towards Market Braithwaite, only stopping to drop Gi off at the disused entrance of the Hall which led to his cottage. He had demurred when Jim invited him to the pub, preferring instead to make the most of the rest of the day on his own and head out for a walk.

By early afternoon he had changed out of his dusty farming clothes and into his equally old walking trousers and boots and was striding across the recently ploughed fields. His route led to a narrow path, which in turn led down towards the reservoir. As a private path, it bore very little traffic so was very overgrown in places, but it was by far the quickest route to his favourite spot for sketching the birdlife that crowded the shoreline. Gulls, waders, cormorants, and more recently ospreys – following the reintroduction of the species at nearby Rutland Water. It was the latter that he was hoping to catch a glimpse of today before they left on their winter migration to Africa.

*

Once she had stashed her bike in its usual place under a hedge at the top of the hill, Jenny weaved her way down the jumble of rocks and fallen timber and settled herself at her favourite spot – her secret place which she was sure was hers and hers alone.

The reservoir was situated at the bottom of a natural valley. The hills on one side were covered in arable farmland and on the other side by deciduous woodland. It was this wooded side where Jenny's secret spot could be found, where the hill climbed steeply between rocky outcrops and mossy boulders. There was a large expanse of rock shaped like a horseshoe which climbed vertically to a height of some thirty feet. A copper beech growing at the top of the crag leant outwards, casting its branches in a giant natural shelter covering the mossy carpet below.

Jenny chose this spot to sit and gaze from the viewpoint down to the reservoir shoreline, whilst also being able to look downwards onto the canopy of woodland which covered the hill immediately below. She loved to watch the foliage change colour as the seasons passed: the gorgeous tanginess of spring when the new shoots were a fabulous vibrant shade of green, the lush fullness of summer and then (her favourite) the palette of autumn colours that could last well into November. Even winter's stark emptiness held a fascination for her with its display of brittle architecture.

On this day she was fully absorbed in sketching the scene before her and was concentrating on the sky dappled with high, grey clouds. They reminded her of the flat, grey pebbles that could be found by the sea where they often holidayed. The sun was still high in the sky, but with this cloud formation, it looked as though the sunset was going to be amazing.

She thought of her parents then for a moment and felt a clutch of guilty dread in her stomach. They always laughed at her with delight when she urged them to watch the setting sun. "But you'll never see another one exactly like this!" She would cry, and then she would sketch frantically as the sky scene changed by the second.

She paused with her pencil clamped firmly in her mouth, and pushing the guilt aside, she addressed the scene again, trying not to consider the consequences of not going home in time for the christening.

In fact, of not going home at all.

It didn't matter how much she thought about it, the idea of going home was intrinsic to going back to school and she couldn't do it. Cheryl Bosworth was going to be waiting for her on Tuesday morning, and the whole nightmare that Jenny had had to endure the previous term would start again.

She sighed heavily, and for a moment, her lip quivered until she twisted it resolutely to one side to sidestep her feelings of despair.

*

Tom Pritchard drove into the car park and, noticing the single other vehicle parked there, pulled alongside, and nodded to the occupant who immediately opened the door of the vehicle and climbed out.

"Mr Pritchard?"

"Yes, thank you for waiting for me."

"It was the least I could do. Will I show you where I found the phone?"

"Please. Let me just put my boots on." He opened the boot of the car, kicked off his flip-flops and quickly donned his Wellington boots. "The police should be here shortly."

"You must be very worried. It's over here, look – where the nettles are trampled down."

"Jesus Christ!" Tom raked his hands through his hair, feeling the last vestige of control slipping away from him. During the short car journey his thinking had see-sawed between *She's fine, it's just a mistake, we'll all be at the christening later and laughing about it* to *I've lost her and failed as a father, where is she? What's happened to her? I'll kill the bastard that laid a hand on my daughter*. His breath rattled shakily in his chest as he struggled to control his emotions and the other man shifted uncomfortably from foot to foot, unsure of how to react or what to say in this most unusual of situations.

"Let's go and wait over by the cars until the police arrive," He paused. "Tom, isn't it? Come on now, no sense in staring at this patch of ground." And he turned and started to walk slowly back to their vehicles in the hope that the distraught father would follow him and at least put a small distance between himself and the area where, for all they knew, Tom's daughter could have been abducted.

*

Rebecca Dawson yawned. She was bored. When she had been appointed acting Detective Inspector on this patch, she had wrongly assumed it would present her with the opportunity to take another stride along her short but successful career path. Three months into the secondment and she realised she could not have been more wrong.

She leafed listlessly through the charge sheets which lay upon her desk, the very tidiness of which reiterated what she already knew – Market Braithwaite was a small rural town, with a population of twenty thousand people of mixed demographics, where nothing ever seemed to happen.

At thirty-two her chosen career was a direct result of both her parents being police officers. Opting not to go to university she had worked in a local supermarket and then applied to become a Police Community Support Officer before finally fulfilling her dream and entering the service at twenty-three. Based in Luton, she knew she had the best opportunity to assimilate knowledge and experience quickly, in what was one of the busiest conurbations in England when it came to law enforcement. She had done her stint in the Rapid Response Team before moving into Traffic and Custody, and then she had sat her sergeant's exams, passing with flying colours. Her superior's encouragement had demonstrated that she was firmly on the promotional pathway.

So, when she had been given the opportunity to transfer, on a temporary basis to cover a maternity leave in Market Braithwaite as acting DI, she had leapt at the chance. Now she reflected upon what this experience had brought her to date. A dairy herd rustler which had involved getting extremely dirty and wet when she reviewed the crime scene. A couple of punch-ups on a Saturday night during what was laughingly called the local nightlife. And the usual reports of missing persons who turned out to be confused pensioners who had escaped from their day care centres or wayward teenagers who had grown tired of their supervision orders. She realised now that this secondment was going to be nothing short of laughable on her profile and would do her no favours at all when it came to the next move.

A light flickered and blinked on the telephone display on her desk, and it continued to wink at her until she leant forward in her chair and laconically picked up the receiver. "Yep?"

The voice of the duty sergeant piped breathlessly down the phone. "Guv, we've got a misper."

"Okay, George, calm down. Usual suspects?"

"No, not at all, Guv, this one's a goer."

Rebecca sat upright in her chair and tucked her chestnut hair firmly behind her ears, scrabbled with her notebook to find a page which wasn't covered in doodles and poised her pencil. "Go on then, out with it."

"Local girl, fourteen years old, out on a bike ride seemingly. Should have been going out with her parents this morning, and when they tried to call her, some bloke answers her mobile – claims he heard it ringing in a ditch whilst he was walking his dog. No sign of her since. But apparently looks like signs of a struggle around the site where her mobile was found."

"Right! George, squad car outside in five minutes and get Gerry on the blower – he'll have to come in."

"Guv."

Rebecca's heart was hammering in her chest, and she could feel the adrenalin coursing through her body. She knew she shouldn't feel elation at the prospect of a girl going missing, but this could be the chance she had been waiting for: national headlines, a high-profile case for her CV – the lot. She picked up her jacket and handbag and marched out of the office, pausing only to call in at the ladies on her way down to the squad car.

*

Gi made his way along the tangled pathway and then headed into the woodland which clung to the steep sides of the hill leading down towards the reservoir. The wood was littered with the detritus of fallen branches, leaf litter and the beech mast that was left from previous years. In many places the moss grew so thickly it covered the fallen wood, the stones, and craggy patches, creating a difficult descent which could only be negotiated with care. The path ended abruptly at the edge of a drop of about a metre, and as Gi was familiar with the stability of the surface below, he paused only for a moment before he launched himself off the edge and landed crouching on the ground below.

At the sound behind her, Jenny let out a small cry and turned to see the man crouching less than twelve feet from her. He was leaning forward and balancing his weight using one of his huge hands, splayed upon the ground. There was a long moment of silence as they stared at each other.

Jenny was afraid and she could feel her heart hammering in her chest, her breath was coming in short gasps.

The man seemed shocked too, and then he straightened up

into a standing position to reveal his full height.

Jenny was completely trapped. The only way out from the mossy area was to scrabble up the bank and back onto the pathway, but that lay behind this man. She thought he seemed familiar to her. He took a step towards her, and she cried out again, only being shocked into silence once more when he said quietly, "The girl from the garden. You're the girl from the garden."

"Don't hurt me, please." She whimpered and started to cry, but she could only call out once more before he crossed the distance between them and grasped her by the arm.

THREE

"You must be Mr Pritchard." Rebecca Dawson strode across the uneven surface of the car park and thrust her hand towards one of the men. Both men were leaning heavily against one of the two vehicles parked adjacent to each other in the clearing within the woodland. She had picked him out alright – just by observing the man's body language as the squad car parked up, she could tell it was this man who must be the father of the missing child. His face was grey and had taken on that look of shock and fear that, unfortunately, Rebecca had seen on many previous occasions. He acknowledged her introduction with a half-hearted handshake in return.

Then she eyeballed the other man. "And you are?"

"Henry Barker. I found the mobile phone; shall I show you where?"

She nodded curtly and indicated with her arm that she would follow him. The small group traipsed across the car park and on into the woodland. On the right-hand side of the path was a ditch and it was clear to Rebecca that the foliage, mostly made up of nettles and other unidentifiable weeds, had been crushed and flattened recently.

"Mr Barker, was the ditch like this when you found the phone?"

"Yes, pretty much. I heard the phone ringing and had to get into the ditch to retrieve it."

"I am going to need you to give a statement down the station."

"Is that really necessary? I told you what happened; there isn't much more to say."

Rebecca regarded him with a severe look. "Mr Barker, a child is missing. I need every bit of information you have in relation to the incident. I need your fingerprints to identify them on the mobile phone and most importantly I need to eliminate you as a suspect."

"I say! Steady on, I was only trying to help."

Rebecca brought her irritation back under control. "I appreciate that, Mr Barker, as I am sure you will appreciate, my job is to find this child without delay."

"Yes, yes, of course, of course."

"If you would like to go with my colleague PC Franks, he will do the necessary." With this she nodded in the direction of the squad car.

"What about my car? What about my dog?" Henry Barker wasn't a happy man, but he wasn't about to incur the wrath of the DI again.

"We can sort the vehicle out later, Mr Barker. For now, your car is part of a potential crime scene and will remain here..." She cast a glance down at the dog which was standing impassively at its owner's side, "Provided it's well-behaved you can bring the dog with you."

With that she turned dismissively to preclude any further protests and spoke to her colleague. "The whole area needs sealing off and we need SOCO down here immediately. And organise a search party asap. Can I leave that with you?"

"Yes, Guv, on it." The young PC turned away and spoke into his radio mike.

Tom Pritchard watched in a catatonic state, letting the comings and goings wash over him. Inside he wanted to scream, yell, fight, do something, do anything to rid himself of his growing sense of panic and frustration.

"Mr Pritchard. Mr Pritchard." Rebecca placed her hand gently on Tom Pritchard's arm to bring him back to her. She noted the gold wedding band on his finger.

"What? Sorry, yes, what?"

"We are going to need to have a chat about what has happened at home to lead up to this situation. How about we go and have a chat with you and your wife. I take it you do have a wife at home?"

"Yes, yes but what can we do to help? When can we start looking for her… please!"

"I've already instructed my colleague."

"I want to help – I've got to help!" Tom slapped his hands against his legs.

"Mr Pritchard, I appreciate how you must be feeling but we need to establish some facts first and leave the searching to my team who are fully trained for it. Come on, let's get you home. I will travel with you and then get a car to pick us up later."

"Us?"

"I will want you and your wife to come to the station with me, so we can take a formal statement and confirm necessary details about Jenny and how close you are as a family. Purely a formality, of course."

For a moment, Rebecca thought the man was going to pass out. White already, he turned a ghastly shade of greenish grey. She knew her implication had sickened him, but she needed to face facts. Most cases of this nature that ended badly often involved the very people who were meant to protect the victim. She hated to do it, but she must; she had to keep a completely open mind, and until each person was proven to be innocent, everyone was a suspect.

She guided Tom Pritchard to his car and left him for a moment whilst she confirmed requirements with PC Franks.

"Wait for Gerry and SOCO to get here and keep me informed every step of the way. Get Gerry to call me the minute he gets here, okay? Then take Mr Barker back to the station and organise fingerprinting and take a statement."

"Guv."

With that she turned away and accessed the phone directory listed on her mobile to locate the Detective Chief Inspector's number. It rang briefly before being answered.

"Critchley."

"Sir, DI Dawson. Sorry to bother you on a Sunday, sir, but we have a girl gone missing in suspicious circumstances. I don't think it's the usual casual runaway, sir." She briefly explained the background of the situation and waited for her instructions, hoping that he wasn't going to take the case away from her at this early stage.

She breathed a sigh of relief as he merely said, "We'll need to brief the press office for a release to the media. Meet me at the station at two, Dawson, and in the meantime, I assume you have everything in order?"

Again, she explained exactly the wheels she had set in motion – the interviews, SOCO on the scene and the search party – to which he said, "Fine. Just keep me informed of any developments."

With that the call was cut so she turned back to Tom Pritchard who was sitting in his vehicle, his forehead buried deep in his hands. She could see his shoulders shaking with the outpouring of emotion, and with as much empathy as she could muster, she climbed in beside him and indicated they were ready to go.

*

The Melchett Arms pub was situated on the junction of the main road that led towards Market Braithwaite and a smaller country road which led down to Melchett Hall. Sundays were generally very busy, both with local patrons and passing trade. The pub served excellent lunches in the lounge and dining areas, and locals were well catered for too, with a bar area containing a pool table, dartboard, and a newly installed flat-screen television. This was currently showing a one-day cricket match between two county teams.

The courtyard of the pub had recently benefited from a makeover and there was a raised decking area which provided covered seating and a view out on to a pleasant garden. The garden edged the same river which wound its way around the Melchett estate. This outside space allowed the overspill of customers to partake of their drinks and food whilst enjoying the late summer sunshine.

The farmworkers from the estate had disembarked from the

trailer which was now parked up on the side of the minor road leading to the hall. They quickly claimed the bar area as their own, ordering pints in readiness for the football game that was due to kick off at one p.m. Whilst they waited to be served, two of them commandeered the pool table and set the juke-box playing, much to the annoyance of a group of domino players who had taken up residence at a round table in the corner of the room.

The landlady watched them tolerantly. She needed their custom and she knew they would be there for the remainder of the afternoon, no doubt consuming several pints of beer or lager. They would probably order some of the hot roast beef and horseradish rolls with which she was hoping to tempt those customers who would not be partaking of the full roast lunch. She turned from the bar, happy that they were sorted for the time being, and brought her attention back to the small queue forming at the opposite side of the bar. She sighed with barely concealed irritation and muttered, "Where is that girl now?" Then she adjusted her persona, brightened her smile, and said, "Sorry for keeping you waiting, sir, what can I get for you?"

The young man acknowledged her smile and nodded towards the gleaming pumps of real ales. "Three pints of Speckled Hen please, two large glasses of dry white wine and a diet coke with ice."

The order was dispatched with efficiency and placed upon a tray. "Will you be eating with us today, sir?"

"Yes please. We're outside, is that OK?"

"Yes, yes of course. Here let me pop some menus on your tray and I'll send someone out shortly to take your order. Whereabouts are you sitting?"

He craned his neck and gestured approximately in the direction of where his party had settled. "Over towards the river."

"It's good that the weather is holding for you today."

"Absolutely! It makes a nice change to be able to enjoy a good summer for once." With that he pocketed the change from the round, carefully picked up the tray and, negotiating the various obstacles, made his way out of the lounge bar and across the garden to where his wife and friends were sitting.

"We thought you'd got lost, Craig!"

"Yeah well, a helping hand wouldn't have gone amiss, y'know. The bloody carrot-crunchers have taken over the bar again."

"Sorry, mate! My round next, okay?"

"Christ, now I know the sun has got to you – here, get this down your neck."

Craig Rogers settled onto the bench next to his gorgeous wife Sally and nuzzled into her neck. "Hello, beautiful, want a date?"

"Please you two save that for later, won't you!"

The group of friends had fallen into the habit of meeting on a Sunday for drinks and lunch when other commitments allowed. The Melchett Arms was one of their favoured watering holes and it was a bonus that the weather was still holding on to the summer warmth for yet another weekend.

Their friendship had originally stemmed from school, with Craig, James and Harry all being alumni from the local grammar school in Leicester. James and Harry were both civil engineers, or, as Craig often put it – just jobbing builders, really. Craig was a freelance reporter whose ambitions to date had secured him a column in the local paper, a few pieces in the red tops and some articles in a journal dedicated to the farming industry. He was determined to carve out a successful career for himself as a journalist and hoped that his caustic writing style would soon be noticed properly by one of the nationals.

The group had just ordered lunch and were starting on their second round of drinks when Craig's attention was diverted from the banter and chat by yet another police vehicle passing by on the main road. His interest was further piqued when two police vans crammed with officers and a police dog unit van sped past in the same direction.

"Something's afoot!" He announced and eased himself off the bench, reaching into his pocket for his mobile phone as he did so. He wandered away from his friends to make a call to his contact at the police station with whom he had an understanding: *you keep me in the loop, and I'll return the favour – it's a win-win situation, mate.*

"What's up then?" Craig didn't bother with any preamble and after a couple of soft expletives and a "Cheers, I owe you!" He disconnected the call and turned back to his companions. He grabbed the car keys off the table and bent to kiss his wife. "Sorry, hun, got to dash – there's something going on and I mean to be there to get the story."

Sally looked up towards her husband and, shielding her eyes from the bright sunshine, exclaimed, "What's happened?"

"Girl gone missing, only fourteen – seems she's been abducted in the woods. This could be my break, Sal!"

"Craig!" She admonished him and shook her head as he disappeared towards the car park. He had a ruthless streak about him, and she didn't like it when it took over.

Within minutes, Craig had parked the car as close to the woodland parking area as he could without bringing undue attention to himself. He wandered over to a young constable who was supervising and authorising entry to the cordoned-off area.

"Afternoon, constable. Craig Rogers, freelance. What's going on then?"

"Can't say, sir." The constable looked confident and calm in his role.

"I've heard it's a missing local girl, is that right?"

"I really don't know, sir. There's a press briefing at the station at four. You'd be best to go there, sir."

"Come on, let's give the local paper a break, man. We can rally the community and get everyone helping to find her."

But the constable remained inscrutable and turned his back, so Craig figured he wasn't going to learn anything worth knowing here. But on the way back to the car, he took a few photographs of the cordoned-off area thinking it could add spice to any story that may be emerging.

*

Maggie Pritchard stared red-eyed at the bagged mobile phone. When the female police officer placed it upon the kitchen table the bag had crackled noisily, and to Maggie, it seemed dirty somehow, defiled by whoever might have touched it when her Jenny had come to harm.

"Mrs Pritchard, may I call you Maggie?" The woman reached across the table as if to grasp her hand, but she hesitated, and the ineffectual gesture petered out halfway so that her hand lay palm down on the rough pine table and then slowly withdrew until it clasped not Maggie's hand but her own.

"I can see there is an unread text message on the phone which I think we should take a look at." Again, the woman leant forward trying to make some show of empathy but instead grasped the bag which crackled again as she drew it towards her.

"A message?" Maggie gazed listlessly at Rebecca Dawson, thinking she seemed far too young and inexperienced to be managing the investigation into the disappearance of her daughter.

"Why aren't you looking for her? FOR GOD'S SAKE!" Maggie's torpor suddenly transformed, and she could feel her whole body shaking with violent emotion.

"We are, we are. I have fifty police officers from three counties searching the woodland right now, Mrs Pritchard. I can assure you we are doing everything we can to find your daughter"—she paused for a moment; it was infinitesimal but both Maggie and Tom noticed— "safe and sound, I am sure."

Tom nodded towards the bagged phone. "What's the message say, Inspector Dawson?"

"Right, let's take a look then." Rebecca smoothed out the crinkled surface of the bag across the keypad and screen and, after pressing a few combinations of keys, managed to access the inbox for text messages. They all held their breath as she opened the text. She read it without comment before sliding the still-bagged phone across the surface of the table towards Maggie and Tom, "This mean anything to either of you?"

They both bent over the display and squinted for a moment to read the text through the reflective surface of the bag. The message was quite simple.

Jen r u ok? Tell yr mum and dad about it, please x

Tom and Maggie made eye contact for a moment, each one silently questioning the other and then they both turned to the Detective Inspector, shook their heads, and said in unison, "No, what do you think it means?"

"It could be relevant or mean nothing. I'm sorry. The number is withheld which is strange. Any trouble with boys that you know of?"

"She's only fourteen." Tom shook his head in denial, but he noted the look of scepticism that fleetingly crossed the young policewoman's face.

"Did… does Jenny have a laptop or computer?"

"Yes, it's in her room. I'll get it."

"Actually, I'd like to see Jenny's room if I may."

"Of course." Maggie stood and for a moment had to grasp the edge of the table to steady herself.

"Okay, love?" Tom reached out to her.

She waved him off. "I'm fine. I'm okay, love, thanks."

By the time Rebecca Dawson had finished at the Pritchard home, it was one thirty and high time she was heading back to the station for her briefing with DCI Critchley. She arranged for a squad car to pick her up and asked Tom and Maggie to be available to come to the station too, so they could be present at the press conference. Painful though this experience would no doubt be, she assured them it would help their inquiries.

She took the mobile phone, Jenny's laptop, and her diary with her, together with a recent photograph of the young girl. She thought the girl was striking to look at which added further speculation to the possible involvement of a love interest. When she left, she had the distinct impression that there was no way Jenny's parents could be complicit in their daughter's disappearance, but she knew better than to come to any judgement at this early stage in her investigation.

*

The press briefing didn't take place until four thirty and lasted only a few minutes but there was at least a sense of something happening now that DCI Critchley had presented the facts of the case.

Jennifer Pritchard, fourteen years old, only daughter of local married couple, Thomas and Margaret Pritchard – he an accountant, she a seamstress – had gone missing whilst on a bike ride on Sunday morning. She had not been seen since Saturday evening when her parents had kissed her goodnight, and her mobile phone had been found in the well-known and frequented Burberry Woods near the reservoir, by a local man who had been walking his dog. Anyone with any information should call the dedicated phone line that had been set up.

The photograph of Jenny was circulated to the small group of press in attendance, Craig Rogers being one of them. As the small group of attendees filtered listlessly out of the door, Detective Chief Inspector Critchley gathered his sheaf of papers and turned to Rebecca Dawson. "A few moments in my office, if you please."

"Yes, sir." She quietly told the Pritchards they were free to go home and that she would keep them informed of any developments, before turning to follow DCI Critchley.

Critchley led as they walked in silence from the press room and down the corridor, before climbing the broad set of stairs which led to the offices. Once inside his office, Critchley positioned himself behind his desk but remained standing with his back turned to Rebecca so that he could look out of the window.

"What have we got then?"

"Well, sir, not much, if truth be told. I don't think the parents are implicated at this stage. Forensics are still at the scene, and I've got someone checking her laptop. I reckon we might be looking at young love, sir. You know the sort of thing: girl falls in love with older bloke and next thing she's in a spot of bother and does a bunk."

"That doesn't explain the discarded mobile, does it?" He turned to look directly at her. "And what about the man who found the phone – could be a smokescreen to divert our attention from him. Check out her friends too – school, and whatever extracurricular things she got involved in."

"That's one thing, sir – she didn't."

"Didn't what?"

"Didn't go to any clubs or play sports or anything like that – bit of a loner, it seems."

"Hmmph. Also check the paedophile register. What's occurring with the locals. Who's in and who's out at the moment, and their movements."

"Sir."

"Look, Dawson, I'm looking for a quick result on this, understood?"

"Yes, sir, of course."

"I don't want your inexperience to slow things down, so keep me fully informed, at all times. I hope that's clear."

"Perfectly, sir."

"Go on then, get cracking. Every minute wasted chatting is a minute we could be looking for the girl."

As she left the office, she closed the door gently behind her and mouthed "Oh piss off!" To the thankfully impenetrable door. "It was *you* who wanted the chat, sir!" She simpered as she strode down the corridor. Of course, what Rebecca Dawson hadn't reckoned on was that his patronising manner was having exactly the impact that he had wanted. She was galvanised by his lack of confidence in her and would spend every available resource tracking Jennifer Pritchard down.

*

When Gi arrived back at his cottage it was already dark. His boots were caked in mud from crossing the ploughed field. He heeled them off by the back door and left them just inside the porch. The aroma of the stew he had placed in his stove much earlier wafted tantalisingly across the kitchen as he opened the door and flicked on the light. The harsh neon tube flickered mercilessly for a few seconds and then pinged into life.

He was filthy. There was a large and deep scratch on his forearm that ran from just below his elbow down onto the back of his hand and he flinched when the sting of soap and water entered the wound. He peered at his reflection in the mirror and for a moment couldn't work out which marks were spots of mud on his face, and which were the ageing flaws in the surface of the mirror.

He was ravenous, but instead of eating, he left the kitchen and stumbled to the small bathroom where he peeled off his clothes and stepped with great weariness into the shower. Once clean and changed into jeans and a soft plaid shirt, he moved back to the kitchen, scooped the pot of stew from the stove and whacked it without ceremony straight onto the kitchen table, pausing only to remove the lid before dipping a spoon into the meat and vegetables. He ate as quickly as he could shovel the food into his mouth, despite the burning temperature.

When finished, he burped loudly, pushed the ancient stew pot to one side and slid the kitchen chair noisily back across the slate floor. He stood and stretched languidly before helping himself to a bottle of beer from the fridge. He flicked the top off the bottle and drank noisily, gulping several times before pausing to wipe the residue of ale from his mouth.

Seemingly satisfied for the moment, he turned his attention to the drawing of the girl in the garden, and taking his sketch pad and pencil, he sat opposite the sketch he had made of Jenny and started to deconstruct her face. Drawing first her eye, then her mouth, and even her hand as it was poised in its own act of artistry. He finally stumbled off to bed, well after midnight, leaving dozens of images of Jennifer, component parts of her really, carefully pinned to the cork board.

FOUR

Daylight struggled to get a hold of Monday morning. The weather had finally broken, and it turned out that the dappled mackerel clouds of the previous afternoon had merely been a presage to the heavy clouds and dull mist which were now slung low across the landscape. A fine drizzle filled the air, the dampness insinuating itself into everything. The bushes and trees were covered with droplets of moisture so that the cobwebs hung like gossamer necklaces strung with tiny crystals oscillating gently in the slight movement of air. The dampness had infused into the ground so that the air held a sour aroma of decay, and in every sense, it appeared that autumn had quite suddenly and unexpectedly arrived.

Gi was already awake, despite the lack of light filtering through the drab curtains which hung haphazardly from the old pine curtain pole in the shabby bedroom. He had been awake for some considerable time, lying on his back with his arms bent and hands resting behind his head, the picture of deep contemplation.

With a huge sigh, he swung his legs out of the covers and stretched before making his way across the room to where he had dumped his clothes the previous evening.

Mondays were always his day off from work on the estate and he generally took a more leisurely approach to getting up and about his business. This usually took him into Market Braithwaite to stock up on supplies, and then perhaps to the pub for a pint and a bite of lunch. Then, invariably, he would attend to his own vegetable garden situated on the slope at the back of the cottage.

He wandered into the kitchen scratching his stubbly chin which rasped noisily as his fingernails encountered the blackish bristles that had sprouted overnight. He yawned again and flicked on the light switch, filled the kettle, and placed it upon the hot plate. Then he turned on the old television set which sat on a small pine shelf in the corner of the room.

An inspection of the contents of the fridge revealed two remaining rashers of thick-cut bacon and some sliced bread, and he grabbed them both with relish. The skillet was upturned on the enamel draining board, so he grasped the handle and placed it on the remaining hot plate, dropping in the bacon and watching with satisfaction as the fat began to render in the heat of the pan.

The news was burbling along in the background, issues with the world – America struggling to agree its budget and all the ramifications this held for the rest of the global economy, a terrorist attack in the Middle East with tragic loss of life. Then the weather forecast began which made Gi turn to give the television his full attention. He was always interested in the weather, more so than the rest of the news as it had a direct and sometimes pertinent impact upon his working life.

Then the presenter cut to the local *Midlands Today* news and Gi turned once more to the stove to flick the two rashers of bacon over in the pan. This encouraged a small and satisfying sizzle and a gorgeous aroma to waft its way to his palate, and he anticipated the meal with his usual enthusiasm. But then his attention was suddenly and shockingly pierced by the story being relayed by the local newsreader to her audience.

"… the girl shown here is fourteen-year-old Jennifer Pritchard who was last seen on Saturday evening at her home. Police are increasingly concerned for Jennifer's safety and her parents have made this emotional appeal." The newsreader's face had taken on a sombre expression as the piece cut to a press conference showing a man and woman clinging together to face the camera and stuttering their plea. "Please, Jenny love, come home. You're not in trouble. Please, anyone, anyone…"

The set flickered once and then died as Gi switched it off. He slumped heavily down into one of the kitchen chairs. His hand was shaking badly as he wiped the broad palm over his face and muttered, "Oh God, God!" For a moment he felt weak, and a bitter regurgitation of bile burnt sickly in his throat.

His mind was working. *What do to, what do to?* He had to go back there. He didn't want to, but he knew he had to. Something had to be done. He took the kettle off one hot plate, placed the bacon in the bread and then lifted the skillet off the other hot plate. But the handle of the skillet had become very hot, and it burnt his hand. He cried out with a vile expletive and hurled the skillet across the kitchen where it now lay, dripping little blobs of fat onto the floor. He had to run cold water over the palm of his hand, where he could already see the beginnings of a blister forming painfully on the tender pad below his thumb.

He cursed again, more quietly this time, and then quickly grabbed the things he would need, tugged on his boots and coat, and picked up the sandwich on the way out. He left the cottage, not even shutting the door behind him as he strode off across the lane, into the fields, and onto the footpath which would lead him to the reservoir.

*

Marion Gamble was also in her kitchen as it was her duty and pleasure to ensure Jim had a decent breakfast in him before he set out onto the estate for the day. Most likely he would barely have time to take a rest in his busy schedule, so she liked to make sure he had a good, cooked meal inside him before she sent him off with his packed lunch.

This way, she would be able to turn to her own busy schedule for the day without worrying about him. She shivered as she peered out of the cottage window, thinking how dank and miserable it seemed compared to the previous day.

"Hey, Jim, thank goodness the weather wasn't like this over the weekend with the festival, hey?"

"You what, love?"

"I said…" She raised her voice but thought better of it. "Oh, never mind, dear." She shook her head and smiled. Jim was getting a bit hard of hearing, not that he would admit it for a moment, of course, and Marion often gave up trying to talk to him when he wasn't in the same room.

Instead, she turned on the television which was tuned to her usual early morning news programme. Often it was just a comforting background noise which sometimes provided a subject for discussion over the breakfast table.

Marion turned back to the task of cooking breakfast but poised motionless, tea towel clasped in one hand and a plate in the other as the newsreader moved on to a bulletin about a fourteen-year-old girl going missing, possibly abducted from woodland near the small rural town of Market Braithwaite.

"Jim! Jim! Come and listen to this." She raised her voice.

"Alright, no need to shout, what is it?" Jim stood in the doorway.

Marion flicked the tea towel towards the television screen to draw Jim's attention to it.

"Dear oh dear, that's bad news – tragic for the parents," He muttered.

The item continued to focus on the disappearance of the girl, and her photograph came up on the screen.

Marion exclaimed, "Oh, she's a pretty thing too! I hope to God they find her safe. What's the matter, Jim?"

Jim Gamble was staring at the photograph. "She looks familiar, but I can't think where I've seen her before."

"Maybe in the grounds, with her family or something?"

"Hmmmm… maybe." He made an exasperated noise in his throat. "That's going to annoy me all day, that is."

"Here." Marion placed his breakfast on the table. "Make a start on that whilst you're wondering, love."

Twenty minutes later, and feeling replete, Jim Gamble opened the rear door of the Land Rover to allow his two working collie dogs, Bill and Patch, to enthusiastically jump into the back of the vehicle. He slammed the door shut and made his way around to the driver's door. He keyed the engine which spluttered into life, and he frowned and shook his head at the various squeaks and rattling sounds which emitted from under the bonnet. He'd tried to talk Toby into replacing it recently, but he knew the request was more in hope than expectation. With the current financial position of the estate, the Land Rover would have to draw its last breath before Toby would consider a replacement. The gears grated horribly, and the Land Rover lurched forwards spasmodically as the clutch finally fully engaged and set about driving the old jeep onwards.

It was daily habit of Jim's to do a circuit of the estate, keeping a careful eye out for any broken fencing that may lead to the longhorn cattle escaping. He also carried out an inspection of work completed by the estate workers the previous day just to check they had followed his instructions and shown the appropriate level of industry. They were all good men, but he liked to keep them on their toes. It was with this in mind that Jim brought the Land Rover to a halt on the road by the side of the walled garden. He wanted to see the progress Gi had made with the clearance of the beds in preparation for bulb planting, and as he surveyed the area that Gi had been working on, he nodded with satisfaction. He might be a strange character, but Jim wished all the estate employees had the same work ethic as Gi.

It was only as he turned to exit the garden that his brain finally made the connection between the photograph shown on the news that morning of the young girl who had gone missing, and the sketched drawing of *the girl in the garden*, as Gi had described her. Jim's head snapped up. It felt like someone had punched him in the solar plexus. His heart pumped as though it might explode, stimulated by the rush of adrenalin. He slumped onto one of the numerous stone benches that were scattered around the garden and waited for a moment to allow the physical reaction to settle. He noticed his hands were trembling as he lifted them to his face to cover his horrified expression.

"Oh my God! No way, not Gi, surely not." But even as he continued to deny the possibility of a connection, he also knew he had to be sure, and the only way he could do that was to go to the gatehouse cottage again and take another look at the sketch. If his worst fears were confirmed, he would have to decide what course of action to take. It could just be a coincidence and mean nothing, but he wouldn't take chances, not when there was the life of a young girl at stake.

He felt physically sick as he retraced his steps back to the Land Rover. The dogs bobbed up again into the back and Jim took a deep and shaky breath before starting up the jeep once more, pointing it in the direction of the northern edge of the estate where the gatehouse stood.

As he drove down the lane that led to the gatehouse, he started to imagine how the next few minutes would play out. Maybe he had been mistaken, and taking a second look at the drawing would allay his fears completely. As he brought the jeep to a halt in front of the cottage, he certainly hoped that would be the case.

The cottage door was ajar, but instead of the warm sunshine spilling onto the stone entrance step as it had the previous day, like a welcoming wash of colour, the scene this morning seemed dank and sinister. There was no sign of life, either immediately inside the cottage or in the grounds which extended all around the dwelling, rising at the rear of the building. Anyone wishing to access the substantial vegetable patch had to climb four damp and mossy steps situated at the end of a narrow passageway that led down one side of the cottage. The other side of the cottage provided support for a decrepit lean-to which housed Gi's old motorbike, the presence of which confirmed that its owner was probably at home.

Jim knew that Gi was probably gardening on his patch of land as that's where he could often be found on a Monday when he wasn't working on the estate. But rather than seek him out in this most likely of places, Jim decided to try the cottage first so that he would have the chance to look at the sketch once again without the unwavering scrutiny of Gi.

To be sure he wasn't mistaken, Jim rapped noisily on the open door, and when this announcement of his arrival drew no response, he pushed the door open with the toe of his boot and stepped over the threshold. The entrance led into a tiny vestibule, big enough to accommodate one person. The doorway immediately opposite the front door led straight on and into the kitchen.

Jim called again, "Ay-up! Anyone at home?" Before pushing the door open to reveal the room beyond. The kitchen was deserted. Jim immediately noticed the skillet lying upside down on the kitchen floor, and it struck him as a very odd place to find the cooking implement.

Then his eye was drawn to the cork board, and its contents made him gasp in mortification. The board was covered with countless drawings, all depicting that girl or, more weirdly, parts of the girl. Jim didn't even want to think what that might mean, but he felt a chill of fear and repulsion so strong that he stumbled from the cottage and didn't stop until he got back to the Land Rover, climbed in, and locked the door.

His hand shook as he scrabbled to reach his mobile phone in the pocket of his jacket. When he finally managed to extricate it from within, he had to hold his trembling finger steady with the fingers of his other hand to unlock the keypad and dial three nines.

*

DI Dawson was just climbing into her car and preparing to drive to the station to carry out the morning briefing when her mobile phone began to vibrate on the passenger seat. When she saw the station number flashing on the display she answered without delay, and after a moment of listening, she reached down into the footwell of the car to grab the notebook from out of her handbag. She left instructions with the caller for the team to continue with the tasks delegated to them the previous day and give them notice that the briefing would be held at some point later. Then she cut the call and immediately dialled another number, this time calling her boss, DCI Critchley. He answered with his usual alacrity.

"Critchley"

"Sir, we have a lead."

She didn't waste time on details but apprised him of the situation and the information that had come from Melchett Hall which, as she pointed out, was a stone's throw from the wooded area where Jennifer Pritchard had gone missing. They agreed to meet at the hall within the quarter hour.

In fact, it took Rebecca just five minutes to arrive at the main entrance to the hall where she paused briefly before shifting the car into second gear and easing it gently over the cattle grid. This indicated the demarcation between the public road and the private lane that curved away to the left and through an avenue of trees. She followed this lane until she arrived at a parking area where she brought her car to a halt, cranked on the handbrake, and waited for her superior to arrive.

Ian Critchley wasn't far behind her, and within minutes, he pulled his BMW into the parking area, cut the engine, and stepped from his vehicle.

"Morning, sir."

"Dawson."

"I've been told that the estate manager and Toby Bursill-Brookes the owner of the hall will be waiting for us in the estate office, sir."

"Come on then, let's see what's what."

They walked quickly from the parking area, following the lane as it continued to sweep through the beautiful mature trees, until it panned out into a wide circle, in the middle of which was a pristine lawn. The house stood in front of them, perhaps not looking its best on this dull, early autumn morning, but it was still an impressive façade which gave them both a moment to pause and admire.

"Wow! Some house," exclaimed Rebecca softly.

"Eighteenth century, local stone. Impressive, isn't it?"

"Ah! It looks as though we have a welcoming party." Rebecca nodded over towards the side of the house where a door located in a brick wall had opened to reveal two gentlemen who were clearly expecting their visitors. Unexpectedly, the younger of the two was the first to introduce himself.

"Toby Bursill-Brookes." He extended his hand and shook the hand of Ian Critchley and then Rebecca Dawson warmly and firmly. "This is my estate manager, Jim Gamble."

Once the preamble of introductions was over, Jim Gamble

led the way through the door and into a single-storey brick-built building that appeared to have several functions, the estate office being one of them. Someone had placed two additional chairs, in readiness for their meeting, in front of the rather tatty desk. Upon the desk there was every imaginable item: seed catalogues, plant bulbs, some of which had rolled onto the floor, a broken padlock, a half-eaten packet of biscuits and three mugs which, judging by the dried-on stains, had been there for some days.

"Sorry about the mess." Jim waved at the chairs, inviting the police officers to sit. "Tea? Coffee?"

"Coffee would be good if it's not too much trouble." Ian Critchley accepted gratefully, having reluctantly left his mug of steaming coffee on the kitchen table at home moments after he had taken the call from his DI.

Toby had been leaning against a bank of very battered filing cabinets with his arms folded, but he stood up quickly and said, "I'll sort that out, Jim. I guess you'll want to get started straightaway?" He directed the final part of his remark to the male police officer who merely nodded his agreement.

Rebecca Dawson delved into her bag and brought out the notebook and pen and poised herself in readiness to take the notes of the impending interview. She was interested to see how Ian Critchley would handle the estate manager. Not having had the pleasure of working with him closely yet, she wondered how he would adapt his rather terse manner to develop a rapport with their interviewee.

Critchley seemed to sense Rebecca's interest, and he shifted in his seat and uncrossed his legs before leaning forwards and addressing the man. "Now then, Mr Gamble, why don't you tell us why you think one of your estate workers may be implicated in this girl's possible abduction."

Jim started hesitantly at first, nervous of the scrutiny of the two senior police officers. He started to explain how he had found this extraordinary drawing of a young girl in one of his employee's cottages.

Rebecca interrupted him. "Hold on there, Mr Gamble –

where is this drawing now?"

"Oh, it's still at the cottage. I haven't touched a thing by the way. It's all just as I found it this morning."

"Okay, carry on. We'll want a look at that in a few minutes."

At this point, Toby appeared with a tray holding four mugs of coffee which he put down on the centre of the desk and indicated that people should help themselves.

Jim inclined his head towards Rebecca to acknowledge the demand that she had made, and he continued. "When I saw the appeal on the television this morning, I couldn't make the connection. Knew the girl looked familiar but couldn't place her until I went to the walled garden and then it hit me. She's the same girl – as the one in the drawing, I mean."

He went on to explain he'd had words with the estate worker about an incident that had taken place on the previous Saturday, some small drama that a visitor had made a complaint about. It was then that he had seen the drawing of the girl, and he had warned his employee off drawing visitors to the park. "As I told him, folk could get the wrong idea. Told him to stick to flowers and the like."

"So, when did you make the connection?" Ian Critchley prompted him.

"This morning when I was in the walled garden, and I hotfooted it round to the cottage. Needed to be sure. And that's when I found the rest…" He looked, for the first time, distressed by what he was recounting.

"The rest?" Urged Critchley.

"I think it's best if I show you; it's difficult to explain, you know." Again, Jim Gamble shifted uneasily in his chair.

"Tell me some more about your employee. What's his name?"

Toby cut in here, explaining that Giovanni Santoro had lived on the estate for more than twenty-seven years and had worked there for twenty of those years. Then Jim chipped in that, all that time, Gi had been reliable, hard-working, and honest.

"But?" Rebecca paused in her notetaking and glanced an apology to her superior for hijacking the interview.

"But what?" Jim eyed her nervously.

"Well, I picked up some note of reservation, Mr Gamble, when you were describing your employee's attributes. Anything else you would like to tell us? Obscuring the facts at this stage in the investigation would be less than helpful."

"Well, what can I tell you about Gi? He's…" Jim shook his head and pulled a face of uncertainty.

"I think what Jim is trying to tell you is that our Giovanni is a bit of an oddball. Solitary character. Moved here from Italy with his parents – they're both gone now – had trouble settling in, spot of bother at school for which he got expelled. We've been, well, I suppose, caring for him ever since."

"I see." She arched her eyebrows to convey her opinion – she may just have well uttered the word *nutter* out loud, her demeanour was that obvious.

"He's a good lad," Jim protested. "I've never had a moment's bother with him."

"Until last Saturday's drama," Critchley stated. "Tell us more about that, Mr Gamble."

Jim unfolded the tale of the visitor complaining about the way Giovanni had spoken to his two girls in the walled garden.

"When did you address this complaint to him?"

"Sunday morning, I think. Yes, it was, because I called round to the cottage to see if he would help us with some harvesting."

"And when was that."

"On that morning. We had half a field to bring in and the weather looked iffy, so I wanted all hands to get the job done."

"When did you finish the job?"

"Oh, let's see, it would have been about twelve thirty, cos we were in the pub in time for the football starting at one."

"So, you all went to the pub?"

"Not Gi. We dropped him off at the cottage on the way past."

"Time?"

"Can't be certain of that, but would guess at about twelve forty-five, something like that."

"And were you with him all morning up until that point, Mr Gamble?"

"Yes! We started the harvest about seven and worked like slaves to get it finished. Gi was with us all morning until we..." Jim Gamble stopped in mid-sentence as though a thought had just occurred to him.

"Mr Gamble?"

"He did disappear, actually, but it was only for five minutes at the most."

"Why would he do that?"

"I've no idea. Maybe needed, you know, to relieve himself or something. It was literally minutes."

"And where is this field on the estate?"

"It's on the north perimeter."

"I see, so, close to Burberry Woods then?"

"Yes, the woods back onto the field. But we were down the bottom end mostly. There's no way Gi or anyone else for that matter would have gone to the woods, no way," Jim Gamble finished lamely and made eye contact with Toby who pressed his lips tightly together and raised his eyebrows, his eyes casting upwards into the upper corner of the room.

"I see. And where is he likely to be today? On the estate somewhere, working?" Critchley leant forwards, grasped the mug of coffee closest to him and took a gratifying mouthful.

Jim Gamble shook his head as he too raised his drink to his lips. "No. Monday is always Gi's day off."

"Okay, so what does he generally get up to? We'd like a word with him, obviously."

"Gardening, bit of shopping, sometimes see him in the Melchett at lunchtime, does a lot of walking out and about."

Ian Critchley sat in silence for a moment before placing his mug on the surface of the desk and standing up. "Right, well, let's take a look at the cottage then. If you could direct us?"

"I'll take you over there myself," Toby explained. "It's right up the north end of the estate and not the easiest place to find."

Rebecca glanced around the estate office as they all trooped out, wondering how long their partially consumed mugs of coffee would stay on the desk before someone tidied them up.

*

The cottage was just as Jim had left it some two hours previously. He and Toby led the police officers across the gravelled approach, and then both instinctively hung back to allow the professionals to take over.

Ian Critchley turned to them. "Thank you for your help. We'll take it from here." He rapped on the wooden door and called out the occupant's name loudly before stepping boldly over the threshold. Rebecca followed closely behind, leaving Toby and Jim stranded on the gravelled drive. They both shifted uncertainly from foot to foot, eyes downcast as they mustered their own private thoughts about the implications of what was happening.

"Jesus Christ! Look at that." Ian Critchley had stepped into the kitchen and immediately been confronted by the drawings that covered the cork board.

"Gruesome! That's just weird, sir."

"And look." He nodded towards the skillet which still lay upturned upon the floor. "Looks like someone left in a hurry." He turned to Rebecca to issue his instructions. "I want SOCO here now and a thorough search of the whole estate, and let's find our friend Giovanni and ask him a few pertinent questions. And let's be discreet about it all, Dawson. I don't want him sussing us out by spotting vans and uniforms, okay? See if you can get a photo of him from somewhere, maybe the employee records or something."

Rebecca was noting down his instructions as he issued them, and at this last one, she nodded curtly and disappeared back through the door they had just entered and called out to Toby and Jim who had gathered by the bonnet of Toby's Range Rover.

"Have you got a photo of this bloke?"

Both men considered the request for a moment before Jim exclaimed, "Yes, actually we have! We won an award last year for our longhorn cattle and the whole team had their photograph taken. I can get that for you?"

She nodded. "If you could, asap, please."

"I'll get Marion to bring it down – it will be quicker."

Next, Rebecca turned to Toby. "Mr Bursill-Brookes, we are

going to need to search the estate, and I will be bringing my team in to start that search straightaway. I trust that doesn't cause you any difficulties?"

"The hall is closed all day on a Monday so that's fine." He breathed a soft sigh of relief. That was something at least.

"Yes, well, the search will take as long as it takes and could well run into several days, so you'd best be prepared for that."

He grimaced at that. He didn't even want to consider the impact of the bad PR and loss of earnings that could ensue, but he knew he had no alternative other than to fully cooperate with the investigation.

By the time Marion arrived with the promised photograph, Ian Critchley and Rebecca Dawson had completed an initial search of the cottage. Apart from the upturned skillet and the extraordinary drawings, the only other indication of any recent activity was a pile of filthy clothes lying on the bathroom floor. Critchley indicated that these should be bagged and taken away for analysis, the usual things: blood, semen, fibres… When Marion handed the photo frame to Rebecca, she pointed out Giovanni. "That's him on the back row with his arms folded."

Rebecca removed the photo from the frame which she handed back. "Thanks, Mrs Gamble. Best to keep quiet about all of this." She nodded her head upwards and to one side to indicate the cottage. "No sense in the whole world and his wife knowing."

"I understand. You don't really think Gi – dear, dear Gi – would do anything to that little girl. He hasn't got it in him. He might look fierce but he's a gentle giant."

"Well, that's what we need to establish, Mrs Gamble. Why did he get expelled from school?"

"He hit someone. Hurt them rather badly actually."

"Not such a gentle giant after all then. So, what was the spat about then, do you know?"

"Oh, my dear, those boys at school could be very cruel. They used to call him names, and he just snapped, I suppose, and that was that."

Rebecca turned from Marion Gamble and looked at the

photograph properly for the first time. Privately, she thought Giovanni Santoro looked like some kind of Neanderthal throwback. She took the photo into the cottage to show Critchley. And as she proffered it to him, she said, "He looks like the missing bloody link, sir! That's him on the back row."

Critchley glanced at the photograph. "He looks like a piece of work, doesn't he?"

*

Toby provided a lift to Jim and Marion, dropping them both at their cottage for a much-needed cup of tea.

Then he headed for the main house. He peeled off his boots, nervously considering how he was going to tell his mother about the unsavoury developments of that morning.

Evelyn was in the drawing room, reading the *Daily Telegraph*, which entirely obscured her upper body, except for her hands which flicked the paper shut as Toby entered the room.

Toby cut to the chase. "It's Giovanni, Mother."

"What's the matter? Not an accident, I hope."

"No. It's this missing girl. The police think he may be involved in her disappearance."

"What nonsense! Giovanni is a good man."

"Well, let's hope they've got it wrong. Jim found some sketches of the girl in the gatehouse, and Gi's nowhere to be found. And we're going to have police swarming all over the estate until she's found!"

"Let's do what we can to assist them. And Toby"—she gave him an imperious stare— "an open mind with regards to Giovanni, please."

"Yes, Mother."

FIVE

Gi approached the slope that led down towards the glade where he had left Jenny the day before. He paused as the sweet smoky smell of a fire, long burnt out and dampened by the weather filled his nostrils.

He felt a sense of trepidation which grew into a deep foreboding with each step down the hillside until he reached the platform from which he had launched himself only yesterday.

Pausing again, he caught his breath as he saw her. She was sitting exactly how he had left her, back supported by a huge beech tree and one leg bent up. Her hand still clutched her pencil and the sketchbook lay on her lap.

With huge misgivings, Gi once again jumped into space to land as before in a crouch. Except this time, he stumbled and ended up on his hands and knees. He stared at her face which was partially covered by her hair.

"I'm practising the feathers like you showed me."

"I thought you were asleep."

"Nope. Just concentrating." She turned to face him then, a brittle smile on her face.

He could see she looked exhausted. Her eyes were red-rimmed and dark circles lay like bruises under them. Her hair was a mass of tangles with bits of moss and twigs stuck here and there. There was the remnant of a fire in the clearing and her face was smudged with soot. He hunkered down next to her and looked searchingly into her eyes. "Jenny, why have you run away?"

Her mouth twisting to one side was the only indication that she had heard the question.

"What do you think? Are these better?" Jenny thrust the

sketchbook towards Gi.

He took it from her and flicked through the pages of feathers she had drawn. He nodded his approval. "Much better. You will be a very good artist one day."

At this comment, she grinned at him and sniffed. "Hey thanks! And thanks for the lesson yesterday."

"Everyone is looking for you. The police, your parents – they are so frightened, Jenny."

She stared off, her mouth downturned in defiance.

"You fell out with your parents?"

"No!" She looked at him stricken. "I love them!"

"Jenny, you can't stay here – you know that don't you? Here…" He remembered the food he had grabbed from the cottage before he left in such a hurry and reached into the small rucksack for half a ginger cake, a bottle of milk, and two apples. "It's all I had; I have to shop today."

She took the food gratefully from him, and immediately opening the package, she split the sticky ginger cake in half, passing a piece back to him. They sat in silence for a while, both eating whilst taking turns to slurp from the bottle of milk.

The dampness had invaded everything in the clearing and Jenny shivered slightly as a cool breeze shifted the leaves overhead. Gi slipped off his waxed jacket and put it around Jenny's tiny shoulders, and she inhaled the smell – a mixture of him and the oiled cloth. The combined aroma was rather comforting.

"What've you done to your arm?" Jenny mumbled through a mouthful of cake, pointing at the deep scratch.

"Just a scratch from a bramble, that's all. Why didn't you tell me yesterday that you'd run away?" He asked, looking out over the reservoir. "It's those girls, isn't it?"

She nodded, and then that was it – the bank of control that had held her emotions in check broke, and great sobs of despair wrenched from her until her whole body shook with the outpouring. In shuddering gasps, she began to tell him everything.

She'd been reasonably happy and settled at school until the spring term of that year when Cheryl Bosworth and her sister Laura had joined, having transferred from another academy on the other side of town. Jennifer clearly remembered the day the nightmare had begun.

It was art class and they had all been asked to draw a still life, getting to choose a bowl of fruit or a vase of flowers. The tutor had brought the items into school and placed them on a table in the centre of the room. At the end of the session, the tutor asked everyone to present their work, asking each of them to stand up in turn and show their efforts to the rest of the class. Anyone could offer any comment about composition or style.

When it was Jenny's turn, she presented her drawing to her peers and there was a collective gasp followed by a spontaneous round of applause. She had smiled her thanks whilst going a deep shade of pink before she sat down again.

Then it had been Cheryl's turn, and it was most unfortunate that her child-like effort had followed Jenny's, because it highlighted the complete lack of artistic flair the poor girl had. There were snickers of stifled laughter around the room and a couple of loud snorts of derision from the boys. Jenny, trying to help, had said, "I think the colours are really good. I like it."

She would never forget the stare of pure malevolence Cheryl had given her as she whispered, "Thanks for that, bitch. Thanks a million."

The poor girl had been completely humiliated, but rather than laying the blame with her other classmates, or the insensitivities of the tutor in making everyone show the class their efforts, she had blamed Jenny. Perfect, pretty, clever Jenny Pritchard.

It was all downhill from there with an unimaginable series of hideous scenarios enacted out to hurt and ostracise Jenny from the rest of her year group.

Her lunchbox was thrown out of the chemistry lab window on the third floor, to the delight of the rest of the class. She was tripped over in corridors until her knees bled. Her sports kit was sliced to shreds and then put back in her bag. Physical assaults – hair pulling, pinching, and slapping, and even a push on the stairs. Money was taken from her purse and replaced with vile notes threatening her with the most horrible things. Dog excrement was put in her outdoor shoes whilst she was playing hockey. It just went on and on.

Whilst Jenny told Gi this, he made no comment, but stared off into the distance, his expression impassive in the face of her suffering.

Finally, she drew breath and whispered, "I can't go back. I won't go back. I'd rather die!" She looked up at him fiercely. "I would, I bloody would – I'd rather die! Please, please don't tell them where I am, please!" Her plea to him was reinforced by her hand which lay upon his knee pressing down hard.

Still, he said nothing, but sighed deeply and rested his chin in the cup of his hands which were clasped together, elbows resting on his knees.

"I was bullied at school," he muttered.

"You!" Jenny stared at him with open amazement. "Why?"

"I was different. Italian – looked different, sounded different, lived on the Melchett estate. I was rubbish at making friends and I got picked on."

"What happened? I mean, how did you get out of it all?"

"I was expelled."

"Oh my God! What did you do?" She looked at him in open admiration.

"I hit a boy, broke his jaw."

"Wow!" She sat in silence for a moment. "Why did you hit him."

He shrugged.

"Go on… tell me."

"He called me…"

"Called you what?"

Again, the shrug, and he glanced down at her face.

"You can tell me." She implored.

He stared down at her then, thinking *I've probably spoken more to this girl than I have spoken to anyone in years*. "He called me Munch."

"Munch? What does that mean when it's at home?"

"It was an insult, a reference to my eating habits. I was always hungry and eating my food…" At this, he mimicked his eating style by making scooping gestures with his hands towards his mouth. "You know… munch, munch…"

"It's horrible, isn't it? When you feel the whole world hates you."

"Hmph!" Gi nodded in agreement.

"So can you see why I can't go back?" She implored him again.

"Maybe talk to your parents? Change school?"

"It won't work. I know what they're like. My dad'll say *never mind, bumble, it will be alright*, and my mum will have a word with the school, and the adults will think it's all been sorted. But those girls are so conniving and cruel; it's like torture and I can't face it anymore!" She lay her head on her bent knees and vented another purge of emotion.

Minutes passed without either of them saying a word, and then they both heard it together – the far-off clatter of a helicopter hovering, searching.

"Jenny, what will you do?"

"I don't know." She said in a small voice, sniffing loudly.

"Come back with me, today."

"No! You haven't listened to a word I've said!" She shook her head at him in dismay. "You've got to promise me, *promise me* that you won't tell them where I am. Please."

He was in a quandary. He could physically pick her up, tuck her screaming under his arm, and take her back himself, but he couldn't face doing it. He could walk away and let her make her own mind up, guessing she would come home eventually.

Or he could help her.

Bring her some more food and warm clothing and make sure she was okay until she was ready to make up her own mind. His life experience had not equipped him for this kind of problem, and he really didn't know what to do for the best.

So, he did what came naturally to him whilst he pondered upon his decision. He took a page from her sketchbook and started to draw the outline of an osprey diving into the reservoir for a fish, and Jenny watched him in fascination with a growing sense of reverence.

SIX

On the instructions of Ian Critchley, Rebecca asked Toby Bursill-Brookes whether there was somewhere on the estate where she could establish an operational centre to direct the search of the grounds. He'd suggested an empty building which was situated adjacent to the estate office.

Once she had made the necessary arrangements to get the focus of the search moved, she commandeered Jim Gamble again, asking him to take her to the field in which the manager and his farmhands had been harvesting on Sunday. The old Land Rover lurched the occupants along the single-track lane which led through the landscaped areas of the grounds and then over a cattle grid and onto the arable land which lay at the far end of the estate.

They bounced across the rough surface of the field until Rebecca felt as though her spine was coming unravelled and she had to clutch the dashboard to retain any sense of composure. Finally, they came to a halt about halfway up the length of the newly harvested area. They both climbed down from the vehicle.

"So, this is where we were working on Sunday." Jim extended both his arms up and outwards to illustrate the extent of the working area. "And the wood"—here he turned and faced towards the furthest corner of the field— "is over there."

"Can we take a walk up there, Mr Gamble? I just want to see how long it takes and how accessible the woodland area is from the field."

It took them a full five minutes to walk the distance from the parked Land Rover to the corner of the field. Rebecca paused and turned to Jim Gamble. "And just confirm for me, how long did you say Mr Santoro was gone?"

"Well…" He tilted his chin upwards and thoughtfully scratched at the loose jowls that sagged slightly beneath his jawline. "I reckon no more than five minutes."

"So, you saw him go then, and come back, presumably."

"Well, not as such, but he wasn't gone long for sure."

"Okay, Mr Gamble, so when you say five minutes, that's your best guess, is it?"

"Well, yes, I suppose, but he wasn't gone long," He repeated.

"Yes, so you've said. Okay, well thank you for your help with this. If we can go back to the office now, I think we're done here."

Rebecca barely felt the roughness of the ride on the way back across the field as she was beginning to assimilate the facts into some distinct possibilities.

Ian Critchley was waiting for her when she arrived back at their temporary command centre which was now buzzing with search activity being directed by a variety of uniformed and plain-clothes police officers. The team had taken on a renewed sense of energy since news of the lead had come through and there seemed to be a determined effort to get on with the search of the extensive grounds, buildings, and farmland which made up the estate. Critchley noted their industry with satisfaction. He took advantage of a quiet moment and turned to Rebecca. "Let's grab a coffee and go through what we know."

Toby Bursill-Brookes (offering the utmost co-operation and courtesy as directed to do so by his mother) had organised an urn of boiling water and the means to make tea and coffee for the search party whilst they were based at the hall.

The DCI and DI helped themselves to tea and coffee respectively and took the mugs of steaming drinks outside where they walked down to an avenue of lime trees, beneath which wooden tables and chairs were set out for visitors. They took advantage of the relative dryness of the seating, although Rebecca could immediately feel the chill seeping through her thin trousers. She shifted onto the edge of the chair, not willing to complain to her governor about the unwelcome sensation in her buttocks, assuming any remark would be bound to illicit some snide comment about the sensibilities of women cops. Ian Critchley felt equally uncomfortable, and he too said nothing, instead staring off towards the river in contemplation of that morning's events.

Then he turned his attention to his new DI. She was still something of a mystery to him, and to date, he had considered her something of a lightweight, but to be fair she hadn't had the opportunity to prove herself through the lack of a real case to get her teeth into. In the current case, thus far, he had been quietly impressed with her professionalism and apparent determination to get quick closure.

"Your thoughts, Dawson?" He invited, nodding down towards the notebook that she was clutching on her lap.

She tucked her hair behind each ear, took a gulp of coffee and a breath. "Right, here's what we have so far. Jenny Pritchard takes her bike and leaves home on Sunday morning, sometime before seven a.m." She glanced up at him at this point to clarify the assumption. "Her mother Maggie found her note at about seven fifteen. The mobile gets found at five past ten – that's the time of the mother's call answered by the bloke walking his dog. So somewhere in between, Jenny gets nabbed or comes to harm in some way."

"Okay and what's the chances that Santoro is involved?"

"So, I reckon he's seen the girl in the grounds of the hall – we know that already from the drawings showing her in that walled part of the garden. Then on Sunday, he's helping with the harvest, needs to relieve himself and takes off up towards the wood. Now maybe the girl is nearer to the harvest than we think, y'know been drawn towards the noise and activity. Anyway, their paths cross, maybe he frightens her, she falls off her bike or something and she's hurt, or he harms her in some way. I'll bet that's where he is today, sorting out the mess, sir."

Critchley leant forwards and put his fingertips together making a bridge of his hand. He placed them over his nose, his thumbs joining together under his chin, "So what's his motive?"

"Well, he's clearly a weirdo, sir. Sex, I guess."

"Hmmm. What makes you think he's sorting the mess out

now when there's so much police activity? Surely, he would stash the body and wait for a few days." He looked at her questioningly.

"I don't think he's got the brains." She tapped the side of her head meaningfully. "Look, his coat has gone, his boots are gone, and his motorbike is still at home. He's gone walkabout, and I would bet my Christmas bonus he's up to no good."

"Christmas bonus?" Critchley smiled despite himself. "You're bloody hoping, aren't you?"

"You know what I mean, sir, it was… figurative."

"Okay, well, keep up the search and have an officer placed by his cottage. I want him brought in for questioning asap." He nodded his head down firmly and raised his eyebrows whilst making eye contact with her.

"Sir." She took this gesture as his dismissal of her and rose from her seat. She picked up her mug and made her way back towards the estate office, trying not to think about the way the seat of her trousers was clinging uncomfortably to her body.

*

Finally, Gi turned to Jenny, his decision made. "Okay, listen to me now – this is what we will do. I promise I will not say anything to anyone about this." He flicked his hand until the palm faced upwards, indicating their present circumstance.

"Thank you! And a promise is a promise, isn't it?" Jenny held eye contact with Gi.

Gi nodded solemnly. "Yes, in my house, my mamma taught me you only promise when you mean it and you can keep it. But…"

"But what?"

"When I come back tomorrow with food for you, you must have made a choice, a decision about what you are going to do, okay?"

"But that's not fair!"

"That's it, Jenny, or you come back with me now."

She sighed deeply and stared off, planting her chin in the cup of her hand. She looked desolate and for a moment he wanted to reach out to her.

"Okay, okay," She muttered.

"I have to go." He nodded towards the upwards pathway, and for the briefest of moments he thought Jenny would go with him there and then. But instead, she took his coat from her shoulders and held it out towards him. He shook his head. "You keep it; it's going to be chilly tonight – you'll need it to keep warm."

Her lip trembled for a moment and her mouth turned downwards. Gi briefly placed his hand on her head. "You sure?"

A nod and a sniff in response.

He put the coat back around her shoulders and left her without looking back. He couldn't bear to look back.

The walk to the cottage was tortuous. He stopped several times, cursed, turned back on his steps, and then, shaking his head, turned, and moved forwards again. He made his way over the ploughed field that sloped down towards the scrappy area of land that lay in front of his cottage. He was so deep in thought that he didn't notice the man partially screened by a large shrub, the leafy branches of which hung over the edge of a raised bed. At the door of his cottage, he bent down wearily to untie his boots.

"Mr Santoro?" A woman stepped forwards from the side of the building.

Gi looked up in surprise.

She reached into the pocket of her coat and flipped her police badge under his nose. "Surely you were expecting a visit?"

"Why?"

"Come now, Mr Santoro, you must know a local girl has gone missing?"

His hooded eyes slid over to hers then away again. He shrugged. "So?"

"I have reason to believe you may be able to help with our enquiries."

Again, the shrug. "No."

"You always a man of such few words, Mr Santoro?"

He turned away from her then, and as he did so, she couldn't help but note the impressive musculature of the man and she made a point of eyeballing the officer who had radioed in that Santoro had returned to his cottage. Once she had his full attention, she mouthed "Back up" to him. He nodded and moved away to speak discreetly into his radio.

"No coat, Mr Santoro?"

Again, the sullen stare from him.

"Just wondered, y'know. Chilly and wet when you went out and no coat hanging on the peg by your other kit, so just where is your coat?"

Gi moved into the entrance of the cottage, pausing briefly when he noted the drawings of Jenny had gone. His heart was hammering in his chest and his stomach was roiling with fear, but he wasn't going to give this woman the pleasure of seeing his discomfort. He ignored her question and moved over to the sink where he grabbed a mug which was lying upside down on the draining board. He filled it with water from the tap, gulping the drink down noisily, partly to satisfy a genuine thirst and partly to buy himself a few seconds of thinking time.

Rebecca Dawson watched him from the doorway and noted the delaying tactic with interest.

*

No one knew how Craig Rogers obtained information about the developments in the police investigation, and that piece of knowledge would remain between him and his faithful snout at the station.

In his kitchen at home, Craig had been about to sink his teeth into a ham and tomato sandwich when the light on his mobile illuminated at the same time as the text message alert sounded. He could see without opening the text that it had been sent anonymously which was always a hopeful sign, so he wiped his hand on the leg of his denims before opening the message which simply stated, *local Melchett estate worker Giovanni Santoro being questioned about disappearance of JP.*

"Yes, get in!" Was his inappropriate response as he grabbed the sandwich, the phone, and his car keys. He slung the sandwich down on the front seat of his car and checked the boot for his camera equipment, then tracked quickly back into the house for his laptop bag and notebooks. With luck, he reckoned he could be at the estate within ten minutes and digging the dirt on this local man. He knew the estate was closed to the public on Mondays, but with a little bit of slyness, he figured he could insinuate himself into the general activities. He reckoned to get himself a nice bag of info on the man and his background for a piece that could very well make the nationals by this time tomorrow. As an old hand at gaining entry to areas where he had no authority to do so, Craig had learnt the best approach was complete confidence and assuredness. He didn't pause at the main gatehouse to the estate but drove straight in and followed the driveway, parking his car so that it faced the exit, just in case he needed to make a swift departure.

He sat in the vehicle for a moment to consider his options and most likely route to success. He figured out that he needed to inveigle one of the employed staff of the estate to spill what information they had about their colleague, so he stepped out of the car and slipped on his black raincoat to add an air of authority to his appearance. That done, he placed his mobile phone in the top pocket of his shirt so that the top of its black leather case was just visible and then he inserted the earpiece leading from his phone firmly into his ear. The final touch was his notepad which was encased in a black leather folder.

Feeling fully prepared he locked the car and strode purposefully across the car park and from there onto the circular gravelled pathway which enclosed the large area of lawn at the front of the house. There was a sign for visitors indicating directions to the ticket office, the estate office, and the café – it was to the latter which Craig directed his attention.

Although the estate was closed to the public on Mondays the café was still staffed, albeit by a skeleton team who carried out the weekly deep-cleaning, date-checking and re-stocking of the facility. This meant the usual team of six staff was reduced to just three:

Lisa Brown the café manager, who was preparing the accounts, and two of her part-time ladies, Penny, and Beryl. These two ladies liked nothing better on a Monday than a good gossip whilst they were washing out the chilled units and re-stocking the shelves. It was hardly surprising then that, on that morning, their chatter was limited exclusively to the unprecedented goings on. Firstly, about the young local girl going missing and then, more shockingly, Giovanni being wanted for questioning in connection with her disappearance, for by now, the whole estate was buzzing with the news. It was rather annoying for them both when their salacious gossip was interrupted by the familiar and seemingly innocent ringing bell from the opening of the door.

"Good morning, ladies." Craig's voice took on a sombre and professional tone and he pressed the earpiece with his thumb for a moment just to emphasise its presence. "I can see you're both very busy, but I need to ask you a few questions, for our records, y'know."

"Oh!" They both sprang up almost simultaneously from their kneeling positions, their faces eager and open. Craig had to prevent a smile from encroaching across his face that would spoil the gravitas that his most serious expression was lending to the moment – it was clear these two old hens were going to be a pushover.

"Now then, if I may take your names, please…" He'd opened the notebook and stood poised with his pen above the snowy white page where it hung like a predator waiting for its prey.

The ladies were still in full flow some ten minutes later when their manager Lisa Brown emerged from the office at the back of the serving counter. She stopped when she saw Craig and frowned. "I'm sorry, may I ask who you…?" She got no further before Craig held up his hand to interrupt her question and pressed his thumb to his ear.

Then he turned away partially from his audience and lifted the collar of his raincoat towards his mouth. "Yes, sir, just finishing the interview with the employees at the café. Certainly, sir, right away, sir."

He snapped the notebook shut and said, "You've been more

than helpful, but I must go immediately. I have been called away to look at some new evidence. Ladies." He nodded his head in the most gallant way and let himself out of the café.

Craig walked briskly back to his vehicle, where he wasted no time before keying the engine of his car. He drove away from the house and back out onto the road, whereupon he did allow a grin to spill across his face from ear to ear.

*

Back in the café, Lisa Brown surveyed her two recalcitrant members of staff with disapproval. "Who on earth was that and what were you saying to him?"

"He's one of the officers on the case, isn't he, Penny?"

"I think so." Penny began to look uncomfortable, possibly privately predicting what Lisa's next question would be.

"Did he show you his police ID?"

"Well, no…"

"Or give you his name perhaps?"

"Um… I don't think… Beryl?" Penny fixed a stare on her colleague, a mixture of shared guilt and accusation.

"What did you say to him?" Lisa demanded again, with a more insistent tone to her voice.

"Oh, nothing really, did we, Penny?"

"Just a few, well, bits and pieces."

Lisa expressed her feelings with an exasperated shake of her head and a rather unladylike guttural noise at the back of her throat. "Hmmm, well, I guess we will see in the fullness of time, who he was and perhaps what you told him. I hope to God he wasn't the press, because if he was and you have spoken out of turn, there'll be trouble, I promise you that!"

She stalked from the room, leaving them in an uncomfortable silence for a few seconds before Penny whispered, "Silly cow, who does she think she is?"

Beryl tittered, their conspiracy complete, but privately, they both felt fearful of just what they had said and, more importantly, to whom they had just said it.

*

Ian Critchley and Rebecca Dawson sat adjacent to each other on the hard plastic chairs which were possibly the most uncomfortable, bottom-numbing articles of seating that had ever been manufactured. Fleetingly, Rebecca wondered why, as the investigating officers, they had to suffer the discomfort of the poorly designed chairs along with the suspect.

The interview room was utterly depressing. Green paint lay heavily on the walls, and the light from the neon strips threw a sickly reflection off the walls and onto the Formica table. The legs of the table had twisted over time so that any drink placed thereon was certain to slop when someone placed their hand on a corner of the table, perhaps to emphasise a point they were making. The Formica veneer was also badly damaged with huge gaping chips down both the length and width. It looked as though someone had taken bites out of it, maybe during a particularly frustrating interview.

The physical presence of the man who sat opposite them dominated the room. He was huge. His legs, bent at the knee and placed wide apart implied masculine aggression. His massive hands lay palms down on the surface of the table, a gesture that looked incongruous but suggesting perhaps that he might use them to lever his body-mass upwards and across the table towards them at any moment.

His facial expression was completely impassive, and his hooded eyes were blank and empty of any expression whatsoever. The 'invitation' to attend the station, as Rebecca had so charmingly put it, to help them with their enquiries, had been met with casual agreement by Gi and he had co-operated demurely when accompanied to the police vehicle. He had been duly cautioned and advised of his rights of representation, which he had declined with a small shake of his head. Critchley and Dawson now prepared the onslaught of questions that they hoped would lead to a new breakthrough in finding the girl.

Rebecca reached forwards to prepare the tape-recording machine, clearly enunciating date, time, and the names of those present in the room together with the reason for the interview. Following this and a small pause in which she seemed to collect her thoughts she launched into her first question. "Where were you on Sunday morning, Mr Santoro? And what were you doing?"

As Giovanni's impassive gaze met hers, she shuddered inside – *God! What a creep!*

He shrugged and then said quite clearly, "Rape."

Both Ian Critchley and Rebecca Dawson visibly flinched and then leant forwards.

What? Rebecca thought, surely it can't be this easy.

"The harvest." He paused and then spoke more slowly. "The harvest of oil seed rape."

"Right. Very clever." Rebecca curled her lip in disgust.

Critchley spoke at this point. "And why did you disappear from the group, *Mr* Santoro?" He placed an emphasis on the mister to imply the reluctance he felt when using the courtesy of a title for this man.

Another shrug and then, "I needed to go."

Rebecca pushed a sheet of paper across the table and turned it over to face their suspect. "You know this girl?"

"It is the girl in the garden."

"When did you draw this picture?"

"Saturday."

"Why?"

"I just did."

"And why all of these?" She scattered the remaining pictures over the table.

"I like drawing."

"Come on! Mr Santoro, we're not stupid! What have you done to this girl?"

Gi slowly stretched out his legs until the soles of his boots were almost touching the officers' own shoes on the other side of the table. He stared at the fingers on his right hand which he moved to tap out a slow but insistent rhythm on the surface of the table. It was his own version of white noise, a coping mechanism which he hadn't had to employ since he'd been at school and fending off the onslaught of snide comments and insults from his peers.

Critchley nodded towards the deep scratch on Gi's arm. "How did you hurt your arm?"

Gi brushed his hand against the scab dismissively. "Bramble."

"And where was this bramble?"

A shrug.

"And where is your coat, Mr Santoro?"

A yawn.

"I am intrigued by the fact that, when we looked in your cottage, there was a skillet on the floor. Do you usually keep your kitchen implements on the floor?"

Gi turned the palm of his right hand towards them. "The handle burnt my hand; I lost my temper."

"Hmmm, you seem to have a history of losing your temper, don't you? You were expelled from school for breaking a fellow pupil's jaw, weren't you?"

The shrug.

"So, you came across Jenny Pritchard in the woods, perhaps you were relieving yourself and Jenny found you in that compromising position. It frightened her and you lost your temper and grabbed her. How am I doing?"

He shook his head and resumed the steady thrumming rhythm of his fingers on the table.

Critchley suggested a break after three hours of questioning which had got them absolutely nowhere. He and Rebecca left Gi in the capable care of two uniformed police officers and climbed wearily up the stairs to his office.

"He's a tough sod, sir."

"Hmmm, and we've nothing concrete on him, until we get his clothing analysed – which may prove to be more conclusive. What do you suggest, Dawson?"

"I think we should let him go and keep tabs on him. If he's stashed her somewhere he's bound to return to the body – his coat must be with her. Everyone on the estate could describe his coat, one of those waxed jackets, y'know? And he's going to want it back, because if it's found with the body, the evidence will be damning."

"It's a dangerous game to play, inspector. If she is still alive it could be placing her at further risk, but as we don't have a clue to where she is…" He smoothed his steely grey hair with his hand and expelled air noisily from his lungs. "Okay, let's do it, but for Christ's sake watch him – don't let him out of our sight for a moment."

"Sir." Rebecca nodded and stood, stretching to try and remove some of the stiffness that had accumulated from sitting in those God-awful chairs.

She moved across the room and placed her hand on the door handle as her superior reminded her, "She's been gone for more than twenty-four hours and that's bad news for us all I'm afraid."

*

If the police thought Giovanni Santoro was a man with limited intellect, they could not have been more wrong. When he was finally allowed to leave the station, following hours of assisting them with their enquiries, he walked immediately to the nearest express supermarket, knowing full well that he was almost certainly being followed.

He loaded up with food and called a taxi from the telephone located in the foyer of the store and less than five minutes later an old Ford Mondeo pulled up to the side of the kerb to take him home to the cottage. As the vehicle pulled away from the last set of traffic lights at the edge of the town, Gi contemplated just what the hell he was going to do.

He had to get to Jenny somehow – without his newfound followers. But first he had to eat before he keeled over from lack of food. He paid the cab driver the fare and nodded his thanks, tugged the bags of shopping out from the back of the car and turned to push the dilapidated garden gate open with his backside. It seemed to Gi, once he had placed the bags of food on the kitchen table, that the cottage had been tainted by the earlier visits of the police

– it hardly seemed like home to him at this moment. He tried to shake off the feelings which were troubling him: the anger and shame from coming under suspicion for taking Jenny, the anxiety about what the ultimate outcome of the whole affair might be, but most importantly, his despair over how he could possibly provide Jenny with the help and support she needed without breaking his promise to her.

He started to grab the shopping from the carrier bags – at least he could solve the gnawing hunger pains in his stomach if nothing else.

*

Craig Rogers was delighted with his piece of journalism. Because of his industry during the past two hours, he was able to send his article to every editor of the major nationals for consideration in time for tomorrow's issues. Now it was just a waiting game to see who would bite his hand off for the exclusive piece of news. He had to admit, even to himself, that although the article was based loosely on the facts he had managed to assimilate, there was also a great deal of supposition and speculation on his part.

There were sections containing the ruthless dissection of Giovanni Santoro which made even Craig wince, despite the fact he had read and re-read the article at least half a dozen times. Still, his justification was simple. The man was clearly a monster if he had snatched this young and defenceless girl for whatever depraved and degenerate intent he had in store for the unfortunate child. So, it stood to reason that Craig's language and commentary about the horror that was unfolding in the tiny, close-knit community had to be emotive and passionate to convey the feelings which were reverberating through this idyllic piece of English countryside.

He'd also managed to snatch a five-minute interview with the girl's parents whilst their family liaison officer was otherwise engaged. He'd poured on the pathos in this section of his piece and sent in a photograph of the couple clutching at each other and looking distraught.

By the time the deadline for copy approached, Craig had received offers from no less than three red tops, four tabloids and a broadsheet to run the story. One had mentioned the possibility of a headline on the front page.

When Sally got home from work, he met her at the door with two glasses of champagne. Once he had finished breathlessly telling her about his article and impending fame and success, he sensed her disapproval. "What?" He asked as he sat carefully on the edge of the sofa and sipped his champagne. "Why are you looking at me like that?"

"It's just wrong, Craig. That poor girl is yet to be found and it's almost… it's almost as though you hope for the worst so you can get maximum exposure in the papers. What's happening to you?"

Before he had the opportunity to respond, she placed her champagne flute gently down on the coffee table and left the room.

*

Gi was still contemplating his options when a sharp tap on the cottage door interrupted his thoughts. He scooped up the various wrappers that were scattered across the kitchen table – the only remnants of the food he had devoured to satisfy his hunger – and pushed them into the kitchen bin. Then two strides took him across the kitchen to the small vestibule and the front door. Upon opening it, he noted Toby Bursill-Brookes and Jim Gamble hovering uncertainly on the threshold. Gi turned away from them and returned to the kitchen where he took three cans of lager from the fridge. The other two men entered the room a little uncertainly but took the drinks from Gi, thankful for the momentary distraction.

"Gi," Jim breathed his name like it was an expression of disappointment.

Gi glanced at the two men before saying quietly. "I have done nothing to this girl. Nothing, except draw her and that is not a crime."

"No, no, I'm sure that's right," Toby agreed before popping the top on his can so that it cracked open like an exclamation in the room.

Silence settled on the threesome for a moment until Jim took a breath and said, "Gi, look, take some time, eh? Some holiday, yes?"

"Boss?"

Toby cleared his throat. "Just until, you know, until it's all sorted."

Gi looked at each of the men in turn. "That will not be necessary but thank you."

"Actually, Gi." Toby squirmed momentarily. "It's actually not a request old boy – I want you to take some time away from the estate. You can stay here, of course, but until things are sorted one way"—a pause— "or the other, I don't want... I *can't* have you on the estate, don't you see?" He extended his hand towards Gi as a gesture of appeal.

"So!" Gi stood up quickly from the kitchen chair which rocked on two legs for a moment before crashing backwards onto the slate floor. "I think you come here to support a friend. But no! You've come here to fire me, yes?"

"No!" Both men shouted out in unison.

"Look here, Gi." Jim Gamble took a breath. "You may or may not have anything to do with this. But you surely must see how it looks, and more to the point, you must surely see the position it places Toby in. This could cost the estate thousands in lost revenue, and the PR..." He pushed his hand through his hair, forgetting he was wearing his cap which spilled off his head and onto the floor. He bent to retrieve it. "And the PR could ruin us, God damn you, man!"

For a moment Gi considered telling them both the truth but what was the point? They had clearly marked him as history as far as Melchett Hall was concerned, so instead, he merely said in a quiet but barely controlled voice, "I see. Goodnight to you both and thank you." With that he took his can of lager and left the room, closing the door firmly behind him.

When the two men left the cottage, they both looked back ruefully, but hurried across the rough ground to the Land Rover, pleased that the unsavoury task had been completed. Toby paused before unlocking the door, the hinge squealed as he pulled it open.

"That wasn't very pleasant, was it?" Jim turned to Toby who was looking thoughtful.

"What? No, no, but necessary, Jim. Something you said in there about PR."

"What about it?"

"Well, y'know, it may not be all bad news for us. This could really put Melchett on the map; we could turn the PR into a positive." He tapped the steering wheel providing percussion for his thoughts.

Jim turned his head sharply in his boss's direction. "That, Toby, is the most revolting thing I have ever heard." He unclipped the seat belt and opened the door of the vehicle. "I think I'll take in some night air. I dare say I'll see you tomorrow."

Toby watched in dismay as his loyal right-hand man disappeared into the shadows, and he felt a deep and bitter sense of shame wash over him.

SEVEN

Jenny was cold, hungry, and very frightened. Running away from her problems had magnified them a hundred times, and it didn't matter how much she considered her options, she simply couldn't find a way back or out of her current predicament.

The fire hissed a soft disapproval as the flames tried to get a hold on the damp wood but the heat and light that ensued were pathetic.

She had three dry sticks left which she had stored in the one-man tent and these she laid in front of the fire. For a moment she imagined that the stick on the left represented going home and facing whatever consequences there would undoubtedly be, but she immediately eschewed that idea and threw the stick into the fire.

The stick on the right, however, represented never going home but finding her way to London or Birmingham, and eking out an existence as an artist or street beggar, eventually to be discovered by some rich benefactor and saved in the nick of time.

"Yeah, right, you're not in *Annie* now, kiddo." And the second stick also landed with some force on the fire.

Then she contemplated the third stick.

What was that meant to represent? She reflected on her new friendship with Giovanni. Now, that was something worth holding on to. Could this third stick represent him? She wondered what he was doing right now. Part of her couldn't wait to see him in the morning, bringing food, warmth, and comfort, but another part of her shuddered, for by then she would have to have made her decision.

She sighed deeply and recalled what she had said to him earlier, that she would rather die than go back. She went cold and shivered suddenly, a little gasp escaping from her lips.

So, okay – she inclined her head to the third stick – I see you now and what you mean. Not go back and not run away but just finish it here. No fuss, no consequences to face, no future to consider. The third stick seemed to take on a new form as she stared and stared at it, and she was sure it started to jiggle and move around in front of her, teasing, teasing. "Come on, Jenny, it's easy. It's for the best. You've shamed your mum and dad; they won't want you back. Follow me and you don't have to go back to school, ever!"

She was mesmerised by her thoughts as they danced in her head. She was caught in a vast, sluggish but slow-whirling pool of despair that took her to a place so dark, so hopeless. It was the blackest place which dropped still further into a deeper and even darker void.

She curled up in her agony and lay by the receding fire, shaking with the utter and shocking certain disbelief that there was only one thing she could do.

*

Gi packed food, drink, a small blanket, and some drawing pencils into the rucksack he used occasionally for walking. He couldn't remember the last time he had used it and the dust billowed up and off it as he opened the clasps to place the items inside. The torch, he placed on the top. Not that he would be able to use it at first and certainly not until he got over the field.

They would be watching the cottage, of course, waiting for him to make a move. But he reckoned on leaving by his bedroom window which was at the back of the dwelling. This would lead him to the vegetable patch and from there the road. Once on the road, he would need to be stealthy, but he reckoned he could use the ditch as cover to take him to the side entrance of the field. Once in the field, he could edge along by the hedgerow which would again provide him with cover and then, making use of the darkness, he could finally risk moving across the final corner of the field and to the path beyond which would lead him to the reservoir. Then he would be able to employ his torch, find Jenny, and bring this whole mess to an end.

That was what he hoped for, anyway.

*

Rebecca Dawson was terrified their plan would go wrong and that Giovanni would disappear, the consequences being that they would never find Jenny Pritchard, alive or dead.

She and Ian Critchley had considered the likely steps their suspect might take, and as a result, two detective constables were located at the main entrance of the hall, with another two uniformed constables placed near the front of Giovanni's cottage. There were two dog units on standby, and the helicopter ready to be scrambled at a moment's notice.

The rest of the team were in the sparse facilities that had been provided for them by Toby Bursill-Brookes. As nine o'clock turned to ten o'clock, Rebecca glanced nervously at her watch for the umpteenth time and let a stream of air exhale noisily from her lips, watching it billow outwards. Her radio crackled briefly into life, and for a moment the quiet chatter and movement in the room ceased. The message was from the helicopter unit to inform her that there had been a road traffic collision on the motorway, and the unit had been diverted to assist with traffic management in the resultant chaos. It could be some hours before they returned to base, sorry.

"Damn!" She cursed softly and beat a rhythm out on the table using her fingers to vent her frustration. Her team had been asked to radio in every hour unless anything, anything at all, happened in the intervening period. The radios were all quiet and another hour passed on the clock.

*

Gi was also playing a waiting game. He'd tried to sleep but had found his mind just wouldn't rest, so he sat at the kitchen table and occupied his mind by sketching. He quite deliberately left the kitchen curtains open so anyone wishing to could quite easily look in and see his bulky outline sat motionless at the table, or moving about the kitchen from time to time, returning to the table with a drink or some supper.

He planned to make a move early, around five. It would still be dark enough to obscure his escape, but by the time he reached Jenny, the dawn would be bringing its soft light to help him negotiate the steep bank down to her hiding place. At midnight he stood up and audibly locked the outside door, shooting home the rusty bolt which made a terrific grating sound that pierced the quietness of the night. He hadn't used the bolt for years, if ever, but he wanted his watchers to know he was shutting up for the night and going to bed. He drew the kitchen curtains and switched off the light, instead putting the light on in the hall and bathroom. He left these on to provide some light for later which would mean he wouldn't have to put his bedroom light on to complete his preparations for escape. Once inside his bedroom, he eased open the catch on the window and left it so the window would just need to be pushed noiselessly ajar for him to climb through. He also pulled the old dining chair which he kept in his bedroom over to the window so he could stand on its seat to gain him the additional height he would need to squeeze his frame through the window opening.

Earlier in the evening he had thrown a pile of old sacking onto the concrete pathway which ran around the cottage so the sound of his landing would be muffled. Then there was just the matter of getting to the field without being seen and then he reckoned he would be home and dry. He pulled on a thick jumper and his walking socks and boots and then switched off the light in his bedroom and lay on top of the bed, his mind fractiously working through his plans, repeatedly.

At four forty-five Gi rose from his bed. He had managed a few minutes of light sleep but had been awakened by a tawny owl's unmistakable *quee-wick quee-wick* call just outside the bedroom window. It felt for a moment as though his heart had squeezed itself into his throat as it pounded its rapid and throbbing beat.

He took a deep breath and bent down to pick up the rucksack and the old black fleece which he hoped would help his outline fade into the pitch blackness of the night. Every noise he made seemed amplified: from the squeaking of the old chair as it bore his considerable weight, to the sigh of the window which creaked slightly as he pushed it open to its furthest extent.

He first lowered the rucksack onto the pathway below the window and then he began to manoeuvre himself through the tiny opening, first placing one leg through, then his torso and head so that for a moment he was balanced halfway and sitting on the sill. Then using the frame of the window to brace himself he pushed outwards, letting his leg drop further and further down until the tip of his boot met the sacking on the hard surface of the path below. Whilst still holding on to the frame, he pulled his other leg through until he was standing on the path and looking back into his bedroom.

He shoved the sacking back in through the open window, so it dropped like a whisper onto the bedroom floor, carefully pulled the curtain so the emptiness of the room was obscured and pushed the window closed until there remained only a crack of the opening showing. That would have to do as he simply could not close the window fully from the outside.

That being done, he crouched down and felt for the rucksack which he grasped and eased carefully onto his back. One last glance at his reflection in the window shocked him into realising his face shone out like a beacon from the rest of his dark clothing and hair. So, feeling rather foolish, he grasped a handful of earth and rubbed it across his forehead and face so that his features were hidden behind its peaty layer.

He listened, acutely aware that his actions could be discovered at any moment. Hearing nothing, he crouched, and half walked, half crawled diagonally across his newly dug vegetable patch. He reached the furthest corner of the garden where the compost heap lay, a mound of decaying vegetation. There was a small gap between the wooden slatting that retained the compost and the hedge, and it was into this gap that he squeezed, and then, using the rucksack and his broad back to part the branches of the hawthorn, he managed to slowly force his way backwards through the hedge.

Unfortunately, he hadn't reckoned on a four-foot drop into the ditch on the other side and as he made a final push to release the rucksack which had become caught on a branch or bramble there was a loud snap before he found himself falling backwards and landing with a wet thump in about four inches of brackish water. He quickly scrabbled up and out of the worst of the water which had immediately seeped through his clothing and was now running in cold little rivulets down his back and legs. He swore softly but continued to creep along the bottom of the ditch which ran alongside the road that led down to the Melchett Arms and towards the entrance to the field.

When he reached the end of the ditch, the ground rose to meet a narrow lane which Gi would have to cross to get to the large aluminium gate that heralded the entrance to the field. He knew this part of his journey presented him with the greatest degree of danger as he would be fully exposed, both when crossing the lane and then climbing the gate.

He paused for a full minute and then took a deep breath; his hand grasped a large tuft of grass at the top of the ditch, and just as he was about to haul himself up and onto the lane, a beam of light spread across the road in front of him. He flung himself back into the depths of the ditch, not caring in the least about the water this time. The sound of a vehicle approaching made his breaths come in heavy shaking rasps and he tried to control his body which was also shaking with adrenalin and the fear of being discovered.

But no, the vehicle continued past and on towards the hall. He allowed another few minutes to pass to calm down his heart rate and breathing and to be sure the vehicle wasn't about to make a quick return trip. Nothing.

So again, he employed the tuft of grass and cautiously pulled his body up and onto the narrow lane which he skittered across until he reached the gate. Then without pause, he swung himself over the gate by grasping the top rail and leaning headfirst over it and swinging his legs up and over into the field beyond. As soon as he planted his feet into the earth, he moved quickly into the shadow of the hedgerow and began to walk softly but quickly up the field and away from the road, his heart hammering and sweat coursing down his grimy face.

*

Rebecca Dawson yawned until her jaw cracked noisily. Five thirty, and still nothing. She picked up her radio and called up the officer at the main gate, "John, nothing, I suppose?"

"Only the milk van, guv."

Then she radioed his colleague at the rear entrance to the hall. "Mike, anything?"

"Nothing at all. Quiet as the grave out here, ma'am."

Finally, she radioed the two constables positioned at Gi's cottage, "Derek, what's happening?"

"He's still in bed, guv."

"Okay, let me know the minute anything changes."

"Guv."

He turned to his companion. "I could do with a smoke, Brian. Think I'll stretch my legs and have a wander."

"Okay, be my guest, mate."

Derek Manning opened the passenger door of the panda car and stretched his lanky frame out of the vehicle. Then patting his jacket pocket, he located a solitary cigarette, which was rather squashed, and a cheap lighter. It took several attempts before it flared and ignited the tip of the cigarette.

He leant against the bonnet of the police vehicle and enjoyed the sensation as he drew the smoke into his lungs. He tipped his head upwards and expelled a stream of smoke into the darkness. Smoking was his guilty pleasure, and he knew his mother would go mad if she knew. When he had finished, he chucked the butt to the mud and ground it into the earth with his heel before wandering towards the cottage.

The occupant had left a light on in what the young policeman assumed was the hallway. The gloom of the kitchen was backlit by the soft creamy light spilling in from the partially open door. His interest piqued, he stepped onto the concrete pathway which seemed to lead along the side of the property and then up four mossy and very slippery steps. Here, the path turned a sharp right angle and continued along the back of the property. He walked down this path until he came to another set of steps which led him to a lower path running adjacent to the wall of the house.

There were two windows situated within the back wall of the cottage. One small one that was glazed with an opaque pattern of leaves – Derek presumed this was the bathroom. The other window was larger and the drawn curtains on the inside implied this was a bedroom. He stood outside this window for a moment, uncertain of what had caused him to feel a growing sense of something being not quite right.

He could see that the window was not fully shut, not unusual perhaps. Many people liked to sleep with a window open. But then he remembered the sound of the bolt shooting home in the front door earlier and how that had seemed to imply that the occupant was security conscious. Would that same person leave a ground-floor window open, a window that was big enough for someone… Derek's eyes widened at the implication of his thoughts. He slotted his finger carefully into the corner of the window and pulled it gently so that the window opened. With his other hand, he reached up and quietly pulled back the curtain. It was very dark inside, except for the light from the hallway which shone through the partially open door and across the bedroom floor. He stood on tiptoe and peered into the room from the open window and he felt sick when he saw the empty bed and, worse still, the chair positioned in an obvious way to allow the incumbent to climb out of the window.

"Shit! SHIT!" He raced back up the rough steps, along the

back of the cottage and flung himself down the steps at the corner of the property. He slipped down the last two and grazed his knee when landing heavily on the rough concrete surface. He hardly felt it when a stone bit through his trousers and into his knee. PC Brian Watterly saw his colleague appear from the corner of the cottage and immediately realised something was wrong, terribly wrong. He leapt from the car. "What's up, mate?"

"We are in so much shit, Brian."

"Why? What?" He looked at his colleague's distraught face. "Bloody hell, no! Tell me he's still there."

"He's gone! Back bedroom window. Christ knows how long for." He pointed to his radio. "So shall I radio it in, Brian, or would you like to?"

"Oh! Christ Almighty, she's going to go bloody crazy, and I don't even want to think about what Critchley will say."

"No sense making matters worse." Derek Manning took a deep breath and pressed the communication button on his radio whilst his colleague issued forth an invective of the worst possible expletives he could muster as he imagined the chances of his promotion to sergeant disappearing down the toilet.

*

At the moment when the two young PCs came undone, Gi reached the top corner of the field and paused for a moment as he took off and unclipped the rucksack so that he could reach in and grab the solid rubber handle of the torch. He closed the clasps again and wielded the rucksack back onto his shoulders, then stood perfectly still for perhaps half a minute, listening hard before he nodded with cautious satisfaction and pressed the rubberised button on the torch. He'd need the light now he was on the narrow and overgrown pathway which would lead him down towards the reservoir and to Jenny. He reckoned it would take him at least forty minutes to reach her, by which time the dawn would be creeping over the eastern horizon.

They would have a chat, something to eat and then hopefully

they could walk back together to face the consequences of their adventure. He kept the beam of the torch low and shining just in front of his feet, and set off once more, feeling the most difficult part of this particular journey was over.

*

"He's what?" Rebecca uttered the question in a low growl, and the whole room immediately became still and tense as the assembled group sensed something had occurred, and by her demeanour, it definitely wasn't good news.

"How the hell did he manage to get away, with two of you watching the cottage?" She snorted. "Oh, don't even try and answer, Manning. I expect you were all nice and cosy in the panda car playing eye spy or something, too bloody lazy to get off your arses and check around the place. I'll have your bloody balls on a plate for this." She closed her eyes and breathed slowly twice. "I'll be there in five minutes. In the meantime, at least try and find out which direction he's gone in."

Ian Critchley crooked his finger. "A word, DI Dawson, if you please."

She followed him into the chill of the early morning air. "Sir." She waited for the onslaught.

"Get the dog unit and the rest of the team together. We've cocked up for sure, but he's made a move so let's get on his tracks."

She looked away for a moment, feeling the bitterness of disappointment crushing her throat. She wished he'd railed her for her ineptitude – she could have borne that. Instead, his objectivity and tolerance were almost too much for her and she had to turn her back on him so she could quickly wipe the tears of frustration away to clear her vision.

Thankfully, the dogs picked up Giovanni's scent almost immediately. The shamefaced constables had found the disturbed soil on the freshly dug vegetable patch and followed the footsteps into the corner of the garden. It wasn't difficult to surmise that Giovanni had pushed through the hedge and into the ditch from where it was impossible to see what his next course had been. But the dogs, having been provided with some clothing and an old pair of boots were excitedly leading their handlers along the ditch and then across the narrow lane and into the field. The search party followed on closely behind to be sure not to sully the trail. It wasn't long before the dogs, their handlers, and then the posse of police officers led by Ian Critchley and Rebecca Dawson emerged onto a narrow pathway. The dogs hesitated for just a moment before plunging onwards and down towards the reservoir.

*

Jenny Pritchard sat in the little tent. The fire had long since gone out and there were just a few embers that glowed now and then when the breeze blew through the remains of the sticks and leaf litter. She had hung the torch on the hook, designed for such purpose at the highest part of the tent, so that she had free use of both of her hands. These were occupied by shredding and then plaiting the inner lining of the tent. She had also removed her shoelaces and tied these securely to the lengths of plaited material. She played out the length of material in her hands and gave a small nod of satisfaction. Then she took the torch and the plait out into the clearing where she began to search for a suitable branch upon which to tie the strands.

The shoelaces would form the business end of the ligature and she just needed something to act as the leverage she would need to do the job properly. Finally, she found a branch that was low enough for her to throw the strands over the top, after which she tied the rope in a knot underneath the branch, leaving the remaining length and the shoelaces hanging down in two separate lengths. These she tied together so that the plaits met and were joined by the shoelaces. All that remained was for her to place her head through the noose, take up any slack by wrapping the material around her throat and apply her body weight.

She paused momentarily – not because she had changed her mind, but to look towards the sky which was beginning to show a pale strip across the eastern edge of the horizon. It seemed quite fitting in a way that she would be ending when a new day was just beginning. She knelt and inserted her head through the space, wrapped the material around her throat twice and then she fell forward, immediately feeling the pressure on her windpipe.

Suddenly there was a kaleidoscope of colours in her field of vision, and it felt surreal – she was floating away, and all her troubles were floating away with her – it would all be over for her in moments.

*

Gi paused at the top of the bank and, using the beam of light from the torch, searched for Jenny. She wasn't there. He jumped down and into the clearing, noting the extinguished fire and empty tent. His coat was lying just inside the entrance to the tiny shelter and as he bent to pick it up, he noticed with a frown that the inside of the tent was shredded, and that scraps of material lay on the rug inside. He stood up and turned to face the reservoir, casting the beam from his torch across the clearing once more. He stopped moving the torch when he saw Jenny kneeling by one of the trees near the edge of the clearing.

For a moment he didn't move towards her but watched with curiosity, trying to establish what she was doing in such a peculiar position. Praying perhaps? But then he cast the beam of the torch upwards, and he saw the flutter of rags, and something bound around the low-slung branch of the tree. In a gut-wrenching horrible moment, he realised what she had done. He let out a cry of horror and lurched across the space between them. Then dropping to his knees, he lifted her weight upwards into his arms to release the pressure on her throat.

"Jenny, Jenny, what have you done?" He cried out and felt something break inside of him.

Her eyelids flickered and she opened them to gaze upwards into his face, then they closed again so that two tears glistened on her lashes before sliding down her cheeks. She smiled and whispered, "Gi you came back. You're my best friend in all the world…" She squeezed her tiny arms around him and pulled herself into his embrace.

He shuddered with emotion and began to loosen the ligature from her throat which had so nearly taken her life. The thought that delaying his journey by half an hour would have certainly meant he would have been too late made him gag with horror. He sat Jenny into a more comfortable position and stroked her tangled hair away from her face, "Jenny, it will be okay. I promise you; everything will be okay."

She looked up at him, her features drawn, pale and incredibly sad. "I've been so stupid, haven't I?"

He shushed her and shook his head. "Thirsty?"

She nodded gratefully, and Gi pulled the rucksack from his back and loosened the clips. As he reached in to grab the bottle of water he had packed, the clearing was suddenly and terrifyingly illuminated with the light from several heavy-duty torches. At the same moment, the excited barking of dogs filled the air.

Jenny cried out, "You told them! You promised me!" She pushed away from his protective embrace. "I thought you were my friend and you betrayed me!"

"No! Jenny, no, I didn't!" He protested. "They must have followed me, Jenny, please!"

She didn't hear a word of his protestations which were drowned out completely by the chaotic noise, and there was no further opportunity for explanation as the team of police officers poured over the lip of the clearing, three of them with German shepherds which were growling and barking viciously, straining at their leashes. The remaining men were carrying huge flashlights, the beams of which were strobing through the woodland and casting long black shadows that seemed to dance with grotesque movement. Then the shouting began.

"Get down, get down, armed police. Lie on the ground, keep your hands clear!"

It was too much for Jenny. She stumbled to her feet, looked in horror at the storm of light, sound, and activity, turned to Gi and screamed. It was the most blood-curdling sound Gi had ever heard, and it made him feel sick with the horror of it. And she didn't stop, barely even to breathe, just tilted back her head and screamed and screamed. Then just when he thought his head would implode, she fell like a stone and he had to lurch forwards to catch her, and at that moment, three police officers launched themselves at Gi who roared with rage as he tried to protect Jenny from damaging herself any further.

*

Rebecca Dawson also felt the horror of the scene. Looking down from the top of the clearing was like watching Armageddon unfold before her. She would replay those few minutes repeatedly in the days to come. The child tethered to a tree by a ligature around her neck, the hulking form of the suspect engulfing her in some kind of sick embrace when the lights from the torches were switched on. Then the noise. The child shouting something and Santoro shouting and gesticulating back to her. The dogs, the caution shouted by her team leader and then the screaming. Rebecca didn't think she had ever heard such a gruesome sound. The poor child screamed herself into a dead faint, at which point the suspect flung himself at her, maybe in one final futile attempt to finish it.

And then it had taken how many of them to pin him down? She reckoned there were six or seven men holding on to Santoro before they manage to cuff him and bind his legs together at the ankles and knees. Even then, he was bucking and twisting to be free and shouting Jenny's name over and over. Rebecca felt rooted to the spot before Ian Critchley held out his hand to assist her in jumping down and into the clearing.

As they approached their suspect, Rebecca took in the details: the girl lying prone on the ground, the ligature having been severed from the tree by one of her team who had been quick enough to see it was throttling her, Rebecca's team brushing dirt and debris from their clothing and she caught their mutterings,

"Bloody hell, think he's broken my hand…"

"Reckon there were eight of us at one point…"

"Should have let the bloody dogs on him, bastard…"

And then there was Giovanni Santoro, sat amid it all, wearing that impassive expression on his face. But she couldn't fail to notice the tears streaming down his face, and his eyes, turned towards Jenny whose tiny frame seemed so insignificant in the melee.

Ian Critchley turned to Giovanni. "Giovanni Santoro, I am charging you with the abduction, false imprisonment, and attempted murder of a child. You do not have to say anything, but anything you do say that you later rely on in court may be taken down and used in evidence. Lads get him out of here." The men glanced at their boss, wondering just how the hell they were supposed to transport this monster of a man back up the hill, but as they pulled him to his feet, it appeared the fight had gone from him, and as they cut the bindings that had held his legs together and led him away, his most defiant gesture was to look back again and again towards the child lying on the ground.

Rebecca bent over Jenny and gently removed the ligature from around her neck. It seemed to her such a curious device and not something she would have expected a man to make. Plaited, it seemed, from a nylon material and then finished off with boot laces, it was the most bizarre thing. She placed it in an evidence bag and directed the paramedic, who had been waiting for the area to be made safe, to approach the child.

Rebecca looked at the paramedic's facial expression as he examined Jenny to see if she could tell what his assessment of the little girl was.

"Is she okay? What's wrong with her?"

"She's got a good pulse. There's some bruising around her throat but her breathing seems steady enough. She'll be fine, physically, I think. This has been a very traumatic experience for her, poor little thing." He placed an oxygen mask over her nose and mouth and brought a blanket out from his bag.

"Here." Rebecca noticed another rug lying on the ground by the rucksack which Gi had been wearing. "Have this for her too."

"Cheers. I'm going to see how close we can get the ambulance so we can get her to the hospital and looked at properly as soon as possible."

Rebecca barely heard him but nodded her agreement. She was inspecting the contents of the rucksack. There was food, drink, the rug which she had already removed and some drawing implements. Hardly what she would have expected, under the circumstances, and she frowned, pensively sucking her bottom lip over her teeth in quiet contemplation.

EIGHT

Maggie Pritchard had finally managed to fall asleep when the telephone rang. She and Tom sprang up from the bed and looked towards the radio alarm clock whose lit display showed seven a.m.

They knew the next few moments would be pivotal to the rest of their lives and they grasped at each other as Tom took a shaky breath and picked up the receiver. He identified himself and listened for a moment, with Maggie holding her breath beside him and digging her nails into the palm of her hand. Then he cried out, "Thank God! Thank God! Yes, thank you, we will, thank you." He put the receiver down and wept. "They've found her, Mags, she's fine!"

And then they collapsed together allowing the tension and anxiety of the last forty-eight hours to spill from them in a torrent of emotion. Thirty minutes later they were on their way to the hospital where their daughter had been taken.

*

Gary Bosworth always called in to the garage on his way to work usually to buy food to supplement the healthy lunchbox his wife had packed up for him, and a daily paper. There was a queue at the check-out, so Gary unfolded his usual red top and was stunned to see a photograph of Giovanni Santoro and the headline *Local Man Questioned Over Missing Girl*.

He paid for his purchases and headed back to his work van where he sat head bent over the article, the reading of which made him whistle softly. It was certainly hard-hitting, and he glanced at the foot of the page to note the reporter's name and email address. It could be to his advantage to contact this Craig Rogers to give him some more ammunition to really sink this guy. He reckoned the reporter would love the story about Giovanni stalking his girls at Melchett Hall and some more salacious details about his schooldays. Gary reckoned the reporter would probably be prepared to pay good money for such information.

Gary picked up his phone and tapped a brief message and his contact details, then inserting Craig Roger's email address, he pressed the send key and smiled as he considered how he would be able to enthral his workmates with his inside knowledge of the man whose image was plastered all over the daily national papers. Just as he had parked up the van in the yard, his phone began to ring, and he snatched it up eagerly to take the call. "Gary Bosworth."

"Ah, Mr Bosworth, Craig Rogers here. You emailed me a few minutes ago? I understand you have something you'd like to impart about Giovanni Santoro."

"That's right! Think you'll like it. I'll want some cash for my trouble, mind."

"Don't worry, we'll sort that out when you pass me the information. Where can I find you?"

Gary Bosworth suggested meeting at a café that was in the same road as the yard of the electrical contractors he worked for, and they arranged to meet within the hour. Gary was late for work, but it was well worth the rollicking he got from his boss, his wallet bulging with the four hundred pounds that Craig Rogers had paid him. His somewhat exaggerated version of his family's recent encounter with Giovanni Santoro and any other dirt he could dig up from his schooldays had been received with relish by the reporter.

*

Tom and Maggie clasped hands as they sat in the back of the squad car whilst it sped them to the hospital. Tom felt unaccountably nervous at the prospect of being reunited with his daughter.

It reminded him of the very first time he had seen Jennifer as a tiny baby in the special care unit. Her birth had been difficult, culminating in an emergency caesarean section, a somewhat different birth experience to that which he had been expecting. He had prepared himself as a dutiful modern man to be present at his daughter's birth, but Maggie had been rushed off to theatre when the baby's heartbeat became worryingly slower at each contraction.

He recalled how, with Maggie still in theatre, he had been led by one of the nurses to an incubator in the unit. The nurse had assured him it was just a precaution. His infant daughter had needed a blast of oxygen to help her breathing but was fine, a healthy five pounds and six ounces in weight. The nurse had left him at his daughter's side and, laying a compassionate hand briefly against his elbow, had said, "I'll leave you two to get to know each other."

He had almost immediately felt a sense of concern, almost of panic, as he stared down at this tiny bundle of human life. What the hell was he supposed to do if she woke and cried? How did one pick up a baby safely and without dropping it? He had been crushed by an overwhelming sense of responsibility and the realisation that his life and that of Maggie's had fundamentally changed.

Now he sighed deeply and thought, *I feel the same way now. What do we say, how do we overcome this horror? How will she have been damaged – physically, mentally?* He felt completely out of his depth and glanced across at Maggie to note with trepidation that she too looked pensive and drawn.

Maggie was also worried. Her child had been taken and kept against her will by a man and there was no telling what monstrosities he had inflicted upon her whilst she was in his clutches. She felt physically sick when she considered the implications and possibilities. The police had said very little to them other than they had found her, and she was safe. Maggie realised that, depending upon what that creature had done to Jenny, the term safe may take on a different perspective when they took into consideration the long-term effect that the whole episode may have upon her daughter, on all of them. This could just be the start of a very long and difficult time for them, and in a way, she dreaded seeing her daughter because then she would have to face the reality of everything that had occurred in the last two days.

They were met at the rear staff entrance of the hospital by Rebecca Dawson to avoid the growing number of newspaper and television reporters who were milling around the main entrance. Before taking them to be reunited with their daughter, Rebecca showed Maggie and Tom into a private consultation room within which Ian Critchley was already located, standing at the window with his back to the room as was his habit. He turned when he heard the door open and strode forwards to shake first Tom and then Maggie Pritchard's hand.

"We don't know how to thank you both for finding her so quickly and unharmed." Maggie held on to the Detective Chief Inspector's hand for a moment, clasping both her hands around his outstretched palm.

Tom was more circumspect. "How is she? We'd like to see her please. Can you tell us what happened?"

It was Rebecca who spoke. "We haven't been able to question Jenny yet, so the details are unclear, but we have a man. This man…" She passed them over a copy of that morning's *Times* newspaper, "in custody. We followed him and he led us to Jenny. She was… look, this could be quite difficult to take on board, so please sit down." Rebecca indicated that they should take a seat on the low-slung sofa which took up one half of the room.

Maggie sat down almost immediately; her handbag clutched on her lap like a shield. Tom pulled his fingers through his hair and took the paper from the DI.

"Jesus! This…" He gulped, quite unable to continue but dropped the paper and turned, seemingly without thought, to thump the wall before crying out in pain. Maggie stared at the image of Giovanni Santoro as it lay on the floor.

"What did this man do to my Jenny?" She whispered, revolted by what she saw.

"Mr Pritchard, please, sit down," Ian Critchley implored. "Come on, man, before you hurt yourself."

Tom sat shakily on the edge of the sofa, cradling his fist which was smeared with blood. He reckoned he'd probably broken his hand, but he didn't care. All he knew was that he would kill this man if he ever came across him – mild-mannered as Tom was, he would have no compunction about that.

Rebecca took a deep breath and looked guardedly over towards her boss before starting to speak quietly. "Here's what we do know. She was tethered by her neck to a tree to prevent her from escaping and there is some swelling and bruising around her throat. It's not serious but just to prepare you when you see her, okay? She has some cuts and bruises and a bump on her head, but other than that her physical injuries are minor. Jenny was"—she searched for the right words— "distressed when we found her, and she did pass out for a time. She is exhausted and sleeping peacefully now, and the psychologist has been spending some time with her, to help her overcome the trauma of what she has experienced."

"Why? Why did that man take her?" Maggie shook her head in confusion.

"Mrs Pritchard, we are questioning Giovanni Santoro regarding your daughter's disappearance. It appears he saw her at Melchett Hall when you visited at the weekend – we found some drawings of Jenny in his cottage. We believe he came across her when she was on her bike on Sunday morning, and for some reason, he took her then. Rest assured we will get to the bottom of this, and he will be remanded in custody for sure. We will want to question Jenny when she feels able to respond to us. It's likely the doctors will want to keep her in for observation for a while, just to be on the safe side. Come on now, I'll take you to see her." Rebecca held out her arm in a gesture for them to follow her from the room.

They passed along a wide and brightly lit corridor and then through a set of double doors at one end. This led them into a small, square entrance lobby which had four doors leading off, one of which was being supervised by a uniformed police officer.

Their nerves jangling, they allowed themselves to be led into the room. And there she lay. Diminished somehow, her hair tangled and filled with leaves and twigs still, a bruise on one temple and a scratch underneath her eye. Her nose was smudged and her mouth downturned in repose. Worst of all, the angry and provoking mark that the ligature had left around her throat. They both approached the bed hesitantly. Maggie grasped Jenny's hand, noticing the dirt encrusted nails and a graze on one knuckle, and she gently lifted the hand to her face and pressed the palm to her cheek and lips.

Tom stood at the end of the bed and covered his mouth with the cup of his hand, swallowing hard several times to contain the emotion broiling within – love and pure relief that his daughter had been returned to him, coupled with vicious hatred of the man who had done them this great injury.

If they had expected Jenny to wake gently and smile softly as they were reunited, they were bitterly mistaken. In one movement her eyes flew open in unseeing terror, her hands clutched at the bedclothes, she sat upright and screamed and screamed until Maggie grasped her by the shoulders and pulled her, still screaming, into her arms.

*

"This is a common symptom of post-traumatic stress."

The psychologist had taken Tom and Maggie out of the room whilst Jenny was being sedated. "This is the third episode we have recorded since Jenny has been admitted and is an indication of her feelings of extreme fear and her reaction to her security or self-esteem being threatened. I know it's very disturbing and upsetting for you, and I'm sorry that I didn't get the opportunity to explain her condition to you before you witnessed her distress."

Maggie and Tom sat grim-faced as the psychologist explained the reasons for Jenny's frightening behaviour. They had known the reunion was going to be difficult, but her extreme reaction to waking and the fact that it was the third time it had occurred since she had been rescued gave them cause for grave concern.

*

Jenny was exhausted and confused. Her mind kept rewinding to the chaos in the woodland clearing. The shouting of the police, the lights, the dogs, had all given her the impression she was in so much trouble. And yet since she had arrived at the hospital everyone had been so kind and gentle, and no one had mentioned the fact that she had caused a lot of people an awful lot of bother by running away. For a moment she thought about Gi. What he had done was unforgivable. He had promised not to give her away and yet had led that throng of people to the very place she thought she was safe.

She had thought… oh never mind what she had thought, but she was heartbroken that someone who she had finally felt a connection with, a soulmate, had betrayed her.

The Sunday afternoon they had spent together, sketching, talking about art and her ambitions to become a professional artist, had felt so special to her. He had watched her drawing and given her some great advice on improving her technique and when he had demonstrated some of these techniques, she had become transfixed by him and his artistic skill.

She just couldn't understand why he had gone back on his word. So much for new friendships, huh!

She sighed deeply. Either way she looked at it, she was faced with nightmares. The outlandish fantasies of her dreams where, it was not the police, but rather Cheryl Bosworth and her cronies who found her in the woodland or the waking nightmare of having to face her parents, the school, the police, and God knew who else.

She curled up on her side and pulled the covers up past her ears in the vain hope that it would all go away. No such luck though as she had barely hunkered down under the covers when Rebecca Dawson came back into the room. The psychologist was with the police officer, and when they each pulled up a chair so that they could sit adjacent to the bed, Jenny knew she was in for a grilling. But what ensued was completely different to her preconceived assumptions.

Rebecca Dawson smiled at Jenny and reached out to touch her hand. "Hi there, Jenny. My name is Beccy and I'm a police officer. I've come to ask you some questions and Dr Lovat is here to help. Is that okay with you?" Jenny offered the tiniest of nods by way of assent. "I know you've had a tough couple of days, and you probably don't want to talk about some of it but it's important that we know what happened." Again, Jenny nodded cautiously.

"What time did you leave your home on Sunday morning?"

Jenny looked sideways and upwards, considering her response.

"Was it before seven?"

A nod.

"And where did you go? To the woods?"

Another nod.

"Now this is the difficult bit, Jenny, so bear with me, okay?" Rebecca Dawson, desperately trying to gain an empathetic connection with the young girl, took her hand and squeezed it gently. "Were you hurt by the man, Jenny; can you tell me that?"

Jenny shifted under the bedclothes to hide her confusion. She was bewildered by the question. She had been expecting a ticking off for wasting police time. What did the police officer mean? What man? She felt vulnerable and afraid, and the question completely befuddled her.

The police officer squeezed her hand again pressing for a response. "Did that man hurt you? He did, didn't he?" Jenny looked at the policewoman and then the doctor and then lowered her gaze to her hands which were twisting the bed sheet into a tight knot. "It's okay, Jenny, take your time, just tell us in your own time. Did Giovanni Santoro hurt you in any way?"

Jenny gasped. Gi! Giovanni hurt her. She was angry with him, and in a way, he had hurt her, hadn't he? Jenny suspected the police officer had something other than a broken promise in mind, but even so, the betrayal had hurt her, very much, and she allowed herself to be misled by the question. After all, Gi's breach of his promise had led to the horrible culmination of the police and the dogs and the shouting, and now this stay in hospital… So, yes, whilst she was being disingenuous and deceitful, and in hindsight, she would live to regret this moment for the rest of her life, she had to agree that Gi had hurt her.

Rebecca Dawson took the young girl's gasp as a sign of her distress and placated her. "Hey! It's okay, he's never going to hurt you again; I can promise that. You don't have to tell us just now, just confirm for us if he hurt you, Jenny."

And God help her, she closed her eyes, nodded, and whispered, "Yes, he hurt me." Then she turned her face into the pillow and sobbed.

The doctor shook her head quickly at Rebecca and frowned, mouthing, "No more, that's enough for today."

Rebecca left the room and walked to the window which provided a rather depressing view across the town. She made a brief telephone call to her superior officer who was on his way back to the station to give confirmation of her conclusion. "We got him, sir, lock, stock, and barrel."

NINE

Gi could feel the hostility and repugnance emanating off the custody sergeant as the two arresting officers presented him at the desk. Once he had been divested of what minimal personal belongings he had with him, and these were bagged and labelled, the two uniformed constables guided him with considerable force to the cells, where he was relieved of his shoes and belt before being shoved into the tiny windowless room.

Once alone, he could hear the distant and muted sounds of activity in the police-station corridor and beyond: someone banging a metallic object against a wall, a voice shouting aggressively and, in the distance, a police siren as its occupants deployed the vehicle's blues and twos to announce the urgency of their journey. The noises seemed to exacerbate his solitude.

The light in the cell came from a dull circular aperture sunk into the grimy ceiling, the dim bulb hidden behind thick, unbreakable glass. The room was chilly and smelled vile. The furniture comprised a concrete base, which presumably was meant to be a bed, and a basic toilet which was stained and chipped. Gi squatted down onto the edge of the concrete shelf, noting the worn and grimy edge. He shook his head and sighed deeply.

Of course, it was only a matter of time before Jenny put them in the picture and he would be free to go, with the authority's abject apologies for his unnecessary and wrongful arrest. He would probably receive a caution for wasting police time, but he was confident that he would be released within the next hour or so.

It was somewhat of a surprise to Gi, therefore, when the same two constables returned to the cell some forty minutes later and marched him to the interview room where Ian Critchley and

Rebecca Dawson sat grim-faced and ready, it appeared, to interview him again.

Again, the formalities were dealt with, and again Gi demurred when he was offered access to a solicitor. The two detectives exchanged a glance of surprise between each other, and it was only then that Gi wondered whether perhaps he had misjudged the situation, and he felt a small curl of nervousness flutter in his belly.

"Mr Santoro. Why don't you keep things simple for all of us and tell us what happened between you and Jennifer Pritchard."

"How is she?"

"Pardon?" The senior officer seemed outraged by the question.

"How is Jenny?"

Ian Critchley laughed bitterly and shook his head. "Do you really think, *really think*, that you have any right to ask?" His tone was incredulous.

"Yes, I do. I tried to help her, that is all I did."

"Mr Santoro." Rebecca smiled, except there was no warmth in the expression, more a bleak pity for him. "You may be unwell; you are certainly deluded but let me help you with some salient facts so that you can start being more accommodating with your responses to our questions. You first came across Jennifer Pritchard at Melchett Hall on Saturday, 29 August in the walled garden, yes?"

Gi nodded in agreement.

"You were attracted by her... well, whatever... her innocence, her looks, and this attraction turned into an obsession, am I right."

"No! I drew her, that's all." He protested, throwing a hand in the air.

"You came across her again on the Sunday and took her to your little secret spot, where you tethered her by the neck for your own deviant purposes."

"No, she was already there; I found her there."

"Okay, so you found her there. You kept her there against her will, and you placed a ligature around her neck, then you returned to finish your work today, isn't that right?"

"No! Ask Jenny what happened."

"We have." They both eyeballed him.

There was a pause when nobody spoke or moved.

"What?" Gi could feel his heart hammering in his chest, and he could almost sense what the inspector was going to say next.

"I have spoken with Jenny, which wasn't easy in her traumatised state, I can tell you, but she was able to confirm that you kept her against her will and that you hurt her. Once we have—"

"No!" Gi leapt upwards from his chair and thumped the table. The two constables in the room immediately grappled with him as he strained against their hold. He fell, half sprawled across the table and half in the chair.

"Mr Santoro. Sit down!" Critchley barked the order.

The fight suddenly went out of Gi, and he slumped into the chair, his shoulders collapsing forwards in defeat, his voice shuddering with effort and emotion. "I did not hurt her; I didn't hurt her. Please let me tell you what happened."

"Yes, in good time. How do you explain the ligature if you say you didn't hurt her?"

"Jenny…" Giovanni pulled the palms of both his hands across his face, leaving his fingers pushed deep into the sockets of his eyes. When he pulled them away, Rebecca was surprised to see that his eyes were swimming with tears. With great difficulty, he said, "Jenny… It was Jenny who did that."

*

As they made their way back up to the offices, Ian Critchley touched Rebecca on the shoulder. "Well done, Dawson. First big job as a DI and you did a bloody good one. We'll leave him stewing tonight and wait for some of the forensics and then question him again tomorrow. But yes, well done."

Rebecca glanced upwards to her superior. "Thank you, sir. Made a few mistakes along the way."

"But you're pleased?"

"Pleased? God, yes! Really chuffed with the result, sir."

"Only you don't seem… Well, how can I say this? You don't seem quite as upbeat as I would have expected."

As he said this, he pushed open the door to the communal work area whereby a raucous cheer hit them at the same time as warm cans of lager were thrust into their hands. There was a general pushing and shoving and whacking on the back and cuffing on the arm as the team allowed the tensions of the last couple of days to leave them through the celebration of their collective success.

Ian Critchley stayed with the group for a few minutes before quietly excusing himself and taking himself off to his private office where he could make his report to his own superiors and prepare a statement to the press.

Rebecca drank the lager thankfully, wondering just how many hours it had been since she had managed to have anything to eat or drink. She took the drink over to the window and stared out across the mixed architecture of the town. The community would be relieved and grateful to their local police service for performing well to achieve this happy ending. Jenny would hopefully make a full recovery over time, and Rebecca hoped both she and Critchley would receive a glowing report outlining their contribution to the whole affair. The only person who ended up on the losing side was Giovanni Santoro, but then he surely deserved to be treated like the depraved creature he was. She was exhausted and turned away from the window as the light began to leech from the sky. There was a report to write, and she at least had to make a start on it before she could even think about going home.

TEN

Gary Bosworth couldn't help the smug expression which was plastered across his face as he walked up the path towards the front door of his house. Not only had he purchased Prosecco (already chilled) and chocolates, but he had also rashly picked up a bunch of flowers for Louise too, something he had never done in their fourteen years of marriage. He burst in through the door, clattered his keys onto the hall table, and betting Louise and the girls would be in the kitchen-cum-dining area, he strode down the hallway and pushed open the door. Louise was preparing dinner whilst the girls had homework spread out on the dining table.

Louise turned and eyed the armful of purchases sceptically. "Won the lottery, have we?"

"Nearly as good as! Hey girlies, first day back at school okay?"

Cheryl shrugged and said nothing, but Laura looked up at her father with tears brimming in her eyes. "It was horrible, Dad. Jenny Pritchard's gone missing, and they think someone's taken her. We had a talk from the head about it and we had a minute of silent thought after. Poor Jenny!"

"She's in your class, isn't she, Cher?"

Cheryl nodded as she studiously bent over her maths workbook. Laura took a breath seemingly to impart some further piece of news but cried out suddenly and clutched her leg as her sister's eyes drilled into hers sending an unspoken message across the table.

"Don't fight, you two," Louise admonished as she sliced carrots and potatoes on a chopping board, then she spoke softly to Gary as she continued her task. "What then?"

"What?" Gary looked confused for a moment as he plonked

the chocolates on the kitchen side and put the wine in the door of the fridge.

She turned and pointed the knife. "This. What's all this in aid of, Gary?"

His expression took on a smug look as he leant against the side of the worktop. "I sold my story to the nationals."

"Story. What story?" Louise looked sideways at him, her voice wary.

"Munch. I told them all about Munch."

"Oh Gary!" Louise said in dismay.

"What? What have I done now?"

The girls were watching their parents from the table with interest.

"What has that man ever done to you?"

"You are joking! He's been questioned about that missing girl. He's a bloody monster; he threatened our girls at the weekend, unless you've forgotten."

"He may have been questioned but that doesn't make him guilty of anything, does it? For God's sake, Gary, you, and your cronies always did have it in for Gi. You were bullies, the lot of you!"

It was Laura's turn to kick her sister. "Must run in the family, wouldn't you say, Cher?"

"Shut up, you cow!"

Gary pushed himself off from where he was leaning against the side and placed his hands on his hips. "Gi! Gi is it now? Since when were you on first-name terms with him? The bloke's a bloody caveman."

Louise carefully placed the knife down on the side and folded her arms. "That man has got more sensitivity and compassion in his little finger that you and your bunch of thugs ever had in your whole bodies put together. Just because he was a bit different from your tribe, you hated him."

Gary let out a bark of incredulous laughter, and pulling a hand through his hair, said, "You bloody fancied him! Oh my God, Louise, don't tell me that you and him…" He cocked his head on one side and gave an exaggerated wink. "You did, didn't you? Jesus!"

She stared at him, and as she began taking off her apron, she said quietly, "And what if we did, Gary?"

Before he could respond, she turned and left the room.

Upstairs, she closed their bedroom door and opened her bedside table. There it was. Still there – a little ragged around the edges – but still there. She gently drew the paper from the envelope and opened it out. The image still evoked the familiar sensation. A glow, a memory of him, his gentleness, his complete masculinity. She smiled softly as she traced the image of her face, as it had been portrayed in its youthful beauty, drawn by the man she wished she could have spent the rest of her life with.

She would always regret listening to the counsel of her girlfriends who had teased her for liking Gi. And when her parents forbade her from seeing him, she had reluctantly finished their friendship. She often wondered what life would have been like if she had stayed with him, and she smiled softly as she refolded the drawing and carefully replaced it in the envelope, which she pushed to the back of the drawer.

ELEVEN

Craig Rogers had already been privy to the headline that was going to be on pretty much every national paper in the morning. He thought it was genius: *Monster Munch!* If anyone had thought his previous piece had been hard-hitting it would pale to nothing against the story that would run tomorrow.

He had summoned every vicious and vitriolic word he could think up to describe Giovanni Santoro.

He'd touched on the fact Santoro was a migrant which was a nice link to the current hot political topic of immigration.

He'd focused on the working-class upbringing, implying of course that a life without privilege was almost certain to lead to depravity and crime.

He'd covered off the incident at Melchett Hall, where in a flagrant abuse of a position of trust, Santoro had preyed on little girls as they visited the hall with their families. Adding here an acerbic criticism of the management who obviously didn't vet their employees suitably.

Then he reiterated the abysmal school record, how the boy who was educationally obtuse and socially inept had been given the unfortunate moniker of Munch by his peers because he couldn't even feed himself with any modicum of grace. Little wonder then, as he had grown and matured, that his physical needs could only be satisfied by snatching little girls.

And poor, poor little Jennifer Pritchard who had been rescued in the nick of time by a crack team of police officers who had found the young girl tethered like an animal by a ligature wound tightly around her neck by this... this monster! It was only a matter of time, sensitive questioning and physical examination before the true atrocities that had been inflicted on her by this animal would be revealed.

The whole piece was an absolute gem and Craig had been invited to join the journalistic team at one of the leading red tops as a result.

*

The local community had also reacted to the horror of having a paedophile in their midst. There wasn't a soul who didn't have an opinion about the situation and that dreadful man, and these opinions needed airing. Whether it was in the supermarket, the Melchett Arms, the hall or at the school gates, the consensus was it was a miracle that the little girl had been found safe and well, that the police had done a fine job, and the man – the monster – who had done her harm deserved to be locked away for a very long time.

Some of the more radical views were translated into action in the form of revolting hate messages sprayed across the walls of the estate perimeter and the little cottage where Gi lived.

*

Rebecca Dawson was past exhaustion. As she drove home after the completion of her report her eyes felt loaded with grit. She parked up on the driveway of her rented accommodation and sat in the car for a full five minutes before she could muster the energy to open the car door, swing her legs out and then haul her body upwards and out of the vehicle. She grabbed her laptop bag and handbag from the rear seat and locked the vehicle before she traipsed up the short slope to the front door.

Once inside she disengaged the intruder alarm, slung her bags down at the bottom of the stairs and shrugged off her jacket which she let drape over the newel post at the base of the staircase. She eased off her shoes and padded in stocking feet to the kitchen. She hadn't eaten for hours and hours but didn't really feel hungry enough to cook a proper meal so she opened the freezer door more in hope than expectation and was pleasantly surprised when she saw a Marks and Spencer ready meal which would only take seconds to prepare in the microwave. She plonked the packet on the side and made the necessary preparations before popping it in the microwave.

Then she grabbed the half-full bottle of white wine from the fridge and, whilst opening an overhead cupboard for a glass, closed the fridge with her backside. The wine glugged deliciously into the glass, and she took a mouthful, savouring the tangy acidity as it flowed across her palate.

She grabbed a knife and fork directly from the draining board together with a plate and stood watching the meal rotating slowly around inside the microwave. Her colleagues had wanted to go out for a meal to celebrate their result, but she couldn't muster the enthusiasm.

In fact, she wondered why she felt so low. Maybe, she reflected, she was coming down from the adrenalin rush of the last couple of days. Maybe she was still cross with herself for not instructing her team more clearly when directing them to watch Santoro's movements. Maybe she was wondering about the rapport she was beginning to establish with her senior officer and his comment to her as she had left that evening about staying on as permanent DI.

In fact, she knew it was none of these things that were niggling at her. There was something, something off about their investigation. She had that itch that, somehow, they were not quite on the right track. There were things emerging that just didn't fit together, a thread at the back of her mind... if she could just grasp it.

The microwave timer pinged and broke her thoughts, and she dismissed her dissatisfaction with a tired shake of her head and another gulp of wine as she reached for her supper.

Whilst she ate her meal, she watched the evening news. Their story was the headline piece, and it was strange to see the familiar locations of the police station, the hospital, and Market Braithwaite being shown on the television screen. There was a brief interview with Jenny's parents as they emerged from the hospital and the headteacher at Jenny's school speaking about their community's great relief that all had ended well. A live report came from the imposing gates of Melchett Hall where the journalist postulated on the fact that Santoro would be remanded in custody and that the trial would probably take place early the following year.

Rebecca thought of Jenny, how they had found her and how she had reacted when Rebecca saw her at the hospital. She scraped the last vestiges of the meal from her plate and licked her fork, downed the remainder of her wine, and switched off the television. If she didn't go up now, she reckoned she would wake up tomorrow morning still on the sofa. She placed her plate and glass in the washing-up bowl and splashed sufficient water onto them to ensure they would be easy enough to clean in the morning. Then grabbing her jacket on the way past, she checked the front door was locked and wearily climbed the stairs. She was in bed in minutes, not even bothering to remove her make-up – that could wait until the morning too.

She clicked off the bedside light and tried to relax. First, she curled up and on her right-hand side but then only minutes passed before she moved onto her left-hand side. She tried lying on her back and even on her stomach, but she could not seem to settle. Her mind was still pushing her to think about the case, the circumstances. Finally, and with a degree of bad language, she pushed the covers back and padded downstairs where she opened her laptop bag to grab her notebook and pen.

As she grasped the outer cover of her notebook her hand brushed against the evidence bag that held Jennifer Pritchard's mobile phone. Rebecca cursed softly. She should have returned that to the station along with Jennifer's laptop. It was a breach of protocol which could have caused an issue if the girl had still been missing. But as she had been found and the items would be returned to their rightful owner in a day or so, Rebecca concluded that it was a moot point as the phone didn't really need to be returned to the station now.

She shrugged, turned, and climbed back up the stairs and into bed. The covers were still warm so she snuggled down but raised her knees so she could use them as a support for her notebook. On the top of a fresh page, she wrote *loose ends* and then considered the aspects of the case that were bothering her. The plaited ligature – surely Santoro would have used something more secure and less ad hoc. The rucksack contents – items that showed care and concern for the victim, food, drink, a rug. And now she came to think of it, the little tent, which surely belonged to the girl, and the text message on the mobile phone. What had it said? She lay back and closed her eyes for a moment and her exhaustion finally took her into a deep and immediate sleep.

She had no idea how long she had been asleep when she woke with a start, her heart hammering in her throat. The mobile phone and the message on it – they weren't loose ends! Again, she swore and climbed out of bed, padded down the stairs and grasped the evidence bag from her laptop bag.

When she clambered back into her bed, she ripped open the bag and tipped the phone out onto the bedcovers. The battery was flat, but as luck would have it, her own mobile phone charger was compatible, so she plugged it into the phone and switched her charger on at the plug by her bedside table. A long beep indicated the phone was connected to the electric and then a battery symbol appeared pulsing with energy. Rebecca pressed the on switch of the phone which vibrated for an instant before the screen lit up and the introductory notes heralded its awakening.

She lay it on the bed for a moment so she could reach across for her notebook. The phone shuddered and gave a trill, then shuddered and gave another trill. New messages appeared in the inbox. Rebecca frowned as she noted the date they had been sent was the Sunday that Jenny had disappeared. She hesitated for a moment before taking a breath and opening the first message, which seemed innocent enough – *hope yr looking forward to Tuesday meet you at the gates like always* – but the second one was shocking – *yr for it bitch, gonna break your fingers bad.* She checked back at the previous message which read – *Jen r u okay? Tell yr mum and dad about it, please x*

All the numbers were withheld. Rebecca felt sick. And then

a sudden and horrible thought struck her. She hadn't handed in this phone as evidence. She hadn't even remembered it had been in her bag since Sunday. That meant that no one had interrogated the information on the phone, which meant no one had checked the message folders. She placed the phone carefully on the bed in front of her and sitting cross-legged she rested her head in her hands as she stared down at the glowing display. Then carefully, with one finger, she gingerly and reluctantly guided the cursor over the folder marked read and pressed the button. There were several messages stored in the folder, and as Rebecca read each of them, she could feel her stomach begin to churn and her heart begin to hammer.

She sat quite still as she mentally berated herself. Not only had she not considered the phone message as a lead or even a loose end, but she'd also missed its significance entirely in her pursuit of Santoro, so completely convinced had she been of his implicit involvement. But what if these horrible messages were in fact leading them in an entirely different direction? The implications of this just didn't bear thinking about. She would be in so much hot water she'd be lucky if she kept her position as sergeant, never mind that permanent promotion to Detective Inspector.

She flipped onto her back and stared at the ceiling whilst considering her options. She ought to contact Critchley right now and confess her monumental faux pas, except she would then be pilloried by not only her colleagues, but the press, the local community – Jesus God, the shame and humiliation. Just when she had thought her career was on the up and up, and that the result from this case would have pushed it on further.

She bunched her fists together and pummelled the bedclothes. "Think! Think, you stupid woman. It was not thinking that got you in this mess." Minutes passed before she rolled resolutely out of bed, pulled on her clothes, and ran down the stairs, pausing only to grab her bag and the car keys on the way out. She nearly twisted her ankle as she pushed her feet into her slip-on shoes as she moved down the driveway to the car.

Gi had at least been provided with a coarse woollen blanket, and by bunching up his fleece, he had managed to fashion a kind of pillow. Exhaustion had finally taken him into a deep sleep despite the alien noises still reverberating around the station.

Since he had been returned to the cell some hours earlier, he had been trying to fathom his emotions: outrage, despair, hurt, bewilderment? He reckoned, in the end, that all these emotions, and more, were flowing through him.

He held countless conversations with Jenny in his head but only one word stood out: why? Why had she told them a lie which had dropped him in so much trouble? He didn't even want to consider what was going to happen now – almost certainly remanded in custody, then a public trial, and a prison term. He didn't think he could face that.

When he woke, he had no idea of the time, but judging by the reduction in the general comings and goings up and down the corridor, he reckoned it must be beyond the kicking-out time in the pubs and clubs. He was surprised then when the clunk and grind of the lock being opened from the outside of his cell announced a visitor. Again, two uniformed officers stood at the door and indicated that he should follow them, and again, they led him to the interview room.

As he was shown into the room, he was intrigued to see Rebecca Dawson sitting alone; he was even more fascinated when she indicated to the officers that they were to leave her and Gi alone. The officers glanced at each other, silently acknowledging the lack of compliance with procedure, and she reasserted her request in a tone that made it quite clear she didn't expect any insubordination. They shrugged simultaneously and left the room, closing the door behind them.

"Sit down, Mr Santoro." A pause. "Please."

He sat without taking his eyes from the DI. Her demeanour seemed very different from the caustic and confident interrogator of earlier.

"You asked us earlier to listen to your explanation. Perhaps you would like to take this opportunity to do that now."

Gi glanced sidelong towards the tape machine and then back to Rebecca Dawson.

"This… meeting, shall we say… is just an informal off-the-record chat between you and me, so why don't you just tell me what's been going on."

He looked down into her face and she noticed for the first time the warmth of his eyes which were a deep and rich chocolate brown. He sat for perhaps two full minutes without saying anything at all, and just as she thought he was going to remain silent; he began to speak. His voice was quiet but clear with a deep timbre and Rebecca realised that she had misjudged more than one aspect of his character. He chose his words carefully but was fluent and articulate, and as he continued to provide an explanation of his part in Jenny Pritchard's disappearance, Rebecca could feel a dread settling in her stomach like a stone.

He admitted to having been fascinated by Jenny when he saw her in the walled garden and that this fascination was driven by his artistic compulsion to capture images which gave him pleasure. He usually limited his sketching and drawing to flora and fauna, but on this occasion, he had been captivated by Jenny's innocence.

It wasn't until he came across her quite by accident the following day by the reservoir, that they realised they had a common interest in art, and he had been able to provide some helpful advice for Jenny in artistic technique. He had been completely unaware at that stage that Jenny had run away from home, and it wasn't until the following morning when he heard the news that he realised she was in trouble.

He had returned to Jenny to try to persuade her to go home but she had been adamant, and it was at that point she had explained her life was a living hell because of a group of bullying girls at Jenny's school. He paused here and swallowed noisily, clearly distressed as he recalled the memory. She had said she would rather die than return home, and at the time, Gi had thought her statement had been figurative.

Anyway, he had promised not to alert the authorities but return the following day with food, but only on the basis she would decide then what she would do.

When he returned to his cottage that evening, he had first had the pleasure of meeting Ms Dawson and her colleague. Once released from questioning, Gi explained, he had felt it was imperative to return to Jenny. That was when he found her with the ligature around her neck, almost passed out from trying to throttle herself. He shrugged. "And of course, Ms Dawson, you are quite well aware of the rest."

Rebecca didn't say anything for a moment but passed her hand briefly over her face, leaving it covering her mouth. Everything he had said rang true, and she realised with shame and regret that rather than threatening Jenny Pritchard's life as they had all assumed, Giovanni Santoro had saved it. And it didn't matter how this mess was ultimately sorted out, he would always be a pariah in the eyes of the local community. An element of doubt would forever colour peoples' opinion of Giovanni Santoro.

She sighed deeply. "I think we may have made a mistake, Mr Santoro, and for that I am truly sorry."

He inclined his head in acknowledgement and then said, "I don't understand why Jenny lied."

Rebecca smiled ruefully. "You were her scapegoat to get her off the hook?"

"Sorry?" A frown formed on his face.

"Okay, so she must have realised she was in a lot of trouble, and then the circumstances provided her with a get-out-of-jail-free card. She's not the naughty runaway but the poor little girl who got snatched and found in the nick of time. Faced with those same options… well… who knows what any of us would have done."

"Ah yes. Poor Jenny. Don't be hard on her please."

"That's a very honourable attitude if I may say so, Mr Santoro. Are you sure you mean it?"

"You need to find out what that poor girl has had to put up with from those… those girls!" He spat out the word in disgust.

"Hmmm. Let me explain what's going to happen next. I must

return you to the cell for now – sorry about that. I need to speak directly with Jenny so she can verify what you have just told me, although I don't think there will be any doubt this time. Can I organise some food and drink for you in the meantime? I hope to be able to release you later this morning and prepare a press statement that will exonerate you completely from any involvement in her disappearance."

Gi scratched his chin disconsolately but brightened slightly with the promise of food. "Food would be good, and a paper perhaps?"

"I'll see to it." She stood up and strode over to the door to call one of the officers back to collect Mr Santoro, return him, with all due respect, to his cell and to arrange some food, drink, and a paper for their guest.

When Gi received a tray of sandwiches with crisps and a cake, he ripped open the packets with relish and wolfed down the first sandwich in seconds. He took a noisy slurp from his coffee, and feeling a little happier, he pulled the paper over towards him and unfolded it.

The headline, *Monster Munch!* was boldly printed across the front page in block capital letters and it hit Gi like a punch to his solar plexus. By the time he finished reading the article, the meal he had just enjoyed was spattered across the floor of the cell.

He knew life was never going to be the same again.

TWELVE

Rebecca made a call to the hospital to confirm that Jenny Pritchard was well enough to be seen. The on-duty nurse confirmed that Jenny was due to be discharged later that morning, but if the inspector would care to come immediately, the patient would still be there and available to talk. Jenny had rested well during the night and there had been no more episodes of her waking screams – all of which implied she was beginning to recover from her ordeal. The doctor would like to speak with the inspector if she had time when she arrived.

Some forty minutes later Rebecca parked her car in the still relatively empty hospital car park. She had managed to avoid Ian Critchley and most of her team by leaving the station well in advance of their usual time of arrival. Now she spent a few moments considering the approach she would take with Jenny to verify Santoro's story. Whichever way she looked at it, the ultimate outcome would be messy for everyone concerned and there didn't seem to be any obvious route to take that would avoid that.

A few reporters were still loitering at the front entrance of the hospital, and they perked up when they saw the young DI approaching. She cut off any questions by shaking her head and saying curtly, "No comment, so don't ask."

One young man positioned himself directly in front of her to block her progress through the automatic doors and into the vestibule of the hospital.

"How is your interrogation going with Mr Santoro, Inspector Dawson?"

She glared at him and held up her arm, her palm facing outwards between them as a physical barrier. "Excuse me, please."

"Has he confessed, has Munch confessed?" He shoved a Dictaphone forward and into her face.

She pushed it away. "I said no comment and I meant no comment! Now let me pass!"

Craig Rogers sprung back and raised both his arms in the air, yielding to her aggression.

As she strode on past him, his gaze followed her progress with interest. His curiosity was piqued. Would a police officer who had just brought a major hunt for a missing girl to a successful conclusion behave like that? She had seemed… what? Stressed, distracted, embarrassed? He pinched the end of his nose thoughtfully – maybe there was another angle emerging, and if there was, he would be the one to sniff it out first.

Rebecca Dawson reported to the nurse's station and was shown immediately to the consultation room where she had met with Tom and Maggie Pritchard the previous day. She unwittingly took up the same stance as her superior, standing with her back to the room whilst she gazed out of the window. She turned as she heard the soft click of the door opening.

"Ah, good morning, Inspector Dawson, you're here nice and early."

"You wanted to see me." Rebecca really wasn't in the mood for pleasantries.

The doctor paused fractionally and tilted her head slightly to one side which Rebecca supposed was the doctor's way of acknowledging her rudeness. She felt a small pang of guilt.

"Sorry, I haven't slept much."

"No problem," was the brisk response. "I just wanted to bring you up to date with Jenny's progress. Physically, we can find no sign of any sexual assault or interference, her superficial injuries are already healing, and mentally, I feel she is coping better… better than I would have expected, under the circumstances."

"Thanks for the update. May I see her now?" Rebecca wasn't surprised by the information, and it just added further credence to the emerging truth.

"Yes, by all means. I expect to be discharging her this morning so she can continue her recovery at home. I'll take you to her now if you would like to follow me."

The doctor led Rebecca from the consultation room and down the corridor to Jenny's room. "I'll leave you to have your chat. Not too long please." With that she nodded curtly at Rebecca and left.

Rebecca sighed deeply and paused on the threshold before knocking lightly on the door and entering the room.

Jenny was propped up in a half-sitting position staring listlessly out of the window. She didn't even acknowledge the presence of the policewoman as she entered the room and moved across to the window, not until she was in Jenny's field of vision. Jenny watched half-heartedly as the woman, whose name escaped her, delved into her handbag, and brought out a plastic bag containing a mobile phone.

"I thought you would want this back, Jenny." Rebecca walked over to the bed and placed the phone on the bedspread immediately adjacent to Jenny's hand. Jenny stared at the phone whilst a dozen thoughts crowded into her head. She really hadn't expected to ever to see that phone again, thinking it was still lost in the undergrowth exactly where she had flung it some four days previously. Minutes passed and nothing was said, until Jenny looked up into the steady gaze of Rebecca Dawson.

"Do your friends keep in touch on your mobile, Jenny?"

A shrug.

"Mum and Dad got it for you, didn't they? Was that so you could let them know where you were when you went out biking and walking?"

A nod.

"Who's CB, Jenny?"

A frightened look.

"Is she a girl at your school?"

A nod.

"And does she bully you, Jenny?"

Jenny looked up again and into the still steady gaze of Rebecca Dawson. For a moment nothing happened, but then Rebecca saw Jenny's fingers curling the bedclothes tightly into her hands, her breathing becoming rapid and her eyes flooding with tears.

Rebecca considered her options. She could scare the living daylights out of Jenny and threaten her with all sorts of consequences if she didn't come clean, or she could offer compassion, comfort, and understanding. She chose the latter option.

"Jenny." She said softly, "what has happened to you... is awful. But I think I know, and I think you should tell me now... I think I know that this isn't about Giovanni Santoro hurting you, is it? Isn't this about you running away because your life is miserable? Because a girl – this CB – has been bullying you?" Rebecca paused for a moment. "Jenny?" And then she reached out to touch her briefly on the hand.

That was enough. Jenny's bottom lip drooped and trembled, and she tilted her head back on the pillow and closed her eyes. Tears began to course down her cheeks and her shoulders convulsed, and she sobbed as though she was finally and completely broken. Rebecca moved over to the child and sat on the edge of the bed, and in a gesture of rare kindness, she gathered the girl to her chest and placed her arms around her, whispering, and rocking her gently. "It's alright; it's alright, love," But she thought, *It's not alright; it's not alright at all. It's a bloody great mess.*

She waited until Jenny's sobs diminished before reaching into her bag and handing her a wad of tissue. "Here, clean up your face and tell me in your own time absolutely everything."

And so, haltingly at first, and then more clearly, Jenny began to narrate her story, and Rebecca didn't interrupt her until she had finished.

"Why didn't you tell someone, Jenny?"

"I don't know." Jenny's eyes filled again with tears, and she wiped them away as they spilled over and onto her cheeks.

"Why did you lie about Mr Santoro?"

Jenny looked up puzzled.

"When I asked you if he had hurt you, you said that he had, didn't you?"

"He did hurt me."

"I don't understand."

134

"He betrayed me. I asked him to promise he wouldn't tell anyone where I was, and he promised, and he said a promise was a promise and that his mamma had taught him that you only made a promise if you could keep it. And then he brought all those police and dogs and noise – it was horrible. And that hurt me cos he broke his promise to me, and I thought I had found a friend."

"Oh Jenny!" Rebecca looked crestfallen.

"What?"

"Giovanni didn't break his promise to you. We followed him. He didn't know we were following him. We spent many hours questioning him regarding your disappearance, but he didn't tell us where you were. Giovanni didn't betray you, Jenny."

Jenny looked aghast and her small mouth stretched open in horror as she realised what she had done. She had betrayed him!

*

Rebecca was still sitting with Jenny when her parents arrived. They entered the room quietly, both with expressions of concern and empathy etched on their faces, not quite sure of what to do or what to say. But, when Rebecca spoke, their expressions changed to confusion.

"Mr and Mrs Pritchard, please take a seat; Jenny has something rather important to tell you."

"What is it, love?" Maggie Pritchard grasped her daughter's hand and swept Jenny's unruly hair from her face. Tom Pritchard's expression became guarded and clouded as he watched his daughter and noted her eyes flicking from the policewoman then to her mother before finally making brief eye contact with him. He knew that look – it was a look that heralded a confession. He had seen it many times before, during her fourteen years, whenever she had crossed a line or misbehaved.

"What's going on, Jenny? What have you got to tell us?"

And so, they listened with growing disbelief as their daughter repeated the story she had just told Rebecca Dawson. When she had finished, no one said anything for a moment until her mother whispered, "So that man didn't take you?"

Jenny shook her head disconsolately.

"Then why did you say he did? Jenny, I don't understand why you would want to get someone in trouble like that. Did he hurt you in any way?"

"No," she said miserably whilst sniffing and wiping tears from her face.

"I'm sorry, I still don't understand. You had a ligature around your neck, I thought…"

"Actually," Rebecca Dawson interjected, "Giovanni Santoro almost certainly saved Jenny's life."

"But who then…? Oh! Oh Jenny! It was you." Maggie looked from Jenny to Tom in horror, her fingers plucking at her mouth.

"I would rather die than go back to school. And I mean it, Mum. I can't go back there."

"This bully," Tom Pritchard addressed Rebecca. "What's going to happen with her? She can't get away with this – she's only going to do it to someone else."

"Please, Daddy, don't make me go back, please!" Jenny looked up at her father, her eyes pooling again with fresh tears.

He scratched the back of his neck with ferocious energy and shook his head. "Not whilst that girl is there, my love, don't you worry about that. Christ!" Tom raised his eyes to the ceiling and looked across at the policewoman. "This is a mess, isn't it? What's to be done?"

"I need to speak to my superior, Mr Pritchard. But obviously, Mr Santoro will be released without any charges and with complete exoneration. I will be speaking with the headteacher, regarding the problems Jenny has been having at school. Other than that, I can't say at this stage."

Tom nodded and then another thought occurred to him. "So how did you know?"

"Know?"

"Well, what made you think that Jenny hadn't told you the truth?"

Rebecca paused for a moment. "It just didn't quite add up,

Mr Pritchard, and once I'd had my chat with Jenny this morning, well…" She shrugged.

*

Ian Critchley was in his office when Rebecca returned to the station. She knocked and entered at his invitation.

"Morning, Dawson, where have you been?"

"At the hospital, sir, with Jenny Pritchard."

"Ah, how is she doing?"

"They're discharging her this morning. We got it wrong, sir."

He paused in his task and glanced up sharply. "In what respect exactly."

"Entirely wrong, sir."

"Explain."

When she had finished, Ian Critchley leant forward in his seat and eyeballed her. "And precisely what led you down this pathway, inspector?"

Rebecca realised this was crunch time for her. Critchley was not a fool, and she either needed to confess her unforgivable oversight or use a degree of obscuration to cover her tracks.

"It just didn't feel right to me, sir. The ligature was wrong, the rucksack with food and drink, the tent all neatly erected – it just didn't add up."

"So, you had a cosy chat with Santoro?"

"Ah."

"My team like to see due process being followed, inspector. I understand you took it upon yourself to speak with Santoro alone this morning at five thirty."

"I couldn't sleep and… look, I know it was a bit inappropriate, but sir, what he told me enabled me to go and speak with Jenny and that's when the truth came out."

He made a derisive sound at the back of his throat. "And if he'd given you a full confession, inspector, none of it would have been admissible in court. It was a bloody stupid, amateurish thing to do."

"Sorry, sir."

He shook his head in disappointment. "Go and sort out Mr Santoro's release whilst I deal with the press. What a mess!"

"Sir! We all thought we'd got Santoro bang to rights. You can't blame me for that! We would have been putting an innocent man away."

"Just a pity we didn't establish the truth a little earlier – we've all got egg on our faces now and it's my job to limit the damage. I can't help thinking there's more to this, Dawson, more than you are telling me. Is there?"

"No, sir."

Again, the derisory noise, then, "That's it, off you go!" And he cocked his head towards the door dismissively.

Rebecca had to bite back the words she was about to utter, and as she put her hand on the door handle, he said, "Oh, and by the way, Detective Inspector Stephens has just notified us of her intention to return from maternity leave, so it looks like you'll be heading back to Luton, sergeant."

She turned to look back at him and took a breath to reply, but Critchley didn't give her the opportunity; he didn't even look up from his work but simply said, "Close the door on the way out, would you?"

She made it to the ladies' toilet without being seen by anyone on the team, so she was able to splash cold water on her face which was aflame with embarrassment and anger before anyone saw. She hadn't deserved to be humiliated like that and she had to press her lips tightly together to prevent the tears from coming. She took a deep breath and reapplied her lipstick to try and at least give the impression of composure, and with a straightening of her crumpled suit, she turned to the door to finish the job.

THIRTEEN

Gi accepted the offer of a lift back to the cottage from Rebecca Dawson. Melchett Hall was on the way to Jenny's school, Rebecca had explained, so it made sense to drop him off on the way. They sat in silence for most of the journey and it was only as Rebecca pulled the car onto the narrow road that led into the back of the estate that she spoke.

"I am really so sorry, Mr Santoro. I'm afraid life isn't going to be very easy for you for a little while, but I hope now you are home…" Her voice trailed off as she saw the atrocious words that had been sprayed on the walls of his home.

Gi turned and looked at them, his expression once again impassive, but she saw him swallow heavily. He turned back to her. "I don't think this is home anymore, do you, Inspector Dawson? Thank you for the lift."

As she drove off, she saw him aim a kick at the wall, and she thought, *Poor man, what have we done to him?*

*

Head Teacher, Barbara Bradshaw wasn't entirely surprised when her personal assistant had telephoned her office to announce that a police officer was here to see her. A young female police officer, her assistant had added, in that conspiratorial tone she used when she was trying to wheedle her way into her superior's confidences. She'd even had the temerity to hover inside the door with a notebook and pen in her hand, the inference being she would be needed for notetaking, so Barbara had felt a degree of wicked satisfaction when she dismissed her without a moment of consideration. She had caught the look of deflated disappointment on Marian Winchbrook's face as she backed reluctantly out of the room, which she returned with a warm smile of thanks and a gracious incline of her head.

She now turned her full attention to the young woman who sat opposite her and had to admit she did look rather young for a Detective Inspector. She extended her well-manicured hand across the desk, saying rather pointlessly, "Detective Inspector Dawson, Barbara Bradshaw, Head."

Rebecca Dawson thought Barbara typified the persona of a schoolteacher with her patronising air of gracious superiority.

"How is little Jenny Pritchard? She's such a sweet child and we're so lucky to have her at this school. We were all so shocked when we found out she had been abducted. What a dreadful business, Inspector Dawson."

"That's the reason for my visit, Mrs Bradshaw."

"It's Ms, actually, inspector. But perhaps we can forego the formalities – please, do call me, Barbara."

For a moment Rebecca wanted to laugh out loud. From the tone of the woman's voice, it was clearly an honour to be invited into the inner sanctum of first-name terms. *Good grief*, she thought, *do people like this still exist!* She pressed her lips firmly together, thinking, *I'm just about to ruin this woman's day.*

"It appears that Jenny's disappearance wasn't quite what it seemed."

The Head Teacher frowned and briefly closed her eyes, her eyelids fluttering momentarily. "I'm sorry, inspector, I don't understand."

"It would appear there has been some serious bullying going on in this school. Were you aware of a bullying problem, Ms Bradshaw?"

"Here? In my school? I should think not, inspector!" Her expression transformed to one of disdainful haughtiness. "Upon what basis are you making that accusation?"

"You have a pupil here, Cheryl Bosworth?"

"Yes, that's right, and her sister Laura also attends the school.

What of it?"

"Jenny Pritchard has told me of some dreadful things that happened to her at this school last term at the hands of Cheryl Bosworth and her cronies."

Barbara waved her hand dismissively. "Oh, Jenny has such a vivid imagination! I wouldn't be at all surprised if she was gilding the lily to get some attention."

Rebecca had had enough of this sanctimonious woman. She sighed and shook her head in disbelief. "Jenny Pritchard was pushed to the brink of despair and beyond, because of that girl and your attitude of see-no-evil Ms Bradshaw. Now perhaps you could make the necessary arrangements to fetch this girl so I can follow up my line of inquiry."

Barbara Bradshaw met the police officer's assertive stare for several seconds before acquiescing. She reached forward to pick up her telephone and waited a moment before she spoke with quiet severity. "Marian, would you bring Cheryl Bosworth to my office, please." There was a pause as she listened to her personal assistant's objection and Rebecca could only wonder what activity the girl might be involved in that would preclude her from coming to the Head Teacher's office when commanded to do so. She didn't have to wait long before she found out, as the Barbara drew herself upright in outrage before cutting off her assistant's protestations. "Marian! I don't care if she's about to audition for the lead in a West End show, kindly bring her to me immediately and don't question me in future. The audition for the Christmas play can wait!"

She propelled the telephone back into its cradle with some force, leaving Rebecca with no doubt the impact her news had had upon the woman. But then Rebecca noticed a shift in the woman's attitude, and she watched her shoulders sag slightly as she shook her head. "I don't understand it, inspector. Cheryl was moved here early this year from another school in town because she herself had been bullied. Now what turns a girl who understands the horror of being bullied into a bully herself?"

"Maybe it's a question of protection. Y'know – if she's the one dishing it out, no one can get at her. Would you let me speak with her, please? I would appreciate your presence as a witness to what is said and how I handle her, but if you could refrain from speaking whilst I interview her."

Barbara Bradshaw demurred with an inclination of her head, and at that moment, there was a tap on the door of the office.

"Come!" the Head Teacher said tersely. "Cheryl, please sit." She indicated an upright chair that was positioned to the left of her desk.

The girl looked curiously across at Rebecca before she sat in the chair as she had been directed to do so. Her appearance was unremarkable. She was of average height and build and appeared to be suffering from a rather a nasty bout of teenage acne. There was a touch of disrespect in her general demeanour and body language, and she didn't seem a bit fazed to have been called to the Head Teacher's office. Barbara Bradshaw addressed her coldly. "Cheryl, this is Detective Inspector Dawson, and she has come to speak to you on a very serious matter indeed, so do sit up child and pay attention."

Upon the mention of Rebecca's rank and role as a police officer, the girl swallowed quickly, and her head dropped down so she could avoid eye contact.

"What do think about bullying, Cheryl?" Rebecca asked, watching the girl closely. Cheryl simply shrugged by way of a response.

"I understand you moved to this school because you were bullied in the last school you were at, is that correct?" This time Rebecca noted the small nod which made the girl's hair swing gently.

"That must have been horrible for you. What do you think makes people behave like that?"

Cheryl looked up then and met Rebecca's gaze. She took a deep breath and said, "This is about Jenny Pritchard, isn't it?"

"You may be aware we found Jenny yesterday, but you won't be aware that she ran away. She wasn't abducted. She ran away because she couldn't face coming back to school. So, you tell me what you know about Jenny and why she might do that."

For the first time, the girl's equanimity slipped and then folded completely, her eyes flooded with tears and her lip quivered uncontrollably as she cried out, "I'm sorry! I don't know why. I don't know how it even started, but once it did, it all ran away from me. Suddenly people looked up to me and I didn't have to be worried anymore. I don't know why I picked on Jenny. She's just so perfect... just how... just how I wanted to be..." She was sobbing and had laid her head on her arm which was resting on the corner of the Head Teacher's desk. Barbara was looking appalled and repelled by the girl's loss of self-control.

Rebecca found herself feeling sorry for the girl, so she moved to crouch down by her side, and as she gently rested her hand on Cheryl's knee to empathise, she said, "This isn't a case for police action, Cheryl, and I'm sure Ms Bradshaw will see to it that you get some help and support, so try not to worry too much."

The girl took a huge shuddering breath and swallowed before wiping the sleeve of her jumper across her face. "Thank you." She sniffed thickly. "Please say sorry to Jenny if you see her."

Rebecca nodded and stood up. "Well, I'll leave the matter with you, Ms Bradshaw. Perhaps you could see me to the door."

"Yes, yes, of course. Cheryl, please stay there. There are some tissues on my desk that you may help yourself to, and then we'll have a chat."

The two women stood together in the corridor outside the office. "She doesn't need punishing; she needs helping – that's my advice to you."

"I'm well aware of what is required, thank you, inspector." And Barbara swept her hand outwards and towards the door that led to the exit.

Rebecca knew she shouldn't, but she couldn't help herself. "Cheers, Barbara, it's been a real pleasure."

FOURTEEN

The outrageous graffiti on the estate perimeter walls and the walls of the cottage proved difficult to remove and the unsatisfactory outcome of the task of scrubbing it off seemed to sum up how Giovanni was feeling. He may have been a free man, completely cleared of any wrongdoing, but there remained a stain on his character, a stigma which would surely colour peoples' attitude towards him. He finished off the unpleasant task as best he could, but without a tin of paint, it was impossible to complete the cover-up of the remaining marks. Whilst he packed away the scrubbing brush and emptied out the pail of discoloured water, he gave a heavy sigh.

He knew he was deluding himself if he thought his life here would ever return to normal, and as he stood back to observe the outcome of his labour, he allowed his mind to consider what options might be open to him. Eventually he disappeared through the front door of the cottage and into the kitchen within. He didn't delay but walked slowly and determinedly to the bookcase where he withdrew a notepad and envelope, and once he had located a pen, he settled himself at the kitchen table and began to compose a letter. It didn't take long to put the words onto the page and sign it, then he folded the paper in half and slotted it neatly into the envelope. He stood up and stared with trepidation at the missive so easily written, though the implications of delivering it weighed heavy – so he stood the envelope on its end between the salt and pepper pots that sat in the middle of the table and there, for now, it stayed.

Evelyn Bursill- Brookes enjoyed breakfast more than any other meal of the day so it was with her usual degree of relish that she entered the breakfast room and observed the range of dishes which had been carefully arrayed upon the sideboard. *The Daily Telegraph* held its usual position of importance, folded neatly, and placed on the left-hand side of her place setting, together with her reading glasses that had miraculously transported themselves from her bedside table. She smiled her approval as she appreciated the dedication with which her housekeeper cared for her. It was the wonderful predictability of this time of the day that most appealed to Evelyn – the precise orderliness of her morning routine was a discipline that had been honed and polished over the years to the point where it would be most distressing to have it disrupted.

It was therefore rather annoying, having just lifted her knife and fork to begin eating her cooked breakfast, when there was a tap at the door.

"Mrs Mulberry, surely you haven't forgotten anything?" Evelyn enquired, in a tone that gave her housekeeper no doubt of her mistress's disapproval at the interruption, and which matched the imposing glare issued over the top of her spectacles.

"I am so sorry, Mrs Bursill-Brookes, but you have a visitor."

"A visitor!" She eyed the carriage clock with mild surprise. "Rather early."

"It's Mr Santoro." The housekeeper squirmed.

"Ah." Evelyn regarded her plate for a moment then, after selecting a mushroom and popping it into her mouth, she nodded and said, "Well show him in then."

"I thought the drawing room…"

Evelyn stopped chewing and glanced scathingly at her housekeeper who, crimson-faced, backed out of the room, saying, "Of course, of course."

Evelyn heard the diminishing sound of the housekeeper's footsteps crossing the tiled floor of the hall and then a low murmuring and the same footsteps coming back, this time accompanied by a second and more hesitant set of heavier steps. Giovanni Santoro appeared at the doorway and waited.

"Giovanni! Come in, come in." Evelyn indicated that he should sit at the table with her and so he pulled one of the old, heavy dining-room chairs out from under the table and sat down opposite her.

"Tea?" she enquired. "Shall I pour? You like it rather strong, don't you, Giovanni."

Giovanni inclined his head and thanked her. Then, remarkably, Evelyn began to speak as candidly and plainly about his predicament as though she was talking about the market garden or some repair to be made good on the estate.

"What a mess this all is." She tapped the front page of the paper. "Poor girl, yes, poor girl. But it's not all as it seems, is it, Gi? So, you are 'exonerated and beyond reproach' according to the *Telegraph* and it's a bloody good newspaper so that must be right. So... come on, man, tell me what you need to tell me – my breakfast is getting cold."

Gi reached into the inside pocket of his jacket and withdrew an envelope – the very same envelope that had caused him so much agony the previous evening. He placed it on the table and pushed it across the polished surface until it lay in front of Evelyn above her place setting.

"Ah, I see." She sniffed at the note. "Your notice, I suppose?"

"Regrettably, yes."

"Hmmmph!" She sniffed again and nodded towards the teacup, inviting Giovanni to drink his tea. His huge hands couldn't possibly have negotiated the delicate china handle, so he grasped the whole cup and lifted it to his lips. She noted that, although his hands were large and strong, his fingers were surprisingly elegant.

"What'll you do?"

He shrugged, his eyes focusing on the surface of the table, but then he shifted his gaze upwards until he made eye contact with her. "Travel, I think, for a while, find somewhere to settle."

Evelyn focused on her breakfast and speared the last piece of sausage and egg. She chewed on the mouthful of food thoughtfully and said nothing for a full minute, but then she met his gaze too and told him boldly. "You have a talent, young man, a talent to put to good use, so see that you do." And when Gi looked momentarily puzzled she waved her knife at him. "Your drawing and the like. Oh, for heaven's sake man – you're wasted here! Much valued but wasted. You'll not want to delay your departure, I take it."

"Not under the circumstances, Mrs Bursill-Brookes."

"A month's pay in lieu of notice, whenever you like, Giovanni."

He dipped his head in appreciation. There was a moment when something passed between them, unspoken gratitude, the passing of a piece of Melchett Hall social history, the end of the Santoro family's long dedication to the estate, a frisson of sentiment... until Evelyn brusquely dismissed him. "Off you go then!"

It was only when Gi was pulling the dining-room door closed behind him that he thought he heard Evelyn Bursill-Brookes speak again. He may have misheard, but he was sure she had uttered, "God bless you, Giovanni Santoro, and good luck."

He walked away from the house feeling a sense of... what, exactly? Regret, certainly, and an ending of things, but something else too. Someone had expressed confidence in him and imbued a sense of direction, a way to do something different with his life. Whilst he would never have chosen this radical derailment of his comfortable life at Melchett Hall, maybe if he could take the positive out of it, he would find a new path for himself that could provide him with new challenges and opportunities.

He was still musing on these thoughts when he almost walked directly into Toby and Jim as they rounded the corner from the estate office. The two men exclaimed their joint surprise on seeing Gi, and following a moment of awkwardness, Toby suggested the three of them should have a chat in the estate office and perhaps even a nip of whisky to celebrate Gi's release and exoneration. Gi acquiesced reluctantly and followed the two elder men into the confines of the office.

True to his word, Toby opened the top drawer of a filing cabinet and withdrew a half-full bottle of good whisky, and with further scrabbling about in the bottom of the drawer, he located two small tumblers. Jim picked up a mug from the table, swilled the dregs of his morning coffee down and swallowed with a grimace then wiped away the residue with a couple of tissues. Whilst Toby sloshed whisky into the tumblers and the quickly located mug, Jim watched Gi with a mixture of endearment and regret. He had a niggling feeling he had let him down somehow and wasn't sure how he could put things right between them. He remembered how he had promised Gi's parents that he would fulfil the role of watchful guardian over their son, and he suddenly felt a flood of conscience.

"So, lad." Jim tried to inject an avuncular tone into his voice to mask his own feelings of discomfort. "All back to normal, aye? Back to work tomorrow."

Toby concurred enthusiastically. "Yes, we've got the autumn and winter maintenance to work on, and we thought we could make a start on the—"

He didn't finish the sentence before Gi interrupted him quietly. "No."

The two men glanced uneasily at one another. "What do you mean – no? Your place is here, Gi, with us."

Gi shrugged and paused. "I handed in my notice to Mrs Bursill-Brookes just now."

"What!" Jim slammed the mug down on the table, incredulous. "You can't do that, Gi, we need you! I promised your parents that I would..." His voice trailed off under Gi's accusatory stare.

"It's... look, I can't stay, okay, not with what's happened."

Toby stood up and thrust his hands into the pockets of his tweed trousers. "Now look here, old chap, what on earth are you going to do?"

"Travel; find somewhere new."

Toby couldn't help taking a patronising tone. "What with, exactly, Gi? You need funds to do that sort of thing, y'know."

"I have money put by, that's really not a problem."

"Really, Gi, the sort of money you're going to need to—"

"I have three hundred and fifty thousand in a deposit account that will see me clear for a while. Now, if you'll excuse me, gentlemen, I have some arrangements to make." He drained the whisky tumbler and handed it back to Toby. "Thank you, both."

And with that he turned and left them open-mouthed in his wake.

"Bloody hell!" Toby exclaimed softly.

"Still waters and all that. Must have been an inheritance from his parents I should think." Jim shook his head in amazement.

"Yes, that and what he's managed to save. When you think about it, what has he had to spend his money on? No rent to speak of, no hobbies, no social life, so I guess he's been saving all these years." He barked out a laugh. "Bloody hell, he could afford to replace our roof for that, with change to spare."

"We're going to miss him, that's for sure. He's a good man." Jim looked miserable. "And if I hadn't misjudged him and dropped him in it with the police, he would still be here. I promised his parents I would look after him and I don't think I've done a very good job, have I? I feel as though I've betrayed the trust they put in me."

Toby didn't really know how best to respond, so rather than eliciting a platitude, he caught up the bottle of whisky and poured them both another drink.

*

Jenny would have been mortified had she known that her own misjudgement had led to Gi handing in his notice at Melchett Hall. She intended to visit him as soon as her parents would agree to take her, so she could apologise to him, but her parents had been reluctant to take her anywhere whilst the press were still hot on the tail-end of the story.

Tom Pritchard found it ironic that the same reporters and newspapers that had been so keen to rip Giovanni Santoro to shreds were now intent upon getting to the bottom of why he had been exonerated and what part their daughter had played in creating the misconceived ideas that had led to the police arresting him in the first place. It hardly seemed possible that a week had passed since Jenny's safe return, and during this time, Tom had spent most of his days – and nights, come to that – considering the best way forward for them. Jenny returning to school in Market Braithwaite was out of the question, and until the press did finally move on to their next set of victims, they were prisoners at home.

He'd taken a week of leave from the office, and he and Maggie must have drunk gallons of coffee whilst they batted various ideas and solutions back and forth. Finally, they made their decision and Tom left the house as surreptitiously as he could on Wednesday morning so he could meet with the senior partner to discuss a transfer to the West Country branch office. Even so, one determined reporter still managed to accost him as he reached the door of his car.

"Mr Pritchard, would you like to make a comment about why your daughter misled the police and implicated an innocent man?"

Tom Pritchard turned to him. "What's your name?"

"Me?" The reporter looked momentarily confused.

"Yes. I think the question was perfectly straightforward."

For some reason the question had unnerved the young reporter. "It's Craig, Craig Rogers."

A look of incredulity passed across Tom's features. "Ah! Okay, let me get this right, Mr Rogers. You are the reporter who wrote that vitriol in the papers about Giovanni Santoro, most of which was utter fiction. My daughter made a mistake under the most difficult of circumstances, but it was you"—Tom poked his finger into the reporter's chest— "y'cold-hearted bastard who systematically destroyed that man. So don't you dare ask me to comment on my daughter's conduct in this matter. Now, if you'll get out of my way, I have a job to go to!" He stepped forwards until he was chest-to-chest with Craig Rogers who, for once in his life, had the discretion to step backwards to allow Tom Pritchard to gain access to his vehicle.

As Tom started the engine and drove off, Craig Rogers looked on. He felt a twinge of regret, possibly even guilt for the way he had handled the story. But then he shrugged and smiled lopsidedly – it was his job to investigate and report, and that's what he had done. He wasn't to know the girl had been lying all the time, and after all, the story had propelled him into a high-profile position at one of the leading red tops, so the end justified the means in this case.

When Tom Pritchard returned from his office some two hours later, he nodded briefly to Maggie who closed her eyes in relief. Jenny was writing a letter to Gi – the suggested compromise her mother had made when Jenny had once again asked if she could visit him to apologise.

Jenny had settled herself in the conservatory to take advantage of the warmth of the autumn sunshine, but whilst it warmed her skin, it did nothing for the coldness she felt inside. She had asked herself a thousand times why she had blamed Gi for what happened, when in fact he had saved her life and had turned out to be the first person she had ever met who she felt truly connected with. She'd blown it completely, she reflected, and let everyone down. She didn't think she would ever get over the way she was feeling now.

Jenny barely noticed when her parents entered the conservatory together and carried on writing her letter. Her father didn't prevaricate but sat down in the chair opposite Jenny and began to explain his plan. "Right, young lady, I've got some news for you."

She didn't even bother to acknowledge him, but he continued determinedly. "I've got myself a transfer to Exeter which means we will have to move."

Jenny paused momentarily in her letter-writing but said nothing.

"And me and your mum have been looking at schools in the area."

This time Jenny did look up at her father, a mixture of expectation and fear on her face.

"We've managed to get you a place at Devon Art College."

This announcement did elicit a response from Jenny: a small but positive "Oh!"

Her mother pushed a prospectus for the college across the table towards Jenny who looked at it for a moment before her curiosity got the better of her and she pulled the pamphlet over the top of the letter she had been composing and opened the booklet at the first page. Her parents could see the flicker of interest move to excitement as Jenny flicked through the information about the different types of courses for students from fourteen years upwards. She finally looked up and caught the expectation and hope in their faces, "This would be wicked if I could go here, absolutely wicked!"

FIFTEEN

Jim Gamble slowed the Land Rover as he approached the disused turning into the estate, beyond which was the cottage that Giovanni and his parents had lived in for almost thirty years.

Parked outside was a campervan, the tailgate and sliding side door open as the vehicle was seemingly being prepared for a journey. He pulled the Land Rover off the road and parked it across the lane, killed the engine but then paused for a moment as he contemplated the conversation he would like to have with Gi. What he wanted to say in his heart of hearts was simple. *Don't go. Stay and we will work through this together. You're like a son to me and I can't bear the thought of not seeing you again. I'm sorry I doubted you, Gi, but please – please stay.*

He sighed and plucked the ignition key from the steering column, then he pulled the catch on the door, which swung open with a creak. He climbed down from the vehicle and closed the door behind him, walking the short distance towards the back of the cottage. Gi was packing two small boxes, that sat upon the kitchen table, with what appeared to be all his meagre kitchen utensils and equipment. Gi and his parents before him, no doubt, had used the utensils to cook hundreds, probably thousands of meals over the years. This simple task seemed, to Jim, to mark a significant change for him and Gi, so much so that it brought a sudden and unexpected lump to his throat. Gi turned as Jim cleared the emotion from his voice and nodded a greeting.

"You're off then?" Jim thought, *that's stating the bleeding obvious.*

"Yes, just about ready to go."

"Nice motor you've got." Jim tipped his head in the direction of the campervan.

"Yes, it's okay, it'll do me anyway."

Jim noted the emptied bookcase and again felt a pull when he considered the Italian books of renaissance art that had been there for as long as he could remember, and yet he had never asked to look at them, not once. Suddenly, he wanted to look at them now, to gain a better understanding of the young man who was preparing for his departure. All those years, Jim had felt there was an undercurrent to Gi's character he didn't understand, and now he realised it was his artistic flair, his quiet astuteness that had eluded him and now it was too late to get to know him. Jim knew he would regret that for the rest of his life.

"I should have come to you, Gi," he said quietly.

"Sorry?" Gi was carrying one of the boxes across the kitchen and towards the back door, and somehow it felt easier for Jim to bring up the events that had led to this moment whilst Gi had his back to him.

"I mean, I should have come to talk to you first about the pictures I found, instead of going straight to the police. I'm sorry for that."

Gi shrugged and continued to walk out of the kitchen and out to the campervan. Jim followed him.

"Where will you go?"

Again, the shrug. "Just where the road takes me to begin with, and then, who knows? I may settle somewhere, or I may go back to Italy."

"Will you stay in touch, Gi?" Jim grabbed his arm. "Please, Gi, please stay in touch."

Gi looked down at Jim Gamble and thought suddenly, *He's the nearest thing I've had to a father since Papa died*, and so instead of turning away, he grasped the old man by the shoulder and squeezed it affectionately. "I'll do my best, but we'll see…"

Jim cleared his throat and pulled his cap down over his eyes. "Well, good luck t'you. You're a good man, so, well… I'll let you get on."

With that Jim turned and walked away from the van and

back through the gate to the Land Rover. It was only when he had driven the vehicle a hundred yards up the road that he pulled over and sobbed into his hands in frustration and sadness that, even in those extreme circumstances, he still couldn't express his innermost feelings.

*

Giovanni spent the last evening in the cottage contemplating the bare bookcase, the empty cupboards, and the resultant echoing effect of the absence of his personal effects. He wondered what would happen to the little house once he was gone and who would replace him within the estate gardening team. He acknowledged he would miss the predictability of his job and the relative ease with which his life had trundled along. But now – and at this thought, his stomach did a little flip – he was entering a new chapter in his life, completely unknown, utterly unpredictable. It was terrifying and yet, at the same time, exciting. He drained his glass of beer and went to bed.

*

In the morning he awoke early and only had to shower, dress, and grab a coffee from the dregs remaining in the coffee tin. He ditched the remainder and rinsed the tin out then stood it upside down on the draining board. Then he grabbed his jacket and opened the back door.

The sky was burning with a vivid red sunrise, the grey clouds shimmered like embers in a furnace, and the colour seeped across the whole sky so that even the clouds towards the western edge of the dawn were dappled pink and grey. A dead tree that stood in the garden was in the forefront of the most intense area of light, starkly silhouetted like a great shard of charcoal. The vision made Gi's fingers itch, so desperate was he to draw the image. But he knew to delay now could make him falter in his determination to leave. He looked towards the cottage for the last time, said a silent prayer for his parents, and then turned to look at the sunrise once more. The intensity had already begun to fade so he turned and opened the driver's door of the campervan, fired the engine, and with a slight grate of the gears, he manoeuvred the van around the tight turning circle on the rough parking area at the front of the cottage and out onto the lane. He didn't pause to look back, fearful of the doubt that might cast on his plans.

*

That same morning, Jenny posted the letter she had written to Giovanni, begging him for forgiveness and expressing the hope that they might become friends, if he felt like it of course. She provided him with Devon Art College as a forwarding address, not knowing where they would be living when they moved to Devon. She paused at the post-box, the letter resting on the cusp of the opening, partially in and partially out, and then she pushed it gently and heard the whisper as it landed on top of the drift of paper inside.

As she turned to walk back to the house, she gasped when the colours of the sky seemed to fill her soul, and for the first time in ages, she felt her fingers twitch with the desire to draw. She raced back home and barged through the front door. Her mother looked up in surprise and concern. "Jenny? What's wrong, love?"

"Nothing, Mum! You've got to come and look at this – the most amazing sunrise. Come on!" Jenny dragged her mother by the arm to the conservatory and they stood together, arms around each other watching as the sky shifted from intense burnt orange to flamingo pink. Maggie gazed down at the top of her daughter's head feeling the surge of love only a mother can feel.

"Don't you wish you could paint it, Mum?" Jenny murmured.

"I don't need to paint it, darling, when I've got you to do it for me." Maggie squeezed Jenny tightly to her.

"Are we going to be okay, Mum?"

"Yes, love, we are going to be just fine. Now why don't you get your pencils out and sketch that beautiful sky whilst I get some breakfast ready."

Jenny looked up at her mother and smiled. It felt like her face was cracking – it had been so long since she had smiled. She felt a sense of trepidation for the future, but excitement too, and as she grabbed her sketchbook and pencils, she fleetingly thought of Gi and hoped the future would be good for him too.

*

The missive Jenny posted that morning was delivered to Melchett Hall the following day and safely handed to Evelyn Bursill-Brookes, who in turn entrusted it to Toby's care. Giovanni had already gone, and with no forwarding address, the letter would have to wait for his eventual return.

The letter would remain in the safe-keeping of the Bursill-Brookes family in the battered old bureau for sixteen years before being handed to its intended recipient.

PART TWO

ONE

Jenny stood with her back to the window, a cascade of brilliant sunlight flooding the room with a golden, flickering shimmer. She turned, fascinated by the dapple of light and shade, and smiled as she noted the vivid intensity of the spring foliage through which the sunlight was glittering. It was late in March and the warmth of the sunlight in the room belied the chilliness of the breeze disturbing the leaves outside. That movement of the foliage outside was echoed in the dappled light as it cast mesmerising patterns upon the wall.

She brought herself back to the matter in hand – an invitation. Printed on cream vellum card, the wording was crafted in beautiful calligraphy in an attractive bronze pantone, the embossed letters raised from the card in delicious curls. She traced her fingers over the wording and sighed with resignation. Having been told that the venue had been booked, the press release sent, and the local dignitaries invited, she guessed it was a fait accompli and that she would have to cooperate with her fiancé's plans.

Simon! What was she to do about Simon? She sat down in the armchair and placed the invitation on her lap. Allowing herself to be bathed in sunlight, she closed her eyes against the glare. She could still detect the flickering play of light and shade even behind her closed eyelids. Anyone entering the room may have assumed she was sleeping and would almost certainly have spent those moments observing her beauty as the corona of light shone around her head.

Far from sleeping, Jenny was considering her current position as an artist who had quickly earnt a reputation for a unique style whilst also gaining an established foothold in the commercial world of art. She'd left Devon Art College and gone on to study her undergraduate and master's degrees at Bournemouth, graduating eight years previously. She smiled softly as she recalled the early days: a few commissions, too few and far between to make meaningful money. Then she had taken a risk and booked a stand at Badminton Horse Trials. She had sold dozens of prints, three originals, and taken four commissions. But she had to admit, even that hadn't been the true turning point for her.

It had been Simon. She recalled now how he had appeared at the stand that Sunday afternoon, just when she had begun to pack away her remaining stock of paintings.

He'd sidled up to the corner of the display whilst her back was turned, so made her jump in surprise when he exclaimed, "I say! These are pretty good, very good, in fact." And he had proceeded to dip his hand quickly into the breast pocket of his jacket and produce a business card which he passed to her with a flourish. "Simon Fellows. I am a fine arts agent." He'd thrust his hand enthusiastically towards Jenny who had taken it somewhat hesitantly.

From that moment, he had insinuated himself into her life. At first his attentions had been purely on a professional level, and he had quickly established himself as her agent, which she had to admit had been lucrative – for them both. He seemed to know everyone who mattered in the elite world of art and had managed to introduce her work into several high-profile galleries from which she had received some great critiques, a couple of interviews for the Saturday papers, and a brief appearance on a breakfast television programme. It seemed to her that she had made a meteoric leap from ignominy to relative fame in a very short space of time.

She would have been quite happy to keep their relationship on this level, but Simon, it seemed, had had other ideas, and once her future success as an established British artist was guaranteed, his behaviour towards her had begun to change. Little things at first, so that she barely noticed his advances – touching her hand or arm, kissing her on the cheek as usual but lingering a little too long.

Then he had taken her out to dinner and halfway through dessert had suddenly placed a ring box in front of her, accompanied by his best disarming smile, which had made Jenny feel queasy. She'd been completely thrown off balance by the gesture and her heart had fluttered in her throat nervously.

"Simon?"

"Jennifer."

"What's this?"

He'd laughed heartily so that some of the other diners had turned to look, and Jenny saw them smile and nudge each other. One woman had whispered rather loudly, "Oh, how lovely, a proposal!"

"Darling, you know I can't even think about life without you."

"I thought… Oh, Simon… this is…" She'd fluttered her delicate fingers across her mouth to disguise the little twist of her lips which would betray her distress to him.

"Well at least open the box!" He'd taken on the sulky tone he used whenever he wanted his own way.

"Sorry, yes, of course! Sorry, it's just such a surprise…" And so, with reluctance, she'd reached out for the box, feeling as though the very act of opening it was committing her to something. The ring was beautiful, if rather ostentatious – how like Simon to determine her fate and give her no choice in the matter. Then he'd grasped the box away from her and removed the ring, almost grabbing her hand to slide the ring onto her finger. Jennifer recalled how it had caught on her knuckle rather painfully before Simon managed to push it home and then twist her hand this way and that so that the diamond glittered beautifully in the light.

"Simon, it's lovely really, but—"

"Jen, don't say no!" He'd let go of her hand and pulled his fingers through his hair, then unbelievably, he'd pushed his chair back and left the restaurant, leaving her in possibly the most embarrassing situation of her life, alone at the table as the room fell excruciatingly quiet. She'd dabbed her lips with her napkin, folding it with much care and precision, before grasping her handbag and exiting the room with as much dignity as she could muster. The bill settled, she walked out of the restaurant and across the car park to Simon's car where she could see him hunched over the steering wheel seemingly breaking his heart. She had to admit now that her heart had gone out to him then – poor Simon!

She opened the passenger door, "Simon."

He'd turned his face to her, his reddened cheeks streaked with tears. "Sorry, Jen, had to get out of there before I made a fool of myself."

Jenny just stopped herself from saying, *So, you thought you'd make a fool of me instead.*

She had laid her hand on his arm. "Dear Simon, you know I think a great deal of you and all you have done for me, but I'm just not sure that this is right for us."

"Okay, Jen." The tears were momentarily gone, replaced by a look of regret in his eyes, his demeanour reinforced by the moue of disappointment he'd created with his mouth. "Of course I understand, my darling, but I don't think I can work with you, knowing I can't have you in the way I want you. Jen, I think you're going to have to find a new agent – it'll be torture for me otherwise!"

She'd been shocked. "Simon! Just because I don't feel ready to marry you doesn't mean we can't carry on with our professional relationship."

"I can't do it, Jen. I can't bear the thought of seeing you every day and you not being mine."

"Look, Simon." Again, the hand lay on his arm. "Why don't we see how we go. These things take time, and you've rather jumped it on me I'm afraid."

"Do you mean that, Jen?" He'd clasped her hand and squeezed it tightly.

"Well… yes, I mean if we can take things slowly and see how it goes…" She'd finished rather lamely, glancing down at the ring which seemed to weigh heavily on her hand. What on earth had she just done? Allowed herself to be practically blackmailed into a relationship – possibly even a marriage, if Simon got his way… and as she knew only too well, he almost always did.

She opened her eyes and sighed. That episode had taken place the previous November and Jenny had realised how completely trapped she was when Simon used his PR machine to announce their engagement to the media the very next day. So much for taking it slowly! She'd felt completely manipulated by him, and although he was attentive and cared well for her, she couldn't say her feelings for him had changed. She supposed their relationship was always going to be one of convenience and mutual benefit rather than any real affection or love. When she had mentioned to Simon recently that their physical closeness hadn't developed to more than an occasional kiss, he had been so cross with her, accusing her of wanting it both ways – "For Christ's sake, woman, do you want me to take it slowly or not?" had been his shouted question.

It was terribly shallow, but they had somehow arrived at a point where, in public, they behaved like a doting couple, and in private, they behaved like business partners. Oh well! Things could be worse she supposed.

And now she had this event to get her head around. As promised, Simon had booked a country house for her next big launch entitled Seasons, but she had nearly fallen off her chair when she'd seen the name of the place – Melchett Hall!

The door opened and Simon's florid face appeared around it. "Ah, there you are. What do you think to the invites?"

"Well, they *are* lovely – it's the venue I'm not sure about."

"Why ever not? It's beautiful, central, and well-known on the circuit. It's too late anyhow – the invites have gone out."

"Yes, so you told me."

"What's wrong with it?"

Jenny framed her reply carefully. She'd been scant with the information about her childhood, not wanting to cast any doubt in Simon's mind about her suitability as a client and so he was completely unaware of her successfully buried past. Now she needed to decide just how much of that past she needed to tell him.

"I used to live nearby, and I don't have particularly happy memories of that time in my life."

He smirked. "God, don't tell me you've got the proverbial skeleton in the cupboard."

"Not exactly, Simon. But if you must know, I was bullied at school and we moved away soon after, so going back isn't exactly what I would choose."

"Anyway, never mind all that. I've managed to get you an interview with the *Sunday Times* Arts Editor. The piece goes in the week before the exhibition so will really drive the publicity. What do you think to that?"

Jenny had to admit Simon was good… very good at his job, and she knew her success and developing profile were very much down to his hard work and talent as her agent. She smiled at him with genuine warmth. "Darling, that is amazing, thank you. What on earth would I do without you?" And then she moved across the room and tilted her head upwards to kiss him on the cheek.

He squeezed her arm affectionately and laughed. "We don't make a bad team really, do we, Jen?"

She laughed and moved away, agreeing with him of course but also pushing away that feeling of something being fundamentally missing from her life. She hoped the return to Melchett Hall wouldn't be a visit to regret.

*

There was a great deal to organise before the day of the event which was to be held at the end of April: flowers, refreshment, the presentation, and where each piece of art would be displayed within the hall to present it at its very best. Jenny was preparing the content of the presentation to describe her work which would include the techniques she'd used to create the vibrant images using oils and the unusual method she had developed using minute pixels of colour and form to develop the broad landscapes and wildlife with beautiful accuracy in delicate colours.

Simon had arranged for them to visit the hall at the beginning of April when they would meet with the various agencies to ensure everything would run smoothly on the day. He had arranged for them to travel up during the afternoon, aiming to arrive at their accommodation for early evening, visiting the hall the following morning. Simon managed all the arrangements, and as always, his impeccable taste had guided his choice of their hotel, which turned about to be the most charming gastro pub with rooms, situated in a quintessential English village located some eight miles from Market Braithwaite.

Jenny gazed at the pub with open admiration. It was built from local ironstone, and the fine stone mullioned window surrounds edged the diamond-paned windows to provide a charming and ancient frontage. The rear elevation was augmented with a contemporary restaurant and bistro that enclosed a patio garden. The whole effect was charming, and when a member of staff showed the couple to their room, their delight was complete. The floor of the room sloped noticeably towards the stone mullioned window, which looked out over the river and dovecote, and in the centre of the room, an enormous four-poster bed dominated.

"Simon! This is lovely." Jenny squeezed his arm affectionately. "How on earth did you find this gem?"

"Good old Google – where would we be without it? Now, come on, let's get changed and go for a walk before dinner."

They walked along the banks of the river, following the path which eventually led them out at a road which crossed the stream by way of a path over a ford. A bridge across the road led them over the stream again and directly into the churchyard, where they followed the path which led them around the church until they re-joined the path heading back towards the pub. They paused on the bridge, both leaning their forearms on the handrail, taking that moment to watch the serenity of the scene and a group of wild mallard ducks dabbling in the stream below.

Simon used the opportunity to glance surreptitiously at Jenny. He could tell she was in a good frame of mind, and he wondered if he dared broach the subject of their wedding day. He took a breath. "I tell you what, Jen…" His pause invited her to prompt him.

"What?"

"Wouldn't this be the perfect place to get married?"

She tilted her head forwards so that a curtain of hair fell over her face, obscuring her from him, until he expected the same distractive behaviour: the change of subject, the delaying tactics. He sighed and reflected, a small rueful smile forming – he was the luckiest man in the world if he could only win her over!

Finally, she lifted her head and turned to him. "Yes, Simon, I think it would be the perfect place to get married."

For a moment he expected her to say *but not to you, you fool*. But she didn't. She smiled and took his arm, turning them both back towards the path again.

He turned to her earnestly. "Do you mean that, Jen, really?"

She smiled softly at him. "Yes, I do. Let's talk it through over dinner."

He leapt away from her for a moment and yelped with surprise and delight – "Christ! Yes!" – showing uncharacteristic boyish enthusiasm.

*

Jenny had had plenty of time to consider her future with Simon on the journey to the Midlands from Devon where her studio was based at their shared home. She'd curled up in the passenger seat, and whilst Simon concentrated on the driving, she'd made a mental list of the pros and cons of marrying him, feeling guilty about the totally pragmatic way with which she was addressing her problem.

He'd been good for her, there was no doubt about that, but there was a lack of chemistry between them, and he could be petulant and difficult when he didn't get his own way. But life without him? She couldn't really imagine how she would cope professionally without him, and she had realised, with a wince, that she placed a far greater emphasis on the value of his business acumen and influence in the art world than any personal feelings of affection or love she had for him. Surely, those feelings would develop over time as they got to know each other.

In truth, she was rather indifferent when it came to human relationships. Hadn't she always been a loner as a child? And it hadn't bothered her one bit.

Maybe, she reflected, there was a vital bit of her missing, the part which made other people crave love and affection. She realised with a jolt then that, apart from the closeness she felt towards her parents, she genuinely hadn't grown close to anyone else. And it was this realisation which crystallised her decision about marrying Simon. What was the point in turning him down in the vague hope that her emotional needs would change? She was in her thirties, for goodness sake! The sooner she accepted her own shortcomings the better, and if Simon would have her and love her as she was, at least she would enjoy the stability and security of a permanent and formal arrangement with him. *God, how cold and calculating of me*, she'd thought as Simon had pulled the car into the hotel car park.

*

Jenny had to admit that Melchett Hall was a perfect choice for her exhibition. The main reception rooms were large, with high ceilings and huge windows which provided a view over the grounds, ensuring the maximum amount of daylight entered the rooms within.

The events manager took great delight in showing them around and finalising the floral arrangements, seating, and catering requirements, and when their meeting was finished, she invited them to look around the grounds at their leisure. It was strange for Jenny to be back here in the gardens, the only part of the estate she had ever been familiar with. She wasn't at all sure how she would feel about going to the walled garden, but Simon insisted they made the most of their morning at the hall.

The same old shabby green door led them into the walled area which was beautifully laid out and full of early colour from narcissi, pansies, and tulips. Jenny felt the memories come back to her in a flood as she recalled this was where her dramatic adventure had started with Cheryl Bosworth and her sister... what had been her name? *Laura*, she thought.

And then there had been the intervention to stop their bullying tactics by Giovanni. She couldn't describe the emotions that were coursing through her. It was like mixing oil with water – one set of feelings causing the familiar tightening of her gut as she recalled the vile things those girls had done to her; the other beginning with the warmth of remembering Giovanni and his friendship before that warmth was replaced by a crushing sense of guilt. She sighed heavily. God, she had ruined that man's life. Her mouth twisted into a moue of regret.

Simon turned to her, smiling, but his expression faltered when he saw the familiar tell that Jenny's emotions were in turmoil. "What's wrong, Jen? I thought you'd like it here."

She glanced across to him, uncertain again of just how much of her past she should reveal. "It's nothing. It's beautiful here, in fact I used to come here to sketch and paint." She nodded. "Sat on that very seat over there as it happens, to draw the flowers."

"So why the face?"

She laughed and flapped her hand dismissively. "The face! For heaven's sake, Simon, you make it sound like I'm about to burst into tears!"

"Well, for a moment there, I thought you were, to be honest."

"Listen, it's nothing. Just some good and not so good memories bubbling up – seeing all this familiar territory has just brought it all back, that's all. Come on, I'm hungry, let's go and get some lunch and we can finalise our plans."

TWO

When the day of the exhibition arrived, they were both up early, wanting to arrive at the hall well before any of their guests arrived. As Simon drove them from their accommodation to Melchett Hall, the full moon was dipping downwards towards the still dim hillside, and its startling brightness shifted gradually to a more mellow and creamy glow. A few wisps of cloud passed in front of the moon, so they too took on the creamy wash of the moonlight.

"Wow! Look at the moonset."

"Moonset!" Simon snorted down his nose and laughed. "I've never heard of a moonset before, Jen."

"Well, that's what it is. Hey, what a great title for my next collection! Have we got time to stop so I can—"

"Sketch it? No way. We've got to get to the hall. But I like the name, Moonset!" He laughed softly and glanced across at her fondly.

By the time they arrived at the hall, a dawn mist had descended, enshrouding the house and the grounds with tendrils of moisture.

"God, I hope this clears before the guests arrive!" Jenny frowned at the sky and indistinct landscape surrounding them.

"It's because the estate is in a valley – it'll go, don't worry."

Simon led her across the sweeping driveway and up the stone steps at the front of the hall then to the huge main doors where the events manager was waiting to greet them.

She felt the familiar flutter of nerves as the invited guests began to arrive. There was to be an exclusive showing of her collection to the press, the local dignitaries, and other VIP guests from the art world. Following her presentation, a questions-and-answers session would take place. Then to round off the event, there was to be a champagne reception. Additional guests who had applied for tickets would be admitted later in the day. She glanced at her watch for the third time in five minutes and decided one more trip to the ladies was advisable to touch up her lipstick and hair. She need not have worried, she looked amazing in a taupe cashmere dress which lay softly against her pale skin. A teal scarf brought out the green flecks in her eyes and her gleaming hair lay loosely about her shoulders.

The weather was still rather disappointing with the mist lying inert across the grounds. Some of the mature treetops were just visible, and every now and then, a pale glimmer of sunlight glowed distantly through the fog. Drips of moisture hung from leaves and the early spring flowers. The grass was thickly coated with dew and Jenny could see the dark footprints where someone had walked across the lawn that morning. She sighed, and then sensing the presence of someone beside her, turned to observe an elderly man.

"It'll clear, miss." He nodded at the mist.

"Oh, I do hope so – the grounds are so beautiful, aren't they?"

"Thank you."

"Ah, I take it this is all your handiwork then, is it?" She lifted her arm and swept her hand across the view from the window.

"Well, now, I don't do the work anymore – my knees y'know – but I still potter a bit and stick my nose in where it's not wanted."

"You must have been here when I lived in Market Braithwaite as a girl."

"My wife Marion and I have worked and lived here for almost fifty years!"

"Gracious! You've seen some changes then?"

The man chuckled and tapped his cane on the floor to emphasise his delight. "Oh, my dear, there's so much I could tell you. In fact, Marion says I should write it all down. Now, look there, what did I tell you?" He nodded over towards the window.

Jenny turned, following the direction of his gaze, and smiled. The sun was filtering beautifully through the diminishing mist, its beams of strengthening light visibly cutting through the drift of fog. The effect was magical.

Jenny lay her hand on the old man's arm. "Do you know I'm going to have come back here to paint one day."

"My dear, the Bursill-Brookes family would be absolutely thrilled if you did. And speaking of which, may I introduce you to Mrs Bursill-Brookes?" Jim turned to face an elderly lady who was walking purposefully down the corridor towards them with the aid of a stick.

She extended her hand. "My dear Ms Pritchard, please call me Evelyn! We are absolutely delighted that you have chosen Melchett Hall to show your new work. I am looking forward to your presentation tremendously."

Jenny smiled. "Well, thank you for making us so welcome, and I must say the event has been organised impeccably."

Evelyn nodded firmly. "Of course, of course."

Simon appeared at the end of the corridor. "Jenny, excuse me, we are just about ready to start."

"On my way." She turned to her new companions. "Would you excuse me? I am so sorry – I don't know your name?" She tilted her head towards the man.

"Jim Gamble, miss. And if you should need anything at all whilst you're here, just mention my name." He nodded and touched his cap.

"I'll remember that, Jim, thank you," She smiled and placed her hand briefly on his arm, acknowledging the warmth of their acquaintance. She held her hand out to Evelyn and was surprised at the firmness of the returning handshake. "Lovely to meet you, Evelyn." Then she turned to Simon and put her hand in the crook of his arm. "Come on then, darling, let's go and see what's what."

The saloon was packed, every seat taken and more people standing at the back. Simon advanced into the room, leaving Jenny waiting just outside the entrance, and the gentle buzz of conversation petered out as he stepped onto the low dais and positioned himself behind the lectern. He waited for a moment to allow the room to fall completely silent before clearing his throat and beginning his welcome address to the audience.

"Ladies and gentlemen, good morning, and a very warm

welcome to Melchett Hall. Thank you to the Bursill-Brookes family who are our fantastic hosts for Jenny Pritchard's latest collection, Seasons. Following Ms Pritchard's presentation, you will have the opportunity to view the collection. Any enquiries regarding commissions etc., please come and find me, Simon Fellows. I am Ms Pritchard's manager and business partner, so will be able to provide you with any information you need." He paused for a moment before going on. "Now, without any further delay, would you please welcome Ms Jenny Pritchard!"

The audience applauded appreciatively as Jenny entered the room passing the rows of seating, before stepping lightly to the front of the gathering. Simon moved away from the lectern and settled into the chair which had been set to one side. As Jenny turned to face her audience, she smiled warmly and made eye contact with as many people within the room as possible.

"Ladies and gentlemen, welcome to my new exhibition, Seasons, and thank you all for coming. I would like to spend some time this morning telling you about my passion for drawing and painting, and I hope to answer any questions that you may wish to ask at the end of my presentation." She turned briefly to the large screen and flicked the PowerPoint presentation onto the next slide before turning back to her entranced audience.

The presentation continued for thirty minutes, and when Jenny concluded by thanking the audience for their interest, there was a spontaneous burst of warm applause. She smiled and nodded her thanks, inviting any questions from the floor. Simon always arranged for one or two questions to be asked by members of the press to ensure there was no danger of an embarrassing silence at this point, so it came as no surprise when an arts reporter from *The Times*, who was sitting on the front row, raised his hand.

"Ms Pritchard, do you have any news for us about your next body of work?"

She smiled. "As it happens, I do have a small announcement to make this morning. The title for my next piece of work is Moonset, and I may well be coming back to Melchett Hall to complete some of the pieces. I have fallen in love with the hall and the surrounding countryside."

Another hand popped up towards the back of the room, and Simon stood up and held his hand out towards the small lady to whom the hand belonged, inviting her question.

"Ms Pritchard, is it correct that you grew up locally?"

Again, Jenny smiled graciously at the lady and said, "That's right! I lived in Market Braithwaite with my parents before we moved to the West Country when I was fourteen."

Several more questions relating to the unusual technique Jenny had developed led the subject back to art which Jenny was mightily relieved about, not wanting to linger on her personal connections with Melchett Hall.

Outside, the sun was burning off the remnants of the mist which now lay like a drift of wispy smoke above the river. A shaft of light spilled into the room and highlighted the deep gold and caramel colours of Jenny's hair as it shone around her like a corona. Simon thought she had never looked more beautiful than at that moment and he suddenly felt a crush of love and desire for her.

There was another question from the back of the room, "Could Ms Pritchard tell us how she developed the magical skill she uses to draw feathers so very beautifully?"

Simon craned his neck to see who had asked the question. A man stood in the far corner of the room, his face partially obscured by the shadows and the fedora hat which he wore at a jaunty angle. He was beautifully dressed in a charcoal three-piece suit, a cashmere coat draped with sartorial elegance over his shoulders. A few people in the audience turned to see who had asked the question and then turned back to focus on Jenny as she prepared to answer. The room waited expectantly and watched as Jenny took a breath to form her response.

"Well..." Then she stopped and leant forwards against the lectern, her eyes wide with shock. The voice, the stature, the unmistakable hair – all so familiar to her – Giovanni!

She stared at Gi with such fierce intensity that the whole room suddenly felt charged. People began to look at one another with quizzical expressions, some turning again to look at the impressive gentleman who had asked the seemingly innocent question.

Simon looked at Jenny who had drawn her hand to her mouth and whose face had taken on a rich glowing colour. What on earth was going on? He stepped towards the lectern and took her arm to lead her to the chair, convinced she was about to pass out, but she put her hand up quickly in a gesture of assertion which clearly indicated to Simon that his intervention was not welcome.

Jenny took the glass of water which sat on the shelf under the lectern and sipped from it before placing the glass shakily back down on the shelf in such a way that it spilled messily onto her notes. She cleared her throat and managed to say with reasonable composure, "Sorry, sir. In answer to your question, I had a very good teacher, but I expect you know that."

Then she acquiesced to Simon and stepped to one side. "Thank you so much, everyone, for coming today. I will leave you now in the capable hands of my manager Simon Fellows who will answer any further questions."

There was a smattering of applause from the puzzled audience who could clearly perceive things had not quite closed as they should have. Simon, being the consummate professional that he was, brought the attention of the audience back, and whilst he invited further questions, he noticed the man who had caused the strange and disturbing reaction from Jenny was quietly leaving the room. He fully expected Jenny to take a seat and wait until the proceedings were concluded, but instead, and to his mortification, she walked quickly from the room. Desperate as he was to pursue her, he could not, not without destroying the integrity of the whole event, so he could only watch in silent fury as she disappeared.

As soon as Jenny left the room, her composed walk deserted her, and she broke into a run. A member of staff looked at her curiously. "Is everything okay, Ms Pritchard?"

"Oh! Did you see a man just now? Tall, a big guy?" She realised she sounded on the verge of hysteria.

The woman eyed her nervously and pointed towards the front door. "A gentleman just went through that door."

"Thank you!" Jenny shot across the reception hall and yanked the massive oak door open, emerging blinking into the bright sunshine. And there he was, sitting on the low stone balustrade which lined both sides of the steps.

"Gi!" Jenny felt the break of emotion in her throat.

"Jenny." He smiled and took off his hat. His hair was shorter and greying, but still a mass of curls. The corners of his eyes crinkled attractively as the warmth of his smile was reflected in the brown of his eyes.

"How are you? I've thought about you so much over the years." She stepped towards him, her hands outstretched. She wasn't prepared for the intense reaction she felt when their hands met. For Jenny it felt like the ground had lurched at a crazy angle and that a shot of some extraordinary elixir had been pumped into her veins. His hands were warm and soft, and they enveloped her own small hands completely.

"Oh! Oh!" It was all that she could manage before bursting into tears.

"Jenny! Jenny! What is it?" He brushed his thumb against her cheek.

"Did you ever get my letter?"

He frowned then shook his head slowly. "Letter?"

His response elicited a fresh burst of tears from her, and she lowered herself onto the balustrade, her head dipping down until her features were entirely hidden by her hair falling across her face, obscuring her distressed expression. Her voice shuddered with emotion. "I am so sorry, so, so sorry for what I did to you."

He shrugged. "It was a long time ago."

"I wrote you a long letter, trying to explain… to tell you how sorry I was. I sent it here."

"I left soon after."

"I ruined your life!" She shook her head.

"No, no, no." He took her arm, and again she felt the pulse of energy, a shock, run through her. "Jenny, you *saved* my life. I'd still be here, in the garden, if I hadn't met you."

"Really?" She sniffed and looked at him long and hard.

He nodded and smiled. "I've been following your progress –

177

my little protégé was what I always said to myself!"

She laughed, brushing the tears from her face. "And look at you! Mr Santoro, you look very different. What have you been doing?"

He drew a card from his breast pocket and presented it to her with a small flourish. She took it from him and read the text before exclaiming, "My God! Arturo D'Arbo! You?"

"It's my middle name and my mamma's maiden name. It just seemed easier to change things after I left."

She shook her head in disbelief. "I've got two of your pieces! I love your work. My God, I don't believe it!" She laughed with delight, and he felt it catch him inside. The feeling was dangerous and pure, and it shook him to the core.

"And I have two of your pieces." He smiled down at her.

"Ah! Let me guess." She smiled mischievously and raised her eyebrow speculatively. "*Feathers?*"

He nodded and she let out a yelp of delight. He smiled. "And?"

"Hmmmm." She tapped her fingers against her lips thoughtfully. "*Barn Owls?*"

"Nope. Good try, though. *Red Kite*, actually."

"Your turn."

"Okay, you have… let me see now… I think you would like *Bluebells?*"

"Nearly – *Christmas Rose* and *Driftwood*. When I saw *Driftwood*, I just fell in love with it."

They fell into an easy silence for a moment, and then both started to talk at once. Simon emerged from the doorway as they were both laughing together. He was livid and his mood was not improved by the stabbing sensation of jealousy that stung him as soon as he saw their rapport. Rapport? No, it was more than that. There was a charge between them, a deep and personal connection which was so transparent it made him feel sick with dread.

Jenny turned to him. "Oh, Simon! Let me introduce you."

"What on earth were you thinking, Jenny, walking out like that, leaving me in the lurch to manage? I have never been so embarrassed!"

"Sorry. Sorry, darling, but this is an old friend of mine, and it was quite a shock to see him after all these years."

Simon looked up at the man and rudely said, "And how did you manage to get in? It was invitation only, y'know!"

"Simon!" Jenny was shocked by his behaviour. "I am so sorry… Arturo."

Arturo shook his head and held his hand out to Simon. "No, no. It is I who must apologise. My friend, Geoffrey Barnes, gave me his invite. He couldn't come at the last moment, and he knew I had purchased a ticket to come this afternoon."

"Oh." Simon wound his neck in a little. "How do you know Geoffrey Barnes?"

"He is my manager."

"Simon, this is Arturo D'Arbo."

Simon's head snapped upwards, and he looked at Jenny for a moment, his eyes wide with shock.

"Good grief! Mr D'Arbo, I am so sorry if I appeared rude."

Arturo laughed. "No, no, not necessary at all."

"Look, we've just popped some champagne, and canapés will be served shortly, so please come in and I can introduce you to some of our other guests."

Arturo shook his head. "Sorry, no. I don't go in for the circuit much."

"Well, that's true." Jenny touched his arm. "In fact, you're a bit of a recluse, by all accounts."

"Not exactly. Just keep myself to myself."

"Well, look, you are very welcome, and if you would rather I didn't mention your name to anyone…"

"Just a glass then, thank you."

Jenny led them shakily back through the oak door and into the gathering of guests who were now in the main hall, sipping champagne and selecting from the variety of canapés that were being distributed by the waiting staff. Simon picked up two flutes of champagne from the nearest tray and passed one to Jenny and one to her companion, then helping himself to another one, he raised his glass to them both. "Here's to talented artists."

They clinked their glasses, and Simon noted as Jenny sipped from the glass that her gaze was focused on Arturo as he turned to look at the surroundings of the great hall. Simon didn't know what their history entailed, and he wasn't sure he wanted to know. The champagne settled sickly on his stomach, and he turned to place the glass down shakily before saying, "So Mr D'Arbo, where is your studio?"

Arturo turned to face him. "I have a small studio and cottage in Norfolk, near to Blakeney."

"Ahhh, wonderful – the light!"

"Yes, it is beautiful there. I love walking along the salt marshes to Blakeney – the seascapes are incredible."

"So how did you two meet then?" He asked the question in a rush, very badly.

Jenny and Arturo simultaneously glanced at each other and then back to Simon, their discomfort and hesitancy obvious.

Jenny said quickly, "Arturo gave me some coaching when we lived here, that's why he asked the question about the feathers. It was Arturo who taught me how to draw feathers."

Arturo inclined his head in acknowledgement.

Somehow, Simon didn't believe them, but any further enquiry was interrupted by the old gentleman who had been speaking to Jenny before her presentation.

"Excuse me, Miss Pritchard, is everything quite alright for you?"

"Quite wonderful, thank you, Jim."

Arturo stared at the man transfixed. "Jim?" His hand reached towards the old man.

Jim turned at the sound of his name, a vague and quizzical expression on his face as he acknowledged the fine-looking man in front of him. "That's right, sir, I'm sorry, I don't think…"

Simon stood back a little from them observing this small drama as it played out. There was something strange here, something off, but he couldn't quite figure out what it was.

"Jim!" Now Arturo was more animated and stepped forwards to embrace the old gentleman. "Jim, it's me, Gi, Giovanni."

The man looked confused for a moment then gave a strangled cry which caused several guests to turn around. He staggered slightly so that Arturo had to catch his arm to prevent him from falling backwards.

"My boy! Good God, lad, just look at you, Gi! Gi!" His voice cracked with emotion. "I can't believe it!"

If Simon had been confused before, it was nothing to how he was feeling now. Just who was this man and what was his connection with Melchett Hall and, more importantly, with his Jenny? And why the change of name – was this really Arturo D'Arbo or… what had the old boy called him? Giovanni? He was confused beyond belief and lowered himself slowly onto the arm of one of the old leather sofas that sat adjacent to the great fireplace in the hall.

He looked across at Jenny who looked almost as flustered, her discomposure only rescued when two of the guests approached her to ask her a question about a particular piece of art. She seemed quite relieved to accompany them across the hall and into the long, wide corridor which contained many of her works. As she walked away, she glanced back towards Simon who was staring after her, the quizzical look slowly transforming into one of petulant disapproval. She recognised that look and dreaded the moment they would be alone together when he was bound to press her for an explanation.

"How have you been, Jim?" Arturo, or Giovanni as he would always be known to Jim, clasped the old man's arm and squeezed. "Why didn't you stay in touch?"

Arturo shrugged. "It was difficult. I wanted to leave this part of my life behind and I travelled for a year before settling in Norfolk. Here…" He pulled a business card from his jacket. "I changed my name, so I am Arturo now, see." He pointed to the name on the card.

Jim peered down at the card. He passed it back. "I'm no good without my glasses lad."

"Never mind." Arturo smiled indulgently. "How is everyone else? Marion, Toby? Is Mrs Bursill-Brookes still with us?"

Jim laughed. "God, yes! She'll outlive us all. We are all well, thank you. Hey!" He grasped Arturo's arm. "I've got something for you. We've kept it safe all these years. Come on, let's go and find Mrs Bursill-Brookes and Toby." He struggled up from the chair that Arturo had guided him to and crossed the hall chatting to him as they passed between the guests and left the room. They walked through the doorway that was marked *private* and on into the west wing of the hall which was dedicated entirely to the private quarters of the Bursill-Brookes family.

Gi watched Jim shuffle across the expansive hallway leaving him to reflect upon the last time he had been here, handing his notice to Evelyn Bursill-Brookes. He could barely believe it was almost sixteen years since he had last crossed this hallway. He shook his head and exhaled sharply – his life had changed beyond recognition since then. Jim, sensing he had left Gi behind, stopped and turned. "Come on, lad, I've got something to show you."

Arturo followed him then, still feeling like an imposter in the house of his former employer. They entered the library together and Arturo was immediately struck by the familiar aroma of worn leather, smoke, and a slight mustiness that stemmed from the aged books, the worn furniture, and the vast fireplace which was set with paper and kindling.

"Have a seat, Gi, I'll just go and find Mrs Bursill-Brookes and Toby."

Jim left the room without giving Arturo the opportunity to do anything other than shift uneasily into one of a pair of large wing chairs that were placed either side of the fireplace. He looked around the room, allowing the memories of working on the estate, life with his parents here, and the circumstances which led to him leaving this place to come flooding back. Then, inevitably, he thought of Jenny.

When he had decided to attend her exhibition at Melchett Hall, he hadn't really thought through the possible ramifications. It had been brilliant to see her again and listen to her presenting with such calm assuredness. Her work was outstanding and wonderful to view. What he hadn't anticipated was the pure and powerful emotional reaction he had experienced when he saw her, and then when she had grasped his hands, it had felt like a lightning bolt going through him, and he was sure that she had felt it too. Even now, he felt different, changed somehow, as though his emotions had become suddenly molten and charged by their connection. He passed his hand across his face and uttered a soft expletive. Maybe it would have been better if he hadn't come, after all.

His cogitation was brought to an abrupt halt as the door to the library swung open and Jim re-entered, closely followed by Toby who strode into the room, his hand extending towards him. "Good heavens, Giovanni, how marvellous to see you after all this time!"

"Toby." Arturo stood and grasped the man's outstretched hand. "Good to see you again. You're looking well."

They chatted for a few minutes about the estate, the gardens, of course, and the staff who still worked there. Toby politely enquired after his circumstances and exclaimed with surprise when he presented him with his business card. The name Arturo D'Arbo didn't mean much to Toby, not being interested in art, but the visible change in the man's appearance and demeanour certainly implied that Gi had found a degree of success since he had left them. Whilst they spoke, Toby slowly moved over towards the bureau and, finally after much searching, grasped a letter from within the depths of the papers stored there. He stared at the front of the envelope for a moment before passing it over to its rightful owner.

"Glad I kept hold of it."

"I appreciate it, Toby, thank you." Arturo took the envelope and fingered the seal whilst their conversation continued. Finally, he could make his excuses, citing the need to get on the road again before the light began to fade. Handshakes were exchanged, with shallow assertions of keeping in touch and revisiting when he was in the area. They all knew it was most unlikely to happen, but it seemed like the polite thing to do.

Once he had bid his final goodbye to them, Arturo made his way out of the hall and through the formal gardens until he came to the old green door at the entrance to the walled garden. When inside, he smiled with pleasure, able to fully appreciate the industry required to create the order and beauty within. He found one of the benches and settled himself on the cool stone surface before pulling the letter from his coat pocket and peeling back the sealed flap. He withdrew the letter and unfolded it, laying it on his lap as he reached into his breast pocket for his reading glasses.

Evelyn Bursill-Brookes entered the walled enclosure, and when her eyes lighted on the figure of Arturo, she struck out along the path, using her stick to aid her walking. In her hand, she clutched the business card which Arturo had handed to Toby.

Arturo sensed her presence and turned, standing at once to greet his previous employer. "Mrs Bursill-Brookes, how good to see you again!"

She waved the business card. "I knew it! I knew you had the makings of a fine artist! Just look at you now. I should call you Arturo, I suppose. I've seen your work, magnificent stuff."

He inclined his head and smiled. "The advice you gave me the last time I saw you, it put me in good stead."

"Nonsense! Here." She proffered her arm to him. "Take me back to the house, there's a good chap. We can have a good old gossip on the way."

*

Jenny had spent an hour chatting with guests and welcoming the additional visitors as they arrived. Simon had been able to observe her for most of the time from a distance, and he could clearly see that, whilst to anyone else she was being the consummate host, she was in fact distracted and not focusing on her role as she usually would. Every few minutes, she would glance across the room as if to seek someone out, and each time the large door was pushed open from outside, her head would turn to see who had entered before turning her attention back to the person she was with. Simon had never witnessed this behaviour from her, and it filled him with a certainty that his hold upon her had slipped irrevocably.

The event had, commercially at least, been a great success, and by mid-afternoon most of the guests had bid their thanks and goodbyes so that only a handful of stragglers remained. Arturo made his way slowly back to the hall, the letter from Jenny folded and tucked into the inside pocket of his jacket. Things may have worked out differently for him, for them both, if he had received the letter before he left all those years before. He shrugged – he was a fatalist and accepted that the fate that had separated their paths then was the same fate which had brought them back together now. This ambivalence didn't prevent a heaviness from falling across his mood – all those years when they could have been friends and now too late to do anything about it.

He paused, his enormous hand engulfing the brass door handle before he pushed the vast door open to re-enter the main hall. The caterers were clearing away the detritus of the event, clattering crockery and glasses with noisy efficiency. Arturo glanced across the room to where his gaze fell upon Simon who nodded an acknowledgement in his direction and then began to weave his way through the remaining guests until he stood in front of him.

"Good event?"

"Very successful, thank you!" Simon effused, although he seemed distracted and on edge.

"Is everything okay?" Arturo inclined his head, demonstrating his concern.

Simon's response was to rake his fingers through his mousey hair leaving it comically askew.

"What?" Simon frowned at Arturo, affronted by this man's directness. "Yes, yes, of course, just whacked. Lot of organisation goes into an event like this – as I'm sure you know."

"Yes, well – good job, Simon. Just wanted to say thank you and let you know I'm off now." He held out his hand, steady and huge, towards Simon in a gesture of farewell. Simon stared at it for a moment. It felt like a challenge to his authority, his masculinity even. He knew his own hand would be swallowed up by this stranger's grasp, and he felt hostile; he couldn't wait to see him go. He grasped the outstretched hand and winced inwardly as he felt the clamminess of his own skin against the soft dryness of Arturo's palm.

"Good to meet you, Arturo, and best of luck. Do give my regards to Geoff when you see him, won't you?"

"Of course. I'll just go and say my goodbyes to Jenny."

He held eye contact with Simon for a just a fraction longer than normal social etiquette would generally expect. To Simon, it was a clear challenge, and he could feel the hairs on the back of his neck bristling with outrage. Arturo didn't give him the opportunity to express this outrage, simply turning his back and walking away across the hall and down the corridor. Simon felt pure hatred for the man surge through him and had to sit down for a moment to try and quell the urge to run after him.

*

Jenny was in the saloon talking animatedly to an elderly couple who looked entranced by her presence as she pointed here and there to the features of the vast painting which the three of them stood in front of. Arturo waited patiently whilst their conversation continued and he smiled softly as he absorbed Jenny's loveliness: the gentle swing of her hair, the elegant litheness of her figure and the glow of her skin as it reflected the late afternoon sunshine that was still seeping through the window and casting a pool of light across the wooden floor.

Suddenly, and to his horror, he felt tears gathering in his eyes, and his throat constricted with a desperate ache. What on earth was happening to him? He passed his hands roughly across his eyes, embarrassed and shocked by the display of emotion and not understanding the reason for it. He managed to compose his demeanour during the few minutes that Jenny took to accompany the couple to the door and thank them for their attendance. She paused with her hand resting on the door frame before entering the saloon once again. She walked across the vast room and stood next to Arturo as he gazed across the landscape of formal gardens and parkland.

Neither of them said a word, each separately and privately savouring the presence of the other and committing the moment to memory. Finally, Arturo turned to her and said, "They kept your letter for me."

"Oh! Have you..?"

He nodded and reached into the breast pocket of his jacket to withdraw the envelope again, then he held it out towards Jenny. "Here."

She shook her head and smiled. "I don't need reminding what I put in it. I pretty much think I could recite it to you, off by heart."

"Did you mean the things you said?"

"Of course."

"Jenny, we could have been such good friends and—"

She interrupted him. "We still can be, can't we?"

Arturo turned back to the window, using the view as a distraction. "Of course, of course." He murmured, and then as if a sudden determination had come upon him, he picked up his hat and turned. "I must be off, Jenny. I'm glad I came. Thank you for today." He gave a stiff little bow of his head which Jenny mistakenly thought was the precursor for a kiss and she tilted her head up towards him. There was a moment of embarrassed uncertainty and then Arturo did bend and brush his lips against her cheek. Then he stepped swiftly back and away from her, and as he did so, he muttered something whilst his face was momentarily obscured in the process of positioning his hat back upon his head. Jenny felt the most extraordinary sensation of piercing intensity; she had to lean momentarily against the long windowsill, her hand fluttering in front of her mouth.

"I need to see you again." She blurted out rather clumsily.

He looked down at her and sighed. "Please, yes, you and Simon must come to the studio when you are visiting Norfolk. I would like that." But he looked, she thought, rather miserable, and she wondered if the letter had stirred up old and unhappy memories and that the last thing Arturo wanted was to see her again. And much to her chagrin, she found herself thinking that she hadn't considered Simon for one moment when she expressed a desire for them to meet up again.

"I have your card, so I'll call you, if I may? We could walk together by the sea!" Her enthusiasm wilted when she sensed his hesitancy. "Or if you would rather I didn't…"

"No, no, of course you must come and see me, I mean it, Jenny." And with that he strode purposefully from the room, closing the door behind him.

It was like the sun had gone out.

*

The supervision of the packing and loading of the artwork was a welcome distraction for them both and they barely had a moment to speak to each other before the vans were loaded up and homeward bound. Simon collected the paperwork together and then went in search of Jenny whom he found in the saloon; she was staring out of the window as the evening light cast its gloom upon the gardens.

"All ready, then."

Jenny half-turned at the sound of Simon's voice not knowing whether his comment had been a statement or a question.

"Sorry," she said softly.

Simon in turn wasn't sure whether she had misheard him or whether she was making a weak apology for her behaviour. It seemed to him that suddenly they were off kilter, out of tune with each other. He wanted to bring up the drama with Arturo D'Arbo, but it felt like such dangerous ground for him to tread on. Instead, he capitulated and touched her arm.

"Come on, you're tired. Let's go home."

She smiled wearily at him and nodded, but his heart lurched. He felt her resigned acquiescence was just another sign of a deep and perturbing unhappiness that had engulfed her, and he was at a loss how to handle it.

Simon drove them home, most of the journey completed in a strained silence. It was purgatory, each one of them knowing the very subject they both needed to discuss was getting in the way of them saying anything at all. Finally, when Simon found the compulsion to say something, he took a breath and glanced at

Jenny only to find she was asleep. The moment had gone, and they never spoke of that day again.

THREE

Spring moved slowly into summer and Jenny tried to busy herself in the creative process of planning her new body of work. But Moonset was proving difficult to grasp, and by late August, she felt frustrated and mentally exhausted. Simon had kept her extremely busy on the circuit, appearing at art shows, speaking at conventions, appearing on radio and television, and featuring in two magazine articles. He was always looking for the new angle which would whet the press's appetite and keep Jenny in the limelight. She found it tiresome but understood the need for it on a commercial level, even if she did find it shallow.

It was just such an event that led to a spat between them. Jenny had experienced yet another fruitless day in the studio, considering several ideas that had simply fizzled out into nothing. She was sitting on the patio enjoying a few moments of warmth and relaxation in the evening sunshine and had treated herself to a glass of chilled white wine. At last, she started to feel her tired muscles relaxing as she prised off her shoes and curled her legs up and into the chair. She allowed her thoughts to turn again to Arturo. She had lost count of the times she had played out their meeting, except in her imagination the ending was different. In her imagination he didn't stride from the room, not looking back, but turned and took her into his arms and… She smiled softly as she let her unbridled thoughts loose.

So, it was an unwelcome interruption when she heard the front door bang and keys rattle as they were tossed into the bowl which stood on the consul in the hallway. She hoped Simon might go directly upstairs and shower and change as he often did. It would give her a few more minutes of peace. But no, he came directly through the patio doors and onto the terrace, and as she glanced his way, she noted his look of mild disapproval at the glass of wine.

"Hi, darling, you're starting early, everything okay?" He sat down opposite her, shielding her from the best view of the garden. It was always about Simon; it always had been. *And it always would be*, she thought tiredly.

"Hey, I just fancied a few minutes relaxation and a glass of wine, and it is six o clock – since when is that too early on a Friday evening?" She couldn't help but let a slight note of petulance creep into her voice.

"No, that's fine, darling, of course. Normally I wouldn't comment but…"

"But what?" She sat up now and looked directly at him. "Come on, but what?"

He stood up suddenly and tugged at his tie, flinging it across the patio and into a chair. Jenny was used to his diversion tactics and sat quietly until he was ready to say what was on his mind. He sat down again and pulled his chair closer to hers so he could grasp her hand in his. "I have just got you *the* most amazing gig!"

"Gig?" Jenny spluttered into her wine glass, looking at him with a mixture of incredulity and scorn. "Right… I can't wait for this." She said carefully, preparing herself.

"Don't make fun, darling. You know the chat show, *Saturday Night Live?* I've only got you a slot on that!"

"Simon, you know I don't like that sort of thing. I don't think it does anything for my credibility as an artist."

"No but think of the exposure!"

"If I'd wanted exposure, I would have been a model." She regretted the sarcasm as soon as she had uttered the words. "Sorry, darling, I know you work incredibly hard to build my profile, but I don't think this is right, not this time."

"You'll be fine."

"Simon, I said no, not this one, okay."

"Well, it's a bit late for that actually."

"What do you mean?" She asked, knowing full well what he had done.

"Well, I've already agreed."

"Well, you will just have to tell them I've changed my mind. I am not doing it."

"But it's tomorrow night! You can't say no now – think of my reputation!"

"Jesus Christ, Simon! It's always about you, isn't it? About *your* ego and *your* reputation and *your* status!" She was livid with him, and she let it show. "No wonder I can't get my creative mind in place when you parade me round like some fancy performing pony! I am *not* going on that show, not now and not ever! So, get that into your head, once and for all!"

She knew she had said too much, and there was an awful moment when they stared at each other with unveiled hostility, whilst a whole world of uncertainty opened between them.

"I didn't realise that you felt so strongly about my efforts to make you a success."

Jenny moved to respond but stopped when Simon held his hand up to stop her. "Don't worry, Jenny I will get one of my other clients to step in. I'm sure they will be delighted at the opportunity. If you will excuse me now, I have a few phone calls to make." And he turned, his posture a picture of self-righteous indignation as he strutted back into the house.

"Oh, get over yourself!" Jenny called after him, just loudly enough to satisfy herself, but she hoped not quite loudly enough for Simon to hear.

"Sorry, what was that?" His head re-emerged from the patio doorway; his expression suffused with rage.

"Nothing." She replied sullenly, suddenly feeling like a naughty child caught backchatting a parent or teacher.

He remained there, poised, and ripe to deliver his retort when his mobile phone rang. He glanced at the display and turned from her and back into the house. "Hi, Peter! How are you? Long time no speak – how's Heather and the children? Oh great, that's great! Anyway, I'm so glad you called; your timing couldn't be more perfect. You're not going to believe this but…"

His words became inaudible as he disappeared further into

the house and Jenny heard the study door close behind him. For a moment she felt like she had been abandoned and a sliver of jealousy cut into her. But then she shook her head admonishing herself silently for her capriciousness. It wasn't only Simon who misbehaved in this relationship, she realised. And how many times had she been grateful for his support and his talent for getting her noticed. Her vision blurred with tears, a mixture of self-pity, remorse, and sheer exhaustion. She tipped her head back and sighed heavily. She knew what she needed to do; she just needed the courage to do it.

They managed to avoid each other for most of the evening. Simon was seemingly busy on the telephone and then he announced he was going out to meet with a client. He paused in the doorway of the kitchen-breakfast area and leant against the frame with both hands before saying quietly, "I'm popping out to see Peter. Don't wait up, I may be late."

Jenny had been preparing an evening meal, and she paused, the knife poised mid-air in the midst of slicing vegetables at the kitchen table, before affording him the courtesy of a glance in his direction and a brief acknowledgement. "Aren't you going to eat something before you go? I was just preparing stir fry."

Another frisson passed between them. Remorse? Regret?

"No, sorry, I should have said." Simon looked momentarily uncomfortable.

"Don't worry, it will keep until tomorrow. I'll just have a snack instead." Immediately, Jenny thought, *that wasn't necessary*.

"Well, you've got to eat, so go ahead. Just chuck what you don't want, for heaven's sake."

And then they could both feel it building again, this new and horrible animosity between them.

"I think I can make up my own mind about what I eat, or do you want to start organising that for me as well!"

They stared at one another for a moment.

"For Christ's sake, Jenny!" Simon shook his head and turned away. Moments later, the sound of the front door banging reverberated around the house.

Jenny laid the knife down, pulled off her apron and sat down. Her head coming to rest on her arms, she wept, finally venting the tension and unhappiness.

*

It was the following morning at breakfast before they referred again to the previous evening's argument. Jenny had made a special effort, squeezing fresh orange juice, grinding coffee beans, and putting croissants in the oven from the freezer. It was a beautiful late summer morning and Jenny had already been for a run with her dog who was now lying at her feet whilst she continued to prepare the meal.

She could hear Simon upstairs moving from the bedroom and into the bathroom before finally coming downstairs. Jenny felt a sense of nervous anticipation as she heard his footfall coming along the passageway and was relieved as she heard the study door open, giving her another few moments to compose herself and prepare what she had to say.

She clicked on the radio, hopeful that the music would be a welcome distraction that would relieve some of the tension she felt. If nothing else, the melodious noise would fill the void of silence that had pervaded the house since the previous evening. And then he was there, poised at the doorway and looking tired and a little sad.

"Good morning, darling." She tried to sound bright and cheerful, but her voice was false and brittle.

"Hi. You alright?" Simon moved across the room and took her elbow in his hand.

"Simon…"

"No don't – I am sorry, Jenny. I am sorry about last night. You're right, I shouldn't try to railroad you into stuff I know you don't enjoy." He squeezed her arm and she thought he looked exhausted.

"I'm sorry too. I was horrible and ungrateful, and I said some things I wish I hadn't." She turned to him, and they hugged.

Simon couldn't help noting that she hadn't said she had not meant them, only that she wished she had not said them. He closed his eyes and held on to her. It was like holding on to sand, he thought – the harder he tried to clutch on to her, the more quickly she seemed to be slipping through his fingers.

Jenny could almost have been reading his thoughts as she pulled away from him and, taking a deep breath, said, "I think I need a break, a holiday. I am just… well, I just feel I am burning out before I've even come anywhere near achieving my potential. And I am so scared I will wake up and just never be able to paint again." She could feel the emotion welling up in her throat.

"Hey! Jenny, come on!" Simon pulled her back in. "That is not going to happen, okay." He stroked her hair. "A holiday is a great idea. We could both do with a break. Where do you fancy going? I could book that clipper cruise we've looked at before, or what about..?" He trailed off as she pushed back from him again.

She placed her hand on his chest and then looked up steadily into his face and sighed. "Simon…" She said slowly, feeling her way around her words. "When I said I needed a break, I meant, well, I meant on my own. I need to get back into my creative frame of mind, and much as I love our holidays together, they are about relaxation. This getaway is about work. Sorry, darling, I don't want to hurt your feelings."

He did look hurt, just for a moment "Oh, okay. I understand. Where were you thinking of going? Would you like me to book somewhere for you?"

He sounded so crestfallen she almost changed her mind. "Thank you but no. I think I need the spirit of adventure, the not knowing. I am just going to take the car and head off for a week or so. I'll take the dog, so you won't have him to worry about."

"Okay, that's fine. I guess it gives us a bit of space too. Fresh start, yes?" He looked at her with concern.

"Yes, that's right, fresh start." She turned back to the task of preparing breakfast.

"When are you going?" He sat down at the table and casually flicked open the newspaper.

"I thought tomorrow. I know it means clearing my diary, but I've checked and there is nothing too major on for the next couple of weeks. The end of August is always a bit thin on the ground for appointments, and I don't have any outstanding commissions so I thought I may as well."

"Any ideas where you will go?" Again, the casual question.

"No. Maybe the Cotswolds, Wales – I haven't decided."

Simon studied the paper with great intent, but he read not a word. His mind was filled with dread as he silently pleaded – *Don't go to Norfolk, Jenny, please don't go to Norfolk.*

FOUR

The journey was ridiculous for what would amount to a little over a week in a hotel, but as Jenny travelled up the M5, she reflected she would have driven a great deal further if the prospect of seeing Arturo at the end of it was the prize.

She stopped the car at the services near Bristol to walk the dog, freshen herself up, and telephone the hotel she had picked out the evening before. The choice of hotel had been deliberate in that she knew it was on the coast and not far from Arturo's studio.

She keyed in the number on her mobile phone and waited for the call to be answered, and then proceeded to book herself a bed and breakfast room whilst explaining she had a dog with her. The receptionist was charming and explained they had dedicated dog-friendly rooms in the courtyard of the hotel. The hotel was on the outer edge of Blakeney, near to the quay, and once the accommodation was booked, she could feel a rising sense of excitement and anticipation. When she gave her name to the receptionist she was surprised when the young lady said, "Oh, Jenny Pritchard! I don't suppose you're Jenny Pritchard the artist, are you?"

"Oh, well, actually, yes, I suppose I am."

"Oh, how lovely. The hotel owners will be delighted you have chosen our hotel for your stay, Ms Pritchard. Are you coming here on holiday?"

"Well, hopefully a bit of relaxation and a bit of work too, who knows!" She laughed, pleasantly surprised that she should be so widely known. She mentioned as much to the receptionist.

"Well, it's such a great place for artists – we are quite familiar with the scene. It will be lovely to welcome you as our guest. What time do you expect to arrive, so I can ensure your room is ready."

"Oh gosh, I think my room will be ready by the time I arrive. If I'm lucky, I'll get there for about seven, traffic permitting – and I'm talking M25!"

"Oh dear, well, the very best of luck with that. In which case, I will make sure there's a warm welcome and a glass of chilled wine. How does that sound, Ms Pritchard?"

"That sounds just about perfect, thank you so much. See you later."

As she terminated the call, she noticed her finger shaking slightly when it pressed the button on her mobile phone.

She had thought about this decision, long and hard, until she'd thought she would go mad with the constant arguments and counterarguments that flicked backwards and forwards in her head. Then she'd realised that in her current state of mind she wouldn't be starting her new project any time soon. She had already wasted eight weeks producing absolutely nothing except some scribbled notes and a few rather poor commissions. In the end, the answer had been clear to her. One way or the other she had to know if the immediate and intense emotions that she had experienced when she saw Arturo were reciprocated.

As she steered the car back onto the motorway, she recalled the moment when they had grasped hands outside on the terrace at Melchett Hall. It had been like she'd lived in a darkened room all her life and suddenly someone had opened a hatch in the roof to allow a shaft of bright light to pierce the gloom. My God! She remembered now the impact had sent her completely off balance. And then afterwards on the way home in the car, when she had pretended to sleep, she had rerun the day over and over again in her head until she realised that for the first time in her life she got it – she finally understood the term 'chemistry'.

Jenny stopped again for her final planned break at the services where the M25 and A1 met. She opened the hatch of the Discovery cautiously so she could grab the dog before he jumped into the road. "Good boy, good boy!" She ruffled the top of his head where his fur was deliciously black and curly. He shook and stretched before yawning widely and looking up at her with the liquid brown eyes that she had first noticed at the animal rescue centre. He'd been just a puppy then. Simon hadn't been keen on having a dog, but Jenny smiled as she recalled saying to him – *love me, love my dog*.

He woofed softly and nudged her hand. "I know you're hungry, aren't you, boy?" As if in answer, he immediately sat down and let his tongue flap pinkly before licking his lips in anticipation. Jenny laughed at him and reached into the back of the Discovery to grab his food bag. As she set about dishing out a portion of his food, she heard a girl's voice nearby saying, "Oh, Mummy, look! Look at that dog, isn't he gorgeous?"

"Don't go near, darling, careful now!"

Jenny re-emerged from the car and, looking towards them, smiled. "He's friendly and you can stroke him if Mummy says it's okay?" She glanced at the mother and smiled reassuringly.

The girl, who must have been seven or eight, didn't need any further encouragement. She petted the dog's huge head that stood easily as high as her waist.

"Hello, boy, hello!" She bent towards him and smiled as he tried to lick her hand.

"He is lovely. What breed is he?" The mother enquired.

"Oh gosh!" Jenny raked her hand through her hair. "They said at the rescue centre they thought he was part cockapoo, part labradoodle and a bit of something else thrown in, so I call him a cocka-poodle-doodle!" They laughed, and the dog woofed in agreement.

"Awww, he's lovely! What's his name?"

"Ahh. His name is Munch." Jenny smiled fondly at him.

"Munch?" The girl enquired quizzically.

Jenny laughed. "Yes, I'm afraid he's rather fond of his food."

They all laughed again, and the mother and girl said goodbye as they continued their journey.

"There you are, Munch – you've made two new friends. Now sit down whilst I get you your dinner."

Munch sat down obediently, his brown eyes regarding her

with love and loyalty. She smiled down at him. "You don't fool me, y'know – you only ever look at me like that when I have food for you!"

She leant back against the car watching him wolf down the food, and she tipped her head back, suddenly feeling the tension from the last few weeks begin to drain away. She had no one to please but herself and Munch for the next few days, and the thought was liberating.

Once Munch was safely stowed in his crate, Jenny settled back into the driver's seat to continue the journey. She leant over to open the glove box where she rummaged through the collection of CDs inside. As she flicked through the various artists, the diamond in her engagement ring glittered in the sunlight. Jenny stared at the ring and for a moment she resented it and all it stood for. She felt only a small degree of guilt when she slipped the ring off and placed it into the glove compartment. She pushed the chosen CD into the player and closed her eyes briefly when music flooded the car, then she tucked her hair behind her ears, flicked on the indicator and, checking her mirrors, continued her journey.

*

Seven hours after she had left her home in Devon, Jenny steered the car into the car park at the back of the Cley Cross Hotel in Blakeney. She was tired but felt content as she cranked on the handbrake and stepped out into the cool evening air. Her senses were immediately assaulted by the moist saltiness blowing in off the marshes and the nearby coast. She turned her head to feel the soft breeze brushing deliciously against her skin; she was looking forward to going for a long walk with Munch, but not this evening. This evening she would settle in, have supper, and maybe have a glass or two of wine before having an early night. She stretched and suppressed a yawn as she let Munch out of the back of the car and grabbed one of the holdalls she had brought with her.

Jenny looked around with pleasure at the pretty courtyard of the hotel. There was a brick and flint circular wall in the centre which retained a stone fountain and pond. A profusion of lilies grew in an abundance; pure creamy flowers and buttercup-yellow stamens, their wide leaves crowding the surface of the water. Jenny could hear the faint burble of the fountain as it splashed into the water. The hotel itself was constructed with the same local materials, and the red brick and flint decoration was pleasing to the eye as its lines and folds cobbled and corrugated across the exterior of the building. Hanging baskets of summer flowers draped their colourful contents in such generosity that the trailing petunias almost brushed the ground in places. The beds were crammed with crocosmia that draped over and, in between marigolds, the burnt orange and red clashing stridently.

As Jenny paused to absorb the scene, she acknowledged to herself that she had made absolutely the right decision to get away. She felt a frisson of excitement knowing that Arturo's studio was just a short walk away. The dog was sniffing the air with relish. "Come on, Munch, let's go check in and get settled for the evening."

Munch looked up at her with his gorgeous eyes, the colour of melted chocolate encircled by a ring of pale gold. Jenny smiled at him as his tongue lolled from his mouth and he smacked his lips together. "You needn't look at me like that and think you're going to get round me. You've had your dinner for today, you old devil."

She clipped the lead onto the leather collar and waited whilst Munch enjoyed a vigorous shaking and then they crossed the courtyard together, passing through the dappled patches of light and shade as the last vestiges of the evening sunlight cast little pools of pale orange upon the flagstones and flowers.

The reception area was bright and welcoming, and as Jenny approached the desk, a young woman emerged from what was presumably a back office to greet her. "Good evening. Is it Ms Pritchard?"

"That's right." Jenny smiled warmly.

"We spoke earlier on the phone, Ms Pritchard." The girl placed a sheet of paper upon the desk, indicating the information that needed completing, and then she passed the key over to Jenny. "We have given you Roses as your room. If you cross the courtyard to the far corner, it's the room at the very end. It's got a lovely private terrace overlooking the marshes and the sea – we hope you'll like it."

"It sounds perfect!" Jenny smiled and clasped the key fob which clicked softly in her hand.

"Now I promised you a glass of chilled wine – please feel free to use our bar and restaurant facilities, or you may wish to have a quiet supper on your terrace?"

"I think supper on the terrace sounds nice."

"There is a menu in your room so just let us know what you fancy. There is a bottle of wine in the fridge for you, so it's nicely chilled already – with the compliments of the management, Ms Pritchard."

"How lovely! That really wasn't necessary but thank you very much."

The door to the back-office area opened again and a man emerged. He was middle-aged, extremely well-dressed, and clearly, from his demeanour, the manager of the hotel.

"Ah!" he exclaimed as he saw Jenny. "Ms Pritchard, welcome to the Cley Cross Hotel and thank you for choosing us for your stay. My name is Geoff Stevens, hotel owner-manager." He moved around from behind the desk and stood before her, his hand extended in welcome.

Jenny took it briefly and thanked him for the welcome.

"Here, let me help you with your bag. Do you have any more luggage?"

"Thank you so much. Yes, some more in the car – perhaps we can pick it up on our way to the room." She turned. "And thank you, for making me feel so welcome."

The receptionist blushed deeply and grinned at both Jenny and her manager, pleased with the compliment.

They collected two further bags from the car as they re-crossed the courtyard, one of which contained clothes and the other artist's materials. The sun had slipped much further towards the horizon, and the quality of the light had taken on a burnished shade as the coppery remnants of the day shimmered across the landscape.

Jenny paused for a moment to absorb the colours and movement of light.

The room was lovely; spacious, and newly furnished. Jenny thanked the manager for his assistance, and as soon as he had wished her a good evening and left her, she dumped the bag she had been carrying and explored her surroundings. In addition to a king-sized bed, there was a large easy chair, a desk, and another chair, and a huge bathroom with spa bath and walk-in shower, and then there was the terrace. Double doors folded back upon themselves to maximise the opening between the suite and the outside space. The terrace was large enough to contain a small wrought-iron patio table with two matching chairs and a sun lounger. Two hanging baskets, which were suspended from the wall by wrought-iron brackets, cascaded purple petunias downwards towards the flagstone paving. It was just perfect.

As Jenny walked to the edge of the terrace and leant against the pretty railings, she looked out across the salt marshes which were now only dully visible in the gloaming of the day. And there was the moon. Huge and palely reflecting the coppers and burnt orange of the fading sunset. It hung on the horizon seeming to almost touch the sea. She felt her fingers twitch and the familiar feeling of the need to paint course through her, a transfusion of energy.

*

Simon arrived home at about the same time as Jenny was checking in to the hotel. His keys clattered noisily into the bowl on the table as he tossed them tiredly from his grasp. The house was silent. Not even the clickety-click of the dog's claws on the wooden floor sounded a greeting. Simon hadn't been keen on a dog, but he had grown to like Munch – *what a name*! He slung his laptop bag into the chair and quickly dispensed with his tie, flinging that across the back of the same chair; then the linen jacket, also placed on the arm of the chair. He pulled his hand wearily through his hair and expelled a burst of air through his lips, but the act just seemed to exacerbate his tiredness and general feeling of malaise.

The evening was close, and a gathering bank of dark clouds presaged an approaching storm. Simon, noting the dullness of the kitchen, flicked the switch that illuminated a bank of soft lighting under the units and a comforting glow was cast across the work surfaces, spilling a sheen onto the floor. He went to the fridge and glanced at the contents, selecting a bottle of cold beer from the door. Then searching for and locating the bottle opener in a nearby kitchen drawer, he flicked the top off the bottle. He watched listlessly as it spun noisily on the kitchen side, finally whirling slowly and coming to a rest with a metallic click.

He walked to the patio doors, beer in hand, flicked the catch, pushed the door open, and stepped out into the closeness of the evening. Thunder rumbled in the distance and a breeze shook the trees at the bottom of the garden, the leaves sounding like rushing water. Simon sat down and took a swig of beer, glugging it noisily from the bottle. He wondered what Jenny was doing and where she was. She had texted him to say she had arrived at her destination but had failed to elucidate further as to her whereabouts.

He cast his mind back to when they had first met. He had seen her potential almost immediately, and yes, admittedly, he had inveigled himself into a relationship with her to exploit that potential. And yes, his proposal had been quite deliberately calculated to ensure he would continue to benefit from her growing profile as an important British artist. But now? He shook his head slightly as he took another swig of the beer. He couldn't say for sure when it had occurred, but his feelings for her now were real – he loved her, and it shook him to the core to realise that he could lose her. He realised now that he needed to stop treating her like a client and start treating her like his fiancée. Maybe he should find her a new agent – after all, he had plenty of other clients to look after without Jenny.

His musings were interrupted by the trilling of his mobile phone, and he snatched it up quickly to look at the display. But he was disappointed to see not Jenny's name flashing but Peter Calcott's name instead. He rejected the call, letting it go to voicemail, not wanting to talk to anyone, except for the one person who hadn't called – Jenny.

A moment of idle curiosity motivated him to dial into his voicemail to see what Peter had to say for himself. A few clicks of his phone took him to the new voicemail message. There was a lot of background noise, but he could make out Peter's voice shouting over the din, "Hey, mate! Bloody fantastic show. Just finished recording *Saturday Night Live*. Very edgy; the audience went wild. Thanks for the gig, man! I thought you'd be here, but I'll catch you next week."

Simon snorted. God, what kind of shallow world had he become enthralled by? He knew for sure that, under normal circumstances, he would have been at that party with his client enjoying the status of being a minor celebrity. It was a kind of epiphany as he sat in the garden surrounded by the darkening sky. Of course, Jenny would hate that kind of plastic publicity, the C-list circuit. What on earth had he been thinking? He would change. From the moment she returned, she would see a different kind of man.

Simon tilted his head back and let it rest for a moment against the back of the chair as weariness dragged at him. He sighed deeply – he'd let her down.

The thunder grumbled again, more loudly this time. He must have slept because the next thing he was aware of was the large spot of rain as it landed with a loud splat upon his hand.

In his confusion between sleep and wakefulness, he thought it was a tear, and he lifted a hand to wipe his cheek. His confusion was dispelled a moment later when thunder crashed again, and a torrential burst of rain sent Simon dashing into the house for shelter.

FIVE

Jenny was awakened early when the pale, buttery light of dawn seeped into the room. She turned over to check the time from her wristwatch which lay on the bedside table, and the softly illuminated dial read ten minutes to six. She lay for a moment contemplating the appeal of snuggling back down under the bedclothes but then the desire to explore overcame her drowsiness and she threw back the covers and padded across to the patio doors to pull back the curtains. It was a beautiful morning, the sky dappled with pale grey mackerel clouds and beyond them a backdrop of an endless sky the palest duck-egg blue.

Jenny washed quickly then pulled on black walking trousers and a grey cashmere jumper with a cowled neck. She pulled her hair back and fastened it into a ponytail, and as an afterthought, she grabbed a small bottle of fresh orange juice from the fridge which she gulped down quickly before finding Munch's lead and her walking boots. Within minutes she emerged from her hotel room with Munch pulling excitedly at his leash into the early morning.

Outside, the air was pure and fresh, and as Jenny walked through the courtyard and down toward the quay, she noticed the row of little dinghies and yachts moored in the tiny harbour. The soft onshore breeze plucked at the cleats that lay against the masts of the boats, resulting in a rhythmic metallic plinking noise. It was strangely appealing and reminded Jenny suddenly of family holidays spent at the seaside.

Jenny paused and looked overhead as a flock of oystercatchers flew over, piping excitedly before they dipped downwards and landed by the shoreline where they scurried here and there whilst probing the sand with their brilliant red-orange bills. There were other smaller wading birds on the estuary too, but they were too far off for Jenny to identify them, and she cursed softly when she realised she had left the binoculars in the boot of the car. *Never mind*, she thought, turning her attention to the pathway that lay ahead, *plenty of time for birdwatching*.

The path curved away from the village and seemed to take a route towards the sea, but it wound, rose, and fell as it dipped across the salt marsh, turning this way and that to avoid the boggy pools of briny water. Jenny let Munch off his lead as soon as they were away from the road, not that she needed to be concerned as they seemed to have the whole expanse of watery marshland to themselves.

Jenny walked on for a mile or so before the path came upon a river and turned to the right. The tide was out, leaving a vast expanse of sand and mudflats populated by huge numbers of birds. Gulls, waders, eider-ducks, and geese were all feeding at the shoreline or within the shallow pools of water that had been caught in the dips and troughs of the muddy, weed-strewn shore. The banks of the river were covered by rushes which whispered and rustled together as the onshore breeze gently pushed them, their heads dipping in submission to the wind. It was a magical place, desolate yet beautiful, and as another flock of oystercatchers shrieked overhead, it felt to Jenny that this morning had been made especially for her and she let her soul fill with the feeling of pure joy of being here in this place at this moment.

Out to sea, a fog bank hung on the horizon. A billowing, shifting wall of moisture that silently and insidiously began to roll towards the shore. Hastened by the strengthening breeze, it was soon racing across the beaches and heading quickly into the estuary, the river almost seeming to act like a conduit to aid its progress inland. Jenny noticed the bank of whiteness with some discomfort. She was hardly dressed for adverse weather, and although the pathway had been easy enough to follow, she hoped the fog would hold off long enough for them to retrace their steps to the turn by the river, after which, she was confident of the way back to the harbour. She whistled for Munch who had run on ahead and when he didn't immediately appear she called him again. In the distance, and it seemed a long way off, she could hear him barking excitedly.

Suddenly the fog was there, wrapping itself around her, seeming to penetrate her as its chilliness struck. Her jumper was soon covered in droplets of moisture. The change of scene was disconcerting, and in a matter of seconds, Jenny was disoriented and beginning to feel frightened of moving in case she stepped off the path and into the marshy ground beyond. With rising panic in her voice, she called the dog again. "Munch! Munch! Come on, boy, come here... MUNCH!"

Still the dog did not appear, and worse still, his barking seemed even further away. She turned left and right, for now she could not work out which way they had come. She knew the path would ultimately loop back and around to the main road but that was surely some distance to walk, especially in these conditions. She stepped forwards and gasped as her foot sank into a patch of boggy ground, and before she knew it, her right leg had disappeared up to her knee in mud and water. Fighting a rising feeling of panic, she called the dog again. "Munch, Munch, come on, come here, MUNCH!" Her voice rose shrilly as the panic swelled within her. Suddenly a vast shape loomed out of the fog and Jenny held her hands in front of her face in defence against whatever it was that was reaching down towards her. She squealed and would have toppled backwards and into the bog if not for a pair of enormous hands grabbing her and pulling her upwards and out of the mud.

"What the hell...?" A face loomed down towards her. The voice belonging to the face sounded angry and aggressive, but then there was a sudden and complete shift and a cry of surprised incredulity. "Jenny? *Jenny?*" The voice rose in disbelief as Jenny fell against the body to which it belonged.

"Arturo!"

He hugged her towards him for a long moment giving them both the opportunity to wonder at the surreal situation.

"What are you doing here?" He demanded.

"Walking and then the fog came down and I got a little

disoriented." She took a deep breath and only then noticed that Munch was by her side wagging his tail as though there really wasn't a problem at all.

"You naughty dog, where'd you go?"

"He was introducing himself to me. Why did you call that name, Jenny?" Arturo was frowning at her, a confused and hurt expression on his face. "I don't understand why you come here, near to where I live, and you shout that name. I thought, well, I didn't know what to think."

"Oh. Oh!" She flung her hand to her mouth suddenly understanding his discomfort. "Well, it's the dog's name." She explained weakly.

"The dog's name." The frown on Arturo's face deepened.

She stepped back and crouched down, putting her arms around the dog. "Look he has black, curly hair, and look at his brown eyes. Arturo, what can I say, he reminded me of you when I got him."

"But Munch, Jenny, really? Munch!"

"Well, I couldn't very well call him Giovanni, could I? And I didn't know you had changed you name, and even then, Arturo for a dog? I'm sorry. I never thought our paths would ever cross."

"Munch." Arturo shook his head and crouched down so that he was eye level with the dog. "Hmm... hello, Munch." He scrabbled his hand through the damp curls on top of the dog's head.

Jenny shifted uncomfortably. "There is something else actually..."

Arturo looked across the top of the dog's head and into Jenny's eyes, his expression wary as he waited for her further explanation.

"Well, yes...well, when I got him – the dog that is – well, he was only a puppy, really, but he was... well, he was rather greedy, actually, and when he ate his dinner, he..." She mimicked the action of eating by making snapping gestures with her hands. "So, it just seemed to be a perfect name for him... Sorry." She finished rather lamely.

Arturo stared from Jenny to the dog, his namesake, trying to prevent his mouth from twitching into a smile but then finally his self-control imploded, and he let out a booming laugh. He grasped her arm. "Come on, let's get out of this fog." He continued to hold Jenny's arm as they negotiated the path together.

"Why didn't you tell me you were coming?" He looked down towards her, hardly believing she was here. One minute he had been taking his solitary morning walk and the next he had been accosted by a very large black dog, only to find the dog belonged to Jenny. It was like a weird dream.

"I wasn't sure I *was* coming, to be honest. I just needed some time away on my own. It's been so hectic, and Simon doesn't always understand I need time away from everything. My painting has just dried-up lately, and he pushes, pushes for me to do the circuit."

She sounded miserable, he thought, and he stopped and turned to her, staring with great intensity at her face. "You do look tired." He brushed his thumb along the purple crescent beneath her eye. She shivered.

"Cold?"

"A little." She muttered, catching her breath at his touch.

"Come on." He grasped her arm again, sending little shocks coursing through her. "I'll show you the seals."

"What? In this?" She eyed the fog doubtfully as it continued to swirl around them.

"Ahh, it may blow away. Come on, we'll take a chance."

They walked for a mile or so along the footpath towards Blakeney point, until Arturo paused and pointed towards the headland. "If we're lucky and the fog clears a little, we may see them."

They watched in silence, listening to the call of the birds which resonated eerily in the closeted atmosphere. The sun was like a lemon drop, a pale disc of light shrouded by the mist, a poor imitation of itself, but suddenly, the breeze turned offshore. The effect was quite magical. The fog, shredded and torn, began to reveal the distant headland, and the calling birds were unveiled as they continued to forage for food whilst the tide was out.

Arturo shielded his eyes from the strengthening sunlight and then pointed out towards a sandbank immediately ahead of them.

"There!"

"I can't see," Jenny protested.

"Here, climb up, lean on me." Arturo indicated a large wooden post for Jenny to stand upon to give the height advantage she needed to see the top of the sandbank as it curved away. He grabbed her hand and pulled her upwards, so she was perched on top of the wide post.

"I see them!" She exclaimed, turning to Arturo, and smiling. He was still clasping her hand and glanced down as Jenny stared out across the headland.

"Where is your ring, Jenny?" He asked quietly.

She said nothing but her mouth twisted a little and she drew the corner of her lip inwards, biting down on it.

"How does Simon feel about you coming here?"

Again, no answer except a barely audible sigh.

"He doesn't know, does he?"

She shook her head fractionally.

"You're running away again, Jenny."

She became suddenly and furiously animated. "I am not!" She protested angrily. "I rather thought I was running to something, actually." She placed her hand on his shoulder to emphasise her point.

He stared off at the headland, his expression brooding and closed, eyes hooded.

"I wish you had told me you were coming." He muttered.

"Why?" She looked at him, hoping for a glimmer of something that might tell her that her feelings for him were reciprocated.

"I must go away tomorrow for four days. An important commission." He shrugged. "I could have rearranged it if I'd known you were coming to see me. I'm sorry I can't now – it's too late notice for the client."

"Of course." Jenny was crestfallen. "When will you be back?"

"Thursday – sometime." Still, he stared off into the distance, until she felt he was deliberately avoiding her gaze.

Then he turned to her, the dark expression momentarily gone.

"Have you ever seen a murmuration of starlings?"

"No. Isn't that when they flock together?"

"Yes, and in huge numbers. On Thursday, I will take you to see them if you like."

She had left her hand lying upon his shoulder and squeezed him again as she responded. "That would be lovely, thank you. And can I come and see your studio and work; I'd love to see where you work?"

"Maybe, yes, that may be possible."

A silence opened between them until Arturo said softly, "You need to tell Simon, don't you? Where you are, I mean."

"I suppose I should. It's just he will get the wrong idea and go off on one.".

"What is the wrong idea?" It was a dangerous question and Arturo immediately wished he hadn't uttered it.

"Well, that I came here because… well, I came to see you and he will think that I…" She trailed off.

An oystercatcher flew past them, its piping call a rude interruption, but it somehow seemed to galvanise Jenny and she took a deep breath. "I love you, Arturo. I think I always have."

Her statement seemed to hang in the air, surprising them both.

"Oh Jenny!"

Before he could prevent her, she fell against him so that he had to place his arms around her waist to stop her from falling from her precarious position on top of the wooden post.

From her elevated position, her head was level with his and it seemed the most natural thing to kiss him. For a split-second he seemed to flinch away but then, as her mouth found his, he groaned, and they melded together, passion quickly rising between them with a ferocious energy. He grasped the back of her head, cradling it in his massive hand, and pulled her even closer. Never had Jenny experienced a kiss that held such sheer power, and for a moment she thought she might faint, but then Arturo pulled away from the embrace.

"Jesus!" He touched his mouth, his hand shaking badly.

"You feel the same." She whispered, her fingers tracing the outline of his face.

He closed his eyes and sighed deeply "This can't happen, Jenny!" He shook his head and lifted her down from the post.

"Why?" She cried, suddenly mortified. "I know you're older, but I don't care! And I know I hurt you a long time ago, but I'm going to spend the rest of my life making up for that."

Arturo shushed her and shook his head, placing his fingers on her lips. "It's not that, Jenny. What happened between us then was a lifetime ago. There is nothing to make up for, trust me."

"Then why?" She demanded.

At that moment a man rounded the corner on the path and came towards them. Arturo raised his hand in greeting. "Morning, Geoff!"

The man eyed them speculatively. "Morning, Arturo, pleased to see the fog has gone."

"It's going to be another lovely day."

The man walked on, his little terrier dog trotting after him.

Arturo was glad of the break in their conversation, and he indicated that they should start walking back. As they approached the quay, there were a few more walkers and several people preparing their dinghies for trips out to sea, and they walked in uneasy silence until they paused outside Jenny's hotel.

"This is where I'm staying." She indicated with a flick of her hand.

"It's nice."

"Yes."

She laid a hand on his arm. "Will you come to my room, Arturo?"

The invitation was met with silence, and again he stared off, distancing himself from her. Then he shook his head – it seemed with great reluctance – and shrugged. "Jenny, I have to go – my things need to be ready for tomorrow and I have work to do." He touched her cheek with such exquisite gentleness that Jenny felt her eyes fill with tears. "I will see you on Thursday. Be ready for six, and I'll come and collect you, yes?"

She nodded, not trusting herself to speak, and then watched as he walked away, back down the pathway they had just walked along together. She waited until his figure had disappeared, and she touched her mouth which was still tingling and swollen from their kiss. Then she turned to go back to her room to compose herself before breakfast.

*

By eight thirty, Simon had picked up and put down his mobile phone a dozen times. He knew Jenny had gone away for some peace and quiet, but his desire to speak with her overwhelmed him. Finally, he picked his phone up again and scrolled to her name in the address book. His stomach felt tight with nervous tension as the phone connected and began to ring. To his relief she answered his call.

"Hiya! How are you?" She answered brightly.

Perhaps a little too brightly, he reflected. "Good, and you?"

"Just having breakfast actually."

"Oh sorry."

"It's alright. I'm heading off to do some drawing after this."

"It's nice then, where you are?"

"It's lovely, Simon."

"So, whereabouts are you?" He held his breath.

"Oh, I'm in Shropshire, actually." The lie came easily which surprised her.

"Shropshire? What on earth made you go there?"

"I've never been, so it seemed like as good a place as any. Anyway, how was your show?" She changed the subject quickly.

"Oh, it went well, by all accounts. I didn't go, actually, but Pete was over the moon."

"Why didn't you go? It's just your sort of… what did you call it… 'gig', isn't it?"

Simon winced. "Tired."

"You okay, you sound down?"

"Missing you, Jen."

217

He sounded gruff and fed up, and Jenny felt a pique of sympathy for him. "Missing you too." Even to Jenny her response sounded empty and trite. "Well, I'd better go, love. I'll call later in the week, okay?"

"Jenny, are we okay – you and me, I mean? You would say, wouldn't you, if there was something wrong?"

"Of course!" She laughed off her discomposure.

When they finished the call, Jenny stared at the blank screen on the mobile phone. Now what on earth had that been about? Then she glanced at the pale line around her finger left by her engagement ring and suddenly felt guilty. In the space of twenty-four hours, she had lied to Simon twice and kissed another man. And she knew with complete certainty that, if Arturo asked her to stay, she would without a moment of hesitation.

SIX

The following four days were a kind of exquisite torture for Jenny as she anticipated the moment when she would see Arturo again. She did however manage to fill her days with drawing, taking photographs, and sketching, and was pleased with the plan that was beginning to form for Moonset. Most days she walked in the morning with Munch and then set up her easel in the afternoon, either working from the terrace or from the quayside where she could watch the various comings and goings to and from the busy harbour.

On Thursday morning she took one of the many boat trips which took tourists out to the point where the seals could be seen basking on the mudflats. It was lunchtime when the boat deposited them back at the quay, and feeling hungry, Jenny walked along to one of the pubs scattered throughout the village, bought a cider, and ordered some sandwiches before finding a seat outside in the warm sunshine. As she relaxed and enjoyed her lunch, she absentmindedly scrabbled the top of Munch's head, making him squint his eyes shut in ecstasy.

She had not spoken to Simon since their conversation on Monday and was reluctant to do so before her planned return home to Devon on Saturday. Only then would she be in a better position, she hoped, to know what her plans were. Speaking to him in the interim would only lead to more lies. Instead, she had texted him to say she was heading out into the Welsh borders, and she didn't think she would get a signal, so he was not to worry if she didn't get in touch. She was slightly shocked at the ease with which she could be quite so disingenuous.

As lunchtime rolled into the afternoon, she took Munch

out for a walk and then returned to her room where she bathed and took a ridiculous amount of time to get ready, changing her clothes four times before she was satisfied with her appearance. Make-up (not too much) was carefully applied, and she dried her hair, so it curled softly into a long shoulder-length bob. Perfume and jewellery completed her preparations. She was ready by five in the hope that he might be early, but as five thirty and then six came and went, she began to think he had forgotten or changed his mind.

She was just beginning to feel rather cross when the telephone in her room rang. She sped across the room and picked up the receiver. "Yes?"

"Ms Pritchard, there is a gentleman in reception for you."

"Oh, right, thank you!"

A burst of adrenalin shot through her as she made one final check on her appearance before she grabbed her bag, patted Munch, and left her room, shutting the door gently behind her. She walked across the courtyard and entered the reception area where Arturo was waiting for her.

When he saw her walk through the door his stomach flipped with desire, and not for the first time, he berated himself for arranging to see her again. He would do his very best to keep her at arm's length, but he could already feel his resolve weakening as she approached him smiling.

"Hi there! Good business trip?" She stood on tiptoe and kissed his cheek which smelt of sandalwood.

"Good, yes, good, thank you." He inclined his head and offered her one of his rare smiles which made her heart go crazy. "What about you? What have you been doing?"

She told him about the boat trip and the days spent planning her next project.

"Ahhh, yes, Moonset."

They left the hotel lobby and Arturo guided her to a Land Rover Defender which was parked next to her own Discovery.

"Jump in. Let's go find us some starlings."

He manoeuvred the vehicle out of the car park and directed

it onto the road leading out of the village. When they arrived at the main road, rather than turning onto it, they drove straight across, taking a tiny country lane which led up a slight incline, very quickly taking them into open countryside.

Jenny couldn't help but stare at Arturo's bare forearm as he shifted the gears. The skin was tanned and muscular and covered with fine black hair, and she could see the muscles moving and tensing as he pushed and pulled the gear stick into place. His hands were beautiful – large yet elegant with long fingers and beautifully manicured nails. She wanted to feel those hands on her, on her bare skin. She looked across briefly at the profile of his face. Strong features, an aquiline nose, and those hooded dark eyes framed by black and arching eyebrows, his mouth downturned slightly, his cheeks and chin showing signs of stubble, a mixture of dark and grey. He exuded masculinity and she took a deep breath and turned to look out of the window, suddenly afraid of the intensity of her feelings for him.

He drove on for a further three or four miles, then flicked on the indicator and swung the Land Rover off the narrow lane and onto a farm track. Then he turned the steering wheel, so the vehicle bumped off the track altogether and into the stubble left in the field following the recent harvest. He brought the car to a halt and cranked on the handbrake before turning off the ignition. Then he quickly opened his door and jumped out, moving around the car to help Jenny from her side.

"Here." He held out his hand and she took it willingly.

"We'll sit on the roof; let me help you to climb up."

As the daylight began to leech from the sky, Jenny couldn't help but relish her proximity to Arturo, their bodies almost touching as they perched on the top of the car. She could feel her whole body buzzing with expectation, so was deflated when she heard and then saw several more vehicles bumping along the same farm track that Arturo had negotiated only minutes earlier. They too turned off the lane and bumped across the stubble, until they parked up almost next to Arturo's car. There would be no opportunity for intimacy between them now and Jenny could feel the disappointment course through her.

There was a growing sense of anticipation as the sky became gloomy, and the party fell silent watching in quiet anticipation, looking for the first signs of the starlings coming to roost. Then someone cried out and pointed, and there they were. A huge cloud of starlings was swirling across the sky, twisting, and funnelling in the most incredible patterns. They flew in complete synchronicity like they were drawn by an invisible magnetic force pulling them, turning them in a harmony of movement and direction, coiling and recoiling as they swooped across the sky.

"There must be tens of thousands of them," Jenny murmured in awe.

Arturo nodded. He had been watching her in profile as she tipped her head back to the sky. She was quite the most beautiful woman he had ever seen, and he could feel an outrageous desire for her throbbing painfully through him until he thought he might go mad. He leapt down from their vantage point and walked around to stand by the front of the car where he leant against the radiator grill, folded his arms, and closed his eyes, trying to fight the turmoil, the indecision. All he knew, one way or another, was that he could not bear to be near her and not have her, but that thought left him in an invidious position.

The drive back to the hotel was completed in an uncomfortable and tense silence. Jenny kept glancing at Arturo as he gave his full concentration to the dark country road. He had been far too quiet since gruffly suggesting it was time to go, and she wondered if she had somehow upset or angered him. She couldn't bear that thought and so reached out to touch his leg as she turned to him in supplication.

"I've upset you." She said, half statement, half question.

"No." He responded shortly, which just made her feel worse. "Just a headache, that's all." He touched his temple to emphasise the point.

"Oh, I'm sorry. I have some aspirin, I think, in my bag."

He flicked his hand. "Don't worry, just tired – need to get an early night."

"Oh, okay, I see." Jenny could feel tears and a constriction in her throat. She wanted him so badly and she had thought that perhaps tonight… "Can I come and see your studio and the gallery tomorrow, please? I would really love to."

He sighed and glanced at her briefly. "Come after two."

Then as they approached the hotel, he pulled the car to a halt and leant across her to open her door. The smell of him was intensely provocative and Jenny had to stop herself from burying her fingers in his hair.

"Thank you for this evening. It was amazing. I hope your headache is better soon." She leant across and kissed his cheek, and for a moment, he turned so their lips caught together. He gave a strangled cry and pulled his head back.

"Jenny, please go, please go now!" He just managed to gasp as he pushed her towards the open door.

She had barely stepped from the vehicle when he slammed the door shut and threw the car noisily into gear, speeding off up the road, the tyres squealing as he took the corner recklessly fast.

Jenny stared after him and watched as the taillights flickered and then disappeared into the night.

She just made it back to her room before she broke, sobs of pure guttural misery spilling from her whilst Munch looked on uncertainly, his tail twitching in sympathy.

It may have helped Jenny a little if she could have known that Arturo had driven barely half a mile up the road before pulling the Land Rover into a deserted car park which overlooked the marshes. He brought the vehicle to a skidding and imperfect halt and then leapt from the car, leaving the engine running and headlights on full beam. He kicked the tyres, he thumped the bonnet, he picked up hunks of stone and threw them with all his strength out into the night. But it didn't assuage his rage, and neither did the tears which coursed down his cheeks.

SEVEN

The following morning when Jenny awoke, she went about her morning routine just as she had all that week. Coffee, shower, teeth, hair, dog walk and then across to the restaurant for breakfast. But that morning, whilst she completed these small tasks without any outward change or variance to her routine, there was an insidious feeling snaking through her which she couldn't shake off and which she couldn't quite define. This day, she felt, was going to be seminal – good or bad, she had to push Arturo today to tell her what his feelings for her were. She knew that there was something there, of that she had no doubt, but this confusion was pure agony, and she'd decided during the night that she'd rather know one way or the other: today was the day she would find out. She felt sick with apprehension.

The morning passed very slowly, and she couldn't settle at anything at all, so at one o'clock she changed into her walking gear and readied Munch. She reckoned it would take her almost an hour to walk to his studio which should put her there just in time for their two o'clock meeting.

In the event, it took her only half an hour, and rather than waiting outside until their allotted meeting time, she pushed open the door of the studio and stepped into a large and airy room which served as a gallery to display his work, a sign indicating the studio was located off this room in a separate area.

The gallery was beautifully constructed. Oak beams supported a high vaulted ceiling and large roof lights allowed a stream of daylight to spill into the room. Jenny noticed how the warm sunlight burnished the colour of the natural wooden floor. The walls were crisply white and illuminated by strategically placed uplighting which softened the brightness of the white with a creamy wash. There was a fireplace at the far end of the room and a large wood-burning stove took the place of a more conventional fireplace.

Art was displayed throughout the gallery, on the walls, and in large stands which contained dozens of prints. There was pottery too, beautifully displayed on tables and plinths throughout the room. Jenny's attention was drawn to a large painting that was displayed above the inglenook containing the stove. As she approached it, she could feel blood rising in her cheeks and her heart began to hammer in her chest. It was her, of course, all those years ago in the walled garden at Melchett Hall. He had captured the spirit of her innocence and melded it with something darker and more erotic, and it shook her soul.

She leant forwards to read the small plaque which simply displayed the words, *The Girl in the Garden, Arturo D'Arbo. Not for sale.*

A voice spoke softly behind her. "It is beautiful, no?"

Jenny turned to see a petite, dark-haired woman emerging from the door which separated the gallery area from the studio.

"Oh!" Jenny's hand fluttered to her throat, and she laughed nervously. "You startled me!"

The woman inclined her head. "Please excuse me, mademoiselle." Her French accent was charming "May I help you with something you are looking for? Or perhaps you are just here to browse."

"I would love to look around if I may?"

"Of course." Again, the inclination of the head and a small smile.

"I am actually also here to meet Mr D'Arbo – I'm a little early, I'm afraid." Jenny smiled at the woman warmly.

"Oh, Arturo is not here. He has been a little delayed, I think." She paused and gave Jenny an appraising look before saying brightly. "But you will have a coffee, no?"

"That is very kind of you, thank you."

"And is that your lovely dog outside? I will get him some water also."

"You are very kind, thank you." Jenny felt unaccountably nervous in this woman's company.

"Excuse me, but I did not introduce myself to you." The woman walked forward, her tiny hand extended. "Margo."

Jenny took her hand briefly. "Jenny – Jenny Pritchard."

"Ah! The artist, no?"

"That is right!"

"You're very good. Arturo has some of your work."

"Yes, I know…" Jenny felt a small but definable shift in the woman's demeanour.

"Right, coffee! Please feel free to look around. I won't keep you a moment." And with that she darted, bird-like, back through the door. Jenny could hear the clatter of crockery and the sound of a coffee machine, so she turned with interest to view the remaining pieces of art.

Margo D'Arbo was shaking. She felt outraged. That woman, that bloody woman was here. Here! An imposter in the gallery. She knew who she was, of course. She knew she was the girl in the garden; the girl Arturo had been drawing and painting almost to the point of obsession ever since Margo had met him some ten years previously, and prior to that too, no doubt.

He was a good man. Respectful, a generous and considerate lover in her bed. She knew he admired her skills as a potter, loved her French cooking, liked her as a companion – but she also knew he didn't love her. Never had and never would. She loved him with every cell of her body, but it didn't matter how much she willed and wished him to do the same – she knew he wouldn't. There was no spark, no flame, zero passion in him – except when he spoke of the girl in the garden. Then he became transformed, and there was a light in his eyes that was never there when he looked at her. And she had been filled with dread when he had returned from a trip recently, and that fire – my God – that light had been in his eyes, and he was reluctant to tell her just where he had been. And now, that woman, his muse, was here! The biggest threat to her marriage. She wasn't a vindictive woman, but she just wanted rid of her. So pretty, so perfect, such a talent. She felt a sob of terror bubble in her chest as she imagined losing Arturo to her; she would have no chance against her – his muse for all these years.

She glanced at the clock. It was one forty and Arturo would be home soon as she had her yoga class on a Friday at two. She didn't have much time.

As Margo emerged with two cups of coffee she smiled at Jenny. "Here we are."

"Thank you." Jenny took a cup from her and then, out of politeness: "So you work here, do you?"

Margo laughed – rather harshly, Jenny thought. "In a manner of speaking, I suppose." She waved her hand towards the pottery. "That is my work."

"Oh, I've been admiring them; your work is really beautiful."

Margo inclined her head, accepting the compliment. Then she took a deep breath. "So how did you meet Arturo?"

Jenny took a sip of coffee. "Gosh, years and years ago. He helped me out when I was first learning to paint and then we lost touch. We met again recently – he came to one of my exhibitions."

"He never told me." Margo said flatly and then glanced nervously at the clock – one forty-five! "Where has my husband got to!" She shook her head with exasperation.

"Your husband?" Jenny enquired politely, but she could feel a coldness descending upon her – a horrible dawning realisation.

"Yes," Margo said slowly. "My husband." And then looked directly at Jenny in a challenging way, her head held high, her nose in the air. "Arturo, my husband."

Jenny felt the room closing in on her. It was like she was underwater, sound and sensation muffled in a horrible slow-motion echo. The cup and saucer she held tilted, slipped, and crashed to the floor shattering in shards of white ceramic pieces, coffee splattering upwards and onto one of the display plinths. She coughed, retched, and barely managed to prevent a sob from escaping from her mouth. She bent to attend to the mess, picking up what was left of the saucer and placing the shards of broken crockery in a little pile on top.

"Sorry, sorry." She muttered, fighting to keep the tears at bay. She glanced at the woman's hand, and sure enough, there was a single gold band on her wedding-ring finger.

"Oh, my dear!" Margo exclaimed in surprise. "Are you alright? Let me help you; don't worry about the cup. Oh dear, now you have cut yourself. Let me get you a napkin."

Jenny stood up as soon as Margo left the room and, without another thought, walked, almost ran, over to the door. Suddenly, she was outside gulping in huge gasps of air. She quickly untied Munch's lead and ran from the gallery and back towards the pathway.

Margo, in the meantime had re-entered the gallery with a wad of kitchen towel, and she allowed herself a small smile of satisfaction when she noted that Jenny had gone, the door left ajar emphasising the undue haste with which she had left. She stepped lightly over to it and closed it firmly shut.

Arturo parked the Land Rover in the car park at the front of the gallery at one fifty and, being very aware of the time and the fact it was fast approaching two o'clock, walked quickly around and in through the front door. Margo was sweeping up some small shards of china.

"Breakage?" He enquired, looking about the gallery for signs of Jenny's arrival.

"Silly me, I dropped a cup, but no harm done."

"You'd best get off to your yoga class, you'll be late."

"Yes, of course, I'm ready." She leant the brush against the wall and picked up a bag containing a change of clothing, then stood on tiptoe to kiss Arturo on the cheek. "Be home about five – we are going to have a glass of wine after class."

"Okay, see you later then." He waved her off, relieved that she had gone before Jenny arrived, and guiltily pleased that she would be home later than usual, giving him longer to be with Jenny.

Jenny ran most the way back to the hotel, pausing twice to be violently ill. As she ran, she berated herself. What a fool she had been! It hadn't crossed her mind for a moment that Arturo might be in a relationship, or even worse – married. Another sob escaped her as the realisation came to her again. What a stupid, stupid girl she had been to think, to dream, to even imagine that it was going to end differently for them, that somehow, they would be together at last. For God's sake! She stopped for a moment to catch her breath and wipe her face. She felt bereft. There was nothing left to do but go home.

Two thirty became three o'clock and Arturo stared anxiously from the window of the gallery. He recalled telling Jenny to come after two so maybe she was taking her time. He shrugged and walked away from the window, trying to find something to do to pass his time. He had just moved into the back office and switched on the kettle when he heard the jingle of the bell that announced a visitor had entered the gallery, and he leapt across the room to the door, his heart suddenly pounding with excitement.

But it wasn't Jenny.

An elderly couple had entered the gallery, and the man was clearly delighted to see he was going to get the opportunity to speak with the artist himself. Arturo resigned himself to showing them around his work, but his attention was constantly drawn to the clock. The minutes ticked by ominously.

*

When Jenny got back to the hotel, she went immediately to her room, contemplated a shower, but opted for a quick wash in cold water to freshen her face. Then she quickly packed her bags and loaded the car. Then checking her room one last time for any items left behind, she loaded up Munch and went to reception to check out. There was no one immediately available and rather than ringing the little bell to call for assistance she scribbled a note giving instructions to take her final payment on her credit card, thank the staff for looking after her so well, and apologise for leaving at such short notice due to a family emergency.

That task completed, she quickly moved from the reception to her car, not wanting to be spotted by anyone. Even though she had managed to compose herself, she felt as though someone had stripped her, layer by layer, laying bare her most sensitive and vulnerable emotions, leaving her horribly exposed to anyone who might see her. She started the car, engaged first gear, and released the handbrake – leaving the car park of the Cley Cross Hotel at four o'clock.

Arturo finally managed to complete the tour of the gallery and his subsequent conversation with his customers. They had bought two nice pieces and under normal circumstances he would have been delighted. But the moment they left the shop he sighed with relief, closed the door, and locked it, inverting the open sign to display the negative message on the other side. He contemplated telephoning Margo to ask her if Jenny had called into the gallery prior to his arrival home, or if she had perhaps telephoned with a message of apology. But then he changed his mind and slung his mobile phone down in temper, sending it skittering across the sales counter before coming to rest against the till.

Something was wrong. Jenny would have come if she could.

Impulsively, he snatched up the car keys and left the gallery, locking the door behind him. It took him only five minutes to drive to the Cley Cross Hotel and less than a minute to cross the courtyard once he parked the Land Rover.

He waited, drumming his fingers on the reception desk whilst the young receptionist dealt with another guest. Finally, she finished and turned to Arturo.

"Good afternoon, sir, how can I help?" She enquired.

"I wonder if you could see if Ms Pritchard is in her room, please."

"Oh no. I know she isn't. She checked out earlier this afternoon. A family emergency apparently."

He brought his fist down onto the reception desk. "Damn!"

The receptionist jumped back in surprise, a little frightened by his show of anger. Arturo glanced at her. "Sorry, sorry – I needed to see her before she went, sorry." He turned and left the hotel, not wanting to acknowledge the feeling of desolation which gripped him. She had gone.

*

When Margo returned home, she did so with some trepidation, gingerly pushing open the door to the cottage before walking down the dark corridor to the kitchen-cum-sitting-room.

Arturo was sitting in one of the shabby, comfortable armchairs by the fireplace. He had a large glass of red wine in his hand and was swishing the contents around and around in the glass. Margo glanced at him, noting his morose expression.

"Arturo?" She enquired nervously.

He barely looked up at her before asking, "Did anyone come to the gallery to meet with me today, Margo?"

She paused to consider his question, her heart thumping rapidly with fear. "Anyone?"

He tipped the glass to his mouth, swallowing the contents in two huge gulps before standing up suddenly and banging the glass down on the pine table. "Answer my question!" His eyes were boring into hers.

She shrugged in her Gallic way. "No – no one came to the gallery today, no one at all. I need to shower."

Arturo stepped across her path, his height looming above her petite frame. Struggling to control his emotions, he shook his head and muttered, "If you have lied to me…" He caught her arm.

She pulled away from him and turned to leave the room, hoping he hadn't noticed how her whole body was shaking, her face stricken with guilt and shame.

Arturo placed his head in his hands. He felt torn. Margo had been good to him in their marriage, but nothing could come close to the surge of emotion he felt for Jenny. He knew he loved her to his core. They both had commitments – had he the courage to follow her?

*

Jenny had plenty of time to consider her options as she drove the long and tiring journey home. She stopped just once to feed Munch and walk him, taking no refreshment herself except for a bottle of water. It was only when she turned the car off the M5 some six hours later that she began to feel nervous about the looming encounter with Simon. Simon! What to do? She glanced at her hands as they rested upon the steering wheel, her left hand still devoid of the engagement ring that still lay in the glove box, exactly where she had put it.

At eleven o'clock she finally turned off the country lane and onto the gravel drive that led up towards the house. The gravel crunched under the tyres as she drew the car to a halt. She pulled on the handbrake before she wearily leant forwards to turn off the ignition.

A huge harvest moon glowed softly in the sky, a pale and creamy ochre, its riven surface clearly visible in the darkness. For several minutes she sat there, too tired to move, her eyes filled with the grittiness that night-driving always gave her. Finally, a distant woof from the back of the car stirred her. She reached forwards and opened the glove compartment, scrabbled around in its interior with a growing sense of panic before locating her engagement ring. Relieved, she pushed it back onto her finger, the action seeming to bring her full circle. She took a deep breath and headed for the house.

The house was quiet as she opened the front door. A glow of light from the kitchen seemed to indicate that Simon was still up so she walked softly down the hallway until the she reached the door to the kitchen which she pushed open tentatively with her finger. There was no sign of Simon in the kitchen, but further around the corner of the large room there was a garden room, which contained comfy seating, a stove, and a television. The television was showing a late-night film, the picture flickering rapid patterns of light and shade across the wooden floor, the sound almost inaudible. Simon was sprawled on the sofa, and Jenny was so shocked at his appearance that for a moment she wondered whether it was him. He looked leaner; his T-shirt was hitched up to reveal his belly, and she could see he had lost weight. His hair was shorn very short – his foppish hairstyle gone. His chin was covered in several day's growth of beard which glistened like rusty wire in the diffused light. He was like a stranger to her, and she didn't want to wake him, but Munch had no such hesitation, wasting no time in licking Simon's hand enthusiastically so that he stirred from his sleep and his eyes flickered open. For a moment he simply lay there, confused in his state of semi wakefulness, but then he sat up and looked at Jenny.

"Hi there." She said, feeling almost shy faced with the change in his appearance.

"Jenny, you're home!" He roused himself and stood up.

"Yes, I am."

"I missed you." He touched her arm, thinking she looked exhausted and changed somehow – brittle as though she might break if he embraced her.

"What have you been doing? Look at you! You look so different, Simon; I hardly recognised you."

He brushed at his hair. "Oh, just fancied a change. Cleared the shed out, painted the utility, tidied the garage, pottered about. Coffee? Tea?"

"I'd love a glass of wine actually."

"Sure." He walked through to the kitchen and called back over his shoulder, "Red or white?"

"Red, please, if you'll join me."

"Why not?" He reached down to the wine rack and took a Malbec from one of the apertures, showing her the label.

"Hmmm, nice."

Then, casually, as he reached into the cupboard for glasses, he asked, "So where did you go then?"

She took a breath. "I went to Norfolk."

He turned slowly to face her. "Did you see him?"

There was a long moment of awkwardness. "Arturo?"

"Of course."

"Yes, I saw him."

"And…"

"And what? I saw him, I saw his gallery, I met his wife, I'm home."

"Are you, Jenny?"

"Simon, I'm home and I'm ready to work."

"I have something I want to say to you."

"Don't. Not tonight, I'm tired."

"No, Jenny, please listen to me." He looked at her imploringly and took a glug of wine from his glass.

She acquiesced. "Go on then, say what you want to say." She concentrated on her wine glass, toying with the stem of the crystal.

"I don't want to be your agent anymore." He paused, looking at her for a reaction and noted her sudden glance of puzzled surprise. "Not what you were expecting me to say?"

She shook her head, waiting for him to go on.

"It's not working, Jen. I love you – I realise that now, and I want to be something more than a glorified agent. I've been stupid, trying to drive your career in the wrong direction. I want things to change between us. I recognise, if they don't, then our relationship won't survive. I think I've found a great replacement, a girl called Stella Bedford – young, up-and-coming but a serious and respected promoter." He paused and looked at her, watching for a response, a sign at least. "Say something, Jenny."

She took a sip of her wine, savouring the intense flavour on her palate. "But what about you?"

He shrugged. "I've got other clients, haven't I? And I can get more if needs be."

She nodded slowly. "I was going to ask you to clear my diary." She looked up at him, a sudden ferocious intensity burning in her eyes. "I have got so much work in here it hurts!" She struck her chest.

Simon held his breath for a moment and then said quietly, "I can do that for you."

"I want the Portland Gallery booked for a November launch."

"Okay. We'll do this last launch together, and then that's it – no more pushy agent Simon."

"I'm going to go to the studio tomorrow and you might not see much of me."

"I'll take care of you."

They looked at each other for a long moment, both uncertain

of their future together, but at least feeling the tension that had been so palpable between them fading to a dull aching memory.

"I'm tired – I need to go to bed." She took another sip of wine and stood up.

"Okay, I'll…" He hesitated.

"Come with me." She held out a hand. "Bring the wine, will you?" She gave him a weary smile.

He reached for her hand, and they went to bed together.

EIGHT

The studio was purpose-built, a wooden structure with plenty of windows and roof lights to create the natural light required for Jenny's work. It was located at the bottom of the long garden and backed onto open farmland. It was absolutely Jenny's space and not even Simon would dream of entering without express permission. Jenny had taken herself off to the studio the morning following her return home. Simon wasn't particularly surprised to see her side of the bed empty and cold when he stirred, and he knew where she would be. He was ready for the next few days when she would barely emerge from the studio, her work becoming all encompassing; even poor Munch had to make do with sitting outside the studio, waiting for Jenny to emerge occasionally, so he could push his nose lovingly into her hand for attention.

But Simon completely misjudged the length and intensity of her period of creative work, and by the end of the first week, he was becoming concerned for her. She was practically living in the studio, disappearing before dawn, and often not reappearing until the early hours of the next morning. She barely ate – meals becoming an inconvenience, just a means of providing fuel to work. Even bathing and changing of clothing was becoming a rare occurrence. When he did see her, he couldn't help but feel worried, her eyes burning feverishly, her movements erratic and driven by nervous energy. At the end of the second week, his concern increased. Her clothing was beginning to hang off her, her cheek bones (beautiful as they were) were beginning to protrude unhealthily, whilst her cheeks were hollow and taking on a sallow tinge.

Week three brought little change. If anything, she was even more distant, barely communicating with him at all.

On the fourth consecutive Sunday of this behaviour, Jenny's parents called by to see if Simon and Jenny would like to join them for lunch at a local restaurant. Simon greeted them warmly as he answered the door, showing them into the drawing room. Tom and Maggie Pritchard had aged extremely well. They were great fun and Simon enjoyed their company, so it was with some discomfort he made excuses for not joining them for lunch.

"I would love to… well, we both would obviously! But Jenny… well, she's in the studio working on her latest assignment – has been for weeks, actually."

Maggie picked up his unease. "Simon?" She enquired softly and looked at him with concern. "Is she okay? I know what's she's like when she gets her head in a project."

Tom touched her arm. "Don't fuss, Mags. Simon will be looking after her." He looked across at Simon his expression trusting and guileless.

"Well, yes, of course I am, as far as I am able. She's really immersed herself in it this time. So…"

Then Maggie exclaimed, "Oh who's that coming up the garden? Oh my God! Don't tell me, Simon, that… that apparition is our Jenny. Oh dear God!" She moved her hands to her mouth in genuine shock.

Tom turned and swore. "Christ, Simon, what in God's name?"

They both looked at him with abject horror, their stares accusatory and hostile.

Simon spread his hands. "You try! Go on! You try and get her to eat, sleep, bathe. God knows, I've tried, but she's oblivious. It's like she's on some kind of drug."

Maggie looked aghast. "You don't think…"

"God, no!" Simon rubbed his hand across his hair. "Christ, Maggie, she doesn't need drugs. It's her work, and until she's finished it, this is how she will be."

The door from the patio opened and Jenny walked into the room, pausing momentarily to acknowledge her parents. "Hi Mum, Dad, what're you doing here?" She paused briefly to cast a downward look at her clothes. They were filthy. Her hair was matted, and her skin was covered in paint. And there was a sour and deeply unpleasant miasma surrounding her.

Maggie stared at her daughter for several seconds, blinking in disbelief, then galvanised, she crossed the room and took Jenny by the arm, shocked by the boniness within the baggy sleeve of her tunic.

"Right, my girl! Come on, upstairs with you!" She pulled her daughter across the room and towards the stairs, ashamed of the state of her. It was incredible. Jenny followed demurely.

An hour later, they both reappeared at the door of the drawing room. The men had used the hiatus to their advantage and had all but finished a bottle of red wine between them. Maggie had taken on that look of dominant matriarch who was somewhat satisfied with her control of the situation, and Jenny followed her in looking a little more like herself, but still, her father was shocked by her emaciated and drawn appearance.

Simon had explained whilst the girls had been upstairs that in the previous few weeks Jenny had become impossible to manage. It was like she was burning up with fever the whole time, like she had to work and work and work until she exorcised this thing inside her. Simon confided that he had considered calling their GP on more than one occasion but had bottled out.

"It *will* be finished soon." He asserted.

Tom looked at him, doubt and worry etched on his face. "Yes, one way or the other, Simon. This could kill her, y'know." His voice had caught with emotion at the end of the sentence, and Simon had grasped his arm in a gesture of comfort.

Now, there she was, standing in front of them, looking contrite and at least partially engaged with them. She smiled wanly and leant against the frame of the door.

"For heaven's sake, sit down before you fall down, girl!" Her father admonished.

She crossed the room and sank into the comfortable sofa then waved her hand dismissively. "I'm fine, honestly. I've nearly finished, then I can rest."

"Why don't you come out with us for some lunch, love?"

Her mother looked towards Jenny with a hopeful expression, but Jenny paused before saying, "Not this time, Mum. Thanks and all, but I am on a deadline with this piece of work. As soon as I've finished, I promise we'll all go out for a meal to celebrate."

Tom and Maggie stayed to chat for a few more minutes, but with the time fast approaching when they had booked their table, they made their goodbyes, both threatening Jenny to look after herself and then urging Simon to do the same. Kisses and hugs and they were finally off, with Simon seeing them to the door.

When he returned to the drawing room, Jenny had disappeared, and once Simon had checked the house, he had to reluctantly accept that she had gone back to the studio. He blew his cheeks out in exasperation and shook his head. "Oh Jenny!"

Two further weeks elapsed, and if anything, Jenny became more engrossed in her work. Simon adopted a new strategy, and rather than trying to persuade her to come to the house for meals, he took to depositing flasks of soup, packets of biscuits, bars of chocolate in the small wooden porch of the studio, noting with satisfaction when the items he left there disappeared. It gave him a small comfort that at least she was taking on some fuel.

*

The end of October arrived with a spell of beautiful early autumn weather. Leaves were turning into the palette of colours that heralded the end of the season of growth and abundance and the beginning of the end of the year. Jenny was in the studio, and she glanced out of the window to see the most gorgeous sunset casting deep crimson colours in the western sky.

She lay the brush, which was almost melded into the palm of her hand, down on the easel in front her. Her hand shook. She wondered whether it was from exhaustion or elation – probably a combination of the two she thought wryly. Her work was complete. *Thank God, I finished it before it finished me*, she thought. Still, it had had to be done. Whatever energy lay within her was relentless, her mind simply using her body as a conduit to transfer its ideas onto canvas. And now? She peered down at the clothes that hung from her and wrinkled her nose in disgust at the earthy smell of sweat that rose from her body. Her hair was hanging lankly and even that was giving off a greasy aroma. She stood up and peeled off the paint-encrusted tunic, noting with surprise she wore no bra underneath. Then she stepped out of her pants, bent down and screwed the clothing up into a ball. She walked, completely naked, across the room to the door where she switched off the light before stepping out onto the tiny veranda. Munch jumped up to greet Jenny, his tail wagging furiously as she bent to hug him.

The evening air struck her, deliciously cool as it caressed her body, and she took a deep, deep breath before stepping out onto the lawn and walking towards the house. The dewy grass was a cold balm to her feet. She could see Simon in the kitchen, preparing supper she guessed, and she felt a warm flood of affection – or was it love? – for him. He had looked after her so well during the last few weeks, to the point where she didn't think she would have survived without his snacks and soups and arms-length care. As she approached the house, she dumped the soiled clothing into the dustbin and then stood in the open doorway watching Simon as he chopped vegetables and took wine from the fridge.

"I've finished." She said softly.

He turned with a knife in his hand and looked mildly shocked at her nakedness. "You must be cold. Here…" He peeled off his jumper and brought it across the room. "Arms up."

She demurely obeyed him and allowed him to slip the still-warm pullover over her head.

"Wine? Food? Sleep? Bath?" He smiled at her, thinking it looked like she could break into pieces in front of his eyes.

"Yes, please!" She laughed, and at last the hunted, fevered look began to fade from her face.

"Right! First things first. I'll run you a bath, pour you a glass of Sancerre and then, whilst you relax, I'll cook us supper. How does that sound?"

She frowned and looked askance at him.

"What? What's wrong with that?" He complained mildly.

"Nothing. Nothing at all." And with a shake of her head, she padded towards the stairs then paused. "Simon, what's happened to you?"

He shrugged and smiled. "Don't know. Guess I grew up or something. Go on, I'll bring your wine up."

She was already in the bath by the time Simon brought her glass of wine upstairs, so he placed the glass on the edge of the bath and perched on the side panel.

"Pleased with it?"

"Hmmm?"

"Are you pleased with your work?"

"I don't know…" She frowned and swirled the water around to increase the bubbles. "I'm a bit frightened by it, to be honest. I look at it and it feels like a stranger did it. It nearly finished me off. I don't think I want to paint like that again. I can't explain it, but it just devoured me, and now it's done, it's spat me out and—"

"Can I see it?"

She looked up at him, tiny and diminished. She looked like a child to him, and then, after staring off for a moment, she returned his gaze. "Yes, you can. Go and look at it now whilst I have a bath. Go on." She loaded her hand with bubbles and spattered them on his buttock.

"Hey!"

"Go on then, go and have a look and come back and tell me what you think."

"Okay." He leant over to kiss her and scooped up his own handful of bubbles, pushing them in her face as he left the room. He smiled when he heard her expletive and laughter as he walked onto the landing and down the stairs.

He switched off the cooker and slipped on his flip-flops before crossing the dewy grass to the studio, Munch trotting happily beside him. He unlocked the door, paused, and turned to look back towards the house. The upstairs lights shone a pallid glow across the grass, and he suddenly felt a deep sense of belonging. Then he turned back and opened the studio door, stepped inside, and switched on the light.

He stood rooted, unable to take in the scene before him. The room was filled with paintings of the most extraordinary quality. The subjects were an oblique departure from Jenny's usual gentle style. There was a gamut of emotion here: passion, bleakness, loss. As he moved amongst them, he was gripped by them, until he was shuddering with emotion. He had never seen anything like it – powerful, violent, moving – absolutely, bloody brilliant. He lost track of time as he moved from one to another and then back again. Finally, he was able to draw himself away, wiping the tears off his face. Jenny was stood in the doorway.

"Do you like them?"

He walked over to her, held her at arms-length for a moment and then surprised them both by bursting into tears.

*

Later when they were eating supper, Simon broached the subject of the launch. "So, I thought I should invite Stella Bedford to the launch. What do you think?"

Jenny looked up in mild surprise. "Gosh, I'd totally forgotten you'd recommended her. Yes, I think she should come along. Why don't we meet up with her the day before in London for dinner? I don't want to wait until the event to meet her."

"Good idea. I'll give her a call and see if she's free."

"Has she signed a contract yet?"

"No, I didn't want to agree anything with her until I'd had the chance to run it past you – she'll be *your* agent, after all."

Jenny waved her fork in the air, another delicious mouthful of stir fry delivered to her ravenous appetite. "Oh, Simon, just do it! I know you'll act in our best interests, and if you think the contract is fair, just deal with the paperwork."

Simon paused and then smiled broadly, suddenly feeling a flood of euphoria hit him.

"What?" Jenny took another glug of wine and looked at him nonplussed by his expression, "Why the grin?"

"Nothing, nothing." He said, continuing to smirk behind his

wine glass.

"Come on you! What are you up to now?"

His held his hands up, palms facing her. "Nothing, I promise. Now slow down else you'll end up with stomach-ache and a sore head in the morning."

When they had finished, Simon cleared the table and stacked the dishwasher. He'd hardly been able to take the smile off his face. It was only a small word, he had to admit, but it had packed a punch. She'd said *our* instead of *my* and that meant a lot… an awful lot to someone who had still been so unsure about the stability of their relationship.

NINE

London in November was dreary at the best of times, but when the train pulled sluggishly through the outskirts of the city, great long slashes of rain spattered against the carriage and rivulets of water juddered across the windows, racing in diagonal streams across the glass so that any view of the capital was smeared beyond recognition. Still, it was cosy in the first-class carriage where Jenny and Simon were seated, and with barely another passenger sharing the space, they had been able to relax for the duration of the journey.

Jenny had felt the anticipation building throughout the remainder of October until she'd barely been able to sleep with the level of excitement that was building at the thought of revealing her latest work. Simon had done his usual consummate job with the organisation of the event, and she knew she could relax in the knowledge that his skills and ability to consider every detail would once again provide a flawless occasion. She glanced across at him and smiled indulgently whilst he slept. She wasn't sure which one of them looked the most done in, but she reckoned somewhere between her modest recovery from her own point of exhaustion and Simon's tireless work to ensure a perfect launch, their respective low points must have crossed paths.

As the weeks had passed following the completion of Jenny's work, she'd indulged herself – eating, sleeping, and generally taking life very quietly – whilst Simon had suddenly become completely absorbed in the organisation of the forthcoming event, the details checked and re-checked a hundred times. Whatever the outcome, they would surely both need a holiday to recover.

She looked out of the window again, her eyes following the streaks of rain as they continued their paths across the broad pane, and for a painful moment, she thought of Arturo. There had been no contact between them since she had visited Norfolk, and she couldn't help but wonder what Margo had told him about their encounter. *Nothing, probably*, she mused. It was such an unsatisfactory ending to their renewed friendship, but nothing would entice her to try and contact him, so complete had been her humiliation. And not for the first time, she had unwittingly put Arturo in an impossible situation, messing with his head again, poor man. She had to admit she was rubbish at personal relationships. If she'd had a modicum of intuition about her, she would have realised that he wasn't free to love her, but she'd been so wrapped up in her own emotions she hadn't given it a thought. That she wasn't free herself had meant nothing to her, and that made her squirm with shame. It didn't stop her wondering, though. Was he happy with Margo and did he love her? Jenny thought she knew the answer to that, and the feeling of something lost which had never been hers in the first place made her feel desolate. She sighed and tried to push the thoughts away – they were unhealthy and would always end like this.

*

They met with Stella Bedford later that day at their favourite London restaurant, a small Italian bistro located just off Marylebone High Street. Jenny and Simon had settled at their table in the corner and were looking at the menu when one of the waiting staff showed Stella over. The usual introductions and preamble to conversation dealt with, Jenny allowed Simon to take the initiative so that she could appraise her new agent. She liked what she saw. Confident without being arrogant, knowledgeable with the right amount of modesty – she soon warmed to her. By the time their meal was served, they were chatting easily about Jenny's work and her plans.

"I can't wait to see your new body of work tomorrow."

Jenny pulled a wry face. "It's very different from my usual genre. Not sure what the critics will make of it."

"What did you think, Simon, when you saw it?" Stella turned

to Simon.

"Bowled over, actually. It made me feel very emotional, vulnerable somehow – it's powerful ground-breaking work, seminal." He smiled across at Jenny, thinking how proud he was of her.

"Simon!" She protested, laying her hand against his arm in mild protest.

"Well, I guess I have some big footprints to fill if I am to take your place, Simon. You're a legend on the circuit."

Jenny didn't think she had ever seen Simon blush before, and just for a moment she felt a pinch of something – jealousy? She took a sip of wine as she contemplated this new emotion and what it might mean. She moved her hand from Simon's arm and down to his hand, which was resting on the table. Jenny was conscious that it was a gesture of possessiveness which she underlined by catching Stella's eye just long enough to send the unspoken message to the other woman – *hands off, love, he's mine!* Stella broke the eye contact first by dipping her head down to dab her lip with her napkin and clearing her throat. Simon glanced from Stella to Jenny and then back to Stella, acutely aware of the frisson that had passed between them but oblivious that he had been the cause.

It was only much later when they were at the hotel and getting ready for bed that Simon commented on it. "What was all that about then?"

"All what?" Jenny asked casually, as if she didn't know.

"In the restaurant – you and Stella. You looked daggers at each other."

"Oh that. Just telling her in no uncertain terms to keep her hands off my man!" She smiled at Simon's expression which appeared as a comical mixture of surprise and delight.

"No!" He said, grinning.

"Oh yes," Jenny responded, nodding sagely. "Believe you me, Simon, she would have you in an instant."

"Jenny!"

"She would! I'll take her on as my agent, but the minute she tries anything on with you…"

"She won't get far!"

"I know, but I'm just warning you to be prepared."

Simon climbed into bed and lay on his back, tucking his hands behind his head and watching as Jenny brushed her hair. She paused for a moment before continuing with the long and even stroking motion.

"Simon, can we have a holiday soon? Together, I mean."

He smiled. "Yes, why not? Let's do it and soon. I quite deliberately cleared your diary, so after the launch and the press interviews, our time is our own for a while."

"I fancy the Lake District…" She padded over to the bed and climbed in next to him. She smiled as she leant over to kiss him.

"A nice hotel?"

"No… What about a cottage. Just you and me. Lazy evenings in the pub, walking during the day and toasting our feet by the fire at night."

He smiled. It sounded like heaven to him. "I love you so much, Jenny."

"I know." She kissed him again. "And I love you too." She turned and clicked off the bedside lamp which was a shame because she missed Simon's expression of pure happiness in the darkness.

TEN

"It's no good I can't eat it!" Jenny pushed her breakfast to one side, preferring instead to take a sip of coffee.

"At least have a slice of toast, darling. It's going to be a long day, y'know." Simon gently pushed the rack of toast towards Jenny.

She sighed theatrically and acquiesced to his request by placing a small piece of toast on her side plate. But rather than eating it she pulled it into pieces and then pushed these around the plate in the forlorn hope that it might at least look as though she had managed to consume something.

He smiled. "I'm nervous too."

"I hate this part; it ties me in knots. I'll be fine as soon as we get there. Did you remember I wanted the champagne serving after the launch?"

"Yes." He nodded patiently.

"And the canapés. I don't want them served until afterwards." She chewed at the side of her nail.

"I know." He touched her hand.

"Did you invite the Bradshaws?"

"Of course."

"What time are my parents arriving?"

He glanced at his watch. "Their train gets in at ten. I've already texted them and it's on time and they will meet us there."

"Do I look alright?" She smoothed her hair, and he noted her fingers were trembling slightly.

"No actually."

She looked mortified. "What? What's wrong?"

"Jenny, you look wonderful. Now for heaven's sake, will you stop? Have some more coffee and put that toast out of its misery."

"I've got to go to the bathroom before we go, sorry." She took her napkin from her lap, brushing her lips lightly with it before setting it down on the table. A member of the waiting staff immediately approached the table and frowned with concern at the barely touched food.

"Ms Pritchard? Is there a problem with your breakfast?" Her clipped East European accent sounded rather forbidding.

Jenny reached out and touched her arm. "I am so sorry. Everything was wonderful. I'm just not hungry this morning."

"Ahhh – you have a special day today?"

Jenny laughed. "Yes, I do as a matter of fact."

"Well, good luck and maybe you'll have a big breakfast tomorrow." She smiled as she took the plate of food away from the table.

"Yes, I certainly hope so. Simon, I'll see you in the lobby in ten minutes, shall I? You finish your coffee in peace." She touched his hand and smiled, and then the jangling nerves were there again churning her stomach until she thought she would be ill right there in the dining room.

*

The Portland Gallery was part of a fine Georgian terrace of buildings that stretched the entire length of the one of the many roads that linked Harley Street and Wimpole Street. The stone steps curved elegantly to the front door accompanied by decorative, black iron railings sweeping either side of the steps in the same arching shape until they touched the walls of the building. A brass plate was positioned on the building, its highly polished surface engraved with the moniker *The Portland Gallery*. The elegance of the entrance was complemented by a hexagonal glass lantern whose bevelled edges glittered with the light shining from within and which hung in front of the fan-shaped window light, positioned above the black, highly glossy door. The external frontage of the property was very deceptive, with only one set of windows situated on either side of the door. A first-time visitor might reasonably suppose the interior was rather small. However, upon stepping into the spacious vestibule, the self-same visitor would immediately be struck by the sense of space within and the depth of the building which receded into the distance, and which was serviced by a long, wide corridor. The décor was contemporary, at odds with the external Georgian-style. Walls painted white, modern lighting and avant-garde seating together with a white marble floor created an almost intimidating atmosphere which produced echoes of sound that exacerbated the sense of being transported away from the city's noise and chaos into this rarefied arena of privilege.

It was Jenny's third launch at the gallery, and as she and Simon paused at the top of the steps and pressed the entrance buzzer, she felt the familiar feeling of excited anticipation. The door bleeped softly, and the lock clicked to indicate they could enter.

As they stepped over the threshold, a small man, dressed immaculately, stepped quickly across the lobby to greet them, his hand outstretched in a gesture of welcome, his pleasure in seeing them warm and genuine.

"Ahhh, Jenny, it's so lovely to see you again and what a great occasion – your third launch with us!"

"Peter!" Jenny greeted him warmly and they exchanged kisses.

Then he turned his attention to Simon. "Simon! Good to see you. You both look very well. Come on through and I'll get some coffee organised."

Privately, Peter Haven thought the couple looked dreadful, but as the curator of the gallery, he would never dream of commenting on a client's demeanour or appearance. In fact, if he had seen Jenny Pritchard in the street outside the gallery, he would have struggled to recognise her. Her weight had plummeted and there was a tight and tired sadness around her eyes. And Simon – good grief – how much could a man change in the few weeks since he had last met with him. He must have dropped thirty pounds himself, practically shaved his head of that wonderful soft hair and looked as though he had not slept for a week. He'd always been rather fond of Simon and had been disappointed when he'd found out that he and Jenny were more than just business partners.

Once they had made themselves comfortable in the office, Peter ordered them coffee using the intercom system to speak with his personal assistant and then he stretched back in his burgundy leather chair to make a more critical appraisal of them, his index finger drawing around the outline of his upper lip. Then he clasped his hands together and leant forwards, his eyes sparkling with excitement.

"You have exceeded yourself this time, Jenny."

"Oh. You like them?" Jenny responded modestly.

"Like them? Darling, they are simply out of this world. God knows what the critics are going to say," Peter effused, his hands waving in front of his face in an extravagant circular motion.

"Bit different, eh, Peter?"

"Simon I nearly wept when I saw them!" He eulogised theatrically and Jenny laughed,

"Peter you are so…" She shook her head at him, laughing again.

"But darling, it's true!" He flapped his hand at her and then rolled his eyes and leant forwards as though sharing some conspiracy. "They are going to go wild, absolutely wild, darling."

"Oh, Peter, I've missed you! We had a great time up at Melchett Hall, but I'm so pleased we chose the Portland again, thank you."

"Ah! Speaking of Melchett Hall… somewhere here…" Peter searched the paperwork on his desk, pulling out a cream envelope. "This arrived for you. It has the Melchett Hall crest on it." He handed the envelope to Jenny.

Jenny opened the sealed envelope and withdrew a card; the image depicted a pen-and-ink drawing of Melchett Hall. She smiled with pleasure as she read the message within. "Oh, how lovely! It's a message from Evelyn Bursill-Brookes wishing us luck for the launch. How thoughtful of her to remember us."

Peter Haven smiled fondly at them both. He was a complete professional when it came to running the gallery and was a highly respected auctioneer and collector in his own right. Jenny knew she shouldn't underestimate his opinion and she had absorbed his compliments about her work with quiet pleasure.

There was a soft knock on the door which swung gently open to allow Peter's secretary to bring in a large tray holding three cups of coffee for them, together with an assortment of biscuits on a china plate.

"Hello, Helen, how are you?" Jenny enquired politely.

"Good morning to you both. I'm very well, thank you. You're looking forward to today then?" She glanced up with quiet concern at Jenny as she placed the tray down on a side table.

"You know me, Helen. Nervous as ever, but I always feel better once I arrive here – you all look after us so well."

Helen smiled with gratitude at the compliment and then left the room so Peter could run through the itinerary of the day once more.

*

At twelve thirty, the invited guests began to arrive, and with the launch due to commence at one, the lobby soon filled up with people. There had been a general consternation amongst the guests once they realised no refreshments were to be served until after the presentation of art. Under normal circumstances the champagne and canapés would be freely distributed to keep the guests happy until matters got properly under way. But Jenny didn't want this occasion to be a repeat of others and felt it crucial that she had the undivided attention of her audience as she took them through to the gallery.

The quiet murmurs of the first few arrivals had turned into a crescendo of chatter and laughter by the time Simon led Jenny out to commence the event. Peter clapped his hands and the room fell almost silent. Once he was happy that he had gained the attention of the room, he turned to Simon and gestured for him to take the floor.

"Ladies and gentlemen, once again I would like to thank you all for coming along to Jenny Pritchard's latest launch. I am tremendously proud and excited to introduce this latest body of work by Jenny. As you will be aware from the invitations, the title of the project is Moonset, and I can promise you it is quite unlike any body of work undertaken by Jenny in the past. Jenny will be addressing you once you have viewed the work so if you would like to follow me..."

There was a palpable atmosphere of anticipation as Simon walked across to the closed doors which had been shielding the guests from the purpose of their visit. He opened one of the doors and Peter Haven opened the other with his usual flourish. The lights inside were dimmed so that none of the work was visible, and then, once every guest had inched their way into the vast room, Peter nodded discreetly to his assistant and the room was flooded with light.

Jenny was watching all of this from a distant corner of the room. As the art critics and collectors slowly walked from painting to painting, she tried to judge the impact the work was having upon them. The collective number of the group probably totalled about forty or so individuals, high-profile and influential within the art industry, and Jenny was under no illusion that the next few minutes would be significant to her career as an artist.

She noticed Stella Bedford amongst the guests and raised her hand in greeting, mouthing to her, "See you later."

Stella smiled, nodded, and pointed to the picture in front of her mouthing, "Wow!"

Jenny ventured out to stand beside the last in the series of paintings, and as the guests noticed her presence, they stopped talking and the room fell into an unnerving silence. Then one person began to applaud, and this initiated a chain reaction until the whole room echoed with the thunderous sound of people showing their appreciation of her work. Finally, and only when she raised a hand in acknowledgement, the noise slowly abated until there was a hushed expectation within the room, everyone looking intently at her.

She cleared her throat and started to speak hesitantly. "Well, gosh, thank you so much for that reception. I will take a few questions if anyone would like to—"

"Jenny – Mark Banner, *Times*, Art Correspondent."

She acknowledged him with a smile. "Hello, Mark."

"What made you change your style so radically?"

She stared off for a full minute, and for a moment it seemed she wasn't going to respond. Mark Banner had followed her progress and had taken a real liking to the young woman, so he was disturbed by the change in her appearance.

Finally, she exhaled tiredly and smiled at him. "You know, Mark, I don't know – that's the honest answer. Sometimes it's like the art takes over, and Simon will tell you this project nearly did me in. It wasn't so much an *obsession as a possession*." A few of the guests laughed softly at this but then stopped as they realised she had said it with complete and utter seriousness. "I look at the work now and it feels as though a stranger produced it – I don't even remember doing it. I don't know if that answers your question."

There was a murmur of disconcertion throughout the room.

Another voice piped up at the back of the room. "What are your plans now Ms Pritchard?"

"A holiday soon hopefully – somewhere quiet. But seriously, I don't know what my next project will be."

"Your final painting in this series, Ms Pritchard." A young man had ventured to the front. "Can you tell us a bit more about its meaning. Are the feathers representative of something? Why did you call it *Remains?*"

He was referring to the large painting positioned to Jenny's left. It was a depiction of a vast field, the harvest taken so that only the stubble remained. The scene was backlit by a huge harvest moon and shadows were thrown across the field, obscure and elongated spectres, the backdrop disappearing into a void of blackness. In the foreground, there was a bird – a barn owl – dead. A mangled, soiled debasement – a ruination of the predator it had once been. The feathers were matted and bloody – the gore gleaming darkly in the pale light and corrupting the once beautiful ethereal creature. Not a natural death – the glint of a steel trap could just be discerned, mostly concealed by the corpse lying inertly over it. It was by far the most haunting and evocative image of the set and had stirred even the most cynical art critic in the room.

For a moment she looked immeasurably sad, and her expression took on a bleak look that scared Simon, her mouth twisting in the familiar tell of anxiety. Her head dipped down and the curtain of hair fell across her features for a few seconds before she looked up towards the guest who had asked the question. "I don't know..." She looked puzzled, and then, as though a dawning realisation had just struck her, she whispered, "I suppose it's just that. The feathers are all that remain." What little colour her cheeks had held, seeped from her face, and for a moment, the occupants of the room held a collective breath, all terribly concerned that she was going pass out. There were murmurs of concern around the room and Simon stood up quickly to be by her side. He looked across towards Peter who immediately pushed his way through the throng of guests to take Jenny gently by the arm and steer her towards a chair. She sank down into it and leant on the arm of the chair, using her hand to support her head which was throbbing horribly.

Her parents by this time had also skirted around the outside of the room and her mother bent down and looked up into Jenny's face, her expression awash with worry and concern. "Jen, you okay, love?"

"I'm tired, Mum; I'm tired to death."

Simon stepped into the hiatus, briefly explained how exhausting the work had been for Jenny, and with that her parents led her carefully from the room like she was made from crystal. Simon went on to explain that Stella Bedford would be taking over as Jenny's agent, and that information seemed to bring some normality back into the room. Questions continued, whilst staff entered with refreshments.

It was only after the formalities of the launch had finished and Simon found himself overhearing snatches of conversation and the champagne and canapés were finally being served that he realised just how pivotal this launch was going to be for Jenny's future. His head was snapping this way and that to catch a dozen phrases.

"Most extraordinary launch I've been to for many..."

"Bloody, violent – Christ, you wouldn't pick these out as a Pritchard, would you...?"

"… actually, very emotional…"

"It's visceral, don't you think? So powerful – I tell you what I…"

He had to get out, find Jenny and see if she was alright. She had looked dangerously close to a breakdown in there and Simon couldn't help thinking about the raft of interviews and the photo shoot he had lined up for her for the following day. He doubted whether she would be able to do them.

*

Jenny looked at the assembly of people in front of her, all of whom cared about her and her welfare. She had to suppress a smile when she observed their expressions, worry etched across their faces in unison. "I am fine! For goodness sake, it's one more day in London, sitting in the Portland answering a few questions from art correspondents." She held her hand up to prevent her father from speaking.

"Dad, please. Peter has the auction in ten days, and if I don't do the interviews, it could have an impact on the value placed on the work. That's right, isn't it, Peter?"

Peter Haven squirmed with embarrassment, caught in the invidious position of not wanting to disagree with Jenny – and she was quite right – whilst also considering how she seemed on the brink of complete exhaustion. He glanced apologetically at Simon and Jenny's parents. "Well, yes, of course, Jenny, you are right, but we need to consider…"

"That's settled then!" She looked at them all with that brittle smile they had all come to recognise. "I'll have a quiet rest-of-the-day at the hotel, dinner in my room if I must, but I will complete the interviews and then look forward to my holiday."

There was no point in taking the discussion any further when she was like this so they resigned themselves to ensuring they would be there to support her if she needed them.

*

The photo shoot was the first ordeal of the day. She absolutely hated being photographed, but the publicity machine was in full swing, and she knew there would be no escaping this excruciating exercise. The first interview was scheduled to take place at eleven thirty and each correspondent was allocated thirty minutes of time with Jenny, followed by a thirty-minute interval before the next interview commenced.

There were the usual familiar faces: Mark Banner from *The Times*, Christine Dowler from *Art Auction*, Bob Smethers from *Artists and Illustrators* and then a handful more whom Jenny was not so familiar with. Some of the questions had been very probing, especially from Mark who, of all the art correspondents, knew Jenny best. His style of questioning had been professional and kind as always, but she sensed an underlying agenda which she wasn't altogether comfortable with. As she waited for her second appointment, she ran through the questions again in her mind. What had he asked? Ah yes, that had been it: *Why had Moonset been so draining? When had she realised she was so close to physical exhaustion? When would she paint again?*

Until she had felt the need to challenge him. "Mark, it's not like you to be so personal with your line of questioning. Why?"

He had looked at her long and hard and then, shaking his head, he had responded. "Jenny, I can see what this body of work has done to you, and it concerns me that... well, your talent would be a great loss if you were to burn out so young."

"Mark, you asked me yesterday where I had got my inspiration from, and I told you I didn't know. It's in here." She placed her hand against her breast. "And it's either in there or it's not. I can't just conjure up a piece of work like that."

A silence stretched between them before she spoke again. "I think it's been in me for a long time, actually, and it was just the right set of circumstances that drew it out."

"Like a poison?" He said rather dramatically.

Jenny considered the analogy for a moment before replying, "I suppose." She tilted her head in consideration. "But you are right: as of this moment I don't know if I will paint again – not like that anyway. It would probably kill me."

They had parted like friends, but Jenny couldn't help wondering if she had said too much to him.

She was feeling pretty good about how the day was progressing, and following a light snack at lunchtime, she braced herself for what would be the final two interviews of the afternoon. The best way she could describe her feelings was by comparing them to finishing school at the end of the year. She could feel the relief pouring into her and the excitement that they would be home by nightfall and off on holiday on Saturday.

Simon showed in her penultimate interviewer, a well-dressed lady who was representing a highly respected art magazine *Art Business*. Most of the questions were centred around the value of art, what Jenny's expectations were for the up-and-coming auction and what her opinion was generally about the growing trend in art as additions to investment portfolios. The interview concluded perfectly politely, and Simon showed the correspondent out before returning to Jenny, his face emerging around the opening doorway, a picture of pure contentment.

"One more to go!"

"Yes, who's this one then?"

"Oh, he's a provincial reporter from the Midlands, probably looking for a local angle – you know, local girl made good."

Jenny looked up sharply at Simon.

"What?" He was puzzled by her reaction.

"Nothing. I'm sure it will be fine." She raked her hand through her hair and expelled a long audible sigh. "Phew! I can't believe we're almost there. Go on then, show him in. Let's be done."

Simon laid his hand on her shoulder and leant forward to kiss her. "Okay, I'll bring him in. Can I get you anything: tea or coffee?"

"No, I'm fine thank you. But you can get me a bloody enormous gin and tonic afterwards."

"Make that one for me too!" They laughed with the relief of

knowing this arduous journey was all but complete.

He removed himself from the room, leaving the door ajar, and it was only a matter of seconds before he returned with the final interviewer, showing him towards the chair which was positioned opposite where Jenny was seated. Simon handed the reporter's card to Jenny and indicated that he would return at the allotted time.

Her fleeting first impression of the man who sat nervously in front of her was that he was rather down at heel. His suit was crumpled and shabby, and there was a faint but distinctive aroma of stale sweat which quickly became cloying in the warmth of the room. She glanced at his card and smiled encouragingly.

"Mr Rogers, thank you for coming to my launch yesterday. Perhaps you would like to ask me some questions?"

"Ah yes… um, Ms Pritchard, I thought your exhibition of art was wonderful. Incredible, actually."

"Thank you." She smiled and nodded to further encourage him to commence his interview questions.

"Yes, I found out too late that you had exhibited at Melchett in the spring. Else I would have been there."

"Oh, what a shame." She couldn't help a sigh escaping from her lips. "I don't wish to appear rude, but I am terribly tired and as this is my last interview…" She looked pointedly at her watch. "Perhaps we could continue."

"Ah, sorry. Yes, sorry." He was beginning to sweat, a thin bead of moisture appearing on lip and brow. "Yes, now then…" He glanced nervously at the notebook that was lying in his lap. "You grew up in Market Braithwaite?"

"Yes, till I was fourteen and then we moved to the West Country so I could enrol in Devon Art College."

"Yes, I have followed your career with great interest Ms Pritchard." He said with a sickly smile. "And how much influence do you think your childhood has had on your later works of art?"

Jenny noticed an almost imperceptible shift in the journalist's demeanour, and she struggled not to show her revulsion when his tongue flicked out quickly in a reptilian way to lick his lips – in out, in out.

"Some, I suppose. We all are influenced by our childhood in one way or another, don't you think?"

"So, running away from home at fourteen, did that have a lasting impression upon you?"

Jenny became still. She could feel the beat of her pulse rising rapidly and thrumming in her chest, and her hands, that had previously been relaxed in her lap, now clutched the arm of the chair, panic only a breath away.

"I don't see what that has to do with…"

"Oh, but surely it does. You recklessly ran away – bullied at school, as I remember. Then you implicated a local man, do you remember him? Giovanni Santoro? You implicated him in your supposed abduction and attempted murder. Surely, Ms Pritchard some of the emotions you portray in your art stem back to those memories, no?"

She swallowed thickly, mesmerised by the transformation in this obnoxious little man, so clearly was he revelling in her discomfort. She cringed as he continued.

"Where is he now? Do you know? Do you care? He had to leave the district; I seem to recall. Don't you think the public have a right to know that, whilst you have been able to rise above your troubled past… It would be interesting to track down Mr Santoro, see what he's been able to make of himself."

She finally found her voice. Quiet, controlled and even, she leant forward from her chair until she was eyeball-to-eyeball with the creature. "I know you, Mr Rogers, and I know the vitriol you wrote about Giovanni. This isn't about the public having the right to know about my story and my success, is it? This is your sad, pathetic attempt to resurrect your career as a journalist."

He took a breath to speak, but she held up her hand stopping him. "You have asked me some questions, at least do me the courtesy of listening to my answers."

She was so incensed with this man she failed to notice Simon quietly re-entering the room. He immediately sensed the atmosphere, hostile and tense, the journalist's body odour a damp and warm miasma in the room.

"I do know where Giovanni is now, and yes, I care very much about him. I made a mistake; one I have regretted ever since. Don't you dare blame me for Giovanni being ostracised from the local community. It was the filthy lies you wrote about him! That's why he had to leave. Now. You go. And you write your pathetic little piece of... of shit about me and be done with it. I finished with bullies a long time ago, Mr Rogers. Good day to you."

With that she rose from the chair, her legs stiffly propelling her forwards as she walked out of the room. There was a moment of excruciating silence in the room as Simon looked on aghast, before he shook himself back to his senses and said, "I don't know what has gone on here, Mr Rogers, but I think it best if you leave right now, don't you?"

The reporter smiled queasily and walked from the room. He passed an older man in the lobby who looked at him for a long moment, a puzzled expression forming on his face. Then he stepped out into the autumn sunshine with a look of self-satisfied smugness. It might have been uncomfortable but by God he'd got his story.

Simon followed the journalist until he was satisfied he had left the building. Jenny's father was standing in the centre of the lobby looking strangely confused, until Simon turned to him, "Have you seen Jenny, Tom?"

"What? No. Simon, *who* was that?"

"He's a journalist. I must find Jenny!"

"Why? What's the matter?"

"Him!" He tilted his head towards the front door to indicate he meant the man who had just left the building. "He's upset Jenny. I don't know what was going on before I went back in there, but by God, she was giving him both barrels. God knows what the article will say." He pushed his hand through his hair in exasperation. "Hell! I should have known better than to let a hack in here."

Tom stared at him, realisation dawning. "Oh my God! I know who that was. What was his name?" He stared off, wracking his memory. "Rogers! Oh, bloody hell, no!"

Simon looked at him. "I think it's time someone put me in the picture, don't you?"

They found Jenny in Peter's office. It appeared Peter had just poured her a very large whisky and, thoughtful as ever, had joined her. So they were both sat cradling glasses, whilst it appeared, they were chatting about the forthcoming auction.

"Jenny! What on earth was going on in there? You don't have a full-blown fight with a journalist and hope to get away with it."

"I don't suppose I shall." She responded quietly and looked defiantly up and into his face.

"What happened, love?" Tom was by her side, his hand coming to rest on her arm.

"Simon, sit down. Peter, would you mind if we stole some more of your whisky."

"God, no, darling!" He swiftly moved over to the sideboard that held the decanter and glasses. "Seems like we all need it."

"Where's Mum?"

"She's shopping, love, back soon I should think."

"Good – she doesn't need to hear this again." Jenny paused and took a pull of whisky from her glass then she set the glass down on the table and took a deep breath.

"When I was fourteen, I ran away from home." She noted the glances of surprise between Peter and Simon, and then waited for their respective gazes to return to her before continuing. "I was bullied at school. Horribly bullied at school until I couldn't stand it anymore, and I ran away. I used to go to the local reservoir to draw and paint..." She smiled softly as she recalled the scene. "I loved it there. You could see the water below and the trees. The leaves will be looking lovely just now. Anyway, that's where I ran to – my secret spot. Except it wasn't just my secret. It was Giovanni's favourite place too. He came across me the day I'd left home. We spent the rest of the day together." Again, she noted the exchanged glances. "No, no. It was nothing like that. He was the most fantastically gifted artist and we... well, we just got on... He showed me how to draw..." She took a deep breath. "How to draw feathers. Anyway, he didn't realise I had run away until after he left me there and he saw it on the news the next morning. He came back and tried to persuade me to go home but I wasn't having any of it. Then he got taken in for questioning by the police." She shook her head, trying to piece the story together logically. "He'd drawn this picture of me, you see, at Melchett Hall, in the walled garden, and his boss had seen it and assumed he had something to do with my disappearance." She shook her head and pressed her lips together.

Simon reached his hand across the space in between them. "Jenny, it's okay…"

"No." She remonstrated. "It really isn't. I have to tell you everything and then it's done. He was released by the police, and he came back to me." Her head dropped onto her chest and her eyes were fixed on her hands which were twisting in her lap. "I was very low. Couldn't see a way out of things and I tried to…" She gasped, the emotion barely under control. "I tried to take my own life. I tried to hang myself."

The room was deathly quiet. Only the strong ticking of the clock broke the silence, and then it chimed, the softened striking of the hour exacerbating the tension in the room.

"I was hanging… and Giovanni saved me… but the police had followed him… and he didn't know… and I thought he had betrayed me… and so…" She sobbed, the words guttural noises in between the outpouring of emotion.

"Hush." Her father stood up. "Enough, Jenny. Rest." He turned to Simon and Peter. "It all came out in the wash and Giovanni was exonerated, but the press had a field day and that piece of… that reptile – as soon as he realised Giovanni was innocent, he turned on Jenny. If I'd recognised him just now, I would have flattened him! It was a mess, but we moved, and Jenny went to Devon Art College, and you pretty much know the rest."

Jenny held up her hand again, her familiar gesture when she wanted to command attention. "I blamed him. That is what Dad won't tell you. The police assumed that Giovanni had taken me, and I did nothing to disabuse them of that. It was only the persistence of the investigating officer that ground the truth out of me. Giovanni saved my life, literally, and if that officer hadn't been astute enough to realise the story didn't add up, Giovanni could still be in prison serving a sentence for a crime he didn't commit. I will never forgive myself for that. He has! But I can't."

Peter pursed his lips together and exhaled slowly. "That is quite a story, Jenny. Whatever happened to… Giovanni, you say?"

She looked up then with a new fear in her expression. Her father didn't know, but Simon would have worked it out by now, and she couldn't see any good coming from revealing Gi's new identity. They stared at one another, and Simon moved over to the sideboard where he placed his glass down carefully before turning around to face the room.

"Hmmm, I don't expect we will ever know, will we, Jenny?" His eyes bored into hers, not with hostility and betrayal as she might have feared, but with a fierce and open love. "The most important thing is to get you out of the limelight for a while. The timing isn't great, but hey, you know what I say about publicity!"

Peter nodded quickly in agreement. "I know you won't want to look at it in this way, Jenny, but more headlines mean more attention at the auction! I know it's cynical, darling, but that's the art world for you. I think we can turn any negative publicity very nicely into a positive – you just leave it with me."

ELEVEN

The four forty-eight left London on time, pulling slowly out of Paddington Station, its rolling stock creaking and rattling as the engine manoeuvred the carriages over the points, until finally, it began to work up speed, leaving the city behind. There was only a brief remnant of light glowing on the western horizon until that too faded, leaving the faintest of pink smears as the only residue of the setting sun.

Jenny sighed and looked across at her parents who were already asleep. She smiled, feeling a sudden surge of love for them. They had been so good to her – relocating to the West Country when things had been so grim for them. Meeting that reporter had brought the whole experience back after she had been pushing it away for years.

In fact, she didn't think she had ever spoken about it with the candour she had today, and somehow it had made her feel better. Not that she'd atoned for her mistake but at least there was a sense of an ending. Her musings were disturbed by Simon who was gently brushing the side of her hand to bring her from her daydream.

"You okay?" He asked quietly.

"Yes, surprisingly so, actually." She looked across to him and smiled.

"Why did you never tell me?"

She stared off out of the window, before turning back to him. "When I first knew you, I didn't want to put you off from becoming my agent, and then when you were my agent, I didn't want to destabilise things. And then of course we got to know each other better and on a different level, and it just seemed as though telling you now would only serve to highlight how disingenuous I had been with you all along. I'm sorry." She touched his hand. "I thought I'd buried the past, to be honest."

"Well, it's my fault."

"What! How on earth do you work that out?"

"I booked Melchett Hall, and if I hadn't, that bloody reporter probably would never have got onto his story. I don't think the article is going to look very pretty."

"I don't care." She shrugged, realising that she meant it. "I've made my peace with Arturo, and what's the worst they can say? They won't find him through all of this and thank you for not saying anything in front of Peter and Dad."

"There's nothing to be gained by involving him. One thing I did want to know." Jenny looked across at him quizzically. "Are you the subject of *The Girl in the Garden?*"

She nodded and said quietly, "I saw the original when I went to his gallery. It's a stunning painting."

"Just think." He smiled now. "Ever since I saw that picture, I wondered who that girl was, and you've been with me all the time!"

TWELVE

The Lakes were the perfect choice for their holiday, and although Jenny was completely unfamiliar with the area, Simon knew it well. He had grown up in Bolton and had spent most of his family holidays in the Lake District and then, later, there'd been teenage camping trips with friends in and around Cumbria. For Jenny it was love at first sight. For Simon it was like renewing an old friendship, and he was delighted to show Jenny and Munch his favourite old haunts.

In between exploring the mountains and lakes, they took time out relaxing in the villages and towns that nestled in the hillsides and valleys. Grasmere, Ambleside, Elterwater, Outgate, Little Langdale – Jenny never got tired of spreading the huge Ordnance Survey maps across the kitchen table at their cottage each morning and searching for the next unfamiliar place name that provided the greatest appeal or sense of adventure.

They had been there almost a week and their days had fallen into the kind of indulgent pattern only ever achievable on holiday. They rose around eight, and whilst Jenny cooked breakfast, Simon strolled down to the village stores with the dog to pick up fresh milk, bread, and wood for the fire. Following breakfast, they brewed more coffee and chatted until mid-morning when, depending upon the weather, they either walked directly from the cottage or set off in the car to explore another unfamiliar location. A pub lunch was usually followed by a trip through Ambleside to refresh their supplies and then back to the cottage. There they would light the fire, listen to music, and wander down to the pub for a pint or two of locally brewed beer, before returning for a late supper and a deep and dreamless night of rest.

The morning of their second Saturday seemed to arrive before they had even paused for breath. It was a particularly dark day with the spattering rain thrown so hard against the bedroom window that it sounded like pea gravel. The noise had woken Simon and he quietly left Jenny sleeping making his way down into the kitchen below. He greeted a tail wagging Munch with a pat on the head whilst he clicked on the kettle. He knew that most of the articles from the interviews Jenny had given would be published this weekend in readiness for the auction that was to take place on the following Monday. They had both quite deliberately avoided the subject of the launch, the interviews, and auction, preferring instead to invest their time in recovering a sense of perspective. They hadn't bought newspapers or watched the television except for a few DVDs of old films which had been left at the cottage for guests to enjoy.

So it was with some trepidation that Simon withdrew his tablet from its case and fired it up, logging onto the internet and punching Jenny's name into the search browser. There was a list of entries, the links of which would take him to various newspaper and art publications but there were two headlines which immediately leapt out at him, and Simon clicked on the first one:

Is this Jennifer Pritchard's last ever painting? There was a large photograph of *Remains* next to the headline. The article continued – *I have had the pleasure of reviewing Ms Pritchard's work previously and have always classed her as a first-rate British artist who is destined for renowned success. However, that was before I was invited to preview her latest work Moonset shown at the Portland Gallery – that great bastion of British artists. It was a true privilege to be one of a handful of people to see this momentous piece of work. It is sublime and I urge you all to view it before it goes to auction at the end of the month. We are often accused of using superlatives too easily, but I have no hesitation when I describe this work as a remarkable and important body of art – powerful, emotional, violent at times – it is a radical move away from the artist's previous style…*

Simon skipped some of the details as the piece moved on.

But I fear this may be the last we see of the diminutive artist.

In an interview I held with her, following the launch of Moonset, I sensed the heavy personal price she has had to pay to produce this level of artistry, and my prediction is that she has simply burnt out her creative soul. The depiction of...

Simon sighed and clicked out of that page and back to the other more controversial headline that had grabbed his attention.

Runaway girl is runaway success – Cast your mind back to a story brought to you by me some years ago. A story of a missing local teenager, Jenny Pritchard, the fears a local community had for her safety, the poor unfortunate local man Giovanni Santoro who was wrongly accused of her abduction and attempted murder, and then the sudden disappearance of both from the local area. Whatever happened to the girl who cried wolf? I was fortunate enough to meet her recently at the launch of her latest works of art, a young woman who has certainly made her fortune in that privileged world. Clearly not wanting to discuss her past misfortunes and misdeeds, she appeared unconcerned that her childish lies had all but ruined an innocent man's life. Given the opportunity to apologise to Mr Santoro via this paper she declined to comment. So, Mr Santoro if you are out there and reading this article, we want you to get in touch and we'll help set up a meeting between you and what must surely be your nemesis. And dear reader, if you know of Giovanni Santoro's whereabouts, there's a substantial reward for information received. We know that someone must know...

Had Simon been reading an actual paper copy of the article he would have flung it across the room in disgust. As it was, the tablet he had been holding skittered across the surface of the table coming to rest precariously near the edge.

Jenny stood in the doorway. "What's up? Looked at the articles?"

He glanced up, surprised to see her downstairs. "Hi, I didn't hear you get up."

"Quiet as a mouse me. Coffee?"

"Please, the kettle's boiled. And in answer to your question: yes – our friend has tried his best to make you sound completely heartless."

She peered at the tablet, pausing to read the article which

had so incensed Simon. "I shouldn't worry if I were you. I bet it's already chip paper." She stared off out of the window which revealed the march of the weather as heavy grey clouds scudded rapidly overhead. "Hasn't it been wonderful to be here and out of it all?"

Simon considered her question for a moment and surprised himself when he found he agreed with her. "You're right. I could get used to this way of life. God, I must be getting old – not missing the parties and the promotions – I'll be getting a pipe and a cap next."

They smiled at each other, but then Jenny became serious. "Do you mean that?"

"What about the pipe and the cap?"

"No, silly! About this way of life?"

"I guess so… yes, why?"

"Because I would love to move here. Buy a cottage with a studio attached. Do a bit of painting here and there. What do you think?"

"Crowded in the summer – Northumberland might be better."

"But I need the tourists to sell my work to."

Simon could see that what had perhaps seemed like a light-hearted question belied a more serious intent which Jenny had been mulling over for a while.

"Your parents?"

"They can move here too… or not – they can visit if they don't want the upheaval."

"Property prices are high."

She sighed. "You're right. It's a silly pipe dream. I just feel I need a sense of permanency, somewhere to settle and have a family, move on to a new phase in our lives."

Simon stared across the room at her as she busied herself making coffee. She had said it so casually he wondered if he had heard her correctly and if, perhaps, he had fundamentally misunderstood her words.

"What are you saying, Jenny?"

She turned to him. "Oh! Well, I suppose I'm saying we should stop messing about and get married. Would you like poached or scrambled this morning?" She turned away again to hide the smile of pure mischief that had lit up her face.

"Jenny Pritchard! You minx, come here!" He caught her around her waist and spun her until she was facing him, egg whisk raised quizzically in one hand.

"What? No egg at all this morning?" She mocked and then squealed as he dragged her through the kitchen and into the tiny living area where he unceremoniously dumped her on the sofa. She gasped with laughter, the egg whisk still dangling from her hand, and only stopped when Simon knelt in front of her and said with as much solemnity as he could muster, "Jenny Pritchard, will you marry me?"

"Yes, Mr Fellows, I will indeed."

"Before Christmas?"

"Why not? Yes, before Christmas."

He yelped with delight, and taking the whisk out of her hand, he half jumped, half skipped across to the front door which he flung open and danced out into the rain whooping at the top of his voice and waving the whisk in the air. His eccentric celebrations were brought to an embarrassing halt when their nearest neighbours walked past giving him a polite good morning whilst watching him with slightly worried expressions out of the corners of their eyes. Even their collie dog looked askance at his behaviour.

By this time, Jenny was rolling on the sofa and clutching her sides, bellowing breathlessly with laughter and gasping, "That was the funniest thing I have ever seen. Ow! Oh!"

*

It rained for the remainder of the weekend. A deluge of horizontal curtains of rain swept down the Langdale Valley obliterating their view of Lingmoor Fell.

On Monday, they left Munch at the cottage and drove into Ambleside wandering around the shops, jostling along the narrow pavements, the spokes of their umbrella tangling occasionally with those of the other shoppers. They paused at the estate agents to peer in at the window and Jenny pointed to the details of one of the properties,

"There you are, Simon, there's our Lakeland home!"

"Wow, that is amazing, love, but have you seen the price! Seven hundred and fifty k – I don't think so, do you?"

"What would we get for ours?"

"Six hundred, maybe six fifty, so unless you have a devious plan to find the other one fifty k…"

"Oh well, in that case you can buy me a cup of tea and a cake in compensation, come on." She pulled him along the pavement to the café, and taking care to shake most of the water off their brolly, they stepped into the steamy atmosphere of the bakery-cum-tearoom and settled at once at the table that was pushed into the small bay window by the front door.

"Wonder how the auction is going?" Simon mused.

"You broke the rules." She chided gently, though she had been having much the same thoughts herself.

"I thought the rule only lasted until this morning." He played along with her game.

"I think you'll find, if you check your terms and conditions, the rule applies until noon today, and it's…" She pulled the cuff of her coat back with careful deliberation and smiled. "Oh shame, its only eleven forty-five. That means you have to do the washing-up again tonight."

"You're a cruel woman, Jenny Pritchard."

They placed their order and chatted whilst they waited for their tea and cake to be served. Simon's mobile phone began to ring, and he glanced down at the display and said, "Speak of the devil, it's Peter. I'll take it outside." He pushed the chair back and answered his phone as he was walking out of the door so that Jenny just caught him saying, "Peter, how are you? We were just talking about the auction. How did it go?"

Jenny could see him from the window, the rain falling thickly again and hastening the speed of pedestrians as they trotted along the pavement and past Simon. He was, it seemed, oblivious to the weather, and Jenny tutted and shook her head in exasperation as she could see his shirt becoming soaked through.

The waitress brought over their order, so Jenny busied herself preparing the tea and cutting the cakes into two pieces to share. She was peering gingerly into the top of the teapot judging whether the tea had brewed sufficiently when Simon re-entered the café. His drenched appearance drew some amused glances from the other customers in the café, but it was his demeanour that Jenny noticed. He was as white as a sheet and visibly shaking, and when he sat down, he didn't look at Jenny. She touched his arm with concern, tilting her head to one side to catch his eye.

"Simon? What's the matter? What is it?"

Then he looked up at her and shook his head in bewilderment.

"For heaven's sake, what!" She pressed him, more urgently.

He drew a deep breath and said unnecessarily, "That was Peter."

"Yes… I know that darling… and?"

"He wanted to let us know about the auction."

"Really?" She said sarcastically, and then sighed in exasperation. "For goodness sake, just spit it out, will you – was it a disaster?"

He looked at her and pursed his lips, and then a thought seemed to occur to him, and he smiled softly and said, "No, no it was fine."

"Fine?" She said flatly. "Is that it? Fine?"

"Finish your tea and cake – we need to be somewhere." Simon took a huge bite out of his piece of cake and Jenny noticed his hand was visibly shaking, so much so that he had to pick up his teacup using both his hands to prevent the tea from slopping over the edge.

"But I've only just started it!" She objected.

"Come on, I've got something to show you."

"You are a puzzle to me sometimes." She just about managed to take a bite of cake and a sip of tea before he stood up impatiently and twitched his head towards the door.

"Alright! I'm coming!" She snatched up her coat and bag and was able to pull a ten-pound note from her purse to leave on the table before Simon yanked her by the arm. "Simon!" Her voice rose in incredulity as he practically pulled her down the steps and back onto the pavement.

"Hold on, let me grab the umbrella, will you?" She gasped as she managed to snatch it on the way past. "What's all this about?"

"You'll see, come on."

They had only walked a short distance up the street when Simon paused and pushed open the door of the estate agent whose window they had been mooning through minutes earlier.

Jenny was dumbstruck by this point and then completely perplexed when Simon waited to be greeted by the agent before saying, "Could we see the details of the property in Elterwater, please – the one you are showing in your window."

The young woman turned to a filing cabinet that was positioned behind her, pulled open the top drawer, which glided open noiselessly, and reached into a section before withdrawing a file and laying it on top of the desk.

"This is the one you were interested in, sir?"

"Yes, that's it, thanks."

"It's a beautiful property." She remarked, and then looked across to a second desk where a phone had started to ring. "Would you excuse me whilst I take that call?"

"No, that's fine. We're quite happy looking at the information, thank you."

Jenny turned to Simon as soon as the girl was engaged with answering the telephone and hissed at him, "Have you gone mad?"

He didn't answer her but took out his mobile phone, flicked open the cover and located his incoming text messages. There was one unread message in his mailbox. He prodded the phone over to Jenny and nodded to encourage her to read it.

"Go on." He said quietly, a smile beginning to form on his lips.

She looked at him quizzically before picking up the phone and opening the message. She looked at the message for a few seconds, her mind trying to compute the content. It read simply:

Yes 350k!

She frowned. "What's that mean then?"

He groaned and shook his head. "Jenny! The message is from Peter. That's what the auction of your work fetched."

She clapped her hand over her mouth, her eyes nearly popping out of their sockets and then she squealed so loudly that the young woman on the telephone turned to look at her with a mixture of annoyance and curiosity.

"Sorry!" Jenny held up her hand in apology. "Oh my God, Simon!"

"I know! Isn't it just fantastic? Apparently, there was an online bidding war and *Remains* fetched two hundred k in its own right. And that's just the start of it, love. Peter's been inundated with requests for prints. You've really done it this time, Jenny."

"So…" She looked across at the untouched file containing the details of the house. "So we really could afford this property?"

He nodded and they suddenly both giggled like joint conspirators.

By the time the girl had dealt with the telephone call, Simon and Jenny had looked at the details of the property several times. So, when she re-approached them, looking somewhat unnerved by their peculiar behaviour, they had already decided they wanted to view. She referred to her laptop to check the viewing arrangements and said, "Well, it's vacant possession so there's no reason why you can't go and look at it today if you wish. I'm afraid, as you can see, I'm alone in the office… but if you don't mind viewing it without an agent?"

"No, not at all." They both said together and giggled again.

The girl smiled at them. "I take you've had a bit of good news?"

Jenny nodded. "Sorry about our behaviour, but yes, we have actually had some very good news which means we can look at a property like this and buy it if we want!" Her eyes shone at the prospect.

"There's just a few formalities to discuss and then I'll get you the directions and the keys."

Jenny couldn't remember a time when she had felt so excited, and she looked at Simon and grinned in anticipation.

An hour later and they were driving down the Langdale Valley and turning the car off the road into Elterwater. Jenny had the directions spread out on her lap, whilst Simon negotiated the narrow track leading into the village.

"Left at the pub, it says." She tapped the paper, "Hey, that could be our local! The Britannia Inn – looks nice."

"Never mind the pub, where to next?"

"Oh right. Okay, over the river and then there's a turning, a rough track to the right on a corner. There! I think that must be it."

Simon manoeuvred the car carefully onto the track and proceeded cautiously until they arrived at a large double entrance closed off by wooden gates.

Jenny undid her seat belt and got out of the car. "I'll get them!"

There was a padlock on the gates, and it took Jenny a minute to locate and then use one of the keys provided by the estate agent. A metal loop sat over the shoulders of the two gates which hinged upwards to allow them to be pushed open. She pushed one gate back to its fullest extent and then the other, wedging them open with the large stones lying on the driveway which Jenny supposed were there for just that purpose. Simon drove the car through the gateway and stopped to allow Jenny to climb back in. It wasn't a long driveway, but it was very overgrown, and the house didn't become visible to them until they rounded a large clump of shrubs, mainly yew and laurel.

Once clear of this obstruction the driveway divided into two, one part continuing forwards and then turning to the right and the other branching right and then turning to the left so that the tracks met with each other again to form a rectangular driveway which had grass and a border as a central feature. The house was built of stone and elevated from the grounds at the front. The front door was accessed via six broad stone steps which were pitted and speckled with lichen. The door, which was protected by a stone porchway, was made of oak, and stood at least eight feet in height from the step to the lintel.

Jenny took the key and inserted it into the ancient lock which clicked as she turned the key to unlock the door. The hallway was square with a cantilevered staircase rising upwards from one corner; the flooring appeared to be original terracotta tiling. The downstairs rooms were huge. A beautiful dining room, a drawing room, study, and modern kitchen cum breakfast room were complemented by a cloakroom, and utility area. There was also a beautiful Victorian conservatory that ran the whole length of the back of the house. Upstairs on the first floor, there were three bedrooms and two bathrooms, one of which was an ensuite in the master bedroom. Two further rooms were in the attic.

Once they had explored the house, they moved outside to the garden. A single-storey brick cottage attached to the main house had been converted into separate accommodation, and according to the brochure, the gardens extended to an acre. Neither of them had said a word to each other as they had moved from room to room and then into the garden. Finally, they moved back into the house to get out of the rain, which was still falling in a fine mizzle. They paused in the kitchen, Jenny looked across at Simon, "What do you think?" She looked away and glanced back at him anxiously.

He grunted. "I don't like it."

She looked aghast. "Really? Oh no!"

He looked askance at her and said, "Nah – I LOVE IT!" and scooped her up in his arms, whooping.

"Oh, Simon, it's perfect, isn't it? Not too big but plenty of room. And if Mum and Dad want to come, there's the cottage attached."

"We would need to sort you out a studio but that's no bother at all with those purpose-built log cabins I see advertised everywhere." He stopped and holding her at arm's length, became serious. "What do you think, hey? Is this going to be our forever home?"

Jenny's eyes sparkled with unshed tears. "Oh, Simon, I hope so. It's the loveliest place I've ever seen. Shall we buy it?"

"Shall we?" He mirrored her question, and they grasped hands and shouted "Yes!" in unison.

When they managed to control their excitement, they looked around the property again, making plans for furnishings and even where the Christmas tree would stand. Then, reluctantly, they made their way back to Ambleside to the estate agent who looked up and smiled as Simon pushed open the door and they entered the warmth of the office, pleased to be out of the rain.

"Hi! How did it go?"

"We love it!" Jenny beamed at her as she placed the keys back on the desk. "We really didn't want to come away."

"I know, it is very lovely, isn't it?"

"We would like to put an offer in," Simon said, getting down to business. "It would be dependent upon us selling our own place in the West Country, but on the basis that we know property is extremely sought after where we currently live, I don't foresee that being a problem."

"And your offer?"

"We'll offer the asking price but only on the basis it's taken off the market today, or as soon as you can contact the current owners."

The girl took various details and promised to revert to them as soon as she had a response from the owner. Their delight was sealed when she called less than an hour later to confirm the offer on the house had been accepted.

Jenny couldn't help but muse later that evening whilst Simon stood at the bar in the pub waiting to be served that she really would not have predicted this outcome for them. She thought she did love him now. There wasn't the chemistry that she felt with Arturo – even thinking of him now made her heart contract painfully – but then she guessed there was more than one kind of love. There would never be hot blinding passion between them, but surely the feelings which they had developed for each other over the previous months were more binding. Steady… yes, that was it – steady love. It made her feel wanted and secure and there was a predictability about the future. Not perhaps the most exciting outcome she might have wished for, but it was a great deal better than many people had, and for that she was grateful.

"You looked a million miles away then." Simon returned to the table with their drinks.

"I was just thinking how lucky we are and how content I feel right now."

"We've both worked hard for this success, Jenny. Yes, there's an element of luck of course, but we wouldn't have the opportunities we have now without the work, would we?"

"No, I suppose you're right. Listen, I've been thinking…"

"Dangerous."

"Watch it you!" She poked him hard in the ribs.

"Ouch!"

"Serves you right. Anyway, as I was saying: I've been thinking. I know we have the cottage booked until the end of the week but if we have a wedding to organise, albeit a small one, and a house to put on the market, I wondered whether we should go home a bit earlier."

Simon took a long draught from his beer and nodded, licking the creamy froth from his upper lip before saying, "I agree. It seems silly lolling here for another few days when there's so much to do. What do you reckon – set off tomorrow after breakfast?"

Jenny nodded. "Let's call Mum and Dad and invite them out for dinner. We can tell them all the news and what our plans are and leave them to think about what they would like to do."

"Okay, that sounds like a plan."

As they walked back to the cottage in companionable silence, Simon glanced across at Jenny and smiled. Now they had something they could share – moving up here and the wonderful house – it felt as though the animosity that had often clouded their relationship had gone. It was almost as though the mixing of their professional and personal interactions had confused the dynamics between them, creating an unhealthy and, at times, toxic atmosphere.

He acknowledged to himself that he had been too wrapped up maintaining his professional persona and that had prevented Jenny from seeing him as the person he was. In fact, he thought with sudden insight, he had lost sight of himself so completely that he had become the shallow invention of Simon Fellows the artist's agent. Now he felt for the first time in years that he was back in his own skin, being his own person and feeling comfortable with the discovery that he was alright without the veneer of confident arrogance – the sham that he had become.

He imagined the process as a shedding of his alter ego, layer by layer, until he stood there guileless and straightforward as he had been as a boy. He did wonder fleetingly if he would be able to step back into the role of art promoter and agent with quite so much conviction – and more importantly whether he wanted to.

"Jen?"

"Yes?" She squeezed his arm fondly.

"How would you feel about me opening a gallery up here? We could display and sell originals and prints of your work and maybe some other local artists too."

"What's brought that idea on?"

"Dunno. I just think that coming here, planning the future, gives us both a chance to reflect. I don't know whether I really want the agency work. I rather like the idea of pottering about in the gallery, chatting to people, coming home, and cooking your dinner. Just being me really."

"And this is you, is it?" She stopped and turned to face him.

"What do you mean?" He frowned in confusion.

"Well …" She struggled to frame the words. "You're just so damn different. This time last year I felt confused about us, entirely unsure whether we were right for each other."

"And now?"

"Well, if this is you, the real you, I mean, then you do whatever it takes to stay this way. Because this does feel right to me."

He grasped her hands and pulled her towards him. "Love you, Jenny Pritchard."

She rested her head against his shoulder, and they walked back to the cottage deeply content whilst they discussed their plans for their future together.

THIRTEEN

When Jenny and Simon arrived at the pub, Tom and Maggie were already seated by the open fireplace. They both stood up when they saw the couple enter the room and Maggie breathed a sigh of maternal relief – Jenny looked like her old self. She'd put on some much-needed weight, her hair shone, and her face was glowing with vitality. And most important of all, she looked incredibly happy.

"Hi, you two! Had a good holiday? Looks like it – you both look fabulous."

"I drank pints of beer, Mum!" Jenny laughed and patted her stomach.

The men took themselves off to the bar to buy drinks whilst Jenny settled down to tell her mother about the cottage, where they had stayed. Once Simon and Tom had returned with the drinks and the menus, Jenny took a breath and gazed at her parents with barely concealed excitement.

"Mum, Dad – we've got news."

Tom and Maggie were stunned by the three pieces of news. Maggie was thrilled about the wedding but quietly disappointed that it wasn't going to be a big affair. No church, a small reception for close friends and family and they hadn't planned a honeymoon either.

Tom was just as delighted about Jenny finally deciding to marry Simon, and quietly very pleased that the wedding wasn't going to be a big affair. He'd budgeted for a wedding at some stage and had privately considered the likely cost, then added another five grand to be on the safe side. Now it seemed Jenny's decision to keep things simple would deliver a nice windfall for him and Mags and cover the cost of the trip to Canada they had been planning forever and had never got around to booking.

The second surprise, which Jenny announced with quiet modesty, was the proceeds of the auction and the likelihood of ongoing sales of prints of her latest work. Tom had whistled. "That's a serious amount of money, Jenny. What are you planning to do with it?"

That's when Jenny slipped the brochure of the house across the dining-room table towards her parents. Although this was the piece of news that excited her and Simon the most, she acknowledged the geographical distance it would put between them and her parents, who accordingly may not celebrate the news with quite the same enthusiasm.

"It's beautiful, Jenny. Whereabouts is it located?" Maggie thought the property looked amazing... and very expensive.

"The Lakes, Mum – Elterwater, right in the heart of the Langdales." Jenny thought she saw her mother's smile falter for a moment, so she lay her hand on her arm. "Mum, there's a two-bedroom cottage attached to the house, and we would love it if you came to live with us. Look..." Jenny flicked through the details until she found the page showing the cottage in the grounds. "Here it is. It's lovely and totally separate so we wouldn't be in each other's pockets. What do you think?"

Maggie glanced across to Tom with uncertainty. She would have said yes in a moment, but she knew it wouldn't be so easy to convince Tom to up sticks and move to the other end of the country. He still had five years to go before he reached retirement age, but she would work on him when they were alone, knowing that pushing him now would inevitably lead to a negative.

"We'll certainly think about it, and thank you, darling, for asking us. Thank you, Simon!"

The rest of the evening was taken up with planning for the wedding and the impending sale of the house, and it wasn't until Tom and Maggie were driving home later that Maggie dared to broach the subject of a possible move.

"What do you think then?"

Tom glanced across at his wife and smiled fondly. "That didn't take you long?"

"Well, you know me – cut to the chase!" She laid her hand lightly on his thigh.

"There's a lot to discuss, Mags."

"I know, I know." She nodded quickly, eager to appease him at this stage of their discussion.

"I wouldn't consider it unless we can buy the cottage."

"Right."

"And that would mean selling ours of course."

"What about work?"

"I've been thinking about cutting down a bit, maybe even going out on my own. You know, take a few small clients on, work from home. That being the case, I could do that whether we're here or in the Lakes."

"Of course!" Her eyes sparkled with anticipation.

"And hopefully there'll be grandchildren, now that they're finally getting married. And I know you'll want to be near Jenny when the time comes, and she'll be needing your support."

"Tom Pritchard, are you saying yes?"

"If it stops you nagging me, woman."

She bounced up and down in her seat, practically banging her head on the roof of the car and clapped her hands. "Oh Tom! Thank you! Thank you! You wonderful man! You just wait till I get you home, young man."

Tom grinned at her. "Points?"

"More than you could ever imagine in your wildest dreams. And you know what points make, don't you?"

They chanted out the familiar patter in unison – "Prizes!" – and laughed liked a couple of teenagers.

FOURTEEN

"What time are your parents coming?" Simon called to Jenny over his shoulder as he basted the meat and turned the potatoes alongside the joint where they were roasting and caramelising in the juices of the pork.

"I said twelve thirty, is that okay? They should be here soon."

"Yep, perfect. Are we eating in here or the dining room?"

"Let's eat in here, shall we? I cleaned the dining room ready for the viewing tomorrow."

"That's fine. I like eating in here anyway, it's cosier."

"Can I get you a beer?"

"Thanks, love."

"Oh, here they are already, early as usual!" Jenny watched as her parents climbed out of the car and smiled. "He's said yes."

"How do you know that just from seeing them through the window?"

"Look." She pulled him to where he could see through the window.

He laughed. "Okay, I get you now. Honestly, sometimes your parents are like bloody teenagers."

"I know, it grosses me out and they know it. Look! They're waving now. They knew we could see them all the time!" She laughed and moved to the front door to let them in. "You're too old for that sort of behaviour!"

"That's no way to greet your ageing parents, young lady."

"Yes, Dad, and that's no way for an ageing parent to behave with his wife. Hello." She kissed them both fondly and took their coats.

"Mum, white wine, gin and tonic, or we've got some bubbles

to celebrate."

"Ooh bubbles, please."

Jenny sidled up to her mother and whispered conspiratorially, "I take it he said yes."

Maggie nodded and squeezed Jenny's arm. "I am so excited!"

Simon uncorked the sparkling English wine with a flourish and topped up the four fluted glasses that Jenny had taken from the cupboard. Glasses were raised and clinked and there was a brief silence as each of them drank and contemplated their future together for a moment. It appeared nothing could spoil their plans. Simon whizzed back into the kitchen to finish off the lunch whilst Jenny chatted with her parents.

"Anything I can do, Simon?" She called and tilted her head on one side to hear his muffled reply.

"No, you can all come through and sit at the table though." And he disappeared into the kitchen, whistling whilst clattering the saucepans and dishes in readiness for dishing up.

As they settled at the table, Jenny's mobile phone began to ring and skitter on the polished glass surface of the coffee table in the garden room. She ignored it for a moment and then walked through to pick it up and glance at the screen. A mobile number was showing which was unfamiliar to her, so she frowned and cut the call.

"Who was it?" Maggie asked in idle curiosity.

"Don't know, didn't recognise the number." She shrugged just as her phone began to ring again. "It's the same number, calling me on a Sunday too! Excuse me, I'll just take this for a moment." She wandered out of the kitchen and into the hallway where she accepted the incoming call, a note of hesitancy and minor annoyance in her voice. "Hello, Jenny speaking."

"Jenny."

The resonant timbre of his voice seemed to vibrate in her chest, and she gasped with the shock of hearing him. "Arturo!"

"I am so sorry to call you like this, Jenny." He sounded distraught.

"What's wrong?" She glanced at her hand as she noticed it

shaking.

"It's my wife, Margo… she's had a brain haemorrhage; it's very bad. I didn't know who else to call. I don't know what to do."

"God, no! Where are you?" She threw her head back and closed her eyes briefly.

"Norwich – the General at Norwich. They won't move her now. They don't think…" His voice caught. "It's very bad."

"I'm coming. I'll be with you as soon as I can, and I'll call when I get there. Arturo…" She didn't know what else to say. "I'm coming."

Simon brought the meat to the table with a flourish. "Ta-dah!" And then noticing Jenny's absence asked, "Where's she gone?"

Maggie said quietly, "She took a phone call." And then she glanced at the door, concern etched on her face. She had not been able to hear the conversation her daughter was having but had picked up the cadence and modulation of her tone and intuitively felt something was wrong, that it was bad news.

And then the door opened slowly, and Jenny leant for a moment against the frame. She was pale and shaking.

"Whatever is the matter?" Simon dumped the dish of meat on the table and crossed the room. "What is it, darling?"

"It's Arturo." She said, looking at Simon with anguish. "Margo's had a brain haemorrhage – it sounds very serious."

Maggie looked at Tom and mouthed to him, "Who's Arturo?" Tom shrugged in reply.

Simon shrugged. "That's terrible but I don't really understand why he's called you, love."

"I have to go." She spread her hands to him in appeal.

"You do not!" He looked aghast. "You bloody don't!"

"Hey, you two, cut it out. Who's Arturo?" Tom demanded authoritatively.

Simon turned to Tom and said bitterly, "You probably know him better as Giovanni Santoro."

Maggie stared at Jenny. "Isn't that the man who—"

"Yes, Mum."

Tom shook his head in confusion. "I don't understand."

Jenny pulled one of the dining chairs out and sat down wearily. "He came to my exhibition at Melchett Hall. He changed his name all those years ago to Arturo D'Arbo – you know, fresh start for him after the…" She twitched her head not really wanting to continue.

Maggie's mouth dropped open. "*The* Arturo D'Arbo? The artist?" She was incredulous when Jenny nodded.

Tom said quietly, "I still don't understand – why would he call you?"

Simon jerked his head towards Jenny. "She went to see him in Norfolk, where he lives, didn't you, Jenny? Could say the friendship was rekindled there in one form or another." He regretted the implied accusation as soon as he had uttered the words.

"Simon! That's not fair."

"No, it's not, sorry. I didn't mean that, Jenny, but you don't have to go, you really don't."

"Of course, I must go. I owe that man a great deal – my life, in case you'd all forgotten. I can't just abandon him. He's asked me for help, what else can I do?"

"So, by going up there you think you're buying your absolution."

"No! Yes! I don't know!" She raked her hands through her hair.

Simon sighed deeply and shook his head in exasperation. "I'll come with you."

"No, Simon. We've got people looking at the house tomorrow, and I think this is something I need to do alone."

"I bet you do." He muttered sourly. "At least have something to eat before you go."

"Yes, okay." She agreed demurely, even though food was the very last thing she wanted.

They ate in strained silence for the duration of the meal with a few attempts from Maggie to make conversation. To Jenny, the meal tasted like cardboard, and she struggled to swallow it down, but finally she finished, and she helped Simon clear the plates.

Maggie and Tom struck up a puerile conversation to try and overcome some of the tension in the room.

Simon scraped the plates with ferocious intensity until Jenny touched his arm gently. "Can I speak with you?"

He didn't look at her for a moment but then relented and followed her out of the room and into the study.

"Well?"

"Simon don't be mad at me. I can't stand it, and I think you are being unfair. I must go, darling. I will come back as soon as I can, and then we can get on with our plans. Please, please, don't be mad at me."

He scuffed his foot along the edge of the carpet, head down and biting on his lip, seemingly poised on the crux of a dilemma. Then he suddenly grabbed her and drew her into a crushing embrace. "I'm sorry, it's just that I'm terrified of losing you."

"Don't be silly. I love you, Simon."

"I love you too. Now go and pack a bag before I change my mind."

As she turned to leave the room, Simon felt a shudder pass through him. He hoped he would never look back on this moment and concede this was when it ended for them. Life could be fickle. One minute poised on the brink of everything, on track, and then derailed by one telephone call. He swallowed his emotions and moved back to the kitchen.

Maggie and Tom looked up when he entered the room and he responded to their questioning expressions, saying quietly, "She's going. I can't stop her. I just hope she'll come home."

"Oh Simon!" Maggie walked quickly across the room and embraced him, and for a moment, Simon thought her unexpected display of empathy would be enough to undo him completely.

FIFTEEN

By the time Jenny was turning her vehicle into the hospital car park it was past eight thirty. A thick fog had descended, and the orange glow of the street lighting cast a morbid and sickly glimmer into the air which didn't seem to reach the darkened surface of the parking area at all.

Jenny climbed out of the vehicle and stared across at the vast building emerging from the fog, and she shivered at the chilliness of the evening after the warm cockpit of the car. An ambulance drove into the roadway leading to the casualty unit, its blue lights strobing through the fog like the fingers of an electric storm. It gave Jenny a fleeting sense of déjà vu of that night when the police had found her in the woods all those years ago and the beams of light which had flashed through the woodland, heralding the arrival of the entourage.

She shuddered and pushed the memory away. Then taking out her mobile phone, she scrolled down until she found Arturo's number. She dialled, and it rang briefly before cutting directly to voicemail, so she tried sending a text instead. She let him know that she had arrived, parked up in car park three, and that she would start making her way across to the high dependency unit. Then she called Simon to let him know she had arrived at the hospital but that she had no news of Margo's condition. She promised to call in the morning when she knew more.

She hadn't crossed half of the car park before she noticed Arturo striding towards her, hands thrust deep into the pockets of his coat. When they met, he took her hands in his and breathed her name like it was a relief for him.

"Jenny, you came."

"Arturo, of course. How is Margo?"

He shook his head fractionally. "She died at six thirty."

Jenny felt a well of emotion fill her throat – she had hardly known the woman, but the news was still shocking. "Arturo! I don't know what to say. I am so, so sorry." She grasped his hands more strongly and pulled him towards her. Two, maybe three, minutes passed before he pushed her away and said hoarsely, "I am sorry to ask, but is there any way we could go home. Can you take me home, Jenny?"

"Of course. Is there anything you need to do here before we go?"

He shook his head. "No, I have said my goodbye."

The journey back to the cottage was made in complete silence, and it was only when Jenny brought the car to a halt at the front of the gallery, she noticed Arturo had fallen asleep, the exhaustion of the last two days overwhelming him. Jenny touched his leg gently and he woke with a sudden jerk, his eyes wide with confusion.

"We're back." She said gently. "Come on, let's get you inside."

He led her away from the front entrance of the gallery and down a gated passageway located at the side of the main frontage, pausing momentarily as he fumbled with the lock. He pushed open the door and flicked on the lights to illuminate the long corridor which led down to the living accommodation. He looked dreadful in the harshness of the interior light, his skin a shade of grey and his eyes bloodshot and almost closed against the sudden glare of light.

Jenny took one look at him and led him by the arm towards the door at the end of the corridor. This, she learnt, led into a large airy kitchen and comfortable seating area. The room was chilly and unwelcoming. There was a vase of flowers on the table, but they had wilted and some of the petals had dropped onto the table surface, their care forgotten in the drama of Margo's illness. Jenny gently guided Arturo to one of the comfy armchairs whilst she set about lighting the fire and putting a kettle of water on the range.

"Are you hungry?" She asked, wondering what on earth there was to prepare for him to eat.

He looked across the room at her and shrugged, "Am I meant

to be?"

"Of course. Shall I see what there is?"

"I'm ravenous." He admitted.

They didn't speak again, whilst Jenny busied herself finding eggs and cheese, to make omelette, together with some salad items. The kettle began to burble on the stove. She felt like an intruder in a stranger's kitchen. Maybe it was the faint aroma of Chanel perfume infused into the surroundings or the carelessly discarded spectacles by the cookbook, but she had a sense of Margo's recently departed spirit being here, perhaps trying to express her outrage at the audaciousness of the scene.

When she turned to Arturo, he was tending to the fire, and she felt the familiar surge of yearning for him, much to her shock and disgust at this most inappropriate of times.

"Are you okay?" She said quietly, thinking, *What kind of trite question is that to ask a man who has just experienced the death of his wife?*

He seemed not to hear her and for a long moment fixed his attention on the fire. Then seeming to be satisfied with the heat it was beginning to throw out, he sat back on his haunches and looked across the room at Jenny.

"She was a good woman."

"Yes."

"She took great care of me – I'll miss her a great deal."

"Of course."

"But I didn't love her, Jenny. I never loved her, not like…" He paused, agonising over his choice of words. "That sounds terrible. Of course, I loved her in a kind of way, but I couldn't love her in the way she loved me." He looked sadly into the flames of the fire as if seeking his answers there.

"There are lots of kinds of love, don't you think?" Jenny said quietly, not really knowing how else to respond to his appalling statement.

He stared across the room at her with his piercing gaze until she had to turn away and busy herself at the stove.

During their supper, Jenny said, "I should see if there are

any rooms at the hotel." But as she glanced at her watch, she was shocked to see that it was almost midnight. "Oh goodness! I didn't realise it was so late."

"No matter. there's a guestroom." He said quietly, softly tracing a knot of wood in the kitchen table with his finger.

"Are you sure? It doesn't seem appropriate for me to stay here under the circumstances."

"Where else are you going to go?" He stood up and stretched and then walked across to a cupboard in the corner of the kitchen, opened the door, and grasped fresh towels which he tossed across to Jenny. "I'll show you the way." He said shortly.

The atmosphere was electric as Arturo led Jenny up the stairs, and he paused outside the door which Jenny assumed led to the guestroom. She thought for one horrifying moment he was going to kiss her, and she was so afraid of what might follow on from that. But he didn't. He briefly touched her shoulder and said, "Thank you, Jenny, for coming today, thank you."

She could only smile at him before entering the room and closing the door behind her, her whole body thrumming with the effort of controlling the urge to embrace him.

"Christ, woman!" She whispered to herself, before quickly getting ready for bed and climbing into the coldness of the linen bedsheets. She lay awake for a long time, and try as she might not to, she kept letting the image of Arturo lying in the bed next door drift into her consciousness. Only the thought that, should she dare to venture from her room, Margo would be stood wraith-like on the other side of the door, prevented her from going any further.

*

The atmosphere at breakfast was a little better but there was a restlessness about Arturo until he said, "Do you fancy a walk – I need to clear my head."

"Okay, why not. Let me just clear these things away and get ready."

Within ten minutes they were pulling on their coats against

the biting chill of the onshore wind. They took the long path that wound across to the headland and then dipped down to where the cliff dropped to meet the beach. Jenny couldn't remember the last time she had walked along a beach on a wild and windy day such as this. The crashing of the grey waves as they piled into the groynes was terrific and exhilarating and it made her want to shout at the sea and the wind until their power whipped her voice away.

When they rounded the headland, they left the worst of the pounding and thrashing noise behind as they entered a sheltered cove which was deserted except for a few brave seabirds chancing their luck amongst the weeds and washed-up debris on the shoreline. The smell of salt and seaweed hung in the air here, trapped by the enclosing cliff which encircled the bay.

"We mustn't stop too long; else we'll get cut off by the tide."

"Is there no way out, up there." Jenny turned her face upwards to search the crumbling cliff for a pathway.

"A very steep path, dangerous. Don't worry, we'll just walk to the end of the cove and back."

He paused then and took a deep breath. "You would have liked her."

"Yes, I'm sure I would, if I'd got to know her properly." She realised her mistake as soon as she had uttered the words.

"Properly?" Arturo turned to her, his eyes dark and quizzical.

"I came to the gallery." She confessed. "That day you were going to show me round, but I was early. I had no idea that you were married, and she rather sprung it on me. She was very territorial, but I can understand that."

"I had no idea; she never said."

"I didn't think for one moment she would. I think she saw me as a threat and dealt with me as such. I don't hold a grudge, for what it's worth, I would have done just the same."

An uneasy silence opened between them, and it was as if they were both creeping inexorably onto dangerous ground, both knowing they should avoid it, but neither doing anything to avert it.

Jenny spoke. "What will you do now?"

He had turned away from her. They had arrived at the end of the cove and would need to turn and head back along the beach. But for a long while he stared out to the sea.

"That depends." He finally said, so quietly that she almost missed the words.

Jenny felt the sound of the sea rushing in her ears, part of her willing him to complete the sentence and part of her dreading it. What on earth was happening to her?

"On what?" She prompted him, whilst wishing she had not.

"On you. On us. If there is an us?" He turned back to her then and caught her arms pulling her to his chest.

"Arturo, no!" She remonstrated, placing her hand on his chest. "This isn't right. You're vulnerable."

He couldn't help but notice the engagement ring glistening on her hand. What a fool he had been! He should have taken his chance when she'd come before, ready to give herself to him. Suddenly he was filled with rage, and he spun away from Jenny, a guttural cry of pure frustration venting from him. He'd kept his vows despite every cell in his body telling him otherwise, and then the bloody woman had to go and die on him! Then he felt the shame washing over him and he sank down onto the sand and cried for the good woman he had lost from his life.

Jenny let him grieve, and then, standing behind him, she draped her arms across his shoulders and rested her chin on the crown of his head and stayed there until the shuddering of his great shoulders abated, and finally, he made to stand.

"We should make a move." He nodded to the tide, which was racing across the sand, likely to cut them off. "Come on!"

They broke into a run and just managed to beat the waves before the edge of the cove was engulfed by swirling water. Gasping, they paused for breath, Jenny laughing despite the situation. "I can't remember the last time I nearly got cut off by the sea!" She exclaimed; hair plastered around her glowing face.

Arturo looked at her and felt the same pure and dangerous emotion he had experienced at Melchett Hall. "Jenny, I love you!" His voice rose against the rising sound of the surf and the wind.

Her laughter faltered as she realised this was it; this was the defining moment for 'them', beginning or end – it came down to this.

They walked in tense silence back to the cottage and gallery until Jenny broke the silence by saying, "You never did show me around your studio."

Arturo looked down and held out his hand to her. With a tentative glance downwards, she took it, allowing it to engulf her own small hand, obscuring her engagement ring entirely so that, for a moment, she could forget about everything else except this moment.

"Come on then, I'll show you now."

The studio was via a door positioned halfway down the long corridor from the entrance to the cottage. Arturo paused on the threshold as if undecided about taking Jenny inside, but the hesitancy passed as he pushed open the door and flicked on the light switches. There were two main areas for working – a potter's wheel and kiln in the far left-hand side of the room, the remainder of the room dedicated to artist's materials. Jenny inhaled the familiar and comforting aroma of paints, a mixture of acrylic and oils.

"This is lovely." She murmured, slowly walking around the room, touching his easel, the brushes, the pile of dusty pastel sticks which were stacked untidily into an old wooden tray on the windowsill. He watched impassively as she imprinted her essence upon the room. There was a selection of work leaning here and there, some finished, some barely begun, but when Jenny noticed the framed picture leaning against a wall on its own, she turned to look at Arturo, a question forming on her lips.

He moved across the room and opened another door which led into the gallery. Again, a flick of switches flooded the expansive room with light. Jenny looked immediately towards the space she thought there would be above the fireplace where *The Girl in the Garden* had hung, now removed, and standing on the floor in the studio. But there was no empty space there, rather a new painting hung in its place, and Jenny gasped when she saw it.

"Arturo! You! You bought *Remains*."

He shrugged. "I like it, that is all."

"But it was an incredible amount of money…"

Again, the shrug. "I have the money, and this is an investment. It's the most beautiful painting I have ever seen."

"Thank you." She said quietly, feeling sick with the implication of his generosity.

He moved across the room, closing the space between them and reaching out for her hands. "Jenny, I want us to be together. We can live here or move, move to Italy, or travel, be anywhere – together. I know you have Simon, but will you think about it?"

She nodded and closed her eyes briefly as his head moved slowly downwards. He clasped her face within his enormous hands and tilted her face towards his. Their lips met and they melted into each other's embrace.

*

Simon looked at his phone in utter disgust and despair as he had already done a dozen times that morning. The dog lay his head on Simon's knee, his huge, sad, brown eyes looking upwards to Simon. Jenny had phoned him first thing to tell him about Margo, and although he had never met the woman, he certainly regretted her passing. As far as he was concerned, Arturo being alone exacerbated the risk of losing Jenny. He tried calling her again and left another message,

"Jenny, it's me, did you get my message? That couple who viewed the house this morning, they've put an offer in! Can you call me – please. We need to talk about it. Love you."

The phone flickered for a moment as the message was delivered and then the screen went blank again. He passed the handset from palm to palm for a minute before flinging it with some temper across the room where it landed with a thud against the back of the sofa. It felt, to him, as though the course of the rest of his life was dependent upon a single phone call or a text, either of which would leave him feeling relieved and reassured or destroyed. *Funny what impact a few words could have*, he thought bitterly.

She did call him at ten in the evening. He raced across the room from the kitchen to snatch up his phone where it still lay on the sofa, and his stomach flipped with a horrible mixture of fear and hope when he saw Jenny's name flashing on the screen.

"Hi, are you okay?" He asked, trying to sound casual and laid back, but even he could hear the tension like a taut wire in his voice.

"Hi, love, sorry I couldn't call earlier. It's been all go. Had to take Arturo into Sheringham to meet with the funeral people."

"That's okay. Did you get my message?" He thought she sounded tired and subdued but convinced himself that was a natural reaction under the circumstances, but then again… was this genuinely the first opportunity she had had to return his calls?

"Yes! Isn't that great news? What did they offer?" The quality of the line was poor, and her voice was thin and kept breaking up.

"Five k under the asking price. I hope you don't mind but I've accepted it."

"Why should I mind? After all, it's your house really, Simon."

He considered that a rather strange thing to say but let it pass, preferring instead to establish when she intended upon coming home.

"I don't know. Maybe tomorrow. I'll see how Arturo is first and then let you know. Is that okay?"

"I suppose so. It'll have to be, won't it?" He said, sulkily.

"Oh Simon! Don't give me a hard time. He has literally no one else to turn to for a bit of support. Don't begrudge a few days."

"As long as that's all it is." He muttered.

"I didn't catch that."

"Nothing. I just said don't stay any longer than you must – I miss you."

"I miss you too. Listen, I've got to go. I'll speak to you soon, okay."

"Bye, love you."

The line broke up completely then, and Simon was left holding his handset to his ear, not sure whether Jenny was still on the line, but seemingly, the connection had been cut regardless.

He sat on the edge of the sofa, a picture of complete dejection, and pushed his hands tiredly across his face, rubbing his eyes to relieve the fatigue that suddenly washed over him, and perhaps to kid himself that the moisture seeping from them was because of the vigorous rubbing and nothing more.

*

The following morning, Jenny quietly left Arturo sleeping and walked to the headland. It was chilly but lovely. The bright sunlight glittered off the moisture left here and there from the previous evening's rain, and cobwebs glistened where they festooned the trees and hedgerows.

When she reached the clifftop, she gasped at the view of the sea which looked like a swathe of crumpled blue linen thrown casually to the horizon, the sails of a small group of dinghies like remnants of white material left carelessly to gather in its folds. The sunshine was fractured and sparkling across the surface of the water, creating an irresistible and scintillating pattern of movement and light.

She felt the tell, the familiar desire to paint course through her as powerful as ever and laughed with euphoria at the knowledge she hadn't lost the creative spirit.

The wind whipped savagely at her hair as she made a decisive move to head down to the low cliff and then use the path which would take her once again onto the beach. From there she walked in the same direction they had walked the previous day, and again, the atmosphere in the cove was calmer. The waves fell onto the shingle in their powerful symmetry, the small pebbles scrunching and bubbling as the surf was pulled inexorably back into the sea.

She'd forgotten how much she loved the ocean, the way it stimulated and heightened all her senses until she perceived everything around her in a kind of abstract form, complex yet crystal clear. As she sat down on the rough shingle of the beach, she reflected. She could understand why Arturo had chosen to live here: the sky, the sea, everything conducive to the painter.

She sighed deeply hoping the exhalation of air would relieve at least some of her burden, but it just served to heighten the awareness that she had a decision to make which she really couldn't put off a moment longer. She bent her legs and then rested her hands on her raised knees. Placing her chin on her hands, she stared out to sea. She was mesmerised by the constant shifting, roiling movement of the waves where they lay pre-formed and churning away from the breakwater before curling, growing, and dashing themselves downwards, the sunlight illuminating the water and turning it a gorgeous jade green.

She sighed again. She didn't know what to do. How could she possibly love them both?

Yet she did.

She glanced down at the rocks and pebbles around her and reached out to pick one of them up. It was smooth and white with courses of pink strata running through it and, here and there, ran grey seams of another mineral like veins over its surface. As she twisted it in the light, the surface of the rock glittered softly. She thought about Simon. He was a good man. Steady, reliable, and just lately, good to be with. He had his faults of course, but then at least she knew what they were. He could be petulant and sulk when things didn't go his way, but he was also kind and had been an incredible support to her recently. He was four years older than her, and she could see them having children, and she thought he would make a good father. She didn't doubt her love for him, but she did think it was love without passion. What had she called it? Yes, that was it: steady love.

Another sigh and she looked to her left and noticed another stone. Again, she leant over to grasp it and heft it in her hand. It was a good weight and a strong shape. A mottle of colours, blacks, and greys, distributed throughout, and a hole penetrated the stone just off centre so that, if the stone had been smaller, the hole could have been strung with leather and the stone made into a necklace. Its grey and charcoal swirls were pleasing to the eye. She thought about Arturo. Strong-minded and principled, a fantastic artist and a man whose passion swirled dangerously beneath the surface controlled by a natural reserve. She realised, with a jolt, she didn't really know him at all. But the previous evening he had asked her to stay, to travel to Italy, to be with him, and she knew without doubt, his was a passionate love.

She hefted each stone, one in her left hand, one in her right, and smiled wryly as she realised, she was using them to visualise each of these men. It reminded her of how she had used the sticks in the woodland all those years before to decide her fate, or so she had thought at the time. There was no doubt in her mind having a physical representation of each of them helped her to put her thoughts into logical form and order. She acknowledged it was a rather theatrical and dramatic way to express herself, but she shrugged dismissively – only she was here to know.

So here, the stone in her left hand, the dark and uneven rock with the hole was Arturo; and here, she felt the weight of the other stone in her right hand, was Simon.

"It comes down to your head or your heart, girl." She whispered, feeling her throat close with emotion at the enormity of what she was about to do.

She stood up and faced the sea, looked once again at each of the stones, and then with all her might, she flung one of them, so it rose in an arc before plunging into the depths of the water. She sobbed for the loss, but it would always be there, just under the surface.

Then she took a deep breath and turned to retrace the footprints she had left in the sand. She glanced down at the stone that remained in her hand and squeezed it tightly before placing it in her pocket. She took out her mobile phone, and not trusting herself to speak to anyone, she selected the text icon and quickly formed her message before pressing the send button. She watched as the message left her phone, marvelling that she had just directed the remaining course of her life with one flick of an electronic button.

She turned to climb the cliff pathway again, feeling the burden of her dilemma being left behind. Then she noticed him, at the top of the cliff, like a statue except for the black trench coat flapping wildly in the wind. He raised a hand to her, and she waved back, her heart clutching with longing and desire – her decision had already been made.

MUNCH ACKNOWLEDGEMENTS

I have always enjoyed writing creatively, but the hard work really started when I took the next step in the preparation of publishing my work. I would like to thank a whole heap of people who have helped me to get this far. **Alistair and Debbie Hall**, for their encouragement and guidance. **Kat Harvey at Athena Copy** provided me with invaluable advice and an education in editing to improve content, style, and copy. Thanks too to literary publicist, **Claire Bowels**, whose review gave me the confidence to carry on. To my daughter **Dr Beccy Gavin** and to friend and brilliant landscape artist **Eddie Potts** for their meticulous proof-reading skills and helpful contribution to the finished product. Thank you to **Pauline Brown at Blueice Graphic Design** for her fantastic interpretation of my ramblings to produce a great cover design and the typesetting of the content; and to **Clays** who printed the end product.

My husband Richard, whose support and confidence in me has been unwavering through it all – thank you!

And finally, thank you to you, the reader for investing your time and effort to read Munch. I hope you enjoyed my debut novel and will forgive any licence I may have taken with descriptions of the Lake District, and the north Norfolk coast around Blakeney. The Melchett Estate and Market Braithwaite are entirely fictional, but those of you who are familiar with Leicestershire/Northamptonshire borders may recognise my descriptions taken from my local surroundings.

My next novel, *The Emerald Frog* is in the pipeline – so please track its progress at www.edenvalleypublishing.com

You may also email enquiries to info@edenvalleypublishing.com